Something Tattered

Joel Bishop, Book 1

SABRINA STARK

ISBN-13:

978-1973815518

ISBN-10:

1973815516

CHAPTER 1

I ruined him.

He stood in the drizzling rain, staring at me, as I stood, dumbstruck, on the slick, manicured lawn. I saw it in his eyes – the betrayal, the hurt, the fact that *I'd* done this to him.

Me. Melody Blaire. The girl he'd been rescuing in one way or another, almost from the very beginning.

But now, he had it all wrong. I had nothing to do with this current cluster. I bit my lip. Or, almost nothing. At least, not on purpose.

Damn it.

I gave him a pleading look. "Joel, please. It's not what you think it is."

He made a noise. It might've been a scoff, except it was too raw to convey normal human disbelief. With a slow shake of his head, he turned away, heading for his car.

I lunged after him, clutching his muscular forearm with my trembling fingers. I gave his arm a desperate squeeze. "Just wait, okay? I can explain."

Except, I couldn't.

If I told him everything, it might mean the death of him, literally.

Still, somehow, I'd make it right. I'd make *everything* right. I just needed some time, that's all.

To my infinite frustration, Joel apparently wasn't inclined to wait. Gently, he pried my fingers from his rain-soaked skin. "Forget it," he said. "Not a big deal."

It was lie, and not a very good one. It *was* a big deal. A very big deal. It was written all over his face, and I couldn't exactly blame him.

Lamely, I mumbled, "That wasn't supposed to happen. Not like that, anyway."

Stupid Derek.

Stupid me.

Stupid dreams that were slipping away.

From somewhere near the front of the house, a female voice called out, "Hey Melody! Ask him if he wants pie!"

Oh, for God's sake. Aunt Gina.

Now, she was trying to help? Where was she an hour ago, when everything was going to crap?

But I wasn't being fair. At least Aunt Gina *was* trying to help. It was more than I could say for some people.

Trying not to scowl, I turned toward the sound of my aunt's voice and spotted her, standing in the open front doorway of the crumbling mansion that I called home. With a pathetic smile, I waved her away, hoping she'd take the hint.

She didn't.

"Just ask him," she called. In an overly cheery voice, she added, "It's apple. Everyone's favorite, right?"

I made a sound of frustration. Didn't she get it? Pie wouldn't solve anything. A flamethrower, now *that* might be helpful.

Still, I turned back to Joel, who, thank God, was still there. With a note of desperation, I asked, "Do you? Want pie, I mean?" I sucked in a nervous breath. "We could talk. And, uh, I think there's ice cream in the freezer."

It was a stupid little speech from a stupid little girl – me, even if I was twenty-one years old. Right now, I was feeling more like five, about to be abandoned by the person I needed most.

Silently, Joel shook his head.

Of course, he didn't want pie. Probably, he wanted to strangle me. And all things considered, I couldn't quite blame him. But he didn't know everything that I knew, so of course, he'd be seeing things totally wrong.

And the worst thing was, I couldn't even correct him. Not if I really cared. And I *did* care, more than he obviously knew.

Suddenly, I hated everything. I hated the big, crumbling place that I called home. I hated my last name and everything it stood for. I hated the fact that some guy I'd known for only a few weeks had come to mean more to me than the hollow life I'd been living for far too long.

I watched, helplessly, as Joel turned away yet again.

Short of throwing myself at him, I wasn't sure what I could do.

Sure, I could tackle him, and we could roll around on the front lawn like Aunt Gina's drunken date last Christmas Eve. Or, I could claw at his clothes and beg him not to walk away. Or maybe I could do what Angelina the Skank had done the first time she'd met him. I could beg him for just one blissful night alone – in his arms, in his bed, in his life.

Except I didn't want Joel for just one night. I wanted him forever.

Six weeks. That was how long I'd known him. Six amazing, crazy weeks.

During those weeks, I'd learned a few things – about him, about myself, and about the things in life that really mattered.

And if he left me now, I knew that nothing else would matter, ever again.

I blinked long and hard. I *had* to find some way to tell him. I'd just need to be creative. That's all. Supposedly, creativity ran in the family, right? No matter how long it took, or what I had to do, I'd find some way.

He was worth it. *We* were worth it.

Funny to think that not too long ago, Joel was just some guy who'd beaten the crap out of the closest thing I had to a brother – not that I'd known that the first time I'd seen him, walking into my family's boardroom like he owned the place.

CHAPTER 2

Six Weeks Earlier

I tried not to stare.

The guy didn't belong here, any more than I did. But here he was anyway, standing like some kind of bad-ass, where no bad-ass belonged.

This wasn't a place for brooding eyes and a fighter's build. It was a place of business. A place of art. A place where pompous posers made pompous decisions, all in the name of my overly famous dad.

A sad smile tugged at my lips. If my dad were alive, he'd totally hate this. Probably, he'd call it a crock – or, knowing him, something a lot more profane. But me? I'd been raised to be way too polite, unfortunately.

So, here I sat, with my hands folded and my face schooled into that familiar mask of ladylike interest. Except now, it wasn't just a mask, and my interest wasn't all that ladylike either.

It was real, and it was because of him, the guy who'd just strode into the packed boardroom.

From the room's opposite side, I watched with nearly twenty other people as the stranger exchanged a few whispered words with Beatrice, the grey-haired receptionist who'd just escorted him in.

From somewhere behind me, I heard a female voice whisper, "Talk about hot."

A second voice whispered back, "No kidding. He can paint *me* any time." She stifled a giggle. "I hope he does nudes."

I wanted to roll my eyes. *College interns.* Funny to think, I should be in college, too. In fact, until a few months earlier, I *had* been in college – before the funds had dried up, leaving me with half an art history degree and no guarantee that I'd ever finish.

As the interns whispered back and forth, I wondered why I felt so much older than they sounded. Maybe it was the weight of responsibility. Like for one thing, the boardroom was actually inside my house, which meant that if interns started drooling, I'd be stuck mopping it up.

And yet, they weren't wrong. I felt my knees tremble under the table, and not because of the air-conditioning. I knew this, because the air-conditioning had been on the fritz for weeks now, and worse, I didn't have the money to have it repaired.

In cheerier news, we were in Western Michigan. It was mid-September. If I was lucky, I wouldn't be needing any air-conditioning for at least nine months, maybe more.

I looked down as the flipside of that logic belatedly hit home. I'd definitely be needing heat though – a lot of it, considering the size of the estate. Searching for a silver lining, I reminded myself that at least *that* part of the furnace was working fine – for now, anyway.

Hoping to forget all of that, I returned my gaze to the dark-haired Adonis, who stood, watching Beatrice as she adjusted the lights, making them brighter on his side and darker on ours.

As for *my* gaze, it remained firmly on him.

Was I staring?

I blew out a quiet breath. *Yes. I was.*

But in my defense, it wasn't *only* because he was obscenely good-looking. It was because he looked so far out of place that I didn't know what to think.

This was a formal interview. But he was wearing tattered jeans and a black T-shirt that looked like it had been washed at least a hundred times. True, the shirt looked good on him – maybe *too* good. The dark cotton clung to his finely cut muscles, only to fall a shade too loosely over his slim waist and narrow hips.

Confused, I gave his jeans a better look. They looked good on him too, but that was hardly the point. They weren't exactly dress-jeans, assuming there was such a thing. I saw a hole in one knee and paint smears along his right hip.

I felt my eyebrows furrow. It was like he hadn't gotten the memo, literally. It was beyond odd, but not as odd as my unseemly reaction to him.

His clothes aside, there was something intriguing about his stance – too wide, too defiant, and definitely too masculine, at least compared to what I'd been expecting.

Shifting in my high-backed leather seat, I smoothed down my skirt, hoping to cover not only my skin, but my growing embarrassment.

After Beatrice left, the guy strode forward and claimed the usual spot, standing at the far end of the ornate conference table. His dark gaze scanned the room, passing quickly over the six of us seated at the table, along with the dozen others sitting in chairs behind us.

When his gaze passed mine, I sucked in a breath.

It suddenly hit me that I was nervous. For me? Or for him? Either way, this was a big deal. If he was selected, he'd have a shot at the kind of fame and fortune that most people could only dream of. The next year could literally change his life.

Or, he could flame out like last year's crop of artist wannabes.

Still, I was rooting for him. Of course, I'd also been rooting for the ten other candidates that we'd interviewed today. But when it came to this guy? Well, I was rooting a little harder for reasons I couldn't quite understand.

It had nothing to do with his clothes, or how obscenely good he looked in them. It was those eyes, dark and dangerous, with a hint of sadness that tugged at my heart.

I felt myself swallow. Yup, those eyes were definitely a problem. I wanted to get lost in them and forget everything else – the fact that I hated this whole process, the sad state of my financial affairs, and the awkward truth that, unlike my dad, I couldn't even paint a bathroom, much less a string of masterpieces that had gained him worldwide fame.

It was official. My life was a mess.

Next to me, Derek leaned close and whispered, "I know what you're thinking."

God, I sure hope not.

Derek wasn't just the attorney for my dad's estate. He was the closest thing I had to a brother. He was tall and lean, with blonde hair and light blue eyes. If Derek *did* know what I was thinking, I'd never hear the end of it.

I reached up to touch my face. Was I blushing? Probably. If I was lucky, the dimmed lights hid the worst of it.

I lowered my hand and whispered back, "I'm not thinking anything."

Or, at least nothing I wanted to discuss.

"Right." Derek gave me a faint smirk. "You're thinking she could've been at least *a little* less obvious. Am I right?"

I wasn't following. *She?*

Into my silence, Derek continued. "If you ask me, she's slipping." He gave a small laugh. "But hey, don't tell her I said that."

Who on Earth was he talking about? I gave Derek a questioning look and waited for him to elaborate.

But all he did was smile in that old familiar way. It was the same smile that he'd given me on my thirteenth birthday, just before Aunt Gina had surprised me with a singing clown who stank of whiskey and fell down the front steps.

Oh, my God. Aunt Gina. My stomach twisted, and my hands grew clammy.

Suddenly, I wanted to crawl under the table. Today was my birthday. The big twenty-one. With growing dread, I snuck another quick glance at the stranger.

Insanely hot? Check.

Dressed in a way that didn't quite fit? Check.

Decidedly out of place? Checkity-check-check.

Oh, no.

She wouldn't.

I swallowed.

Would she?

But sadly, I knew the answer to *that* question. Knowing Aunt Gina, she would, even though she'd promised not to.

I closed my eyes and tried not to groan out loud. For a long moment, I kept them shut and wondered what would happen if I ran screaming out of the room.

At the sound of a low chuckle, I opened my eyes and looked. It was Derek, of course, who leaned close to whisper, "Aw c'mon. Be a sport. It'll be over before you know it." He flashed me that familiar grin. "No harm in humoring her, right?"

Oh, there'd be harm alright – to my sanity, if nothing else.

My face was flaming now. I didn't have to touch it to know. Probably, I looked like a human tomato minus the stem.

I recalled my last birthday, when Aunt Gina hired a stripper dressed as a construction worker to greet me at a ribbon-cutting ceremony for the local art center.

The ribbon-cutter had been me, or at least that had been the plan – right up until the Hard-Hatted Hottie began shaking his tool, directly in front the mayor and fifty other horrified people.

Okay, so maybe the tool *was* covered in a G-string, and maybe not *all* of the onlookers were horrified. I mean, Beatrice seemed to enjoy it. But that was hardly the point.

I wouldn't be invited to do *that* again, even if I *was* the only child of Braydon Blaire, the closest thing to a celebrity this town had ever seen.

I snuck another quick glance at the stranger. Growing up, I'd seen a lot of artists. None of them had looked like that. I should've known something was up the moment he walked into the room.

Damn it. My Aunt wasn't slipping. I was.

My shoulders sagged. There were so many things I needed – a new furnace, a new roof, or heck, even a better winter coat. But what did my aunt get me? A freaking stripper.

I wanted to die of despair.

Sure, her heart was in the right place. I knew that. But for once, couldn't she just listen? Couldn't *anyone* listen? I gave Derek a nervous glance. From the look on his face, *he* sure as heck wouldn't be listening.

He looked beyond amused. And the show hadn't even started.

I felt my jaw clench. *Screw this.* This time, I decided, the show *wasn't* going to start, not if I could help it.

I jumped to my feet, sending my chair rolling backwards. Behind me, I heard a soft thud, followed by a female voice squealing out, "Ow!"

Wincing, I turned to look. "Sorry."

She was rubbing her shins. At my apology, she looked up. "Oh." She gave me a shaky smile. "That's, um okay?"

As I turned back around, I heard her companion whisper, "Maybe *he'll* kiss it and make it better."

This was followed by a dreamy sigh. "I wish."

Pretending not to hear, I looked toward the front of the room. Everyone was staring, including the stranger.

I felt myself swallow. *Now what?*

CHAPTER 3

Standing like an idiot, I glanced around the table. Sitting on the left side were Peter and Henry. Together, they owned Chicago's hottest art gallery, where people paid insanely high prices for original artwork, created by established names, along with a few rising stars, like the ones selected by my dad's foundation.

On the other side sat Andy, the foundation's clerk, who would be doling out the award money, once a decision was reached. Next to him sat Claude, the ancient art critic who'd discovered my dad thirty years earlier.

And then, there was the stranger, who stood, watching me with those amazing eyes.

I stiffened. *Forget the eyes. And forget his body, too, while I was at it.*

I didn't care how hot the guy was. And I didn't care how much money my aunt had paid him. And I sure as heck didn't care that Derek was obviously in on the whole thing.

All I cared about now was avoiding this whole fiasco and getting the heck out of here, preferably without making a fool of myself.

Probably too late for that.

Still, I took a deep breath and summoned up a nervous smile. "I, uh, think we've seen enough." I forced some brightness into my voice and added, "So, should we call it a day?"

For a long, awkward moment, no one said anything. Finally, it was Andy who broke the silence by saying, "Actually, we haven't seen *anything* yet."

Right. And I didn't want to, especially with Derek sitting next to me, shaking in silent laughter.

I looked toward him and hissed, "Just shut up, okay? It's not funny."

Still shaking, he replied under his breath, "That's what *you* think."

Idiot.

I looked back to the stranger and said, "Sorry, it's not you. It's me. My schedule. I um, have another meeting, so…" With a growing sense of panic, I looked toward the door.

If I bolted now, what exactly would happen? Would the show go on without me?

Doubtful.

After all, I *was* the birthday girl. Probably, he'd chase me down and strut his stuff on the front lawn. Cripes, it wouldn't be the first time.

Lucky me.

Hoping to end this now, I looked back to the stranger and said, "It's okay. You can go. I'll make sure you're uh, compensated, if you haven't been already."

But the guy didn't go. Instead, he looked toward Derek, who I suddenly realized was no longer laughing. When I looked, I felt my brow wrinkle in confusion.

Derek was leaning back in his chair, with his hands clasped behind his head. He was staring straight at the stranger, and smirking like he knew something the stranger didn't.

My gaze shifted from Derek to the stranger and back again. I felt like I was missing something. But what? Had *Derek* hired the guy?

Before I could make any sense of it, Derek called out to the stranger, "Aw c'mon, don't be shy. Show us your stuff."

What the hell? I turned to glare at him. "Seriously, stop it, okay?"

I gave a nervous glance around the room. If the others were in on the joke, they were doing a pretty good job of hiding it. They looked as clueless as I felt.

Near the front, Andy cleared his throat. He consulted his paperwork and said to the guy, "It says here that you're a painter?"

In a tight voice, the guy said, "That's right."

My mouth fell open. *Oh, my God.* So he *wasn't* a stripper?

It was official. I was the biggest idiot on the planet. And here I was, still standing.

Crap.

Next to me, Derek gave a self-satisfied snicker. Mortified, I looked behind me and spotted my chair a few feet away. I yanked it back toward the table and plopped my butt back down, wishing I could magically disappear.

Derek leaned close and whispered, "Oh man, you should see your face."

"You jerk," I hissed. "That wasn't funny."

"You kidding?" he whispered back. "It was hilarious."

It wasn't hilarious to me. I looked to the front of the room, where the guy was still standing. His mouth was tight, and he was staring straight at us.

Of course he was. We were being incredibly rude, and not only because of that awful misunderstanding. I gave him an apologetic smile. "Sorry."

With a slow shake of his head, he looked away. *Apology not accepted.*

Well, that wasn't humiliating or anything.

Andy looked to the guy and said, "If you'd like to show us your portfolio, we'll get started."

The stranger said, "What portfolio?"

Andy hesitated. "Surely, you brought one?"

Before the guy could answer, Derek spoke up. "What'd you think? That you'd just waltz in and get painting?"

The stranger gave Derek a hard look. "Pretty much. You got a problem with that?"

Derek laughed. "What, you want us to supply the paint, too?"

The stranger's gaze drifted over the room. "That *was* the deal, right?"

Derek called out across the table. "Hey, Andy, you see any paint around here?"

Watching this, I was utterly horrified. Unless the stranger was a total idiot – and it was pretty apparent that he wasn't – he'd obviously been misinformed.

This *had* to be our mistake. And what was Derek doing? Mocking him for it.

All of this was *so* wrong. Before I knew it, I was on my feet again. "It's okay," I assured the guy. "We can reschedule."

Next to me, Derek called out, "But it's gonna cost you."

I whirled to face him. Through gritted teeth, I said, "No. It's *not* going to cost him, because obviously, there's been a mistake."

Derek laughed like I'd just said something hysterical. He turned back to the guy and called out, "Speaking of mistakes, wanna hear something funny?"

The guy's muscles were corded into visible knots. "I dunno. Do I?"

"Oh yeah," Derek said. "Get this. When you came in, *she*–" He flicked his head toward me. "–thought you were a stripper."

CHAPTER 4

At Derek's announcement, I heard myself gasp, and I wasn't the only one.

Behind me, one of the girls whispered to the other, "Hey, can I borrow ten bucks?"

"What for?"

"Oh c'mon." She giggled. "*You* know. Just in case."

"Oh, rats," the other one said. "All I have is quarters. You know, for the snack machine."

Listening, I wanted to scream. We didn't *have* a snack machine. And if they started tucking quarters into the guy's pants, a chair to the shin would be the least of their problems.

The stranger gave me a perplexed look. "A stripper?"

"Yeah," Derek called back. "The kind who shakes his thing and dances for money."

Thunderstruck, I didn't know what to say. But I did know one thing. If the floor opened up right now and swallowed me whole, I'd consider it a huge favor.

But unfortunately, the estate's foundation was one of the few things that *wasn't* falling apart.

Stupidly, I tried to explain. "No, I didn't. Well, I mean, I did. But that's only because of my aunt, and she's not here." I shoved a hand through my hair. "Anyway, I'm so sorry. I feel *really* awful, so…"

"So," Derek called over me, "if you wanna make some extra cash, go ahead. We'll make it worth your while."

It was then that the stranger made his move – but not toward me, toward Derek.

In the blink of an eye, the guy was halfway around the table. Derek jumped to his feet, sending his own chair flying backward. By the time it slammed into the back wall, the stranger and Derek were standing chest-to-chest – and Derek hadn't even moved.

I felt myself swallow. The stranger was fast. Scary fast.

His muscles were bulging, and his fists were tight. He looked like he wanted to mangle something – Derek, in particular.

I couldn't exactly blame him. I wanted to mangle Derek, too.

Desperate to smooth things over, I leaned around Derek and told the guy, "He was only joking." My voice hardened. "And *he's* sorry, too." I gave Derek a not-so-friendly tap to the shoulder. "Right?"

I couldn't see Derek's face, but I could see his posture just fine. He was anything but contrite. Sure enough, no apology came.

Well, that was helpful.

Around us, the room had fallen utterly silent. I glanced around. No one made a move – not to intervene, not to break the tension, not even to call for help.

As for the two interns, they were eying the stranger like he was the sexiest morsel they'd ever seen. The nearest one licked her lips and leaned forward, as if wanting a closer look.

Oh, for God's sake.

I spoke up. "Alrighty then." I forced a smile. "Let's just reschedule, okay? We'll give it another shot."

From the corner of my eye, I caught one of the interns pulling out her cell phone. She held it out, as if preparing to take a picture – of the guy, apparently.

I tried not to notice. "And next time," I continued, "we'll make sure it's a smaller group."

With no drooling interns. And definitely no Derek.

Again, I looked to the stranger. When our gazes met, I sucked in a quiet breath.

Wow. If I wasn't careful, those eyes – dark and intense beyond description – would be my undoing. In spite of everything else, I felt my lips part and my knees go weak.

Cripes. If I didn't get a grip, I'd be mopping up my own drool, too.

Hoping not to show it, I said, "So anyway, thanks for coming. But for now, I think you'd better go."

"Yeah," Derek said. "You heard her. Grab your shit, and get out."

What the hell? I wanted to scream in frustration. *So much for a friendly resolution.*

The guy gave Derek a long cold look. "Didn't you hear?" the stranger said. "I didn't bring any 'shit.'"

Something about that look made Derek take a small step backward. His voice rose. "I *said* this meeting's over."

"Uh-huh." The stranger edged closer. "You're the one who got me here, right? So come on." He held up his hands. "Make me leave."

I felt my eyebrows furrow. *What?*

Over his shoulder, Derek said, "Call security."

I gave a confused shake of my head. "What security?"

"The police," he said. "Whatever."

I frowned. I didn't want to call the police. For one thing, the guy hadn't even touched him. For another, Derek had been a total jerk. If the guy slugged him, Derek would have no one to blame but himself.

I felt like slugging Derek, and I wasn't even the violent type.

My gaze shifted to the stranger. Was *he* the violent type? His muscles were taught, and his eyes were hard. Something about his stance told me he wasn't a stranger to physical conflict.

And now, Derek was panicking. Should I panic, too? Obviously, Derek knew way more than he was saying.

I said, "Derek, what's going on?"

When he said nothing, I looked back to the stranger. Our gazes locked, and for some weird reason, I couldn't look away – at least, not until a flash of light broke the spell.

I turned and spotted one of the interns, shoving a cell phone back into her purse. It was the same girl I'd accidentally hit with my chair. When she saw me looking, she gave a little wave. "Sorry."

What could I say? I heard myself murmur, "That's, um, okay?" It was, after all, the same thing she'd said to me. Probably, she hadn't been any more sincere than I was.

Politeness – it could be really confusing sometimes.

The stranger gave a humorless laugh. "Screw this. I'm outta here."

I turned just in time to see him reach into the front pocket of his jeans and pull out a tightly folded slip of paper. He tossed it onto the floor and turned away, striding toward the open doorway.

And then, he was gone.

A split-second later, the two interns were scrambling after him. As they moved, one of them called back to the rest of us. "Be back in a minute!"

"Uh, yeah," the other one said. "We're just gonna hit the snack machine."

Silently, I stared after them. *Snack machine, my ass.*

CHAPTER 5

Next to me, Derek was laughing. "Oh man, did you see his face?"

I *did* see his face. It was ungodly beautiful, but that was hardly the point. I whirled toward Derek and demanded, "What was that about?"

Ignoring me, Derek announced, "Alright everyone, let's call it a day."

Around the table itself, no one budged. But behind us, the remaining interns stood and began filing out the door. That was fine by me. The way I saw it, the fewer witnesses the better.

After all, I still might have to strangle him.

When the room was empty of students, I turned to Derek and said, "Now seriously, tell me what just happened."

"Nothing," Derek said.

I turned to Andy. "Do *you* know?"

Andy shrugged. "Sorry. No idea."

"Oh, come on." I gave him a pleading look. "Obviously, something went wrong. It was like he didn't get the instructions or something. He *was* on the list, right?"

Andy looked down at his paperwork. "Yeah. Number twenty-two. A late addition."

"But what was his name?"

Andy looked up. "I wouldn't *have* his name. Remember?"

Belatedly, it hit me that of course, he was right. This was all supposed to be anonymous, which had always struck me as incredibly stupid, considering that we met the candidates in person.

Sure, I got the logic and all. It was meant to keep the process free of "undue influence," as Claude liked to put it. But it had always seemed to me that if we wanted to keep it *truly* honest, we'd just view the art by itself, without meeting the candidates at all.

A couple of years ago, I'd actually asked Claude about it, since he was the guy who made the final selections. His response had been typical Claude. "We're not just choosing the art. We're choosing the artists."

I knew what he meant. Sure, an artist's work was the most important thing, but the artists themselves could play a huge role in their popularity – or lack thereof.

Desperately, I looked to Claude, hoping for some insight. But already, he'd gathered up his stuff and was heading for the door.

I called after him. "Wait. We need to find out what happened."

"Good idea," he said over his shoulder. "When you find out, let me know."

I stared after him. What part of "we" didn't he understand? But already, he was gone, along with everyone else, except for Derek, who had fallen back into his chair and was now scrolling through his cell phone.

I stared down at him. "You're a real ass, you know that?"

He didn't even look up. "Hey, *I* wasn't the one who thought he was a stripper."

At the memory, heat flooded my face. "Yeah, because *you* made me think that."

Derek snickered. "I know. Funny, right?"

"It wasn't funny to *me*," I told him. "And I don't think *he* was all that amused either."

"Not my fault if the guy can't take a joke."

"A joke?" I sputtered. It was one thing for Derek to humiliate me. But did he have to involve an innocent bystander? "You know, you were totally awful to him."

When Derek kept on scrolling, I reached out and ripped the phone from his hands. "Stop ignoring me," I said. "This is serious."

With a sigh, Derek leaned back his chair and said, "Alright. You wanna lecture me?" He made a forwarding motion with his hand. "Go ahead. Get it over with."

"I don't want to 'lecture' you. I want to know what happened." I studied his face. "You obviously know more than you're saying."

"So?" he said. "Maybe it's a surprise."

Already, the day had been full of surprises, and not in a good way.

With more than a little dread, I asked, "What kind of surprise?"

"Well, it *is* your birthday."

"Forget that," I said. "I just want to know what's going on."

"And you will," he said, "as soon as I come up with a Plan B."

"A Plan B?" I made a sound of frustration. "I don't even know what 'Plan A' was."

When Derek made no response, I said, "Did you know that guy?"

"I might've seen him around."

Derek was a lawyer, but just barely, time-wise. He'd graduated from law school just last year and had only recently passed the bar exam. As expected, he'd continued to work for his dad's firm – the same one that had been managing my family's estate for as long as I'd been alive.

I tried to think. "Did you go to school with him or something?"

"As in college?" Derek snorted. "That guy? You're kidding, right?"

What an ass.

I was still thinking. This wasn't a big town. Maybe they'd run into each other at a restaurant or something?

Derek made a sound of annoyance. "Can I have my phone back now?"

"No."

Derek gave me a look I knew all too well. It was the why-are-you-being-such-a-brat look.

Nice try. Derek was only five years older than me. If that look hadn't worked in grade school, why would he expect it to work now?

Derek was still eyeing his phone. "You know, I *could* just take that from you."

No doubt, he could. Derek might not play a lot of sports, but he was no slouch. Still, I held onto the phone and waited.

"Fine," Derek said, getting to his feet. "You really wanna know?" He glanced toward the front of the boardroom, where the stranger had been standing just a few minutes earlier. "That guy? I hired him to paint something for you."

I did a double-take. "What?"

"Yeah. As a surprise." Derek's mouth tightened. "You happy now?"

I wasn't happy. I was confused. "So, it was like what, a birthday present?"

"That was the plan. But now, I've got to find another painter." He looked to his cell phone. "So, are you gonna return that or what?"

No. Not yet. I still felt like I was missing something. "So let me get this straight. You hired one of the endowment candidates to do a painting for me?"

Derek laughed. "That guy? Hell no. Are you serious?"

"I don't know," I snapped. "Am I?"

"Oh man, you are, aren't you?"

I was so tired of the games. Through gritted teeth, I said, "Just tell me already. Did you, or did you not, hire that guy to do a painting?"

"Sure, I hired him, but not to paint a painting."

"To do *what*, then?"

Derek gave a little smirk. "To paint the boardroom."

Suddenly, I felt sick to my stomach. "Oh, my God." I glanced around, taking in the pale green walls. It was true that I'd always hated the color, but that was beside the point. "So that guy wasn't even a candidate?"

"For the endowment?" Derek laughed. "Hell no. He was just some painter guy."

Just some painter guy. I let that phrase rattle around in my brain. The more it rattled, the less I liked it. That was just like Derek, dismissing someone because they had a regular job.

What did *he* know about regular jobs, or regular people for that matter?

Nothing, that's what.

Derek had come from three generations of wealth. But with me, it wasn't like that.

Sure, I had all the trappings of wealth, and was often called an heiress. But before my dad hit it big, he'd come from a long line of factory workers, not that anyone liked to remember that, now.

I was still looking at Derek. *What a jerk.*

At something in my gaze, he shifted in his seat. "Hey, you're always griping about the color." He glanced away. "And it wasn't just the boardroom. It was the guest house, too."

The guest house was the least of my concerns. The whole estate needed work, but if *this* was Derek's way of helping out, I wanted no part of it.

I imagined myself in the stranger's shoes. He'd been called out here to do a job, only to be treated like trash and ridiculed for the misunderstanding – a misunderstanding that wasn't even his fault.

What a disaster.

And in front of me, there sat Derek, looking like he'd just had the time of his life. He flashed me a grin. "So, anyway." His tone grew sarcastic. "Surprise."

Oh, I was surprised alright. I gave Derek a hard look. "What did you do? Put his name on the list?"

"What list?"

As if he didn't know. "The list of candidates. Number twenty-two." My jaw clenched. "Remember?"

Derek only shrugged. "Hey, you had to meet him sometime, right? I figured, why not add him to the list, have some fun with it."

"Fun?" I sputtered. "For who?"

Derek laughed. "Well, *I* enjoyed it."

Feeling suddenly overwhelmed, I looked down, only to feel myself pause. There it was, that folded slip of paper, the one the stranger had tossed down earlier.

Still clutching Derek's phone, I bent down and snagged the paper with my free hand. It looked like a business check, folded into a neat little square.

Derek held out his hand. "I'll take that."

"Why? What are you planning to do with it?"

"Rip it up, obviously."

I frowned. Well, that was convenient. So the stranger wouldn't even be compensated for his trouble?

Distracted, I said, "You want something? Take this." I dropped Derek's phone into his outstretched hand, and then unfolded the paper for a better look. Sure enough, it was an official business check, made out from the law firm of Derek's dad.

I zoomed in on the amount. "Only fifty dollars?"

Granted, this wasn't pocket change. But even in my own limited experience, fifty dollars didn't buy a whole lot of anything when it came to home-maintenance.

Derek said, "It's called a down payment."

"Oh." I didn't bother asking what the full amount would be, or who, exactly, was supposed to pay for it. Given my finances, I didn't want to know.

The check was made out to someone named Joel Bishop. I let that name drift around in my brain. I liked it. Or maybe, I just liked the thought of somehow, making things right.

Feeling suddenly inspired, I told Derek, "You can't rip it up."

"Why not?"

I squared my shoulders. "Because I'm going to give it back to him."

"You're not serious?"

But I was, which is why, a few hours later, I'd changed into casual clothes, and was standing in a campground of all places, staring down at a narrow, Earth-colored tent.

Yes, a tent. □

CHAPTER 6

It was nearly nightfall, but I wasn't going to let that stop me. I glanced around, taking in the neighboring campsites. On them, I saw pop-up campers, oversized recreational vehicles, and colorful tents, many that were large enough to sleep eight people.

It was a Friday night, which no doubt explained the fact that the beachfront campground was utterly packed. I'd actually camped here before, exactly one time, thanks to a friend in junior high, whose parents were, as she'd put it, the outdoorsy type.

At the memory, I felt myself smile. Back then, I didn't have a worry in the world. I'd had two parents, loads of security, and a house that was every kid's dream.

My smile faded as a sad fact hit home. At the time, I'd been way too naïve to appreciate any of it. Just three years afterward, both of my parents were gone, along with any real security.

Pushing that depressing thought aside, I zoomed in on the small tent in front of me. Driving through the campground to get here, I'd seen cheerful-looking campfires, surrounded by families and retirees, all enjoying the final remnants of what had been a mild summer.

But at the painter's campsite, there was no campfire, no friends gathered to roast marshmallows, and no happy chatter or kids laughing.

There was nothing at all.

Except the tent.

I stared down at the thing, wondering if the painter – the guy named Joel Bishop – was inside right now. And if he was, what then?

Should I knock, or…?

Behind me, a male voice said, "You looking for someone?"

Startled, I whirled around, and there he was – the painter, standing within arm's reach. His eyes were dark, and his mouth was tight. I craned my neck to look up at him. He was wearing the same clothes as before – tattered jeans and a dark T-shirt.

I tried for a friendly smile. "Uh, hi. Remember me?"

He didn't smile back. "What are you doing here?"

My own smile faltered. "I guess I'll take that as a 'yes'?"

"Take it any way you want."

Okay, I knew that our last encounter had been totally awful, and I also realized that he had every reason to be angry. But for some reason, this wasn't what I'd expected.

"Just so you know," I said, "that whole painting thing, I had nothing to do with it."

He still wasn't smiling. "Right."

"You think I did?"

"I think you're not answering my question."

As I stared up at him, I considered everything that I'd gone through, just to make it out here. I'd postponed birthday plans. I'd made half-a-dozen phone calls to find out where he was staying. And then, on my way out the door, I'd gotten into a final, raging argument with Derek, who'd lingered at my place just long enough to tell me how stupid I was being.

On top of all that, there had been the sticky issue of the check itself, which was now safely tucked into the front pocket of my jeans. During my final argument with Derek, he'd flat-out demanded that I return it. *Not* to the painter. To Derek himself.

And then, when I'd refused to hand it over? He'd threatened to put a stop-payment on it, to make it absolutely worthless no matter what I did.

In the end, I'd actually gone over his head to keep that from happening. Yes, I'd called his dad, which was especially awkward, considering that Derek's dad had known nothing about the check, or what it was supposed to be paying for.

The whole thing had stunk to high heaven, and now, I was dealing with this guy's attitude on top of all that? It's not that I blamed the guy for being angry. It's just that, well, in my happy thoughts of making things right, I hadn't considered that I'd be dealing with *his* hostility, too.

I gave him a pleading look. "Look, I know that you're mad, but just listen. I'm here to make things right."

He looked unimpressed. "Is that so?"

"Definitely." I reached into the front of my pocket of my jeans and pulled out the check, folded along its original creases. I held it out between us. "Here."

He gave it a long look, but didn't take it.

I hesitated. "It's the check you dropped earlier."

"I didn't drop it. I tossed it."

"Uh, yeah. I just mean, it's that same check. You know?"

He said nothing, but from the look on his face, he *did* know, and he wasn't thrilled.

Worse, he still wasn't taking it. The check weighed next-to-nothing, but for some reason, it was feeling heavier with every passing second.

I nudged it a fraction closer. "Don't you want it?"

"If I *had*, I wouldn't have tossed it."

I stared up at him. *Wow.* This was so *not* what I'd expected. What did the guy think? That I was trying to hire him back?

I bit my lip. I couldn't hire anyone, even if I wanted to, and not only because I couldn't afford the labor. I couldn't afford the supplies.

I considered the check's amount. Fifty dollars. It wasn't a fortune, but it was more than I had in my own purse. Surely, the guy could be at least a *little* happy to get it back.

From the look on his face, apparently not.

Beyond eager to get this over with, I said, "It's not for the job. It's for your trouble." Again, I nudged the check closer. Again, he didn't take it. I looked down. One more nudge, and I'd be poking him in the stomach.

His shirt was loose around his waist, but a stomach *had* to be down there somewhere. Right?

From the looks of him, it was probably a flat stomach, with all kinds of interesting ridges and valleys, but that wasn't terribly relevant, was it?

Still, an image of his shirtless torso flashed in my brain, and I felt a rush of heat rise to my face. I looked up and blurted out, "Will you *please* just take it?"

He looked at me for a long moment before saying, "Alright." And then, with cool deliberation, he took the check from my outstretched hand.

I breathed a sigh of relief. *Finally.*

Suddenly eager to make my escape, I turned toward my car, an ancient import that I'd inherited from my mom. It was parked a few paces away, just off the narrow dirt road that snaked its way through the large campground.

I'd taken only a few steps toward it when I heard a sound – a *ripping* sound that yanked my attention back to the painter. I turned just in time to see him scatter bits of paper onto the darkened fire pit.

My jaw dropped. "Was that the check?"

It was a stupid question. Of course, it was the check. I could see it for myself, scattered among the dusty ashes.

The guy shrugged. "Hey, I took it. You got what you wanted, right?"

I stared at him. *What a jerk.*

But what could I say? It was, after all, his check. Technically, he could do whatever he wanted with it.

Still, if he'd been so determined to rip it up, couldn't he have waited? After all, in five minutes, I would've been long gone.

God, I was such an idiot. Little Miss Do-Gooder strikes again. And, as usual, I hadn't done any good for anyone, especially myself.

I felt myself swallow. "Well, I guess you showed me, huh?"

In front of me, the guy said nothing.

Whatever.

I blinked long and hard, and then turned away. The guy had made his point. There was no reason for me to stick around for further humiliation.

In under a minute, I'd be gone, and then, I'd never have to see his face again.

Or at least, that would've been a perfectly lovely scenario, if only my car had cooperated.

CHAPTER 7

Sitting behind the wheel, I turned the key again. But all I heard was that same click, followed by absolutely nothing.

I wanted to scream in frustration.

Already, I'd been sitting in my car for at least five minutes. Technically, it wasn't a long time, but for some reason, it felt like forever. From the corner of my eye, I could still see him, the painter guy, standing in the same spot, watching me.

Yeah – watching me make a fool of myself.

Again.

At least darkness had finally crept over the campground, leaving me sitting in the shadows, rather than on clear display. Happily, the shadows had crept over him too, which saved me the added humiliation of seeing his face.

I knew exactly what the shadows hid. Scorn. Impatience. And maybe some good old-fashioned boredom, too.

I could practically hear his thoughts. *Why won't this chick leave?*

I'm trying, jerkface.

Desperately, I tried the key again, only to hear that same dreaded click.

With a muttered curse, I yanked my purse off the passenger's seat and rummaged around for my cell phone. I pulled it out and turned away from the driver's side window. Away from him. The check-ripper-upper.

Holding my phone in a death grip, I pulled up Cassie's number and hit the call button. She answered with a raucous, "Hey! Birthday Girl! Where the heck are you?"

I paused. I heard noise in the background, lots of noise – music, voices, and glasses clinking. "Where are *you*?" I asked.

She laughed. "I'm at T.J.'s. Where else?"

T.J.'s was one of only two local bars that had dancing on the weekends. I'd never been inside, because until today, I'd been too young to get in. Tonight was supposed to be my first time, except the plan had been for me and Cassie to go together.

Trying not to sound as hurt as I felt, I summoned up a weak laugh. "So, uh, you decided to start the party without me, huh?"

She was practically yelling. "What?"

I tried again, talking louder now. "I *asked*, did you decide to start without me?"

"Heck no," she said. "We can't start anything without you. But I came in early to snag a booth." She paused. "Didn't you get my message?"

I winced. "Sorry, I haven't checked."

"Oh shoot. Hang on a sec, alright?"

I heard fumbling on the other end, followed by more clinking and a rowdy burst of laughter. A moment later, Cassie was back. "Sorry about that." And then, in a louder voice, she said, "Alright everyone, hush. I'm talking to the birthday girl."

I felt my brow wrinkle. *Everyone? Who was everyone?*

Other than Cassie, I had only a handful of friends, and most of them were hours away at college. Even when it came to relatives, the only *good* one I had was Aunt Gina, who now lived hours away – and wasn't visiting until tomorrow.

More curious than ever, I asked, "Who's all there?"

"Everyone," Cassie repeated. "It's your big twenty-one, remember?"

In spite of everything, I had to smile. I still didn't know who this mythical "everyone" was, but it sounded like one heck of a party.

My smile faded with a guilty realization. Already, I'd postponed our plans by a full hour. Now, she was entertaining unknown party guests while I was stuck where? At some ingrate's campsite. That's where.

"So," Cassie was saying, "are you on your way?"

"Um, well, here's the thing…"

A knock on the driver's side window made me jump in my seat. I whirled to see the check ripper-upper, looking down at me through the glass.

On the phone, Cassie said, "What was that? Are you okay?"

I turned away from the window and said, "What was what?"

"You sort of screamed."

"I did not." I hesitated. "Did I?"

"Well, it wasn't a *big* scream or anything." Her tone brightened. "It was more of a yelp."

Oh great, so now I was yelping? Like a dog? Reluctantly, I looked toward my car window. The painter was still there.

I gave him an annoyed look. *Yeah. That's me. The yelper. Deal with it.*

Deliberately, I clutched the phone tighter and turned away. On Cassie's end, the music and clinking had faded to nearly nothing. "Why is it so quiet?" I asked. "You didn't leave, did you?"

"Heck no," she said. "The party hasn't even started." She laughed. "Since you're not here and all."

I didn't know whether to laugh or cry. I'd been planning to ask Cassie to come out here and get me. Now, I wasn't so sure. She didn't sound drunk, but she didn't sound fully sober either.

On the phone, she was saying, "I just ducked into the bathroom." Right on cue, I heard a distinct flushing noise. Cassie said, "That *wasn't* me, by the way. I'm only in here, so I can hear what you're saying."

I gave an awkward laugh. "Well, that's a relief."

Still, I hated the idea of her hunkering near some toilet on *my* account. I was just about to tell her that when I heard another tap on the car window.

This time, I didn't jump. And I didn't bother looking.

I already knew who the tapper was, and I knew exactly what he wanted – for me to just leave already.

Terrific. We had something in common. I wanted to leave, too.

If only I could.

"So," Cassie said, "are you on your way?"

I hesitated. "Hey, a question…By any chance, is anyone there still sober?"

"Yeah." Cassie laughed. "The bartenders."

I tried to laugh, too. "Oh c'mon, they aren't the only ones, are they?"

"Do the bouncers count?"

My shoulders sagged. "Not really."

"But don't worry," Cassie said. "I'm not getting sloppy 'til you show up." She paused. "Although I can't speak for the others." She lowered her voice. "Dorothy? She's on like her third fuzzy navel."

Dorothy? As in the local librarian?

Wow. The way it sounded, Cassie *had* invited everyone.

And they were all waiting. Why? Because I'd tried to do something nice for some jerk who didn't even appreciate it.

Soon, Derek would be saying, "I told you so."

As usual.

Dreading it already, I asked, "By any chance, is Derek there?"

"Um. No. Actually, he isn't." She hesitated. "I invited him to stop by, but, uh…"

"That's okay," I assured her. "We're kind of on the outs, anyway."

"Oh. I guess that explains it."

Explains what? I was dying to ask, but the birthday clock was ticking. So all I said was, "I'll see you in a little bit, okay?"

I only prayed I was telling the truth.

When the call ended, I turned my reluctant gaze to the car window. The painter was still there, looking mildly irritated. I rolled down my window and forced an awkward smile. "By any chance, do you know anything about cars?"

□

CHAPTER 8

With the window's glass no longer between us, I could see his face more clearly now. Of course, it was annoyingly beautiful, which just made everything worse when he said, "You mean *your* car?"

What other car *would* I mean? Still, overly conscious that I was about to ask him for a favor, I tried to sound more polite than I felt. "Yes, actually." I winced. "It, uh, won't start."

His voice was deadpan. "I noticed."

God, did he have to be so awful?

Screw politeness.

"You know," I said, "I'm only out here because I *thought* I was doing you a favor."

His expression didn't change. "You mean the check?"

"Of course, I mean the check." I glanced toward the darkened fire pit. "Not that it's worth anything *now.*" Under my breath, I muttered, "Well, except as firewood."

His mouth twitched at the corners. "Be a pretty small fire."

Oh, so he was making fun of me now? "Fine," I said. "I'll just check the engine myself."

I opened the driver's side door and pushed it outward until it bumped against his legs. When he made no move to get out of my way, I said, "Are you going to let me out or what?"

"Nope."

"Why not?"

He flicked his head toward the front of my car. "Pop the hood. I'll give it a look."

I bit my lip. I didn't know *how* to pop the hood. Probably, I should've considered that before threatening to check my own engine. With growing embarrassment, I lowered my head to study the car's interior. Maybe the hood-popping thingy was near the floor or something?

Sounding almost amused now, the guy said, "Check under the steering column."

Praying he meant the steering wheel, I ducked my head for a better look. Finally, I spotted the latch near my left knee. I gave the latch a pull and heard a metallic pop.

Thank God.

I sat up straighter and watched as the guy strode to the front of the car and lifted the hood.

I poked my head out the window and called, "Do you want me to turn the key or anything?"

But already, he was lowering the hood back down. When it slammed shut, I felt my jaw tighten. Aside from ignoring my question, he'd looked at my engine for like ten whole seconds.

Thanks for nothing, buddy.

When he approached the window, I gave him my snottiest smile. "So, you figured it all out, huh?"

"Yup."

I blinked. "What?"

"It's the distributor cap."

"Oh." That didn't sound *too* bad. Feeling even more awkward, I asked, "So did you tighten it back up?"

"It's not loose. It's cracked."

Of course it was.

At least it was only a cap. That didn't sound *terribly* expensive. I asked, "Do you know where they sell them?"

He gave me a look. "Yeah. The auto parts store."

"Well, obviously," I said. "But I mean, is it something they might sell at a gas station?"

"Doubtful." He shoved his hands into his pockets. The motion made his biceps pop in a way that was stupidly distracting. "My guess? You're looking at a special order."

Disappointment coursed through me. "For a stupid cap?"

"It's not like you're driving a Chevy."

The guy did have a point. The car had been my mom's. It was

foreign, exotic, and from what I gathered, fairly expensive. I didn't even know its exact value, because I didn't want the temptation to sell it.

My mom had adored this car. It had been a gift from my dad for their tenth wedding anniversary. She'd driven it everywhere. Even now, there were days, mostly in the summer, when I swear, I could still smell the ghost of her perfume, lingering lightly on the white leather seats.

Or maybe that was just wishful thinking.

Feeling more deflated than ever, I glanced around. *What now?*

I wasn't *that* far from my house. It was only a few miles. Maybe I could walk?

My stomach sank. No. I couldn't. Even if I ran, it would still take forever. And then, I'd need to shower and change my clothes, unless I wanted to stink up my own party. Plus, I'd still need some way to get to T.J.'s.

Damn it.

Out of easy options, I looked up, stiffened my spine, and made myself say the thing I'd been dreading. "I don't suppose you can give me a ride?"

He frowned. "You're asking *me*?"

Well, that was nice. Apparently, the jerk was back.

I made a sound of annoyance. "Never mind." I turned away and muttered, "Forget I asked."

His voice, softer now, reclaimed my attention. "I just mean, I've been a total asshole."

Surprised, I turned to look. "Excuse me?"

He glanced away. "Sorry."

For what? Swearing? Or being a jerk? Or was that merely a sarcastic comment. Hoping for the best, I said, "Does this mean you'll give me a lift?"

His jaw tightened. "You do this a lot?"

Oh, for crying out loud. "No," I snapped. "I *don't* do this a lot, because normally, I don't find myself at a stupid campsite, giving a stupid check, to a stupid guy who, for whatever reason, totally hates me."

He looked at me for a long moment. And then, in a voice that was annoyingly calm, he said, "You want to hear what's stupid?"

I already knew what was stupid – my grand idea to come out here in the first place. I looked away and muttered, "Just forget it."

Asshole.

After all, that's what he'd called himself, right? No point in arguing.

His voice, more gentle now, drifted over my anger. "Look at me." He paused. "Please?"

Oh, great. He'd said please. Now, I *couldn't* ignore him. *Stupid politeness.*

Reluctantly, I turned to look. In the shadows, he looked dark and dangerous, with his bulging muscles and grim expression.

He said, "What's stupid is to get in a car with some stranger." His mouth tightened. "Some guy you don't even know. At a fucking campground." He made a scoffing sound. "At night, for Christ's sake."

My jaw dropped. "Well, that's rich. I wouldn't even be here, if it weren't for you."

"Yeah? But you still don't know me."

Maybe he had a point, but I was in no mood to agree with anything this guy said. I lifted my chin. "I do, too. You were at my house today." I gave him my snottiest smile. "Remember?"

"Yeah. And you saw how that went."

Whatever. But desperate times called for desperate measures. And I *was* desperate. I wasn't just stranded. I was stranded *and* had a bunch of people waiting for me.

What, exactly, were my options?

Call Derek?

Oh sure, because that would be totally lovely to have him show up here, just to have him laugh in my face and say, "I told you so." And then, I could eat popcorn or something while he got into another raging fight with the painter guy.

Or who knows? Maybe *I'd* be the one fighting the painter guy, and Derek could eat popcorn.

Come to think of it, I didn't even *want* a ride from this guy.

Screw this. I pushed open my car door. Just like before, it bumped against his legs. I said, "Are you going to move aside or what?"

Finally, he stepped back.

About time. I opened the door wider, reached for my purse, and stepped out of the car. I slammed the door shut behind me and began stalking toward the campground entrance.

Behind me, the guy's voice cut through the darkness. "Where are you going?"

I hollered back, "Like you care." And then, ignoring the glances from neighboring campsites, I looked straight ahead and kept on walking.

Jerk.

CHAPTER 9

Ten minutes later, I was stomping along the lonely country road that I'd taken to reach the campground, back when I'd had a working car and a heart brimming with good intentions.

Now, the car was abandoned, and my intentions were mostly homicidal.

Screw you, Painter Guy.

Already, I'd done the unthinkable and called Derek, who hadn't even bothered to answer his phone. So, in retaliation, *I* hadn't bothered to leave a message, because let's face it, if he wasn't available to give me a ride, there was no reason to let him know exactly how right he'd been all along.

After giving up on Derek, I'd called Cassie, who also wasn't answering. Maybe that was a good thing, because I'm pretty sure if she *had* answered, I'd have flat-out begged her to find someone – anyone – to come out and get me.

Surely, *someone* inside T.J.'s was still sober, right?

I heard myself sigh. Doubtful. The way it sounded, even Dorothy was drunk off her ass.

On the bright side, I was officially twenty-one now. So, even if I missed my own party, there was nothing to stop me from hitting the town's only liquor store and getting raging drunk, even if I had to do it alone.

Of course, I'd have to *walk* there, which would make me feel even more like a giant loser.

I glanced to my right, where a wide ditch, filled with darkened ditch-water, ran along the roadside. I rolled my eyes. If only I had a canoe, I could get paddling.

Happy freaking birthday.

I was so lost in my miserable thoughts that I didn't notice the pickup truck roaring up from behind me until it had already passed. Startled, I watched it squeal to a sudden stop a few car lengths ahead.

It didn't take a genius to figure out who it was. So, he'd decided to give me a ride after all, huh?

I lifted my chin. Well, maybe I didn't want one. Not from him, anyway.

I stopped walking and crossed my arms. If he expected me to scurry forward and leap into the truck bed, he had another thing coming.

A moment later, the vehicle shifted into reverse, accelerated, and then squealed to a stop right next to me.

The passenger's side door was so close, I could almost reach out and touch it. But I didn't. Instead, I stood with arms crossed and watched as the passenger's side window slid down to reveal a face that was all too familiar – except, it didn't belong to the painter.

It belonged to Chester Dunn, a guy I'd known back in high school. The guy was big and blond, with a ruddy face that I knew all too well.

Probably, I should've been glad to see him, but ever since that thing at homecoming, he'd been near the top of my people-to-avoid list.

He leaned out of the window and said, "Mel?" He laughed. "Oh man." He turned to whoever in the driver's seat. "It *is* her." He turned back to me and said, "I *thought* it was you."

I wanted to groan. The guy hadn't changed. And, he'd just called me Mel. I hated being called Mel.

Still, I tried to smile. "Hey Chester."

He looked around. "So, uh, what are you doing out here?"

It was a simple question. And yet, I didn't know how to answer. I recognized this for what it was – one of those godawful moments where time stands still as you're forced to choose between two equally unappealing options.

Let's see…Do I want to be eaten alive by Army Ants? Or flattened by a steamroller?

I looked at Chester, who was still hanging out of the passenger's side window. Back in high school, he'd been an all-state wrestler. The way it looked, he was still in prime condition, with thick muscular arms and a chest the size of Texas.

Good for him. And I meant it, too. It's not that I didn't like him. It's that, well, in spite of his size, he definitely fell into that Army Ant category.

I considered asking him for a ride. He'd definitely give me one, no matter who was behind the wheel. There was only one problem. It wouldn't end there. If it turned out anything like homecoming, that little ride would lead to months of grief.

And not only for me. For him, too.

Still, a little voice in my head reminded me that I had at least five more miles to walk and a booth full of people waiting.

Stalling for time, I said, "So, are you home for the weekend or something?" Quickly, I added, "I mean, I heard about your wrestling scholarship. Congratulations, by the way."

His face split into a huge, happy grin. "You knew about that?"

"Yeah." I tried to smile back. "You, uh, sent me the news clipping. Remember?"

He was nodding now. "Yeah. But, I wasn't sure you got it." His smile faltered. "I mean, you never called or anything. You saw the number, right?"

His phone number? Oh, I'd seen it, alright. It would've been hard to miss, considering that he'd scrawled it across the article in big red letters, along with a personal note that may – or may not – have been a joke.

If you want to wrestle, give me a call.

Even years later, I didn't quite know what to say. Going with the less-is-more approach, I managed to mumble, "Well, I was seeing someone, so…" I let the sentence trail off, hoping he wouldn't ask for details.

"Oh yeah?" he said. "Who?"

I gave a nervous laugh. "That was, wow, how many years ago? Three? Who can remember that far back, right?"

"Uh, yeah. Right." His eyes brightened. "So, how about now?" He leaned further out the window. "Are you *still* seeing someone?"

Oh, crap. I wasn't, actually, but I hated the thought of saying so. I made a vague gesture with my hand and said, "Oh, you know how that goes."

But from the look on his face, he didn't. His eyebrows furrowed, and he squinted through the darkness, as if searching for something in particular. But what?

My car? My boyfriend? My sanity?

He could squint all he wanted, but if he saw *any* of those things, he'd be hallucinating, bigtime.

Suddenly, his gaze popped back to me, and he said, "Hey Mel."

"What?"

His voice boomed across the short distance. "Happy Birthday!"

Startled, I stumbled backward. "Uh, thanks. How'd you know?"

"Like I could forget." He grinned. "It was our first date, remember?"

Technically, it hadn't been a date. It had been one dance, literally, meaning one song.

There hadn't been a second dance, much less a second date. It's not that I didn't like him, even then. It's just that when, after one dance, someone shows up on your doorstep, uninvited, wearing a T-shirt with your picture on it, things tend to get a little weird.

Chester laughed. "Man, that was a crazy night, huh? You know, I *still* have that shirt?"

"Uh, really?"

"Yeah. Check it out." And then, to my infinite horror, he reached into the glove compartment and pulled out a blob of white cotton. He shook out the fabric, and there it was, an image of my own smiling face, taken from my junior yearbook photo.

Well, that wasn't creepy or anything.

I took another step backward, even as I managed to choke out, "Oh. You, uh, kept that, huh?"

"What? You think I'd throw it out." He was still grinning. "It still fits, too." Abruptly, he retreated back into the truck and called out, "Don't move. I'll put it on."

Oh, no. That Army-Ant feeling was back with a vengeance, prickling my skin and making me feel just a little bit twitchy.

Seeking some space, I glanced around. If I backed up any further, I'd be dipping my heels in ditch water. Suddenly, that wasn't sounding so bad. The water wasn't *that* deep. Was it?

I was still pondering that when a second vehicle roared out of the darkness and squealed to a stop directly in front of the pickup. Thanks to the pickup's headlights, I could see the new vehicle as clear as day.

It was an old Camaro with a banged-up door and mismatched paint. I felt my brow wrinkle in confusion. It had no license plate. Now, *that* was odd.

I was still staring when the passenger's side door flew open, and I heard a familiar male voice call out, "Get in."

CHAPTER 10

My gaze bounced between the pickup and the Camaro. Stupidly, all I could think was, *"Army Ant? Or Steamroller?"*

I was still standing there, dumbstruck, when two things happened at once – the painter emerged from the Camaro's driver's side, and Chester reappeared in the pickup's window, wearing *not* the dreaded shirt, but no shirt at all.

Was that improvement? Honestly, I had no idea. In passing, I couldn't help but notice that I'd been right about one thing. He *was* still in good shape, in a big, beefsteak sort of way. But that didn't mean I wanted to see him shirtless – I hesitated – or pantless for that matter.

Oh, God. He *was* wearing pants. Right?

My gaze was still bouncing back and forth when I heard myself call out toward the painter, "Oh, hey…" Drawing a total blank, I said the only term of endearment that came to mind. "…Honey."

Honey?

Cripes. He wasn't a honey. He wasn't gooey or sweet. He was, from the looks of him, a steamroller on a mission.

And, judging from his stride, the mission was me.

In cheerier news, he hadn't contradicted the gist of my greeting. Not yet, anyway.

I looked back to Chester, who was hanging out of the pickup, looking ridiculously confused. I forced an awkward smile. "It was, uh, nice catching up. But my ride's here, so…."

Before Chester could say anything in response, the painter was at my side. He draped a possessive arm over my shoulders and said, "Sorry I'm late. Car trouble."

If the trouble involved a vehicle with no plates, I could definitely see what he meant. But of course, I knew his words weren't really meant for me. They were meant for Chester, who was watching us with that same perplexed expression.

Probably, my own expression wasn't much different. Suddenly, I felt so confused. Draped over me, the painter's arm felt embarrassingly nice – firm and strong, with the perfect amount of pressure.

Worse, it fit perfectly, too, resting over me like a warm, protective cocoon. Against all logic, I fought a humiliating urge to lean against him and close my eyes.

Just maybe, if I closed them long enough, all of this would magically disappear. Or maybe, *I'd* disappear.

Talk about wishful thinking.

The painter said, "Baby, is everything okay?"

My breath hitched, and my heart gave a funny little leap. *Baby?* From his lips, it sounded surprisingly good. Too good, all things considered.

I knew it was all just an act. And I thanked my lucky stars that he'd caught my hint. Still, I was liking this way more than I should've, especially considering what a jerk he'd been earlier.

Somehow, I managed to say, "Uh, yeah. Everything's fine." I looked to Chester, who looked as clueless as ever.

Did he even realize he was half-naked?

Hoping to end this, I gave him a little wave. "Alrighty then, have a safe trip back, okay?"

Chester's gaze darted from me to the painter. "Is that your…?"

"Yup," I chirped. "It sure is."

My what? My boyfriend? My ride? My rescuer?

Okay, I knew this wasn't *really* a rescue, because technically, there hadn't been any danger, well, except to my sanity. In hopes of sparing everyone further embarrassment, I turned to the painter and said, "Ready to go?"

He dropped his arm from my shoulders and flicked his head toward the Camaro. "Get in the car. I'll be there in a minute."

Well, that wasn't bossy or anything.

Still, I gritted my teeth and forced something like a smile. "But we're running late. Remember?"

"Thirty seconds then." He turned back to Chester and his tone grew decidedly less friendly. "Where's your shirt?"

Chester looked down to study his bare chest. "Uh…"

I spoke up. "He was just getting changed."

"Uh-huh," the painter said, keeping his gaze on Chester. "Next time, do it somewhere else, alright?"

I bit my lip. I didn't want any trouble. I just wanted to leave. I reached for the painter's hand and gave it a tug. "Come on. We're gonna be late."

"Yeah?" He turned and flashed me a cocky grin. "So why don't you get your sweet ass in the car, and let me finish up?"

I swallowed. If he thought *my* ass was sweet, he should see his own.

Damn it. Not helpful.

Shaking off the distraction, I tugged harder at his hand. "There's nothing to finish up. Let's just go. Okay?"

When he still made no move, I gave a sigh of irritation and dropped his hand. I took a deliberate look around. If nothing else, there was always the ditch.

Under his breath, the painter said, "Don't even think about it."

So, under *my* breath, I replied, "I wouldn't *have* to, if you'd just cooperate."

But already, he was looking back to the pickup. He frowned, like he didn't like what he saw.

Oh yeah? Welcome to the club, pal.

Still, I followed his gaze, only to feel myself pause. A second face had appeared in the passenger's side window. This new face belonged to Mike Lakowski, another wrestler from high school.

His eyes were wide, and his mouth was open. He was staring, star-struck, at the painter. "Hey, I know you."

After a long, awkward pause, the painter said, "No. You don't."

"Sure I do." Mike grinned. "I saw you fight at State."

The painter's mouth tightened. "I never went to State."

"Well, not state-state," Mike said. "It was in that warehouse on the East Side." He gave a low chuckle. "Man, you totally slaughtered that guy."

I tensed. *What?*

Slowly, I shifted my gaze back to the painter. He wasn't denying it. In fact, he wasn't saying anything at all. But from the look on his face, he wasn't thrilled with Mike's comment.

Well, this was just great. So the steamroller was also a butcher? Yes, I realized that Mike wasn't speaking literally. Still, an image of blood and guts flashed in my brain.

Unlike the painter, it wasn't pretty.

I was *so* ready to leave. But I was hemmed in on all sides. I turned and gave the ditch a longer look. Was the water dirty? Or just dark?

Suddenly, a strong hand closed around mine. When I looked up, the painter tightened his grip and gave me a warning look.

Oh, for God's sake. I wasn't *really* planning to hit the ditch.

Well, not without a canoe, anyway.

I met his gaze straight-on, refusing to be intimidated. While I was at it, I also refused to be intimidated by his insanely long eyelashes, that full mouth, or his finely cut muscles – the ones that made Chester's look like budget beef in comparison.

Still gripping my hand, the painter turned back to Chester and gave him a final warning look. And then, he turned away, guiding us toward the Camaro.

As we moved, I snuck a quick glance over my shoulder. Chester was still staring, and he *still* looked perplexed.

Yeah, I knew the feeling.

CHAPTER 11

A minute later, I was sitting in the passenger's seat of the Camaro, watching as the painter shut my car door and then circled the Camaro's front to claim the driver's seat.

When he closed his car door, I blew out a shaky breath. *No turning back now.*

Behind us, the pickup was still there, with its engine running and headlights blazing through the Camaro's back window. I turned in my seat and gave the truck what I hoped was a cheery wave. Under my breath, I said, "Alright guys, just go already."

Next to me, the painter eyed the truck in the rear-view mirror. "Don't bet on it."

"Why not?"

"My guess? They want us to go first."

I gave him a sideways glance. "So…Should we? Go, I mean?"

"Not yet."

"Why not?" I asked.

"Because I don't want them following you."

"Oh." I hesitated. "Honestly, I don't think that matters. I mean, Chester knows where I live, so…" I shrugged and let the sentence trail off.

"So…?" the guy prompted, as if waiting for me to finish.

I hadn't planned on finishing. I mean, what could I say? Still, I tried again. "I just mean that if he wants to find me, he wouldn't have to actually follow me to do it."

The painter was still looking in the rear-view mirror. "You *want* him to follow you?"

"Not really." I tried to laugh. "But he's harmless. I knew him back in high school." I snuck another quick glance behind us. "It's been years since I saw him last. If he really wanted to bother me, he would've already."

The painter pulled his gaze from the mirror and gave me a long, sideways look. "Seemed like he was bothering you tonight."

"Yeah, but that was just a fluke, you know?"

Even as we talked, it struck me that this whole thing was decidedly off-kilter. I *knew* Chester. He'd grown up a few miles from here. His dad was the local chiropractor, for cripe's sake.

But this guy? The painter? He was practically a stranger. He could be an ax-murderer for all I knew. After all, he did "slaughter" people.

I bit my lip. *What the hell was I doing? Probably, I shouldn't even be sitting here at all.*

Trying to get a grip, I reminded myself that Mike had recognized this guy. That pretty much guaranteed my safety, right? I mean, no one would slaughter a girl they'd just been spotted with in public.

I swallowed. *Would they?*

From the driver's seat, the painter said, "If you need 'em, there's nunchucks in the glove compartment."

I gave a little jump. "What?"

His gaze had already returned to the mirror. In a deadpan voice, he said, "Just letting you know."

I didn't even know what nunchucks were. Reluctantly, I looked toward the glove compartment. Should I open it and find out? Or was I better off not knowing?

Trying to avoid looking clueless, I said, "Why would I need those?"

He was still eyeing the truck. "Protection. What else?"

"Protection from who?"

He glanced briefly in my direction. "Well, from the look on your face. Me."

A flash of heat blazed across my cheeks. *Damn it.* It was like the guy was some kind of mind-reader or something.

My shoulders slumped. No. That wasn't it. More likely, my thoughts were just *that* obvious.

Going for a recovery, I straightened and said, "I'm not afraid of you, if that's what you're implying."

"Uh-huh."

"I'm not," I insisted. In a funny way, it was almost true. Yeah, my imagination could run wild sometimes, but there was a reason I was sitting *here*, and not in the pickup.

True, the painter didn't like me. That much was obvious. But it was also obvious that he'd made a special trip to track me down and offer me the ride that I'd originally requested. And, he'd gone along with that whole boyfriend sham, even though he hardly knew me.

On top of all that, there was one fact I couldn't deny. When I'd felt the urge to flee, it hadn't been *from* him. It had been *to* him.

If I'd been truly worried that he might harm me, I would've taken my chances with Chester the Shirtless Wonder and his trusty sidekick.

After a long moment, I concluded that I wasn't afraid of the painter at all. It was just that, well, logic dictated that I *should* be.

I cleared my throat and turned to give him a better look. "Should I be afraid?"

Slowly, he pulled his gaze from the mirror and turned to face me. In the brightness of the truck's headlights, I saw the hint of a dimple on his left cheek and the remnants of worry lines between his eyes. The contradiction caught me off guard, and I blurted out, "Well? Should I?"

"No." Again, he looked to the mirror. "But you'd be smarter if you were."

"What?"

Abruptly, he turned again to face me. His voice hardened. "You shouldn't've been out here."

Well, that was rich. I felt my gaze narrow. "You know, I *wouldn't've* been out here, if only *someone* had given me a ride when I asked."

His jaw tightened, but he said nothing.

Refusing to let it go, I demanded, "So why didn't you?"

"I figured you'd call someone."

"Like who?"

He gave something like a shrug. "I dunno. A servant or something."

I stared at him. "A servant?"

"Hey, I saw your house, remember?"

"Oh, trust me. *I* remember." My tone grew sarcastic. "But unfortunately, it's Jeeves' night off."

If he was amused, he didn't show it. "I'm just saying, I figured you had a driver."

I was still staring. What world did this guy think I lived in? I had no driver. I barely had a car.

And as far as the house? Yes, it was big and impressive, but I maintained it on my own.

I was the maid. I was the gardener. I mopped the floors and mowed the lawn. In a weird, twisted arrangement, the estate actually paid me for some of these services, but the amount sucked, and I was still broke.

I practically snorted. "A driver?"

"Yeah."

"Sorry, but I sent him out." I gave the painter a sarcastic smile. "For caviar."

His eyebrows lifted. "Caviar?"

"Yes." My mouth tightened. "And a yacht."

He looked at me for a long, silent moment. Whether he caught the joke, I had no idea.

Finally, he said, "I'm just saying, you shouldn't be getting in a car with some guy you barely know." His voice hardened. "It's a dangerous habit."

"I don't make a 'habit' of it," I told him. "It was just one of those things. You *do* remember that my car broke down, right?"

"I remember."

"So, what is this?" I said. "A lecture?"

"I'm just saying, someone like you? Should be more careful."

"Someone like me?" My voice rose. "What, like too rich and stupid to drive my own car?"

"No. Like too trusting." He looked away. "And too pretty to be out here alone."

My lips parted, but no words came out. He thought I was pretty? If so, that was news to me. Without thinking, I asked, "Are you serious?"

"Do I look like I'm joking?" He made a point to look around. "This road? At night? With almost zero traffic and a big-ass ditch? It's like something from a bad movie."

His response felt like a non-answer. Still, I knew exactly the kind of movie he meant, the kind where buxom hitchhikers meet their untimely doom, thanks to bad luck and worse judgment.

The thought wasn't exactly comforting.

Behind us, the truck still hadn't moved. I looked to the painter and said, "Can we just go? Please?"

He spared me half a glance. "If you wanna go, buckle up."

Eager to move this along, I reached for the seatbelt and fastened it over my lap. When I finished, I looked to the painter and hesitated. *He* wasn't wearing a seatbelt. "What about you?" I asked. "How come you're not buckled up?"

"No seatbelt."

"Really?" I felt my eyebrows furrow. "Is that even legal?"

He gave something like a shrug. "Don't worry about it."

But I *was* worried. Safety aside, I knew the answer to my last question. And even if I didn't? There was a helpful road sign, literally one car-length ahead. The sign said, *Buckle Up. It's the Law.*

I pointed. "You *do* see that sign, right?"

"I see it."

If he'd grown up anywhere in the state, he would've seen a hundred signs just like it. So I had to ask, "Then why don't you have a seatbelt?"

"Because the car was in storage."

It was then that I recalled something. *Oh, no.* The car had no plates. In the big scheme of things, that was several degrees more serious than a missing seatbelt. My stomach twisted. Was this car even legal?

With growing nervousness, I said, "But you *do* have license plates? Like somewhere in the trunk or something?" I hesitated. "Right?"

He shook his head. "Sorry."

I groaned. "Oh, my God. Is *that* why you didn't want to give me a ride?"

"I never said I didn't want to."

But he had. I racked my brains. Hadn't he?

Feeling suddenly overwhelmed, I said, "What does that even mean?"

"It means, the car had nothing to do with it."

"But then why?" I asked.

"Because I'm a stranger." He made a hard scoffing sound. "And an asshole. Seems to me, you were showing piss-poor judgment."

Well, that was nice. So he was back to insulting me again? I gave him an annoyed look. "Then why'd you come out to get me?"

"Better me than someone else."

I gave him a stiff smile. "Like my driver?"

He didn't smile back. "No. Like a fuckin' psycho. The world's full of them, you know."

"Yeah," I snapped. "I know." In fact, I was pretty sure that I was looking at one now. "But about this car–"

"Trust me. You don't wanna know."

"Actually, I do." I gave a bark of nervous laughter. "You didn't steal it or anything, did you?"

He looked at me for a long, tense moment. And the longer the silence stretched out, the more I wondered if my so-called joke was actually true.

Suddenly, I wasn't laughing anymore. "So, uh, did you?"

He turned away. "Like I said, you don't wanna know."

Oh, crap.

And with that, he shifted into gear and hit the gas.

□

CHAPTER 12

The Camaro roared forward with us inside. I whirled in my seat and saw the truck's headlights fade into the distance.

I whirled back to the painter and said, "You stole this? *That's* what you're saying?"

He was still watching the road. "Did I say that?"

"No."

"Well, there you go."

I stared at him. "That's no kind of answer."

He gave me a sideways glance. "Relax. I didn't steal it."

I breathed a sigh of relief. "You didn't?"

He returned his attention to the road. "Not exactly."

Not exactly? What on Earth did *that* mean? "So whose car is it?" I said. "Do you even know?"

"Yeah. I know."

"Well?" I demanded.

"Well what?"

"Whose car is it?"

"My brother's."

"Oh." Actually, that made a weird kind of sense. "So you borrowed it?"

He was silent for a long moment before saying, "I dunno."

"How can you not know? You either borrowed it, or you didn't."

As an answer, he only shrugged.

I made a sound of frustration. "But you *are* planning to return it, right?"

He gave it some thought. "Maybe."

"Maybe?" I glanced around. "Is there anything else I should know?" I gave a nervous laugh. "I mean, you don't have a bunch of guns in the trunk or anything, do you?"

At this, he hesitated.

Oh, no. I felt myself swallow. "Do you?"

He gave me a sideways glance, but said nothing.

I groaned. "Oh, my God. You do, don't you?"

After a painfully long moment, he said, "I wouldn't call it a bunch."

I sank back in my seat. *Just shoot me now.* No. Wait. Not literally. He did, after all, have guns readily available. I turned back to him and said, "How many *would* you call it?"

He gave it some thought. "A few."

"A few?" I croaked. "As in more than one? How many is a few?"

"Hard to say. I didn't count."

Hoping for the best, I said, "But they're not yours? I mean, they probably belong to the car's owner." I paused. "They do, right?"

I held my breath and waited for his response. *Please say yes. Please say yes. Please say yes.*

He gave me another sideways glance. "No."

I cringed. *Damn it.*

He said, "They belong to my *other* brother."

I was staring again. "How many brothers do you have?"

His voice hardened. "Too many."

I shoved a nervous hand through my hair. Desperately, I tried to look on the bright side. The whole stolen-car-with-guns-in-the-trunk thing had completely taken my mind off the missing seatbelt.

I closed my eyes and tried to envision a glass half full. It was a total waste. I didn't even see the glass. Instead, I saw the painter getting dragged off to jail, with me calling out after him, *"Thanks for the ride, Painter Guy!"*

Right on the heels of *this* thought came another. What if I was arrested with him?

The guy's voice, sounding vaguely amused, broke through my thoughts. "Don't worry. They're legal. Collector's items mostly."

Obviously, he meant the guns. I asked, "But why do *you* have them?"

He shrugged. "Because I took them."

"Why?"

"Because he had it coming." The painter gave me a sideways glance. "It's complicated."

Oh, I had no doubt of that. I glanced around. Maybe I *should've* gone for the ditch. Or Chester.

Heaven help me.

As if reading my mind, the painter said, "You don't need to worry. It's fine."

I gave a bark of laughter. "You mean except for the fact that we're surrounded by stolen goods?"

He hesitated. "Yeah. Except for that."

I rolled my eyes. "Well, that's a relief."

"Trust me," he said. "It's not a big deal."

"Maybe not to *you*."

Oh sure, he could look calm and collected. As for me, I was a mess.

I had no idea what was going on. But I *did* know we were both too pretty for prison. Yes, I realized that I wasn't *quite* as pretty as he was, but I was definitely a whole lot wimpier.

From the driver's seat, he said, "Relax. I'll have you home in five minutes."

But I couldn't relax. My mind was still churning. I'd need a girlfriend. A *tough* girlfriend. But I didn't *want* to be anyone's prison bitch. For one thing, I liked guys.

I was still panicking when his words finally sunk in. *Home* – he was planning to take me to my house.

Oh, crap. I hadn't mentioned it, but I'd been planning to have him drop me off *not* at my house, but instead, five miles further, at T.J.'s., where everyone was waiting.

But there was no way on Earth I could ask him that now. The added distance aside, T.J.'s was located in the center of town, right next to the city's only police station.

I tried to think. *What now?* Assuming I made it home safely – thus, avoiding a life of shower-shanking and muff-licking, how was I supposed to get to the party?

Even if I wanted to, I couldn't blow it off. People were waiting. And they'd been waiting far too long already.

Feeling incredibly overwhelmed, I sank down in my seat.

I was the worst birthday girl, ever.

As we sped through the darkness, I kept reminding myself that things could always get worse, which oddly enough they did, just a few minutes later, when we pulled into the long driveway that led to my house.

As it turned out, I was being robbed.

By my least-favorite relatives.

Again.

CHAPTER 13

Even from a distance, I could make out the familiar white Mercedes as plain as day. It was parked in the turnaround with the doors shut, but the trunk wide open.

Looking at it, I wanted to scream. Instead, I leaned back in my seat and groaned, "Cripes, not again."

"What?" the painter asked.

I gave him a nervous glance. "I've got company."

He stopped the car and turned to study my face. At something in my expression, he cut the engine, along with the headlights. His gaze shifted forward to the Mercedes, and his eyebrows furrowed. "And that's a problem?"

I looked toward the house. Through the eyes of a stranger, there was nothing to be alarmed about. In front of me, there it was, a perfectly pretty scene – a pricey estate with a pricey car parked out front.

Sure, the car's trunk was open, but that wasn't terribly unusual. I'd parked in that same spot countless times, unloading whatever from my own trunk.

But studying that oh-so-pretty picture, I knew something that a stranger wouldn't. If past history was any indicator, the trunk wasn't being emptied. It was being filled.

I just knew it.

I looked to the painter. "It's my aunt and uncle."

He gave me a perplexed look. "And?"

I winced. "And I think they're robbing me."

His gaze shot back to the Mercedes. "You think? Or you know?"

Right on cue, my front door flew open, and a portly middle-aged man with a shock of red hair staggered out through the open doorway. In his arms was a bronze sculpture of a charging war horse.

The man was my uncle. The horse was my dad's – or at least, it *had* been, back when he'd been alive.

I looked to the painter. "Well, I guess that answers *that* question."

But the painter wasn't looking at me. He was looking at Uncle Ernie, who was stumbling his way down the front steps, heading toward the trunk of his car.

Before I could even consider what to do, the painter hit the headlights. Under the sudden glare, my uncle froze in mid-stagger, like a farmer caught screwing a chicken.

Next to me, the painter fired up the Camaro and hit the gas. We roared forward and skidded into the turnaround, only to stop on a dime just inches from the back of the Mercedes.

Uncle Ernie staggered sideways. "Son-of-a-bitch!" he yelled, apparently more in surprise than in anger.

I had to give him credit for one thing though. He hadn't dropped the horse. Then again, this wasn't exactly his first rodeo.

I shoved open my car door and jumped out to demand, "What are you doing?"

He glanced around. "Huh?"

Through gritted teeth, I said it again, more slowly this time. "What. Are. You. Doing?"

He gave me a shaky smile. "Hey, aren't you supposed to be at T.J.'s?"

I eyed the horse. "Aren't *you* supposed to be *not* robbing my house?"

At this, he had the nerve to look insulted. His gaze shifted to the bronze statue, still clutched in his beefy arms. "You talking about *this*?"

Yes. I was. And whatever else he was taking. I turned toward the trunk of his car. Inside, I saw an ancient broadsword and a lace tablecloth.

I felt my jaw clench. The sword was a collector's item, worth more than I cared to consider. But it was the tablecloth that really ticked me off. It wasn't a pricey artifact, but it *had* belonged to my grandmother on my mom's side.

She'd died years before I was born. She hadn't been a wealthy woman. Far from it. Other than a few old photos, the tablecloth was all I had to remember her by. And I actually used the tablecloth, too. I saved it for special occasions, like Christmas, Easter, and the occasional Thanksgiving.

And here, Uncle Ernie was trying to steal it, just like he'd stolen the good china and half of the wine glasses.

Screw that.

I looked back to my uncle and felt my gaze narrow. "How could you?"

He was *still* looking insulted. "I don't know what you think here, but you've got it all wrong."

Sure I did.

A new voice, the painter's voice, cut across the short distance. "Yeah? Then put it back."

I turned toward the sound and was surprised to see him standing just to my right, giving my uncle the look of death.

My uncle gave a nervous chuckle. "Put what back?"

I made a sound of annoyance. "Oh for God's sake. He means the horse, obviously." I pointed. "The thing you're holding."

My uncle looked to the statue. "This?"

I rolled my eyes. "No. The horse you rode in on."

After a long, awkward moment, my uncle's eyes widened to epic proportions. "What? You think I'm *stealing* this?"

I stared in stunned silence. At that moment, I could practically see him wearing a straw hat and denim overalls, pooled around his ankles. *What chicken? This chicken?*

I threw up my hands. "Of course I think you're stealing it. What else would I think?"

My uncle's gaze shifted to the painter. "So, uh, who's that?"

It was the painter who answered. "It's the guy who's gonna kick your fat ass if you don't turn around and put that back where you found it."

CHAPTER 14

The painter's words echoed in the night. Shocked, I whirled to face him. I don't know what I'd been expecting, but this wasn't it.

It hit me like a ton of bricks that it had been forever since anyone had taken my side, or at least anyone who was willing to make a scene about it.

From the look on the painter's face, he was willing to do more than make a scene. He was willing to make good on his threat. Under the glare of the Camaro's headlights, he looked dark and dangerous, with his fighter's build and tight, coiled muscles.

If *I* were my uncle? Well, let's just say I'd be galloping back into the house, pronto.

But was he? I turned to look. Nope. He wasn't galloping. He was staring, thunderstruck, at the painter. As I watched, my uncle's face turned nearly as red as his hair. He choked out, "What did you just say?"

"You heard me," the painter said. "Now, put it back." His voice grew a shade darker. "In one piece. Got it?"

A new voice, this one female and filled with false cheer, sounded from the open doorway. "Oh, Melody, what a surprise!"

I looked up and spotted the thin, ferret-faced woman, standing in the open doorway. It was Aunt Vivian, dressed to kill as usual, in black designer clothes and so much jewelry, it was a wonder she didn't topple over.

I gave her a hard look. "If *you're* surprised, imagine how I feel."

Ignoring the comment, she plastered on a friendly smile and sashayed down the front steps. She claimed the spot next to Uncle Ernie, who was *still* holding the horse. I saw beads of sweat pooling on his upper lip and signs of dampness under the armpits of his fancy white dress-shirt.

Probably, this was the hardest he'd worked all year. My uncle was, to put it nicely, between jobs. In fact, he'd been between jobs for as long as I could remember, even before the death of my parents.

How long ago was that? Only five years? There were some days, like today, where it felt like a million.

My aunt's voice, dripping with sweetness, yanked my thoughts to the present. "Melody, darling. You never said, why aren't you at T.J.'s?"

That was a good question, and I was angry enough to give her a straight answer. "You mean right now? Maybe it's because…" My voice rose. "…I'm too busy stopping a robbery."

Her hand flew to her mouth, and she made a show of looking around. "What? Where?"

"Cut the act," I said. "I mean *you*. Here."

Her smile disappeared, replaced by a look of overblown concern. "Oh, dear." She turned to Uncle Ernie. "I think there's been a terrible misunderstanding." She gave him a meaningful look. "Didn't you explain it to her?"

His face froze. "Uh…"

My aunt continued over him. "We weren't *taking* these things. We were *transporting* them." She gave me a sunny smile. "For you."

"Oh yeah?" I made a sound of disgust. "Just like you 'transported' the good china? Was that for me, too?"

"Oh, stop harping on that," she said. "You don't use it, anyway. And, as I've told you many times, when you plan your next party, just let us know." She pursed her lips. "We'll bring it right back."

"Fine," I said. "I'm having a party tomorrow."

"Don't be ridiculous," she said. "We know you don't entertain."

About this, she was right. I didn't entertain, mostly because I didn't have the money. Forget fancy dinners. I could barely afford pop and pizza.

Pushing that depressing thought aside, I asked, "And how'd you get in *this* time?"

"The front door," she said. "It was unlocked."

It was the same thing she always said. It was a lie, of course. Before leaving, I'd locked *all* of the doors and engaged the alarm.

It hadn't stopped them. It never did. By now, I was almost convinced they had a secret entrance or something.

I gave her a dubious look. "Sure it was."

"It was," she insisted. "You really should be more careful." She looked to the painter, and her eyes narrowed. "I see you have a new friend."

I crossed my arms. "Yup."

She gave a loud sigh. "Well? Might I ask for an introduction?"

Next to her, my uncle muttered, "I wouldn't recommend it."

I looked to the painter and felt a twinge of guilt. He wasn't just "the painter." He had a name – Joel Bishop. I'd seen that name on the check. If he was willing to stick up for me, the least I could do was remember his name.

He was still giving my uncle that ominous look. In passing, I couldn't help but wonder if it was Joel's stare, and not the weight of the horse, that was making my uncle sweat buckets.

Joel moved toward my uncle. "Are you putting that back?" His jaw tightened. "Or not?"

My uncle took a couple of steps backward and cleared his throat. "Uh, sure." He glanced toward the open front door. "I guess I'll just head inside and toss this thing back onto the pedestal."

"Remember," Joel warned, "in one piece."

My aunt spoke up. "Oh, you two, don't be ridiculous."

I wasn't sure who the "two" were. *Joel and my uncle? Me and Joel?* I paused. *My uncle and the horse?* I remained silent, hoping to just end this already.

My aunt turned to me and smiled. "In case you haven't guessed, we were taking that lovely horse to *your* birthday party."

"What birthday party?"

"Why, the one at T.J.'s, of course."

She knew about that? How, I had no idea. But I *did* know that none of my friends would've invited her. They knew better.

I gave a bitter laugh. "Sure you were."

"We were," she insisted. "I thought it would make the perfect centerpiece. We all know how you love horses."

I didn't love horses. They scared the snot out of me. Aunt Vivian might've known that if our relationship didn't consist mostly of her stopping by to pilfer my stuff.

I pointed toward the open trunk. "And what about the tablecloth?"

"Why, it's for the table, of course." She gave a little laugh. "Your birthday *is* a special occasion, is it not?"

I didn't bother hiding my disbelief. "Right." Like I'd let anyone spread out my grandma's best tablecloth over some bar in a booth, where who-knows-what could happen to it.

Still, I just *had* to ask. "And the sword?"

My aunt's gaze shifted to the trunk. "The sword? Well, yes, you see, that's for…" She hesitated, as if unsure what to say next.

Next to her, my uncle suggested, "Cutting the cake?"

My aunt shot him an irritated look, but said nothing.

Again, I looked at the sword, nestled in the folds of the tablecloth. Knowing my aunt, the tablecloth was just padding, something to protect the ancient artifact.

For some reason, that just made everything worse. To me, the tablecloth was priceless. But to them, it was convenient packing material.

As for the sword itself, it was a genuine collector's item. If the notches on its blade were any indicator, it had seen more than its share of action. And yet, I was reasonably certain that none of that action involved cutting baked goods.

I looked back to my relatives. "Forget the party," I told them. "I'm not even going." I reached into the trunk of their car and pulled out the sword with one hand and the tablecloth with the other.

Holding both of them in a death grip, I circled the vehicle, checking for more contraband. I saw nothing else, probably because we'd caught them in the act.

When I finished circling the car, I looked to my aunt and uncle, and felt my brow wrinkle in confusion. The horse was gone.

No. Scratch that. Now, *Joel* was holding the horse, while my uncle sweated alone.

God, what a spectacle.

And for some reason, watching Joel holding that stupid horse, I felt my eyes grow misty, and my bottom lip start to quiver. But it wasn't with sadness. It was with gratitude.

How messed up was that?

CHAPTER 15

Together, Joel and I watched from the front steps as the Mercedes sped down the long driveway and disappeared from sight.

Good riddance.

Until next time, anyway.

With a weary sigh, I turned to Joel, only to feel myself pause. He was still holding onto that horse. He looked ridiculous. And dangerous. And, boyish in a way that warmed my heart.

In words that felt woefully inadequate, I said, "Thanks for that."

"For what?" he asked.

"For everything." I made a vague gesture with my hand. "The stuff with Chester, the ride back. And that whole scene with my aunt and uncle." I gave a shaky laugh. "Honestly, I'm surprised you're still here."

He frowned. "Like I'd just take off? And let them rob you?"

I shrugged. "I dunno. I mean, who needs the drama, right?"

He gave me a long, penetrating look, and then turned to scan our surroundings. As I watched, he took in the darkened yard; the massive house; and the long, stately driveway that contained only one car, his.

Around us, the estate was utterly silent, except for the rhythmic sounds of waves lapping somewhere below the bluff.

As the seconds ticked away, I tried to see the place through his eyes.

Of course, he wouldn't see it as a giant pile of debt and decay. He'd see it the way everyone else saw it – as a waterfront estate with ornate architecture, a stately boardroom, and multiple balconies overlooking Lake Michigan in all its ocean-like glory.

Plus, there was the size of the house itself. It was big, thousands of square feet, with two stories, a wine cellar, and enough bedrooms and bathrooms for a family of ten, maybe twenty if people doubled up.

But there weren't twenty people. There was just me, all by myself.

As if reading my thoughts, he asked, "Where's everyone else?"

I hesitated. "What do you mean?"

"Earlier today, there were what, twenty, thirty people here?"

I gave it some thought. Yeah, I guess there were, counting all the applicants, along with Derek and the others who'd been helping with the interviews.

And then, there was Joel. I recalled the two interns who'd been slobbering at the sight of him. I couldn't help but wonder if they'd caught up with him after leaving the boardroom. I had no clue, and didn't want to speculate.

So instead, I said, "Yeah, well, this time of year it gets kind of crazy."

He gave me a penetrating look. "Crazy how?"

I briefly explained that my dad's foundation was headquartered right here in the estate. And that yes, for a few days a year, the place was pretty crazy during business hours, with tours, applicant interviews, and whatnot. But the rest of the time, the estate was just home sweet home.

When I finished, Joel gave the house another long look. His eyebrows furrowed. "You don't live here alone?"

I did, in fact. But it seemed foolish to admit it. So all I said was, "Well, there's my aunt Gina."

Even saying it, my heart ached. Aunt Gina *used* to live here, back when I'd been underage and required a guardian. Now, she was living five hours south, thanks to an amazing job offer she'd gotten with the help of Derek's dad.

In spite of her objections, I'd pushed her to take it. It really was a great opportunity, even if I did miss her like crazy.

So here I was, on my own, in a house that was way too big for only me. Some days, it didn't feel like a home at all. It felt like a museum, filled with too many artifacts, and not enough people – especially the two people I missed most.

But crying wouldn't bring back my parents. I knew this from firsthand experience.

Looking to change the subject, I pointed to the horse, which was still cradled in Joel's muscular arms. "You're probably tired of holding that, huh?"

Funny, he didn't *look* tired. Unlike my uncle, who'd been staggering under its weight, Joel looked like he could lug the horse around all day and not break a sweat.

I glanced up. "Not that you *look* like you're struggling or anything." I cleared my throat. "But seriously, who wants to carry around a horse all day, right? I mean, aren't horses supposed to be carrying *us*? You know, giddy-up and all that?"

I froze. *Giddy-up?*

Cripes, I sounded like a complete moron. Hoping he hadn't noticed, I clamped my lips shut and tried to look like I *hadn't* just been rambling like a missing mental patient.

In front of me, Joel made no reply, and I fought the urge to squirm under his penetrating gaze. Something in his expression told me that he knew exactly what I was doing – avoiding the gist of his question.

Where *was* everyone? Gone, that's where – at least when it came to people who mattered.

Unable to bear his scrutiny a moment longer, I looked away and let my gaze settle on the long, lonely driveway.

Really, this was none of his business. Just because he'd rescued me – twice, in fact – from people who I'd been hoping to avoid, that didn't mean he was my friend, as much as I'd like to think otherwise.

I was still pondering that when his voice, softer now, interrupted my thoughts. "Hey. Melody."

Surprised, I turned to face him. This was the first time he'd said my name. In fact, until this very moment, I hadn't realized that he even *knew* my name. But of course, he *had* to know. Everyone knew, just like everyone knew that my parents had died in a private plane crash over Lake Michigan.

It had, after all, made national news.

I said, "Uh, yeah?"

His voice was quiet. "Happy birthday."

I felt color rise to my face. Obviously, he only knew because Aunt Vivian had mentioned it. Still, it was a nice thing for him to say.

I heard myself say, "Thanks."

"Listen, I've got a question."

I gazed up at him, wondering what it was. And, as I looked into his amazing eyes, I wondered something else. What would life be like if I were just a normal girl, some no-name townie with a bunch of siblings, crowded into a bustling house that smelled of bacon in the morning and pie at night?

If I were *that* girl, would a guy like Joel ever ask me out? Would he ever say something like, *"Hey, you wanna hit the beach sometime?"*

Would a guy like him – or anyone else, for that matter – ever look at me as something more than Braydon Blaire's only daughter, the theoretical heiress to gobs of money and a massive estate?

Sadly, I'd never know.

But I *did* know one thing. I liked the sound of my name on his lips. I wanted to hear it again, if not now, then sometime soon.

Standing in the quiet night, I gave a little shake of my head. *Damn it.* He'd said something, and I hadn't yet responded. I said, "Sorry, what question?"

"How about that party? At T.J.'s. You wanna go?" He glanced toward the Camaro. "Say the word. I'll have you there in five minutes."

I bit my lip. The offer was so very tempting. Still, I had to say it. "Thanks, but I don't think that's a great idea."

"Why not?"

"You ever been to T.J.'s?"

"Yeah. A couple times."

"Well then you know, it's right next to the police station."

"So?"

So, wasn't it obvious? Again, I looked to the Camaro. With what I hoped was a light-hearted laugh, I said, "So you'd probably get arrested."

He shrugged. "Eh, I'll take my chances."

I turned to study his face. From the looks of it, he meant it, too. I was insanely touched.

Still, he had no idea what he was dealing with. He wasn't from around here. But I was.

On the upside, there was practically no crime. On the downside, this gave the police plenty of time to watch for strangers driving stolen hot-rods with missing plates.

Reluctantly, I shook my head. "Honestly, I'm pretty sure we'd get caught."

"Not you," he said. "Me."

"What?"

He flashed me a grin. "You're just the passenger. Remember?"

I stared up at him. The sentiment was so sweet, it was enough to melt my heart. Would he really risk that? For me? A girl he hardly knew?

From the look on his face, he would.

But this realization only stiffened my resolve. There was no way I'd let him take such a risk, and I flat-out told him so. And then, I glanced around, wondering how on Earth I'd tell Cassie that I wasn't coming.

I was still wondering when my gaze landed on the tall, narrow outbuilding that my dad used to call the lighthouse. It wasn't *truly* a lighthouse, but it sure looked like one.

The building wasn't round, but it *was* three stories high, with a two-car garage on the bottom, a small guest house on the second floor, and my dad's studio on the very top.

Back when I'd been a kid, my dad used to paint out there for hours. But it wasn't the upper level that had my attention now. It was the lowest one, the garage – and more to the point, what it contained.

I felt my lips curve into a smile. Maybe we couldn't take the Camaro. But we *could* take something, even if I wasn't technically supposed to.

CHAPTER 16

When I walked through the front entrance of T.J.'s, Cassie rushed forward to greet me. "Oh, my God!" she squealed, wrapping me in a sloppy hug. "You actually made it!"

Laughing, I said, "Yeah, I took the long way, like the *real* long way." I pulled back to give her an epic eye-roll. "Don't ask."

Around us, the place was absolutely packed. Like most of the buildings in the small downtown area, T.J.'s wasn't huge. But from what I could see, it more than made up for it in sheer energy.

The music was loud and boisterous, classic rock, courtesy of a live band performing on a raised platform near the far wall. In front of the band, a few dozen people were crowded onto a tiny dance floor, moving in time with the music.

I looked around in amazement. It was like every square inch of the place was packed with people. They were everywhere – standing in front of the long wooden bar off to my left, occupying the few small tables directly in front of us, and crammed into half-a-dozen oversized booths, located to the right of the dance floor.

Zooming in on one booth in particular, I felt my face break into a huge, stupid grin. The booth was overflowing, not only with people, but with colorful balloons and long, yellow streamers, hanging from the dark ceiling.

I turned to Cassie. "Oh, wow. You decorated?"

She smiled. "Not just me. All of us."

I looked back to the booth and felt my eyes grow misty. I saw Dorothy the Librarian, laughing with three of my oldest friends from high school. I also spotted a few newer acquaintances, mostly people I'd met over the last few months, since I'd started working part-time at Cassie's Cookie Shop.

I was so touched, I almost didn't know what to say. The friends from high school, in particular, were a huge surprise, because none of them were living in town anymore, or at least, not usually, since they'd all gone away to college.

At one time, I'd been away at college, too, but this was no time to dwell on my interrupted education. My friends hadn't yet spotted me, and this gave me the chance to savor the surprise, watching their familiar faces as they talked and laughed with each other across the long booth.

Were they all here for me? Just to celebrate my birthday?

My smile faded as a sad realization hit home. I'd kept *all* of these people waiting, and not only for a few minutes. I turned back to Cassie and said, "I am *so* sorry I'm late. I don't know what to say."

She laughed. "Don't say anything. It's fine."

I gave her an apologetic look. "But I'm so late. Believe me, if I'd only known…"

She poked me in the ribs. "You weren't *supposed* to know."

"But–"

She gave me another poke. "You know, I can do this all night, right?"

Laughing now, I tried to squirm away. "But why *would* you?"

"Because you're supposed to be smiling, not worrying. Now, c'mon, it's your birthday." She leaned forward. "I made you a cake."

"Really?" Cassie made the *best* cakes. She sold them, too, at her little cookie shop. If *this* cake tasted anything like the last few I'd sampled, I'd be in serious danger of eating the whole thing.

She grabbed my wrist. "Now c'mon." She gave me a tug, only to pause in mid-motion. She was staring at something near the back of the bar.

I followed her gaze and spotted Joel, talking with one of the bouncers – a big, blond guy in a black T-shirt emblazoned with the bar's logo.

Cassie dropped my wrist. "Oh, crap."

"What?" I asked.

She frowned. "I sure hope Derek doesn't show."

"Why not?"

She pointed toward Joel. "You see that guy?"

Hoping for the best, I said, "The blond?"

She shook her head. "Not the bouncer. The *other* guy. You *do* see him, right?"

Oh yeah. I saw him.

Even if I didn't know him, he'd be a hard person to miss. He looked lean and muscular, with a killer body and a perfect face. I glanced around. The way it looked, Cassie and I weren't the only girls staring.

But unlike Cassie, I wasn't surprised to see him. With me running so terribly late, he'd insisted on dropping me off at the front entrance and parking the car on his own. The offer had been so sweet, I couldn't refuse, especially with everyone waiting.

Reluctantly, I said, "Yeah. What about him?"

Cassie lowered her voice. "He's the guy who beat up Derek."

CHAPTER 17

In my mind, the background noise faded to nothing. My gaze darted from Cassie to Joel and back again. "What?"

"Yeah," she said. "And you *know* I saw the whole thing."

I shook my head. "No. I *didn't* know. How come you never told me?"

"I did. Last week. Remember?"

"Sorry, but you didn't. Trust me. That's *not* something I'd forget."

"Oh come on," she said. "You've *got* to remember. It was that thing at the beach."

I still wasn't following. "So that's where they fought?"

"Right," she said. "But I *told* you about it at the cookie shop."

I searched my memories, and finally recalled which conversation she must be talking about. We'd been boxing up cookies when she'd mentioned something about Derek starting a fight with someone, and being totally outmatched.

But for some reason, I'd just assumed it was a verbal fight, not a physical one.

Even now, it made no sense. I saw Derek all the time. If he'd been assaulted, I surely would've noticed. And yet, it *would* explain Derek's hostility toward the painter.

In front of me, Cassie brightened. "See? You *do* remember."

"Yeah. But you never mentioned it was a fight-fight."

"I know. Because I figured you knew."

"What made you think that?"

"The way you reacted when I brought it up."

"I reacted?" I said. "How?"

"Like for one, thing, when I mentioned it, you literally covered your ears." She paused. "And said something like, 'If I hear one more word, I'm gonna scream.'"

"Did I?" That sounded awfully rude. "Gosh, Cassie, I'm really sorry…"

She waved away the apology. "You weren't mean or anything. You said it like you were joking, but I could tell you were really bothered."

It was all coming back to me now. She was right. I *had* been bothered. All summer, Derek had been a total ass-hat. I didn't know what his problem was, but already, I'd had more than enough.

"So anyway," Cassie continued, "I figured it was best to let it drop." She gave Joel a nervous glance. "But now that *he's* here, we can't exactly avoid it." She bit her lip. "Like, what if they get into another fight or something?"

I shook my head. "But Derek's not even coming."

She perked up. "Really? How do you know?"

"Because you told me. Remember?"

Her shoulders sagged. "On the phone? Sorry, but I meant that he wasn't here *yet.* But he *did* say he might stop by." She frowned. "Even if he *was* all funny about it."

"Funny how?"

"You know, just being kind of a jerk, like he was mad at you or something."

Now, that made sense. I gave Cassie a reassuring smile. "Honestly, I doubt he'll come. Earlier today, we got into this huge fight." I tried to laugh. "And just so you know, I mean the verbal kind. It's not like we 'came to blows' or anything." Under my breath, I added, "surprisingly."

"What'd you fight about?" she asked.

"Well…" I flicked my head toward Joel. "*Him*, actually."

Cassie's jaw dropped. "You mean the guy who beat him up?"

"Um…"

"So he's here with *you*?"

Was he? Yeah, I guess he was. He was, after all, the one who drove us here. And, he'd promised to drive me home, too.

But it was more than that. I'd invited him to join the party, assuming that Cassie didn't mind. In theory, I was supposed to be asking her about it, right now. But I'd gotten too distracted, and already, Joel was wading through the crowd, heading toward us.

I was dying to ask Cassie about the fight, but Joel would be here any second, so instead, I asked, "Do you care if he joins us?"

CHAPTER 18

Two daiquiris and a dozen thin slivers of cake later, I was feeling more mellow than I'd have ever guessed, considering how awful the first part of the day had been.

Ten of us, including Joel, were crammed obscenely tight into a long booth designed for eight. For the third time, April called out to Joel, "Are you sure you don't want a beer or something?"

Joel glanced toward me and said, "Nah. I'm good."

Listening to this, I felt a twinge of guilt. To think, I'd invited him here, only to have him sit, stone-cold sober, while everyone around him got totally smashed.

Plus, he was the only guy at our booth. That had to be at least a *little* awkward, right?

Feeling guiltier than ever, I told him, "If you want to drink, I'm sure I could find *someone* here to give me a ride home."

He shook his head. "Not a chance."

"Why not?" I asked.

As an answer, his dark eyes scanned our surroundings. I turned and saw what he saw – people dancing, drinking, laughing, talking, and yes, in some cases, staggering.

The way it looked, there wasn't a sober person in sight.

I turned back to him and said, "Okay, how about this? *I'll* stop drinking, so *you* can."

His mouth twitched at the corners. "Or…" He leaned his head closer to mine. "*You* could have another daiquiri, and let *me* worry about getting us home."

Home. On his lips, that word sounded nice – nicer, in fact, than the reality of it all.

In some ways, the house hadn't seemed like a home for a very long time. But now, gazing into the soulful eyes of a guy who had, until today, been a total stranger, that sad reality seemed blissfully far away.

Joel was close – so achingly close. If I wanted to, I could kiss him. And I was pretty sure I did want to. Sure, I'd have to lift my head a little higher, and lean into him all sultry-like. But I definitely *could* kiss him. And who knows, he might even kiss me back.

I didn't want another daiquiri. I wanted to be someone else, if only for a few hours. I wanted to be the kind of girl who didn't spend her nights lying awake worrying, and her days working seasonal jobs that everyone assumed I did for kicks, rather than for the money.

Sadly, they assumed wrong.

And being the sentimental sap that I was, I couldn't bring myself to correct them – and not only because I was embarrassed. Mostly, it was because it seemed like such a betrayal to my parents' memories, to admit to the whole world how badly they'd screwed everything up.

Damn it. I didn't want to think about this. I wanted a distraction, or heck, even a brand new life with a brand new name. Maybe if I were somewhere else, I could be the kind of girl who did what I wanted, and said exactly what was on my mind.

Or maybe – a crazy thought settled over me – I could be that girl right here, right now. I leaned closer to Joel, and the words I'd been wanting to say tumbled from my lips. "If you wanted, you could kiss me."

On Joel's face, I caught the hint of a smile. His gaze dipped to my lips, and I saw a flash of interest. *Real* interest. But then, he squashed my hopes by repeating the same three words he'd said just a few moments earlier. "Not a chance."

I drew back. "Why not?"

His gaze shifted to the curvy cocktail glass sitting right in front of me. The glass was empty. And next to *that* glass was another glass, also empty. And then, there was that tiny shot glass sitting off to the side.

I looked back to Joel. Trying to laugh off my humiliation, I said, "Are you implying that I'm drunk?"

"You're *supposed* to be drunk. It's your twenty-first, remember?"

As if I could forget. Pushing aside my embarrassment, I looked around the table and felt a goofy smile spread over my face. It was a smile of gratitude. And yes, maybe a fraction of that smile was fueled by the daiquiris. But mostly, I was incredibly thankful for the friends who'd come out celebrate with me.

Already, we'd been here for a couple of hours, and I'd been loving the chance to catch up with old friends and get to know the newer ones better. I'd already had cake, presents, and yes, more drinks than I'd normally want.

This wasn't my first time drinking, but it *was* my first time drinking legally. I looked back to Joel and said, "How about you? Are *you* twenty-one?"

As an answer, he made a point to look around, as if to say, *"We are in a bar, remember?"*

I had to laugh. "Forget I asked. So, when did you turn twenty-one?"

"Last year." He gave our surroundings another glance. "From what I remember, it was a hell of a party."

I bit my lip. "Are you sure you don't want a drink?"

"Nah. I'm good."

"Are you absolutely sure? Because honestly, I'm feeling kind of guilty."

"Why?" he asked.

"Because I'm pretty sure you're the only sober person in here."

With a secret smile, he leaned closer. "You think that's a bad thing?"

"Um, well..." Whatever I'd been planning to say evaporated somewhere between my throat and tongue.

Just maybe, he'd kiss me after all.

I waited.

No kiss.

Damn it.

Maybe he had a girlfriend, or simply wasn't interested. Or maybe, he'd already had enough female attention for one day.

Suddenly, I was dying to know something. Trying to sound casual, I said, "Hey, just curious, did the interns ever catch you?"

"What interns?"

I didn't even know their names, because they'd arrived late and had missed the introductions. And then, they'd left early to chase after Joel.

But had they caught him?

I tried to sound like it was no big deal. "At my house, earlier today, there were a couple of girls who seemed really eager to meet you." I gave a nervous laugh. "I was pretty sure they chased you down in the driveway or something."

"Oh, them?" Joel shrugged. "Yeah, I met them."

"And?"

"And nothing."

"What do you mean, nothing?" From what I recalled, they'd both been quite attractive in that classic college-student sort of way. "Didn't you like them?"

"Eh, they were alright."

Normally, I wouldn't be so persistent, but whether it was because of the alcohol, or because of him, I couldn't bring myself to let it go. "But…?"

"But nothing. They weren't my type."

So, he had a type? Maybe I wasn't his type either. And yet, something in his gaze suggested otherwise.

I was swimming in unfamiliar waters. Usually, *I* was the one backing away. But with Joel, it was different. Everything was different.

I liked having him here. And I loved being close to him. I'd been sitting crammed up against him for at least two hours now. And the longer we sat here, the more my imagination ran wild.

Probably, he was a terrific kisser.

I was still considering this when, from the far side of the booth, April called out, "Hey, Melody!"

When I looked toward her, she said, "You've *got* to tell us. For your birthday, did your crazy aunt get you another stripper?"

CHAPTER 19

I froze. Suddenly, everyone in the booth was staring. I gave Joel a nervous glance, praying that he wouldn't feel insulted all over again.

In his eyes, I saw a flash of humor that caught me off guard. Back in the boardroom, he *hadn't* been amused. But of course, that probably had something to do with Derek, who'd been awful from the get-go.

Before I could even begin to sort things out, April's voice rang out again. "So? Did she?"

Hoping to end this now, I called back, "Nope. Not this year." And then, desperate to change the subject, I made a show of looking around the bar. "So, how about this crowd, huh?"

But April didn't take the hint. Instead, she leaned forward and laughingly announced, "Wanna know my favorite? It was the policeman, for sure."

I cringed. I knew exactly which "policeman" she meant. He'd been my first stripper, a gag gift for my eighteenth birthday.

With a nervous laugh, I said, "Speaking of policemen, did you see the new traffic light?" Into the blank stares of everyone around me, I added. "You know, by the library?"

Dorothy, who actually worked at the library, gave me a perplexed look. "Sure, but what does *that* have to do with anything?"

Nothing, actually. But I was kind of hoping no one would notice. Still, I gave the diversion my best shot. "Well, you know. Like if people don't notice the light, they might get stopped..." I cleared my throat. "...by a policeman?"

April laughed. "Yeah. Maybe." She grinned across the table. "But he wouldn't look like 'Officer Night Stick,' that's for sure."

A newer friend, Francine, asked, "Who's Officer Night Stick?"

I gave a dismissive wave of my hand. "No one. Just a joke." Desperately, I turned to Joel. "Hey, do you wanna dance?"

The corners of his mouth lifted. "You mean *with* you, or…?"

My face was burning now. Feeling like a total idiot, I stammered out, "Well, um, I didn't mean *for* me or anything." I forced an awkward laugh. "I mean it's not like I'm confusing you with a stripper *now*."

Unlike in the boardroom, obviously.

"Yeah?" he said. "Good to know."

Suddenly, April called out, "Hey, Joel!"

He turned to look. "Yeah?"

She laughed. "*You're* not the stripper. Are you?" At this, the whole table erupted in fresh laughter, except for me and Joel, even if he did look vaguely amused. He looked to April and said, "You *see* a cop uniform?"

"It's not *always* a cop," she said. "Like last year, it was a construction worker." She looked to me and said, "Right?"

"Uh. Yeah." I felt my brow wrinkle in confusion. "But how did you know? I mean, you weren't in town or anything."

She smiled. "Get this. My mom sent me the pictures."

"Pictures?" I swallowed. "What pictures?"

"You know," she said. "From the ribbon-cutting ceremony. There was that article in the weekly paper. C'mon, you must've seen it."

"Oh. The article? Yeah, I saw it."

Unfortunately.

And yes, the article *did* have a few pictures. The biggest one showed me, looking absolutely horrified as Mister Hard-Hat strutted his stuff.

Even worse, the article had been picked up by a national news service. This meant the story, along with the photos, soon found its way onto Web sites and gossip pages around the country. Or cripes, worldwide for all I knew.

It was a total nightmare. Just thinking of it, I sank down in the booth and tried to disappear.

"Oh come on," April said, "don't be glum. It was a riot."

For her sake, I tried to laugh. "Maybe for you. But trust me, after a few birthday strip-a-thons, the joke's not nearly as funny, you know?"

I snuck a quick glance at my watch. Soon, it would be midnight. The way it looked, my aunt was actually going to keep her promise.

No more strippers.

Thank God.

I glanced to Cassie, who'd been sitting in relative silence across from me. In the short time that I'd known her, I'd never seen her so quiet. When our gazes met, she winced.

I gave her a questioning look.

After a long moment, she mouthed one terrifying word. "Sorry."

I tensed. "For what?"

Wincing again, she pointed to a spot somewhere past my left shoulder. "For that, actually."

CHAPTER 20

I whirled in my seat and heard myself gasp.

Oh, crap. There he was – an obscenely handsome stranger in an overly sexy cowboy getup. He was lugging a portable music player, and heading straight for us, strutting in a way that I knew all too well.

Praying for some sign I was wrong, I studied the guy's outfit. I saw fake leather chaps and a brown suede vest, open nearly to his navel. No shirt underneath. No cowboy boots. Just black running shoes with white laces.

My eyes narrowed. This was no real cowboy.

I whirled back to Cassie and said, "She didn't."

But obviously, she had.

Aunt Gina.

Damn it.

Cassie gave me an apologetic look. "Sorry. I didn't know." She bit her lip. "I mean, the way your aunt talked…"

Oh yeah. Aunt Gina. The one who'd promised oh-so sincerely that she was done with this sort of thing.

Apparently not.

I glanced toward the nearest exit. Happily, I was sitting at the edge of the booth, with no one blocking my path. If nothing else, I wouldn't need to crawl over anyone to make my escape.

And I *was* planning to escape.

From across the table, April's voice drifted through the noise. "Oh, man. A cowboy." Her voice became almost husky. "I *love* cowboys." I looked to see her eyeing the guy like he was the last pork chop at a meat-lovers convention.

On impulse, I said, "You want him? You can have him."

Her face broke into a huge, sloppy grin. "Seriously?"

Again, I glanced toward the exit. "Seriously." I turned to give Cassie an apologetic smile. "Sorry I'm being so weird about it." I started talking as fast as I could. "But hey, thanks for the party. And the cake. And everything. It was really, *really* thoughtful. I owe you one, okay?"

Next to me, Joel said, "You're not leaving."

That's what *he* thought. With or without him, I was bolting while I had the chance. I turned toward him and said, "Oh yeah? Why not?"

"Because you haven't given me that dance."

I did a double-take. "Huh?"

"Hey, you asked. Remember?"

Yes. Of course, I remembered. And he'd turned me down. Hadn't he?

No. That wasn't right. He'd turned me down for a kiss. About the dance, he'd never answered at all.

Still, I recognized this for what it was – a way to avoid the stripper without hurting anyone's feelings. It was the perfect lifeline, and I was grabbing that sucker while I had the chance.

I gave Joel a vigorous nod and practically leapt out of the booth, only to collide face-first with the chest of the cowboy, who stepped back and said in a big, Texas drawl, "Sorry ma'am."

I stared up at him. "Uh, that's okay."

He gave me a wink and tipped his hat. "So, are you the birthday girl?"

My mouth opened, but before I could say a single word, April's voice, loud and clear, carried across the short distance. "It's me!" she called. "*I'm* the birthday girl! Howdy, howdy, howdy!"

I could've kissed her – and the rest of the table, too, when no one spoke up to contradict her.

Escape time.

I grabbed Joel's hand, and practically dragged him out of the booth. Without looking back, I pulled us into the aisle that led to the dance floor. Walking fast, I didn't look back, and I didn't stop until we'd disappeared into the middle of the dancing crowd.

We'd barely stopped when the band transitioned from a familiar rock number to a slow, steady ballad from sometime before I'd been born.

Thankful for the switch, I fell into his arms and buried my face against his chest. Soon, I was laughing with relief, and yeah, more than a little bit embarrassment.

Against his shirt, I said, "Thanks for that."

"For what?"

"For rescuing me, of course." I pulled back and rolled my eyes. "*Again.*"

His eyes filled with humor. "Who says you weren't rescuing *me*?"

"What? You're not a fan of cowboys?"

"That kind?" He grinned. "No ma'am."

Again, I had to laugh. "Sorry. I guess I panicked back there."

"If *you* panicked, imagine how I felt."

It was a nice sentiment, obviously designed to spare my feelings. But it couldn't be true. I barely knew this guy, but one thing was already obvious. He wasn't the panicking type.

If he'd been truly panicking, he would've taken the quicker way out. He would've simply followed me to the exit and called it a night.

But he hadn't.

So I had to ask him, "Why'd you do it?"

"Do what?"

I glanced around. "This. I mean, you could've just driven me home and called it good."

"Is that what you wanted?"

"No," I admitted. "Not really."

"Well, there you go."

Yup. There I went. And here I was, dancing with the hottest guy in the whole place. And yes, that *did* include the cowboy. Sure, the cowboy was undeniably hot, even in that ridiculous outfit, but Joel was something more, and not only because of his beautiful face and rock-hard body.

He was real, and he was solid. And his hands felt amazing, resting on my hips. True, it wasn't skin-to-skin, but I liked the feel of him *and* the motions of him, too. But most of all, I liked how thoughtful he'd been in aiding my escape.

I gazed up at him, wondering which Joel was real – the jerk I'd left at the campsite, or the nice guy who'd been rescuing me nonstop ever since.

Searching his face, I couldn't be sure. He was full of contradictions, and there were so many questions I wanted to ask.

Where did you come from?

How do you know Derek?

And then, there was the scariest question of all. *If it weren't for the cowboy, would you still be out here, dancing with me?*

But I didn't ask any of those questions. Instead, I leaned into him and rested my warm face against the cool cotton of his T-shirt. His chest was hard, and his movements were smooth and easy, soothing me into a blissful trance that felt way too good, all things considered.

I let my eyelids flutter shut, and tried to block out everything else – the drunken crowd shifting around us, the muted whoops and hollers from the booth I'd just left, and the certain knowledge that the song wouldn't last forever.

Unfortunately.

CHAPTER 21

Sure enough, the song was over way too soon, replaced by a different slow song, newer than the one before. Reluctantly, I pulled back and smiled up at my rescuer. "Thanks again."

But he didn't let go. Instead, he glanced toward the booth and asked, "You wanna go back?"

Through the shifting crowd, I looked toward my party, only to feel myself cringe. It was *almost* as bad as I feared.

Surprisingly, the cowboy was still wearing all of his clothes. But, on the cringey side, he was straddling April's lap and thrusting against her while the others cheered him on. As for April herself, she was grinning like it was her first time at the rodeo, and she'd just won herself a prize bull.

Watching her obvious enjoyment, I had to wonder if something was wrong with me. Why didn't *I* like that sort of thing?

It's not that I didn't appreciate a good-looking guy. And it's not that I was completely inexperienced when it came to sex. It was just that, well, I liked things to be a little more private – and preferably not the result of money changing hands.

I looked back to Joel and said, "I guess I'm not *quite* ready."

The corners of his mouth lifted. "You and me both."

Relieved, I leaned back into him and sighed with contentment when his arms closed tighter around my back, shielding me from the spectacle that I'd been desperate to avoid. Soon, we were moving in time with the new song, and I thanked my lucky stars that Joel hadn't escaped when he had the chance.

And yet, my thoughts remained a jumbled mess. For what seemed like the millionth time, I asked myself why I hated something that everyone else seemed to love.

I was still mulling that over when I heard Joel's voice, quiet against my hair. "Regretting it?"

I pulled back to gaze up at him. "Regretting what?"

His gaze shifted to the booth, where the rodeo ride was still going strong.

Oh, that.

I had to laugh. "Heck no. When you've seen one, you've seen them all."

I froze in mid-motion. *Oh, crap.* That sounded terrible, didn't it? Hoping for a recovery, I resumed moving and tried again. "I don't mean that all guys are alike or anything. I just mean…" Again, I looked toward the booth. "It's just embarrassing, you know?"

As I watched, April threw back her head and laughed as the cowboy shimmied toward her. *She* wasn't embarrassed. *She* was loving it.

Then again, why wouldn't she? Unlike me, *she* had the cloak of anonymity. If *April* were caught ogling some professional hottie, *she* wouldn't wake up the next morning to see her own image in the weekly newspaper, or worse, on some gossip channel.

She wouldn't have to hear how stupid she looked, or see the intrusive articles that accompanied every single photo. *She* wouldn't have to read the one ghastly paragraph they always included, every single time, without fail.

By now, I could recite the thing from memory.

Melody Blaire is the heiress and only daughter of Blaydon Blaire, the world-renowned artist who died with his wife in a private plane crash.

His wife.

My mom.

They never mentioned *that* part. Did they?

But they *did* mention all the other stuff – rumors of affairs, fights, and whatever other drama they could dream up.

None of it was true. But that didn't stop anyone from speculating, even now.

I was so tired of it, I wanted to scream. But I didn't. Instead, I leaned into Joel and mumbled something about loving this song way too much to think of anything else.

Happily, Joel didn't push the issue. Instead, he cradled me tighter and moved against me, soothing my unsettled nerves until I almost forgot all of those things that I couldn't change.

And besides, I had so much to be thankful for. I had amazing friends who'd shown up for my party. I was dancing with an amazing guy. And, I had an aunt who, crazy or not, never, ever forgot my birthday.

When the song ended, I pulled back to tell Joel, "Thanks again. I owe you, okay?"

He smiled. "Why would *you* owe *me*?"

"Mostly for being here." I gave a shaky laugh. "I mean, this can't be your idea of fun."

"Yeah? Why not?"

"Well, for one thing, we're all drunk, and you're sober."

"And that's a bad thing?"

"Isn't it?" I asked.

He leaned his head closer and said, "You want the truth?"

I felt myself nod.

"I wasn't gonna drink anyway. So forget that, alright?"

"Oh." I wasn't sure what to make of that. "Why not? Are you a…?"

"Recovering alcoholic?" He laughed. "No."

"Then what?" I asked.

Without answering, he glanced toward the booth. "Looks like the show's over."

I turned, and sure enough, the cowboy, still fully dressed, was hoisting his music player onto his shoulder. He turned and began walking away, leaving April and the others ogling his backside.

I squinted in confusion. Had the guy stripped at all? If so, he had to be the fastest stripper on the planet, or I'd blinked and somehow missed it.

Regardless, it was time to go back. Together, Joel and I waded through the crowd and settled back into the booth.

April was laughing. She looked to me and called out, "You don't know what you missed."

Her laughter was contagious. I called back, "That's what *you* think."

"No, I'm serious," she said. "The guy was hysterical."

I gave her a confused look. "As in funny?"

"Oh yeah. Totally."

Wow, that was a first. Even the clowns hadn't been hysterical. I was just about to ask for details when, across from me, Cassie muttered, "Oh, crap."

I leaned forward. "What's wrong?"

She pointed past me. "Look who's here."

CHAPTER 22

I turned and spotted Derek, barreling through the back entrance. He looked like a man on a mission, assuming the mission was to kill someone and hide the body.

Next to me, Joel said, "Let me out."

I was sitting on the end of the booth, with Joel squashed in beside me. My gaze remained on Derek. "What?"

Joel gave me a nudge. "I *said*, let me out."

"Why?"

"You've gotta ask?"

Derek's angry gaze bounced around the room, as if he were searching for something – or more likely someone – in particular.

I felt myself swallow. *Me?*

From the look on his face, I sure hoped not.

I looked to Cassie. "Do you think he's here for the party?"

"I don't know." She gave Derek a worried glance. "*You're* the one who said he wouldn't show."

I looked back to Derek, only to feel myself freeze. He was staring straight at our booth, looking angrier than ever. Almost before I knew it, he was pushing his way through the crowd, heading in our direction.

Next to me, Joel muttered a low curse. A moment later, I felt movement beside me and turned just in time to see him shoving himself up and jumping onto the table. His heel bumped an empty daiquiri glass, and it fell sideways – not breaking, thank goodness, but making me nervous, just the same.

I stared up at him. "What are you doing?"

Ignoring me, he stepped across the table and jumped casually onto the floor.

My mouth fell open. "Are you leaving?" With all the drama, I guess I couldn't blame him. In fact, I decided, maybe that was the smartest thing. "On second thought," I said, "that's probably a good idea."

Joel gave me a look. "The hell it is."

Now, I didn't know what to think. Unsure what to do, I slid out of the booth to stand beside him.

He asked, "What are you doing?"

"I don't know," I admitted. "The same thing you're doing, I guess."

His jaw tightened. "Sit back down." He paused. "Alright?"

Before I could even consider it, I heard Derek's voice, calling out over the distance. "Hey! Asshole! I hope you like jail, because you're fuckin' going!"

I whirled to look. Suddenly, I couldn't see Derek at all, because Joel had moved to stand in front of me.

Confused, I peered around his back, only to realize something that I should've picked up on earlier. The way it looked, Derek had been yelling at Joel.

My stomach clenched. Derek was one of my oldest friends. And Joel was – well, I didn't know what he was exactly – but I definitely didn't want trouble for either one of them.

I shifted forward and tried, unsuccessfully, to put myself between the two guys. But no matter what I did, Joel moved with me, blocking my path, even as Derek continued to plow forward.

I made a sound of frustration. "Stop that."

Over his shoulder, Joel said, "No way."

"Why not?" I asked.

"You *know* why."

Okay, maybe I did. It was the sight of Derek, who was still shoving his way forward. A moment later, Derek stopped, directly in front of Joel and demanded, "You hear what I just said?"

Joel gave something like a laugh. "Dude, the whole place heard you." He glanced toward the nearest exit. "You wanna take it outside?"

I blurted out, "No!" I lunged around Joel and placed myself not exactly between them, but close enough to join in their discussion, assuming you could call it that.

Both guys turned to look. Neither one looked happy with the move.

Derek glared at me. "What the hell are *you* doing here?"

Cassie jumped to her feet. "We're *here* celebrating her birthday, not that you seem to care."

"Yeah?" Derek said. "Well, maybe I've got more important things going on."

Cassie glared at him. "Or maybe, you're being an ass."

Ignoring Cassie's insult, Derek turned back to Joel and said, "The cops are on the way, so I suggest you stick around."

Joel looked utterly unconcerned. "Yeah? Why's that?"

"Three words, asshole." Derek straightened. "Grand theft auto."

My stomach sank. *Oh, God.* I should've known this would happen. I should've *made* Joel return the Camaro before anyone spotted it.

Instead, what had I done? I'd let him leave the Camaro at my place while he drove me here in my dad's car.

I froze. *My dad's car.*

Joel laughed in Derek's face. "That's the best you got?" He spread out his arms. "You wanna hit me? Don't be a pussy. Bring it on."

I spoke up. "Wait!"

Again, they both turned to look.

Dreading what I had to say next, I looked to Derek and said, "By any chance, you don't mean the Porsche, do you?"

CHAPTER 23

Derek still looked on the verge of exploding. "Hell yeah, I mean the Porsche." He pointed to Joel. "This *asshole* was seen driving it, *alone*, a couple of hours ago."

Now, it was my turn to glare. "Oh yeah? Where?"

Derek gestured toward the rear of the bar. "In *that* parking lot." He offered up a cold smile. "If we're lucky, we've got it on tape."

My gaze narrowed. "Who's we?"

Derek straightened. "I've got my sources."

No doubt, he did. Derek's dad was a big fish in this tiny pond of a town, which meant that Derek, by association, had this irritating way of finding out everything that went on, even things that were none of his business.

"Yeah?" I said. "Well, maybe he was driving it, because I asked him to."

Derek stiffened. "What?"

"Yeah," I continued, "and it seems to me, you would've figured this out…" My voice rose. "…considering that I'm standing right here, *with* the guy you're accusing of stealing my car."

Derek gave a derisive snort. "*Your* car?"

I hesitated. Now, this is where things got dicey. The whole estate, including the Porsche, was in some sort of legal trust. But I *was* allowed to live in the house, and yeah, use the things associated with it, so I didn't see the problem.

The car was stored in the garage below the guest house, just like the silverware was stored in the kitchen. As long as I put everything back when I was done, it was never an issue. I mean, I drove my mom's car all the time, and no one gave me grief about *that*, did they?

As if sensing weakness, Derek gave me a smug smile. "Well?"

He could smile all he wanted. I wasn't going to back down, not this time. I lifted my chin. "Yes. *My* car, which means it's none of your business."

Derek gave a bark of laughter. "So *that's* the defense?"

"No defense is needed," I told him, "since no crime was committed. So just forget it, okay?"

"Forget it?" he repeated.

Next to us, Cassie chimed in, "Yeah. Just like you forgot her birthday." Under her breath, she added, "Ass-hat."

Derek's mouth tightened. He turned to Cassie and said, "I got her something, so stop harping on me, alright?"

Cassie crossed her arms. "Oh yeah? What'd you get her?"

Derek's gaze shifted to Joel. "I'm still working on it."

Well, that was rich. Was Derek *still* trying to act like that whole painting stunt was for my benefit?

I told him, "Don't bother. I don't want anything painted."

"Forget the painting," Derek said. "We're talking about the Porsche." His voice rose. "And you let that dickweed drive it? What the hell were you thinking?"

Joel's voice cut through the noise. "Hey, *dickweed.* If you're pissed about the car, you can deal with me, not her."

As thankful as I was, I couldn't agree. After all, Joel had only driven the car as a favor to me, because I couldn't drive a stick.

I turned and gave Joel a pleading look. "Thanks, seriously. But no one has to deal with anything, okay?" I turned back to Derek and said, "Besides, you're leaving anyway, right?"

Derek gave me a thin smile. "You'd like that, wouldn't you?"

"Yes. I would, actually."

"Well, forget it," he said. "I'm not going anywhere. Not 'til the cops show up."

I made a sound of frustration. "But why *would* they? It's *my* car."

"Wrong," he said. "It belongs to the trust."

I threw up my hands. "You know what? Fine. I hope the cops *do* come. And I hope they make a big, ugly scene, so you can explain to the whole world why I'm not allowed to use something that my own dad left me."

I almost felt like crying. Maybe it was the alcohol. Or maybe it was the fact that I'd been dealing with too much of this over the last few months.

Derek's voice softened. "Stop exaggerating. We let you live there, don't we?"

Heat flooded my face. Not for the first time, I felt like some imposter, bumbling around in a mansion that wasn't my own. Trying not to show my humiliation, I said, "You're not *letting* me do anything. It's *my* house."

Derek smiled. "Is it?"

Showing a lot more bravado than I felt, I said, "If it's not, take me to court."

Derek looked heavenward. "I can't take you to court. You're represented by *our* firm."

"Great," I said. "Then you can waste lots of money, suing me *and* defending me at the same time." I crossed my arms. "I hope you've got lots of time on your hands."

"That's not the way it works," Derek said, "and you damn well know it."

Actually, I knew shockingly little about how everything worked. I *did* know that Derek's dad was supposedly my lawyer. And he was also the lawyer for my parents' estate.

But I knew all sorts of other things, too – that the property taxes had gone sky-high, and that most of the money set aside for maintenance and repairs had been diverted to pay those taxes, and that, worst of all, I couldn't do a darn thing about any of it until I turned twenty-five.

That's when I'd fully inherit – not just the house, but any remaining funds, along with full control and responsibility.

That was still four years away. Sometimes, it felt like forever.

Cassie said, "Hey Derek." When he turned to look, she pointed toward the front entrance. "Your swat team's here."

We all looked. Sure enough, I spotted Officer Nelson hustling in through the main entrance. He was short and squat, with a big white moustache that covered nearly a third of his good-natured face.

I liked him. He was a regular at Cassie's Cookies and had a real thing for chocolate. I stood on my tiptoes and waved him over.

Derek said, "What are you doing?"

I gave Derek my snottiest smile. "Getting this over with."

"You can't do that," he said. "I'm the one who reported it."

Ignoring Derek, I called out, "Officer Nelson! Over here!"

His face broke into a friendly smile, and he started lumbering in our direction.

Derek was looking almost nervous now. "What are you gonna tell him?"

The sudden change made me pause. "Why? Are you worried?"

"No."

I studied his face. "You are. Aren't you?" And that's when I realized something. Derek wasn't nearly as sure of his position as he claimed. The way it looked, I'd thrown him off by calling his bluff.

Probably, his little script called me to apologize profusely and promise to never, ever take out the Porsche again. After all, that's how things usually went when it came to estate business.

Funny, I'd never really pushed the issue before. So why was I now? Was it because I had Joel and Cassie backing me up? Or because I'd had one shot too many?

Either way, I wasn't giving in. Not tonight.

CHAPTER 24

Five minutes later, it was mostly over.

Derek, in spite of his attitude earlier, had said surprisingly little during the whole encounter, which ended with me giving Officer Nelson an apologetic smile. "So anyway," I concluded, "sorry for the misunderstanding."

"Aw, that's alright," he said. "Got me off the desk for a few." He looked to Cassie. "See ya Monday?"

She gave him a little wave. "See ya Monday."

As Officer Nelson lumbered toward the exit, Derek said, "What's going on Monday?"

Cassie said, "Chocolate day at the cookie shop." She lifted her chin. "Officer Nelson's a regular."

"Well, goodie for you," Derek said, turning back to me. "Speaking of Monday, I'm gonna have a mechanic look over the Porsche." He gave Joel a warning look. "To make sure nothing's damaged."

Joel said, "You should. The clutch is slipping."

I felt my brow wrinkle in confusion. What was a clutch? Sadly, I had no idea.

From the looks of it, neither did Derek. His eyes narrowed. "What?"

"The clutch," Joel said. "When's the last time you had it checked?"

"Hey!" Derek barked. "I don't answer to you."

"Good thing," Joel said, "with the sorry job you're doing."

Derek took a single step forward. "Listen, asshole…"

I jumped between them and looked to Derek. "A mechanic? Great! And while you're at it, have them fix the other car, too."

Derek frowned. "Your mom's car? What happened to *that* one?"

I shrugged like it was no big deal. "It stalled at the campground."

"What campground?"

"You know. The one a few miles from my house."

Derek stared at me. "You took the car camping?"

"No." I hesitated. "I was visiting a friend."

Derek's gaze shifted to Joel. "A friend, huh?"

I nodded. "Yup."

Looking more annoyed than ever, Derek said, "You got funds for the repair?"

No. I didn't, actually. But that was partially my point. I forced a smile. "I dunno. Do I have 'funds' to have someone look over the Porsche?"

"You know what?" Derek said. "Forget it. You wanna deal with the cars on your own? Fine by me."

"Great," I said. "It's fine by me, too."

Was it fine? Probably not. Supposedly, I had two cars at my disposal. Unfortunately, the one I normally drove was stuck at the campground. As for the other one, I didn't even know how to drive it.

I bit my lip. *What would I do now?* Maybe it was time to pull out my bike and get peddling. That *might* work, until winter, anyway.

Derek gave me a long, penetrating look. "What's up with you tonight?"

"Nothing."

"Yeah, whatever. But the attitude's getting old."

My jaw dropped. "*My* attitude?"

But already, Derek had turned to go. Without so much as a goodbye, he stormed out the same way he'd come in, with lots of pushing and shoving.

Next to me, Cassie, "God, what's his deal lately?"

I shook my head. "I wish I knew."

"Well, at least he's gone."

I sighed. "Yeah. Until next time, anyway." I looked to Joel, who had shown remarkable restraint during the whole ugly encounter. I said, "I'm really sorry."

His eyes filled with humor. "About what?"

He had to be joking. Mentally, I ran through the list. Let's see. I'd involved him in estate drama with my sticky-fingered relatives. I'd dragged him to a party where he was the only person not drinking. And then, as the grand finale, I'd almost gotten him arrested for grand theft auto – *twice*, if I counted the thing with the Camaro.

I had to admit, "I'm not sure where to begin."

"Forget it." He smiled. "Not a big deal."

"How can you say that?" I asked. "I've caused you loads of trouble."

"Tonight?" He gave a loose shrug. "That was nothing."

I looked to Cassie, who appeared just as confused as I felt. Reluctantly, I looked toward the rest of my birthday party, who'd been sitting in awkward silence during that whole scene with Derek.

I gave them an apologetic look. "I'm really sorry about that."

April said, "You shouldn't apologize. Derek was a total dick." She frowned. "Funny, I remember him being a lot nicer."

"Yeah," I sighed. "You and me both."

□

CHAPTER 25

I woke to the smell of burnt pancakes. Smiling, I jumped out of bed, threw on a pair of shorts under my oversized T-shirt, and was down the stairs in a flash.

Sure enough, I found Aunt Gina in the kitchen, looking flustered like she always did whenever she tried to cook. She was petite and freckled, with a mop of dark hair that fell loosely over her eyes as she studied the gas stove in obvious frustration.

When I moved closer, she looked up. "Hey! There's my birthday girl!" She paused. "Even if I am a little late."

"Actually, you're early. I thought you weren't coming 'til tonight."

She smiled. "Surprise!" She looked toward the stove, and her smile faded. "Damn it. Those look like shit."

I looked. On the griddle, I saw four black smoking blobs. They didn't look terrific. But they looked a lot better than her last attempt. "They don't look *so* bad," I said.

She rolled her eyes. "Yeah, right." She reached out and turned off the stove. "Screw this. I'm taking you out."

A half-hour later, we were sitting together at a table for two at the local pancake shack. Aunt Gina leaned forward. "So…" She smiled. "You never told me. How'd you like him? He was pretty hot, huh?"

Instantly, an image of Joel flashed in my mind. He *was* pretty hot. And sweet. And wonderful. And yeah, kind of scary, at least when it came to Derek.

I recalled the previous night. The final hours had passed in a blur, with more shots, more dancing, and more laughing with my friends.

Afterward, Joel had driven me home and practically carried me inside, only *after* checking the place for wayward thieving relatives.

At the memory, I felt a warm glow settle over me. Aside from the ugliness with Derek, it had been the best birthday in a long, long time.

Joel was a big part of that. I never got that kiss, but he *had* mentioned seeing me again. If I was lucky, it might even be soon. But obviously, he wasn't the guy my aunt meant. I said, "You mean the cowboy?"

She slapped her hands, palms-down, on the table, making her coffee cup rattle precariously. "Heck yeah, I mean the cowboy. I heard he was awesome."

"Where'd you hear that from?"

"From him. Who else?"

I laughed. "Seriously?"

"Well, yeah. I asked him to call me when it was done." She gave me a wicked grin. "He said you *really* got into it."

I bit my lip. Technically, it was April who really got into it. But I hated the thought of saying so. "Well…" I hesitated. "About that…"

"What?" My aunt studied my face. "He wasn't lying, was he?"

"Uh, no," I stammered. "That's not it. He was great, honest." I let out a long, frustrated breath. "It's just that, well…" I winced. "You promised. Remember?"

She gave me a confused look. "Promised what?"

Did I really need to remind her? "No more strippers. Come on. You *do* remember, don't you?" I tried to laugh. "I'm pretty sure I begged. Literally. On my knees and everything."

"You weren't begging," she said. "You were scrubbing the floor."

Okay, technically, that was true. But still, I *had* gotten up on my knees while the actual pleading took place. That had to count for something, right?

I gave her a look and waited.

After a long pause, she sighed, "Yeah. I remember."

"So…?" I prompted.

"So…?" She shook her head. "What?"

Feeling like I giant heel, I forced myself to continue. "So, last night, even though you promised not to, you sent another stripper."

"No, I didn't."

Okay, when it came to strippers, I was practically an expert, unfortunately. Again, I waited.

Finally, she gave another sigh. "Oh, okay. He was a stripper. But he didn't strip. So it doesn't count. See?"

It made sense, in an Aunt Gina sort of way. Still, I needed to find *some* way to make her understand without hurting her feelings. I searched for the words, but came up empty.

Into my silence, she said, "Hey, I told him, up-front, 'You take off one single thing, mister, and you're gonna hear about it.'"

I gave her a pleading look. "But he was still a stripper."

She was frowning now. "I don't get it. He told me you had a great time last night."

"I did. Honest." *But not because of the cowboy.*

"Then what's the problem?" She gave me a hopeful smile. "Yee-ha."

"No." I shook my head. "No yee-ha."

Her eyebrows furrowed. "No yee-ha?"

"No. Not that I don't appreciate the sentiment." Now that I'd started this, I was determined to finish. "Look, Aunt Gina, I know you mean well…"

"But?"

"But that kind of stuff isn't my thing, you know?"

"Why not?"

"For starters, because it's embarrassing."

"Not to me."

The funny thing was, she was telling the truth. I'd seen my aunt with strippers, mine mostly. When they did their thing, she was like April on steroids.

Desperately, I tried to explain. "Yeah, but I'm *not* you." I took a deep breath. "It's really, really nice of you. And I know you mean well, but I don't want that kind of attention."

"You mean from guys?" She paused. "Want me to send a girl next time?" She perked up. "Because they've got those, too."

Oh, God. As if the *regular* news stories weren't bad enough. "No. That's not it. I just don't like everyone looking at me."

"But that's silly."

I made a sound of frustration. "Why is it silly?"

"Because everyone *always* looks at you."

Sadly, I couldn't even argue. I took a subtle look around. Technically, only a few people were looking, but they were strangers, touristy types mostly. As far as the locals, they treated me just like they treated everyone else.

And I loved them for it.

I considered myself one of them, even if my life was freakishly different than most of theirs.

It was a nice setup, and I had my parents to thank for it. In spite of their apparent wealth, they'd made a genuine effort to have me grow up as – in their words – a normal kid.

That's why they'd settled here, instead of New York or Chicago. And that's why I went to public school, had regular chores, and regular friends. It was why – thank God – I didn't mind working for a living or cleaning my own house.

Aunt Gina smiled. "So, if they're gonna stare anyway, you might as well embrace it, right? You know, have some fun with it."

Fun? My gaze landed on a far table, where an older couple was whispering and pointing – at me, of course. I didn't need to hear them to know what they were saying. *See that girl at the far table? She's the daughter of that rich artist who flew his plane into Lake Michigan.*

The rest of the conversation was equally predictable.

I hear she inherited a ton of money.

Do you think he killed himself?

I hear his wife was screwing their lawyer.

I gave the couple an annoyed look. Far from being deterred, the woman pulled out her cell phone and held it out in front of her. As I watched, she pretended to check her messages or whatever.

Nice try, lady. I'd seen that trick before.

Sure enough, the telltale flash came a moment later. As I watched, she and her companion studied the photo. Soon, she was holding up her phone again in the same exact way.

Another flash, another look, another urge – from me, to rip that thing out of her hands and shove it where the sun didn't shine.

Aunt Gina said, "Did you hear what I just said?"

I blinked. "Sorry. What?"

"I *said*, you always *were* more like your mom."

Instantly, I felt that familiar pang. My mom was Aunt Gina's sister. But where Aunt Gina was crazy and flamboyant, my mom had been the introverted type. She played the piano and the flute, and sang beautifully from what I recalled.

As if reading my mind, Aunt Gina said, "You know why they named you Melody, don't you?"

I did know. I'd been told a hundred times. But it was a story I loved to hear, so all I said was, "Because my mom loved music, right?"

My aunt got that familiar faraway look in her eyes. "Oh yeah. She loved music. And your dad loved her. They were so crazy together. I never saw anything like it." Her voice grew quiet. "I really miss her, you know." She smiled. "Your dad, too."

She reached across the table and gave my hand a tender squeeze. "But at least I have you."

A sad smile tugged at my lips. "And I have you."

My aunt gave a weak laugh. "And don't forget the cowboy."

"Uh, yeah," I said. "About him. Will you promise? I mean *really* promise this time?"□

CHAPTER 26

"So," Cassie said, "did she promise?"

"Sort of."

It was late Sunday afternoon, and I was sitting on the front porch steps, talking on the phone with Cassie.

I'd called to verify that she still needed me to work tomorrow. Or at least, that was my official reason. My *unofficial* reason was that I was dying to hear more about that fight she witnessed between Joel and Derek.

On the night of my birthday, I never *did* get the chance to ask.

But first things first. I thanked her for the party and apologized for being such a bad sport about the stripper. One thing led to another, and I ended up telling her about my conversation with Aunt Gina.

"But I don't get it," Cassie said. "What do you mean she 'sort of' promised?"

I sighed. "She promised to do better next year."

"But that's good, right?"

"Knowing my aunt? I'm not so sure." I tried to laugh. "Do you know, when I was younger, she'd always get me a clown for my birthday?"

Cassie paused for a long, silent moment. "You're kidding."

"I wish," I said. "And just so you know, I don't mean a clown doll. Or a clown cake. I mean a real, live clown."

"Like a professional?"

"Sometimes," I said. "But other times, she'd have one of her friends dress up and surprise me. It was really crazy, too, because–" I paused as I spotted a car turning onto my driveway.

"Because what?" Cassie said.

It was an unfamiliar black sports car, and I got to my feet. My aunt had left only minutes earlier, and I wasn't expecting company. Into the phone, I said, "Sorry, someone's here."

"Who?" Cassie asked.

I was still watching the car. It looked sleek and expensive, with wide rear tires and dark tinted windows. "I don't know," I said.

"Do you need to go?"

"Actually, I'm not sure." I watched as the car pulled closer and came to a stop in the turnaround. The driver's side door opened, and a familiar figure stepped out.

I felt myself smile.

It was Joel.

Getting out of the car, he looked like every girl's dream – lean and muscular, with a face that made it impossible to look away.

I gave him a wave and said into the phone, "Actually, I probably should go. Can I call you back later?"

"Oh, my God," she said. "It's him, isn't it?"

Already, Joel was moving toward me, striding forward like a man on a mission. I gave the phone a distracted squeeze. "Uh-huh."

Cassie laughed. "You know, I can totally hear you drooling."

I snapped back to reality. In a low whisper, I said, "Oh, shut up. I am not."

"Hey, I don't blame you," she said. "If I were you, I'd be drooling, too."

Ignoring her comment, I gave her a quick goodbye and disconnected the call. And then, I looked to Joel. He was dressed nearly the same as Friday night, in tattered jeans and a thin T-shirt. As he moved, his shirt clung to him, giving me a tantalizing hint of his tight abs underneath.

Who knows, maybe I *was* drooling.

Smiling, I stepped forward to greet him. "Hi."

He didn't smile back. "Hi."

I felt my own smile fade. "Is something wrong?"

His mouth tightened. "Yeah. I don't know how to tell you this…"

My stomach clenched. "What?"

"Your car," he said. "It's gone."

A wave of guilt washed over me. "Oh, no. Didn't they tell you?"

"Tell me what?"

"Derek had it towed."

Joel frowned. "To where?"

"Supposedly, to a repair shop."

He gave me a questioning look. "Supposedly?"

"Yeah. I mean, probably." I paused. "But it's not like I know which shop or anything."

"Why not?"

"Because all I had was a message from Derek on my voicemail." I tried to laugh. "Get this. He had it towed Friday night, right after leaving T.J.'s."

In front of me, Joel wasn't laughing. "The guy didn't waste any time, did he?"

"Apparently not." I sighed. "But mostly, I feel sorry for the tow-truck driver. Knowing Derek, he probably dragged some poor guy out of bed." I paused as something occurred to me. "But wait. That was two nights ago. You just noticed?"

"Yeah, because I just got back."

"From where?"

"Detroit." He smiled. "I told you Friday, remember?"

Did he? Probably. My brain *had* been a little fuzzy.

I considered the timetable. The way it sounded, he hadn't even returned to his campsite after driving me home in the Porsche.

I glanced at the car he was driving today. "Let me guess. You returned the Camaro?"

"Sorry, you'd be guessing wrong."

"But you're driving a different car." I pointed to the car in the turnaround. "So whose car is that?"

"Mine."

"Really?" I gave it a closer look. It wasn't just expensive. It was exotic. I didn't know what to make of it. I looked back to Joel. "It's a lot different from the Camaro."

"Yeah," Joel said. "It's got plates."

License plates? Was that a joke? If so, I was too distracted to appreciate it. "But about the Camaro," I said. "Why didn't you return it? I mean, if you have a car of your own–"

"That's not why I took it."

I felt my brow wrinkle. "So why did you?"

Joel's gaze darkened. "Payback."

"Oh." The Camaro had been a total heap. Obviously, his brother didn't have a lot of money. It seemed almost cruel to take his car, regardless of the circumstances. Unless I was missing something?

"Payback?" I said. "So like your brother owed you money?"

"No. But he owed me *something*."

I bit my lip. "But isn't your brother missing it?"

"The Camaro?" Joel gave a low laugh. "Oh yeah. He's missing it."

I didn't get the joke. "What's so funny?"

"If you knew my brother, you wouldn't ask."

"But I *don't* know him," I said. "Does he know you have it?"

"Oh yeah. He called."

"When?" I asked.

Joel gave it some thought. "A few weeks ago."

My jaw dropped. "You stole it – I mean, *borrowed* it, or whatever – a few *weeks* ago? Doesn't he need it back?"

"No." Joel smiled. "But he *wants* it."

I stiffened. "I'm sure he does. Are you *ever* planning to return it?"

Joel considered the question. "I dunno. Maybe. Maybe not."

I almost didn't know what to say. It was like Joel had two personalities. One was a total sweetheart, and the other was a cold-hearted bastard.

At something in my expression, he said, "Trust me. He can do without it."

I looked at the car Joel was driving today. It was beyond nice. I considered the car he'd swiped from his brother. It was a hunk of junk – something you'd only drive if you were destitute.

I crossed my arms. "If you say so."

His jaw tightened. "So, you're taking his side?"

Was I? Probably. I couldn't help it. I felt bad for him. It was true that I lived in a mansion, but I knew what it was like to worry about money – and now, cars too.

The thing with the Camaro was hitting too close to home. Aside from towing my mom's car on Friday night, Derek had sent someone over on Saturday to pick up the Porsche.

Supposedly, both cars were being looked at. In reality, I wasn't so sure. Either way, I'd be riding my bicycle to work.

Was Joel's brother doing the same thing? Or was he walking to work?

Did he even have a job? Maybe he couldn't *get* a job with no vehicle.

How awful was that?

In front of me, Joel was waiting for my answer. Was I taking his brother's side?

I couldn't help it. When it came to this, I guess I was. But I hated the thought of saying so. I tried to smile. "Well, as you said, I don't even know him."

Joel was frowning now. "Yeah. And you're not gonna."

I drew back. "What does that mean?"

"Nothing. Forget it."

"No." My eyes narrowed. "I'd really like to know."

"Yeah?" Joel said. "Wanna know what *I'd* like?"

"What?"

"To talk about something else."

I didn't *want* to talk about something else. I wanted to know what he meant. Was he sending me some sort of message, like, "*I hope you don't expect to meet my family.*"

Talk about arrogant.

It was time to end this conversation before I said something regrettable. "Alright." I gave him a stiff smile. "Thanks for stopping by."

He looked at me for a long, silent moment before saying, "If you want me to go, just say so."

At this point, I wasn't sure what I wanted. So I said nothing, wondering if he'd tell me what I was missing.

But he didn't.

Instead, he turned away and began stalking toward his car. As I watched, he opened the driver's side door, got in, and fired up the engine. Almost before I knew it, he was pulling away.

And then, he was gone.

Staring at the empty driveway, I had to ask myself, *"What just happened?"*

The sad truth was, I had no idea.

CHAPTER 27

April said, "Hey, you're still listening, right?"

I gave a little shake of my head. "Uh, yeah. Sorry. What were you saying?"

It was still Sunday, an hour before sunset, and I'd called April to thank her for being such a great sport about that whole stripper thing.

My intentions were good, but my performance was pathetic. We'd been talking for less than ten minutes, and already, I was beyond distracted.

Ever since Joel's abrupt departure a couple of hours earlier, I'd been waffling between anger and guilt, hatred and longing, and satisfaction and regret.

It didn't help that April had spent the last ten minutes telling me how totally hot and amazing Joel was. I couldn't disagree with the first part. Hot? Definitely. But amazing? Well, the jury was still out on that.

As she rambled on, I didn't have the heart to tell her that I probably wouldn't be seeing him again.

Hoping to change the subject, I said, "Hey, I meant to ask you something. You called the cowboy hilarious. What'd you mean by that?"

"Oh, that," she said. "Well, you probably saw, he didn't take off a single thing, not even his hat."

"Yeah," I said. "And do you know why?"

"Why?"

"Because my aunt told him not to."

"Oh man, what a bummer. But I guess that explains it."

"Explains what?"

"Well, the whole time he's dancing and stuff, he's describing what he *would* be taking off, if only we were alone in some cow patch or something."

In spite of everything, I had to laugh. "What's a cow patch?"

"Heck if I know," she said. "And you wanna hear something funny? I don't think *he* knew either. But anyway, he's going into all this detail, even as does his thing."

I recalled the spectacle from Friday night. From the little I'd seen, his "thing" involved a whole lot of straddling and thrusting.

April continued, "And he's all like…" She mimicked a masculine drawl. "'Then, I'd take off my pants, and *you*, my little filly, would wanna ride me around, rodeo-style.'"

I burst out laughing. "That makes no sense."

"I know," she said. "But it was awesome." Her tone grew more serious. "You're not sorry you missed it, are you?"

Now, it was *my* turn to imitate the cowboy. "No ma'am."

April laughed. "You know what? I think *your* cowboy voice was better than his."

I couldn't resist. "Thanks partner."

Suddenly, she burst out, "Oh my God! I almost forgot to tell you. You know my favorite zombie movie, right?"

"How could I forget?" I smiled at the memory. "You dragged me to see that thing like five times."

The movie's name was *Flashbang*, and zombies were just a small part of the plot. It was a huge cult favorite from a few years back, some low-budget indie flick that somehow managed to gross a fortune.

On the phone, April was saying, "I know, it was awesome, right?"

It *was* awesome – not the movie, but the fact that April loved it so much. As for me, I was more of a vampire girl. Still, I said, "Yeah, it was pretty awesome."

"So get this." She squealed, "I saw the car!"

Ouch. I held the phone away from my ear. "What car?"

"The one from the movie! You remember, right?"

I tried to think. From what I recalled, the hero had driven this beat-up Camaro across the Mohave Desert, all the while being pursued by gangs of zombies, mutants and pissed-off bikers. "Yeah, it was–"

I froze. A Camaro. *The* Camaro? *No, it couldn't be.*

April said, "Sorry, what was that? You cut out for a minute."

My mind was whirling. Still, I managed to say, "It was a Camaro, right?"

"Yeah, totally. See, I *knew* you'd remember."

"And you saw it?" I said. "Where?"

"A few miles from your house. Crazy, huh?"

I was so distracted, I could hardly think. "Uh. Yeah. Crazy."

"I know," April said. "I mean, who expects to see something like *that* around here. So, are you surprised or what?"

Oh, I was surprised, alright.

And yet, it *couldn't* be the same car. I surely would've noticed, right?

Or maybe not.

When Joel had picked me up, it had been dark, and I'd been distracted. Maybe I *wouldn't* have noticed.

"So?" April said. "Are you? Surprised, I mean?"

"Yeah." I gave a weak laugh. "Stunned, actually." I was still trying to sort things out. "So, when did you see it?"

"This morning. On my way out of town. So in a way, I have *you* to thank for it."

"Why me?" I asked.

"Because if it weren't for your birthday, I wouldn't've been in town, so I wouldn't've been driving down that road at all. See?"

"Uh, yeah. *Which* road? You never said."

"The one along the lake. You know, where that campground is."

Oh, crap. So much for a poor, destitute brother, walking to work.

April said, "You know the road, right?

Did I ever. "Oh yeah," I murmured. "I definitely know."

"Anyway," April continued, "I'm passing this storage place – you know, the one across from the campground – and what do I see? That car! And I'm thinking, 'No freaking way!' But I hit the brakes and turn around. And like half-a-minute later, I'm pulling into that storage place, and I ask the guy driving it–"

"Wait," I said. "Which guy?" It couldn't be Joel, or she would've already mentioned it. Maybe this *was* just a coincidence.

April said, "The guy who works at the storage place. Apparently, I'd caught him moving it from one unit to the other. But that's not the point." She gave another happy squeal. "I got to sit in it!"

Yeah. Me, too.

My mind was a jumbled mess. "Do you have any pictures? Like a selfie or something?"

April sighed in obvious disappointment. "No. The guy wouldn't let me take any. He acted like it was all top-secret or something." She paused. "But you *do* believe me, right?"

Oh yeah. I definitely believed her.

But now, I felt like giant idiot.

□

CHAPTER 28

After getting off the phone with April, I spent the next half-hour scouring the internet. There, I found countless pictures of the Camaro, movie stills mostly. But as far as the Camaro's owner, that remained a mystery.

So I started researching the movie itself. At last, I discovered something that made me sit up and take notice. One of the movie's financial backers was a guy named Jake Bishop.

Staring at the screen, I said his last name out loud. "Bishop." Like *Joel* Bishop. Coincidence? Unlikely.

After that, my research got a lot easier. While hunched over my computer, I learned that Jake Bishop was a big internet star, with a rabid fan base of frat boys, groupies, and mixed-martial arts fans.

Apparently, he was some sort of fighter, or prankster, or both. Scrolling through the promo images, I saw blood and plenty of it.

I gave a shudder. I hated the sight of blood. And I wasn't a fan of fighting at all.

Bracing myself, I clicked on a random video. After five minutes, I hit the stop button and turned to look out my back window.

Outside, the view was amazing. The sun hovered just above the horizon, casting a shimmering glow over the endless water. But no matter how hard I tried, I couldn't bring myself to appreciate it. Not now.

I'd made a huge mistake.

Joel's brother was nothing like what I'd assumed. He wasn't some poor slob, stranded on the roadside. He was rich and famous – and a total jerk.

The way it looked, he made his money by pushing people's buttons and beating them senseless when they finally took a swing at him. Oh sure, the guys he encountered were rich and famous in their own right – sports stars mostly. But the whole thing was crude and ugly, even if the guy himself wasn't.

He was, to put it mildly, quite attractive, with features that were strikingly similar to Joel's.

I sighed. Yup, he was Joel's brother, alright.

With growing regret, I considered Joel's claim, that he'd taken the Camaro as some sort of payback. I bit my lip. Probably, his brother had it coming.

And what had I done? I'd gotten on my high horse and acted like Joel was the bad guy in all this. As my thoughts churned, I stared out over the horizon. Soon, it would be dark. I had no car. And yet, I *had* to see him.

Before I knew it, I was outside, pulling out my bike. With growing resolve, I began peddling toward the campground. If I was lucky, I'd reach it before darkness fell.

Or not.

By the time I peddled breathlessly up to his site, it was officially dark and worse, I saw no sign of Joel's car.

I stopped and straddled my bike while I gazed out over his campsite. It didn't look nearly as barren as last time. The tent was still there, but now, I saw two lawn chairs facing the darkened fire-pit, along with a loose pile of logs and kindling a few feet away.

Unable to resist, I got off my bike and leaned it against a tree. And then, I walked forward to check out the fire-pit. Among the ashes, I saw a few scattered remnants of that torn check. Against all logic, I felt a wistful smile tug at my lips.

That whole scene had been utterly awful, and yet, it had led to an amazing night.

It would make for a great story someday. But how would the story end? My smile faded. For all I knew, the story was already over.

Behind me, a male voice – Joel's voice – cut through the darkness. "What are you doing?"

I whirled around and saw him standing within arm's reach. "How'd you do that?" I asked.

"Do what?"

"Sneak up on me like that."

"I wasn't sneaking. It's my campsite. Remember?"

I glanced around. "Where's your car?"

"Across the street."

"You mean at the storage place?"

"Yeah. Why?"

"I'm just wondering, why would you park *there*?"

He shrugged. "Why not?"

"Well, I'm just saying, most people park right there at their campsites."

"Not if they want privacy."

I drew back. If that wasn't a hint, I didn't know what was.

Joel's expression softened. "I didn't mean you."

I studied his face. Did he mean that? Or was he just being nice?

He glanced toward my bicycle. "You didn't ride your bike here?"

"Well, yeah. I mean, it's not like I have a car."

He frowned. "But it's dark out."

I gave him a tentative smile. "But it wasn't when I left."

He was still frowning. "You've gotta be more careful."

"Why? It's perfectly safe."

"Well, you're not biking back," he said. "Hang on, I'll get the car."

What was this? A dismissal? "But wait, you haven't asked why I'm here."

"I *know* why you're here."

I gave him a perplexed look. "Why?"

As an answer, he reached into his back pocket and pulled out a credit card. Wordlessly, he handed it over. I took a look. It wasn't just any credit card. It was *my* credit card, the one I kept tucked in the front pocket of my purse for emergencies.

"Where'd you find this?" I asked.

His voice was deadpan. "In the Camaro."

Oh. The Camaro.

Obviously, it was still a sore subject, and I could totally see why.

About the credit card, I was beyond grateful to have it back, even if I hadn't realized it was missing. I met Joel's gaze. "Thanks."

"You're welcome." He glanced toward my bike. "You ready to go?"

"Actually, not yet." I tucked the card into the pocket of my shorts and said, "I'm not here because of the credit card. You want the truth? I didn't even know you had it."

"Then why *are* you here?"

I gave him a shaky smile. "I was awful earlier, wasn't I?"

Joel shoved his hands into his pockets. "I wouldn't say that."

"Oh come on," I said. "You would, too. Because I was." I cleared my throat. "Anyway, I just wanted to say, well, I'm sorry."

"Forget it. Not a big deal."

I studied his face. Did he mean it? I wasn't so sure.

"No seriously," I said. "On Friday, you were so great about taking my side, and I should've done the same for you, with the Camaro, I mean. I don't know why you took it, but I'm sure you had a good reason." I took a deep breath. "And lastly, I never thanked you."

"For what?"

"Where to begin?" I gave a shaky laugh. "Let's see, you gave me a ride, went to my party…" I rolled my eyes. "Saved the horse."

His eyebrows furrowed. "What horse?"

"You know. The one my uncle was swiping."

His lips lifted at the corners. "Oh yeah. That horse."

While I was on a roll, I figured I might as well cover everything. "And also, for coming by today to tell me about my car. That was really great of you, and I should've been nicer about it."

I shoved a nervous hand through my hair. "So, I guess that's everything." I glanced around. "So, if you still wanted to give me a ride home, that would be really great."

Joel gave my bike a long look. "You're giving me too much credit."

"I am not," I insisted. "It's all true."

"Nah." He lowered his voice. "I'll let you in on a secret."

"What?"

"Today, about your car, that wasn't the only reason I stopped by."

"It wasn't?" I cleared my throat. "I mean, was there something else?"

"Yeah."

"What?" I asked.

He smiled. "Marshmallows."

CHAPTER 29

The campfire was at the perfect stage, with cheerful flames and a glowing bed of red embers. Joel and I each had a marshmallow on a long stick, and were turning them over the flames.

I gave mine another slow turn. "So, do you camp a lot?"

Sitting in the lawn chair beside me, he looked easy and relaxed as he gazed into the fire. "The truth?" he said. "It's my first time."

The answer surprised me, not because he looked like an avid outdoorsman or anything, but mostly because he'd whipped up a fire in no time flat.

"Really?" I gave him a curious look. "What made you start now? Did you just need a vacation or something?"

A shadow passed over his features. "Something like that."

Obviously, there was a lot more to this story. "So why'd you pick this place?"

Joel glanced around. "Why not?" And then, he returned his gaze to the fire and said nothing more about it.

I studied his face in profile. Thanks to my internet research, I knew more than he realized. Obviously, this had something to do with his brother.

I returned my own gaze to the fire and was surprised to see that my marshmallow was almost done. I gave my stick a few more turns, making sure the marshmallow was roasted evenly all around.

I pulled it back and gave it a closer look. I smiled with satisfaction. It was almost perfect, just like it was the perfect night for a campfire. The evening was cool and clear, with almost no breeze. In the background, I heard crickets chirping and people laughing from a few campsites away.

The place was a lot less crowded than it had been on Friday night, but that was no surprise.

Technically, it was no longer summer, which meant that kids were back in school, and camping would be mostly confined to retirees and weekend warriors.

It was Sunday night, and the weekend was almost over. Most people, including me, had to work tomorrow. I gave Joel a sideways glance. Did *he* have to work tomorrow?

After that whole scene in the boardroom, I'd been reluctant to mention his job at all. And yet, the longer I knew him, the more confused I became.

On one hand, he wasn't from around here, and he seemed to be on vacation. But on the other hand, he'd somehow been hired to paint the boardroom. Those two things didn't quite mesh.

While thinking this over, I nibbled at my marshmallow, loving the taste and texture of its warm, semi-crunchy exterior. Next to me, Joel pulled his own stick from the fire and gave his marshmallow a closer look. It was darker than mine and smoking at the edges. Even so, he plucked it off the stick and popped the whole thing into his mouth.

I had to laugh. "Isn't that too hot?"

He shook his head. "Nope. It's just right."

"Oh yeah?" I teased. "Is it the best one you've ever had?"

"Sure." He leaned his stick against the side of his chair. "The worst, too."

"How so?" I asked.

"It was my first one."

"Your first marshmallow? Seriously?"

"My first *roasted* marshmallow." He flashed me a grin. "Big difference."

I didn't get it. While making the fire, Joel had mentioned in passing that he'd grown up on the other side of the state. I knew for a fact they had plenty of campgrounds over there, too. And yet, he'd never gone camping? Or roasted a marshmallow?

I just had to ask, "What else haven't you done?"

That same shadow passed over his features. "Trust me. I've done plenty."

I had no doubt of that.

He returned his gaze to the flames. "You wanna know why I'm here?"

"Yeah. I mean, if you feel like telling me."

"Alright. Here's the truth." He turned and gave me a smile that chased the shadows away. "I'm in hiding."

I laughed. "Oh stop it, you can't be."

"Yeah? Why not?"

"Okay, let's say you are. Who would you be hiding from?"

He gave a rueful laugh. "My family."

Given what I knew, that actually made sense. I recalled the little he'd told me on Friday night. He had multiple brothers, who he didn't seem to like very much. Other than the guy who owned the Camaro, I knew nothing about any of them. But I *did* know that the car wasn't the only thing that Joel had taken.

I said, "Can I ask you something?"

"Yeah, what?"

I lowered my voice. "We talked about the Camaro, but what about the other stuff?"

"What other stuff?"

I glanced around before whispering, "You know, the guns."

Unlike me, Joel didn't feel the need to whisper. "What about them?"

While peddling out here, I'd given this a lot of thought. By the time I reached the campground entrance, I was pretty sure I'd figured it out.

I said, "I have a theory. And I'm wondering if I'm right."

"Yeah? What's the theory?"

Again, I lowered my voice. "That the guns were an accident."

He was silent for a long moment. "An accident?"

"Yeah. Like, they were in the trunk already, and you just happened to take the Camaro at a bad time. So now, you're stuck with them, and don't know how to give them back." I gave Joel a hopeful smile. "So, am I right?"

"No."

"Oh." I bit my lip. So much for my cheerful little theory.

Joel looked vaguely amused. "Sorry to disappoint you."

"I'm not disappointed."

He gave a low laugh. "Right."

"Well, okay," I said. "Maybe I'm a *little* disappointed. I mean, who likes to be wrong?"

"No one," he said. "But that's not the reason you're disappointed."

"What makes you say that?"

"I can see it on your face."

"Oh." *Busted.* I cleared my throat. "So are you planning to return them?"

Joel gave it some thought. "Maybe."

Maybe? What kind of answer was that? I tried again. "But those belong to a different brother, right? Doesn't he want them back?"

"Oh, he wants them. But whether he *gets* them…" Joel gave a loose shrug. "I'm still deciding."

More confused than ever, I looked back to my marshmallow. I'd already eaten its crispy shell, so all that remained was a small shapeless blob on the end of a cold, dark stick.

Lost in thought, I held out the stick and positioned the blob over the fire. As I turned it over the flames, I asked, "Aren't you worried?"

"About what?"

"Getting in trouble."

"From who?" he said. "My brothers?"

I turned back to Joel. "Them, or someone else."

He gave me a cocky smile. "I'm not worried."

He looked so confident that I had to laugh. "Oh yeah? If that's the case, why are you in hiding?"

"Because I don't want them bugging me."

In spite of everything, I couldn't help but tease him at least a little. "Well, maybe they *wouldn't* be 'bugging you' if you didn't have their stuff."

Joel shook his head. "I know them. You don't."

His words reminded me of something he'd said at my house. The reminder stung, but I tried to laugh it off. "And I guess I never will, huh?"

"What do you mean?"

"Well, when you stopped by earlier, you said that I'd never meet them."

"No. What I said was, you'd never meet the one."

For some reason, the distinction made me feel a whole lot better. "You mean the one with the Camaro?"

"Yeah. Him." Joel's voice hardened. "I wouldn't let him within ten feet of you."

"Why not?"

"Because he's a dick."

I don't know why, but I laughed. "Oh. Okay."

"And I don't trust him." His gaze met mine. "Not with someone as sweet as you."

My heart gave a funny little flutter. "You think I'm sweet?"

He leaned his head a fraction closer to mine. In a quiet voice, he said, "You know I do."

Our chairs suddenly felt way too far apart. I leaned toward him, wondering if he'd say anything else, or even better, if he'd kiss me. But I must've leaned too far, because my chair practically toppled over, leaving me laughing in embarrassment, even as Joel reached out to steady me in my seat.

His hands were on my upper arms, and he wasn't pulling away. I dropped my stick, marshmallow and all, and ignored the telltale sizzle of it being consumed by the flames.

My chair was steady now, but I wasn't. And I was feeling less steady with every passing moment.

Joel smiled. "You alright?"

His hands were large, but his grip was gentle. The feel of his touch, even as innocent as it was, warmed me far more than the fire.

I felt myself nod.

He said, "Remember what you asked me?"

With him so close, I was having a hard time remembering anything. I whispered, "When?"

He leaned closer. "At that bar."

I tried to think. He meant T.J.'s of course. The night of my party was mostly a blur. I didn't recall asking him much of anything, except to kiss me, and – . "Oh." I felt a shy smile curve my lips. "Sorry. I guess I was a little drunk, huh?"

His eyes warmed in the firelight. "How about now?"

I hadn't had a single drop of alcohol since my party, and yet, I was having a hard time forming any coherent thoughts. Somehow, I managed to say, "You mean, am I sober?"

Joel shook his head. "No." His gaze dipped to my lips. "I mean, do you still want that kiss?"

I felt myself nod. *Did I ever.*

CHAPTER 30

In the soft glow of the firelight, Joel leaned forward, and slowly, seductively, pressed his lips to mine. His lips were warm and soft, and as sweet as I'd imagined.

His hands slid from my arms, up to the back of my neck, and soon, and I felt his fingers sifting through the long tendrils of my hair.

As our lips moved, I let my eyelids flutter shut. Desperate for more, I reached out, wanting to pull him closer. And as I did, my chair toppled, leaving me clutching at his shirt and kissing only air. I fell forward, straight into his arms.

No. Actually, that wasn't quite right. Because now, we were both standing. He'd not only caught me. He'd pulled me to my feet. And I'd barely had time to think.

He was fast. Unnaturally fast. He'd caught me before I'd even fallen.

I glanced around and spotted my chair, now toppled onto its side. As for *his* chair, it remained upright.

Showoff.

I gave a shaky laugh. "I hope I didn't trash your chair. I mean, the one I was sitting in."

"It's not my chair. It's yours."

I looked up to study his face. "What?"

"I bought it for you."

My breath caught. "You did? When?"

"On my way back from Detroit."

I smiled. So this wasn't just an impromptu thing? Thinking it over, I recalled how the campsite had looked when I'd peddled up to it. There had been the lawn chairs, the firewood, and even the sticks, resting up against the wood-pile.

I felt a warm glow that had nothing to do with the fire. *Two* chairs. *Two* sticks. One for me, and one for him. How had I not realized?

It was so sweet that I didn't know what to say. So I didn't say anything. Instead, I lifted my face and kissed him again, more slowly this time, leaning into him as much as I wanted, and savoring the rush of pleasure when his arms closed tighter around me, wrapping me in a warm, wonderful embrace.

I kissed him a lot that night, and he kissed me back, like a guy who definitely knew what he was doing. But that's as far as it went, and I was thankful that he didn't push it.

Or at least, that's what I told myself, even as he was driving home just past midnight. It was funny really, because there were so many things I'd been planning to ask him. But somehow, the hours had slipped away with most of my questions still unasked, at least for now.

But I wasn't worried. Already, we'd made plans for the following afternoon, which meant that I'd be getting my answers soon enough.

Still, there was something I wanted to get out of the way, so it didn't come up later on. Just as we were pulling into my driveway, I turned to him and said, "I meant to tell you, I heard about that fight."

Joel stiffened. With his eyes still on the road, he said in a carefully neutral voice, "Yeah? Which one?"

I stared at him in profile. *Which one?*

How many fights did he get into, anyway? I suddenly recalled what Mike had said during that whole roadside encounter with Chester, the Shirtless Wonder. Mike had made some crack about Joel 'slaughtering' someone at State. With everything else, that had almost slipped my mind.

But now, it came rushing to the forefront. I wanted to ask about it. But something – maybe the hard set of Joel's shoulders – told me that now wasn't the ideal time.

So all I said was, "You know, the one between you and Derek."

"That?" Joel's shoulders visibly relaxed. "That was no fight."

I still hadn't gotten the whole story from Cassie, *but* I did know that it wasn't just a yelling thing. And yet, Joel didn't look like he was lying. Trying to be diplomatic about it, I said, "Are you sure? Because Cassie was there."

Joel gave me a sideways glance. "You ever see a real fight?"

"No," I admitted.

"Trust me. A real fight? Looks nothing like that."

I didn't know what to say, and already, we were pulling up to the house. When the car stopped, Joel got out, retrieved my bike from the trunk, and then, walked me *and* my bike to the front door, where all of my questions were soon forgotten, thanks to an amazing kiss goodnight.

Tomorrow, I decided, I'd get the full story – if not from Joel, then definitely from Cassie. □

CHAPTER 31

Standing in the back room of the cookie shop, I stared at Cassie. "But he told me it wasn't a real fight."

We were decorating sugar cookies for a bridal show that was being held at the stately brick hotel across the street.

Cassie shook her head. "Oh, it was definitely real."

So far, I'd learned nothing, except that Cassie was still insisting that the fight was a physical one, and not just some verbal altercation.

I gave her a pleading look. "Just tell me the whole story, okay? You said you saw it. But what happened?"

"Alright, let me start from the beginning. You know how the ice machine's been on the fritz lately?"

I nodded. As her only part-time employee, I *did* know. At the cookie shop, we sold not only baked goods, but smoothies when the weather was warm enough to justify it.

Smoothies needed ice, sometimes, lots of ice. Unfortunately, a few weeks ago, Cassie's ice machine had died a long, noisy death, and she hadn't yet replaced it.

"Right," I said. "And?"

"So, you *also* know that I've been buying all of my ice from that dispenser near the beach, right?"

Again, I nodded. Occasionally, it was *me* getting the ice. This involved lugging a blue, plastic cooler – luckily, a cooler *with* wheels – four blocks to the beach and back again.

I didn't mind. It was actually sort of fun. But what this had to do with the fight, I had no idea. "So…?" I prompted.

"So," Cassie continued, "I'm there, filling the cooler, and I see Derek at the hot dog stand. And there's this huge line behind him." She paused. "You know which stand I mean, right?"

"Yeah." I made a forwarding motion with my hand. "Duffy's Dogs, I know."

She gave me a look. "Hey, don't get all impatient. It's relevant to the story."

I gave her an apologetic smile. "Sorry."

She reached for a tube of icing and began drawing pink flowers on the cookies that I'd just frosted. "So you know the guy who owns the stand, right?"

"Yeah. Duffy." I wasn't a huge hot dog fan, but I'd chatted with him a few times. He seemed like a nice guy.

"Right," Cassie said, "but that day, it's not Duffy manning the stand. It's his son, Spencer."

I tried to think. "Skinny kid? Maybe in junior high?"

Cassie nodded. "Right. That's him. He works the stand sometimes, you know, on weekends and stuff."

I did know. But I still didn't know why this mattered. "And?"

"And, like I said, there's this huge line." She frowned. "And guess who's at the front."

"Who?" I asked.

"Derek." Cassie looked up. "And he's with Angelina the Skank. You know her, right?"

Angelina DeLotta? Did I ever. I'd gone to high school with Angelina. She was loud, obnoxious, and very popular, in that easy good-time sort of way. "Yeah, I know her."

"Doesn't everyone," Cassie said. "Anyway, Derek's totally giving Spencer a hard time."

"How?" I asked.

"Oh, you know. The usual stuff." She gave it some thought. "Like, from what I heard, he'd already rejected like five hot dogs before I'd even got there."

I felt my brow wrinkle. "Rejected? What do you mean?"

"Well, from the bits people told me after, he was like, 'This one's overdone. *This* one's not done enough. *This* one's got a mashed-up bun…"

"You can reject hot dogs?" I said.

She gave me a look. "You ever been to a restaurant with him?"

I had, in fact. And so had Cassie. By unspoken agreement, we almost never went with him anymore. It was just too painful to watch, him running the servers ragged, just because he could.

"Point taken," I said.

"So," Cassie went on, "even from the next stand over, I can see that Derek's being a total jerk. Like, he grabs the kid's tip jar and says–" She imitated Derek. "'–If you want it back, you're gonna have to earn it.'"

I felt my jaw clench. "God, what an ass."

"No kidding," Cassie said. "And all this time, Angelina's there, laughing like she always does."

I rolled my eyes. "Like a coked-up hyena?"

"Oh yeah." Cassie's mouth tightened. "And then the innuendos start."

"You mean from Angelina?"

"I wish," she said. "I mean from Derek."

"What do you mean?"

"Well, he starts making all these cracks about hot dogs, and wieners, and asking the kid if he sees a lot of wieners at home." She made a sound of disgust. "Stuff like that."

I stared at her. I almost didn't know what to say. Even for Derek, this was a new low. I asked, "Were you tempted to say something?"

"Oh, I was *more* than tempted," she said. "I left my cooler, marched over there, and told him, flat-out, to give it a rest."

"What did he do?"

"Nothing," she said. "You know how he is. He ignored me and kept on going. And all the while, Angelina's still laughing, the people behind him are grumbling, and the kid, Spencer, he's looking like he wants to run, or jeez, even cry." She winced. "It was *that* bad."

Listening, it occurred to me that this was exactly why I'd been reluctant to hear this story the first time around. Cripes, I almost wanted to cover my ears *now*. It was vintage Derek, but worse.

Still, a huge part of the story seemed to be missing. I gave Cassie a perplexed look. "But what does this have to do with Joel? You still haven't said."

"Right. Because I was saving *that* part for last."

"Why?"

She smiled. "Because it's the only *good* part of the whole story."

I gave her a dubious look. "There's a *good* part?"

"Oh yeah," she said. "And you're gonna love it."

CHAPTER 32

So far, I wasn't loving anything about this story. Derek had been spiraling out of control all summer. I was accustomed to him giving *me* a hard time, but the thought of him harassing some kid at a hot dog stand was almost more than I could stomach.

Across from me, Cassie reached for a new tube of icing, and began drawing green leaves around the pink flowers. "So, Derek has the tip jar, and he's holding it high over his head, making all these stupid cracks. And finally he says, 'Hey, dog-boy, you wanna fetch *this*?'"

I frowned. "Please tell me he didn't actually throw it."

"Well, he does, and he doesn't."

"What do you mean?"

"Okay, picture this. He's got the jar in one hand, high over his head, right? And he winds back, like he's gonna hurl the jar halfway to Chicago. But..." Cassie smiled. "...When he goes to throw it, it's gone."

"What's gone?" I asked. "The jar?"

"Yeah," she said. "So instead of throwing the jar, he's throwing nothing. And it totally messes up his momentum." She laughed. "He loses his balance, and takes a dirt-dive right there on the beach, in front of like fifty people."

I could almost picture it. "But what happened to the jar? Did he drop it behind him or something?"

"No. What happened was this guy – Joel, I mean – had come out of nowhere. And all ninja-like, he'd plucked the jar right out of Derek's hand." Cassie's eyes brightened. "And he did it so fast, and so quiet, that Derek didn't even notice until it was too late."

Knowing Joel, I could totally believe it.

Cassie was laughing again. "You should've seen it. Derek's stumbling around trying to catch his balance, and…" She paused. "…Did I mention he was drunk?"

I shook my head. "I don't think so."

"Oh yeah. He was. I could tell. But anyway, Angelina's laughing her face off, except *now,* she's laughing *at* Derek, who totally 'loves' that. And a few feet away, there's Joel, just standing there – dripping wet, no shirt, by the way – holding the jar, all nonchalant-like."

An image of Joel, wet and half-naked, flashed in my brain. It was a nice image, with all kinds of details that I'd like to consider later on, preferably after returning home and turning off the lights.

Damn it. Focus, Melody.

I asked, "So, he'd just come in from swimming or something?"

"Apparently," Cassie said. "He *was* wearing black shorts, or maybe a swimsuit that looked like shorts." She waved away the question. "But that's not important. The thing is, Derek's royally ticked off. He gets up and lunges for the jar. Totally misses, by the way."

She paused, as if thinking. "You know what it reminded me of?"

"What?" I asked.

"A bull fight."

"Huh?"

"You know," she said. "Like a bull-fighting scene from a movie. Like there's Joel, the matador, cool as a cucumber, moving the jar just out of Derek's reach a split-second before Derek gets close enough to grab it."

At this, I had to laugh. "So, the tip jar is what? A shiny red cape?"

Cassie grinned. "Exactly!"

I could just picture it, too. "So, how many times did 'Derek the Bull' charge?"

"A lot," Cassie said. "And by now, everyone's laughing, even Spencer." Cassie was still grinning. "It was so awesome."

It *did* sound awesome, actually. The way it sounded, it wasn't so much a fight as a spectacle. I smiled with relief. "So *that* was their fight?"

Cassie shook her head. "Sorry. There's more."

My smile faded. "Oh."

"So this goes on for who-knows-how long, and finally, Derek gets so mad, he hauls off and punches Joel right in the stomach."

I gasped, "Oh, my God."

"Yeah, but get this. Nothing happens."

"What do you mean, nothing happens?"

"I mean," she said, "that Joel just stands there, like he didn't even feel it."

"How could he not feel it?" I asked.

Cassie lowered her voice. "If you saw his abs, you wouldn't ask."

And just like that, another image of Joel flashed in my brain. Now, he was half-naked and wet, with drips of water falling suggestively down the well-defined ridges of his stomach. Before those drops could head lower, I blew out a nervous breath and admitted, "You know, I can actually see it."

"Yeah." Cassie rolled her eyes. "And you know who else could?"

"Who?"

"Angelina. By this point, she's totally ditched Derek, and is doing her best to show off for Joel instead."

"How?" I asked.

"Well, she's laughing, and giggling, and…" Cassie paused. "Um, bouncing?"

From experience, I knew exactly what Cassie meant. This was a small town with only one public beach. Over the last few years, I'd seen Angelina out there, plenty of times, working her special brand of bouncing-bikini magic.

I felt myself frown. *Did it work on Joel?*

Before I could dwell on it, Cassie continued. "So now, Derek's going totally nuts, swearing and yelling, and just generally making an ass of himself. He winds up and hits Joel a couple more times, and misses even more than that."

Okay, that made no sense. "What?"

"Well, like Derek swings a dozen times, but mostly he's hitting air. And by now, he's totally unhinged, especially because Joel's just standing there, utterly unfazed."

"So he didn't fight back?"

"Not at first," Cassie said. "To be honest, he looked more amused than anything. But then, Derek takes a wild swing, misses, and grazes this older guy, standing a few feet away."

I frowned. "Was he hurt?"

Cassie waved away my concern. "Nah, like I said, he was just grazed.

But Joel gets this look, like the fun's over. And he clocks Derek right in the stomach."

"You mean in the same way that Derek punched him?"

"Yeah," Cassie said, "except with Derek, it doesn't bounce off him. He doubles over and…" She gave a little shudder.

I leaned forward. "And what?"

"Well, he staggers back, and then, well, barfs all over his own feet."

At the image, I was feeling kind of queasy myself. "Seriously?"

Cassie gave me a solemn look. "Seriously."

I was almost afraid to ask. "So then what?"

"So then, everyone's totally grossed out. And Derek, he's trying to kick sand over the barf, like if no one sees it, it didn't happen. But we all know it happened, because we saw it ourselves, and even if we didn't, there's Angelina making a huge deal about it."

"How?" I asked.

"Well, she's pointing and laughing and making all these cracks about how gross it was. And finally, Derek tells her to shut the hell up, unless she wants to find her own ride home. And *she* tells him that she's moving on anyway, because he's a pussy, and besides, she's found someone new."

My jaw clenched. I could only guess who that someone new was. "Joel?"

Cassie nodded. "Yup, you guessed it."

I was almost afraid to ask, "So, then what happened?"

Cassie shrugged. "I don't know."

"What? How could you not know?"

"Because my ice was melting, and some guy in a baseball hat was eyeballing my cooler."

"So you just left?"

"Sure," she said. "The show was over, right?"

"But wait, did Joel leave with Angelina?"

"Sorry," Cassie said. "I didn't see either way."

Damn it. "So what about the tip jar? Did Spencer get it back?"

"Oh yeah," Cassie said. "Didn't I tell you? Joel tossed it back to Spencer when the barfing started."

"Was he okay?"

"Spencer? Oh yeah. He was laughing his ass off." She smiled. "Then again, so was everyone."

Stunned by the whole story, I murmured, "I can't believe I'm just hearing this."

"Don't blame *me*," she said. "*You* were the one who covered your ears."

Well, there *was* that.

Still, I was dying to know, did the story end with Joel and Angelina frolicking on the beach? Or worse, frolicking naked somewhere else?

I was still mulling that when Cassie perked up. "You know who else was there?"

"Who?"

"Terry. You know, from the ice cream place."

I leaned forward. "Do you think *she* knows what happened with Angelina?"

"I'm not sure, but it's worth a shot."

Yes, it *was* worth a shot.

Suddenly, I was desperate for ice cream.

CHAPTER 33

I held out the white paper bag. "I brought us a snack."

Joel smiled. "Yeah? What is it?"

His smile made me feel warm all over. "Sundaes. They *were* hot fudge."

His eyebrows lifted. "Were?"

"Well, I bought them like four hours ago." I glanced down at the bag. "But they've been in Cassie's freezer, so they're not melty or anything. It's just that, well, the fudge isn't technically hot anymore."

During my lunch break, I'd dashed over to the ice cream shop in search of answers. Unfortunately, Terry hadn't been working, so I'd left with the next best thing – something cool and sweet for the walk on the beach.

After all, I had to buy *something* from the ice cream shop, if only to be polite – and to learn that Terry *would* be working tomorrow. I didn't care how much ice cream it took, I was determined to get those answers.

In front of me, Joel said, "Cold fudge sundaes, huh?" He gave a slow nod. "Works for me."

"If you want," I said, "we could eat them on the end of the pier."

He reached out and took the bag from my hand. And then, he closed his other hand around mine, entwining our fingers as we walked along the sidewalk, heading toward the public beach.

It was funny. I wasn't on vacation. But with Joel at my side, I almost felt like I was.

At my suggestion, we'd met outside the cookie shop, which meant that I was wearing the same thing I'd been wearing at work, navy shorts and a white polo shirt. As for Joel, he was wearing black shorts and a gray T-shirt, emblazoned with the name of some gym that I didn't recognize.

As we strolled, we talked about nothing in particular, but I loved every minute of it. I especially loved the fact that for once, strangers were staring at him, not me.

It was easy to see why. He was pure perfection, both in the way he looked *and* in the way he moved. There was something about his demeanor that made people pause and take notice, even as we moved from the sidewalk, to the beach, and finally onto the long wooden pier.

A half-hour later, the sundaes were gone, and we were still sitting side-by-side on the pier's edge, watching the boats skim along the waters of Lake Michigan.

It was nearly six o'clock, and the sun wouldn't be setting for hours yet. But a cool breeze was coming off the water, and I felt more relaxed than I had in forever.

I knew why. It was because of Joel, sitting beside me like some kind of mystical, protective force, as crazy as that sounded. For so long, I'd been on my own. Technically, I was still on my own. And yet, with him beside me, everything felt different.

It was strange to think that I never would've met him if it weren't for Derek and that whole painting fiasco. That reminded me. I still didn't know how Joel had gotten that job.

I turned to Joel. "Hey, can I ask you something? How'd Derek end up hiring you? You know, to paint the boardroom."

"That?" Joel gave a humorless laugh. "I wasn't hired. I was set up."

Knowing Derek, this wasn't a huge surprise. He hated to see anyone get the best of him, especially in public. I asked, "Do you know how he did it?"

"Yeah. With help."

"From who?"

"From this guy I know – a painter who's been keeping an eye on my stuff."

His stuff? Meaning the Camaro and its contraband? Probably.

I asked, "So how'd the guy do it?"

"The truth?" Joel said. "With a sob story."

"What kind of sob story?"

"The usual. Sick kid, schedule conflict, needed someone to cover for him."

"Was any of that true?" I asked.

"No. But like a dumbass, I believed him."

"So just like that, you agreed to paint the boardroom?"

"Hell no," Joel said. "I tell him the truth, that I'm not a house-painter. And he says, 'Yeah, but you're still a painter, right? You'll figure it out.'"

"Wait a minute," I said. "So you *do* paint?"

"Yeah, but not houses," Joel said. "Anyway, I tell this guy, 'Sorry, you'd better find someone else.' But he gives me this story, on how he can't reschedule because it's in the contract. And he says the job's too important, a big one in a fancy house."

Heat rushed to my face. Obviously, he meant my house. And he was right. The house *was* fancy, even if it did need a ton of work.

Joel continued, "And this guy tells me how he might lose his own house if he can't get the job started."

I blew out a long breath. "Wow, no pressure there."

"Tell me about it." Joel turned away, gazing out over the water. "You know what it's like to lose your house?"

The question hit a little too close to home. I *didn't* know. But lately, I'd been wondering if I might eventually find out.

Still, I shook my head. "No. Do you?"

"No. But I know what it's like to worry about it."

For some reason, that surprised me. "You own a house?"

"Not mine. My dad's. Back when I was a kid."

Of course. That made a lot more sense. "So you felt sorry for the guy?"

"Not just him," Joel said. "He's got a wife and three kids."

"Are you sure?" I asked. "I mean, how do you know that wasn't a lie, too?"

"Because I met them last week." Something in Joel's voice warmed. "The kids are pistols, cute as hell."

The warmth in his voice surprised me, and I couldn't help but smile. I loved kids. I wanted ten of them – okay, maybe not ten. But I wanted a lot. If I had my way, I'd keep the house and fill it with a giant family to call my own.

Feeling almost shy about it, I said, "So you like kids?"

Joel gave a loose shrug. "Eh, depends on the kid."

I studied his face in profile. The answer felt like a copout, like he didn't want to admit, maybe even to himself, that he had a huge soft spot under that rough exterior.

Or maybe that was just my own wishful thinking.

I said, "So you took the job because of the kids?"

"Not just the kids," Joel said. "This guy? He's got two part-time jobs and a beat-up truck that's always breaking down. The house-painting, he does on the side. The guy's no slouch, but he's having a hard time catching a break, you know?"

I nodded. And even though I lived in a mansion, I could almost relate.

"Anyway," Joel continued, "just before I head out there, the guy hands me this check from the firm who hired him. I look down, and I see *my* name. When I ask about it, he tells me he worked it out so I'd get something for showing up. And I tell him, 'Keep it. I don't need the money.'"

"You don't?"

Joel gave another shrug. "I'm doing alright."

Was that true? I realized that Joel drove an expensive car, but that didn't necessarily mean anything. I considered my own situation. I lived in a huge house, and yet, I could hardly afford ice cream.

I asked, "So then what happened?"

"You saw what happened. I get to that meeting, and who's there? The douchebag from the beach."

"Right. Derek." I tried to laugh. "I'm almost surprised you didn't bolt the minute you saw him."

"Yeah. Me, too." Joel gave a wry laugh. "I was actually pretty proud of myself."

"So why *didn't* you leave?" I asked.

"Because I didn't want to screw over the guy who sent me. So I figure I'll let the douchebag have his fun, and get on with it." Joel smiled. "And who knows. Maybe I'd catch the douchebag later on, after the job's done and paid." An edge crept into his voice. "We could 'talk' again."

I didn't ask about what. But somehow, I doubted any actual talking would be involved.

I considered his explanation. Finally, so many things made sense – in particular, the amount of crap that Joel had taken before losing it.

Thinking out loud, I said, "But then, at some point, you realized…"

"That the job was a crock?" Joel made a scoffing sound. "Yeah."

I almost didn't know what to say. "Wow."

Joel turned to face me. "You know, I might've realized sooner, except there was this girl, sitting next to the douchebag, distracted the hell out of me."

I felt myself smile. "Me?"

"You've gotta ask? There was something about you, made it hard to think."

My breath caught. "Really?"

Joel nodded. "And I could tell you were embarrassed as hell. It reminded me of something."

"What?"

"How embarrassed *I* used to get when *my* family made asses of themselves."

I hesitated. "But Derek and I aren't related. You didn't know that?"

"I do now. But I didn't then."

"Let me guess," I said. "You thought we were brother and sister?"

Joel shrugged. "Or cousins."

"We get that a lot," I said, "probably because our families grew up so close. Sometimes, he almost feels like a brother."

"And other times?" Joel asked.

"Other times?" I forced a laugh. "I'm pretty sure I want to strangle him."

After a long pause, Joel asked, "You two ever date?"

I drew back. "Heck no. Never. Me and Derek?" I gave a little shudder. "It would be like dating your brother." I paused. "Well, not *your* brother. But *my* brother, if I had one, that is."

"Yeah?" Joel smiled. "Good to know."

I smiled back. "Why?"

"You *know* why." He leaned closer. "Less competition."

I rolled my eyes. "Like *you* have to worry about competition."

"You think I'm joking?"

"Aren't you?"

Joel gave a slow shake of his head. "Not with you." He stood and pulled me to my feet. "Now come on. I promised you dinner."

He *had* promised me dinner. But I felt almost guilty taking him up on it. I still knew nothing about his job, or whether he even had one.

At last night's campfire, I'd asked in a roundabout way, but he'd dodged the question by joking that his only job now was to be on vacation.

I bit my lip. Maybe he didn't even have a job. Looking to conserve his money, I said, "Well, technically, we've already eaten."

"The ice cream? Sorry, that doesn't count." He looked around. "So what's good around here?"

I tried to think of what would be affordable. "We could hit the taco stand, and then eat right here on the beach."

He gave me a look. "Is that what you want?"

"Sure." I turned to gaze out over the water. "I mean, it's a great view, right."

"Yeah," he said. "It sure is."

But when I turned to look, he wasn't looking at the water. He was looking at me. And *I* was looking at him. If he thought his view was nice, he should see mine.

Over tacos, Joel told me the rest of the painting story. Apparently, the painter – who also worked part-time at the storage place – was under the mistaken impression that Derek and Joel were old friends.

He'd gotten that impression from Derek, who'd hadn't really hired the painter at all, except for slipping the guy a hundred bucks to get Joel out there. Apparently, Derek had claimed the whole thing was a harmless ruse to get Joel out to my place for a surprise party.

Some party.

And yet, that whole sorry fiasco was the reason that I'd met Joel at all. Who knows, maybe I'd thank Derek someday, assuming I didn't strangle him first.

CHAPTER 34

"So?" Cassie said. "How'd it go?"

I'd just arrived for my afternoon shift at the cookie shop. At the memory of last night, I felt myself smile. "It was nice."

"*How* nice?" she asked.

I couldn't stop smiling. "*Really* nice."

I went on to tell her how Joel and I had tacos on the beach, and had then returned to his campsite for another campfire.

"And?" she said.

"And what?"

She lowered her voice. "Did it get romantic?"

It had. But not in the naked sense. Mostly, it was a repeat of the previous night, except this time, Joel had pulled out a blanket, and we'd sat a whole lot closer while watching the fire.

Yeah, there had been kissing, and a little petting, but nothing I'd be ashamed to do in public.

When I relayed this to Cassie, she said, "I wonder if that's because of what April told him."

I froze. I was almost afraid to ask. "What do you mean?"

Cassie hesitated. "Are you sure you wanna hear this?"

"No," I admitted. "But you'd better tell me, anyway."

"Alright, remember at your party? When you went to the ladies room?"

I shook my head. "Which time?"

"It was that last time, near the end of the night. So anyway, you're gone, but Joel's still there. And April leans across the table, and she warns him that you're a nice girl, and that he'd better behave himself."

My jaw dropped. "She didn't."

Cassie nodded. "She did."

With growing trepidation, I asked, "Did she say anything else?"

"Oh yeah. She told him that he shouldn't be expecting any nookie – her word, not mine – for at least another month, because you're not a sack-jumper."

I cringed. "You mean like, um, a ballsack."

Cassie stared at me. "God, no." She burst out laughing. "Like someone who 'jumps in the sack' on the first date."

My face was burning now with embarrassment. "Oh. Yeah. I knew that. Sorry."

"You should be." She snickered. "Dirty girl."

I wasn't dirty. I was humiliated, and not only because of my stupid mistake. Technically, what April told Joel was accurate, but did she *really* have to announce it to him in front of an audience?

I didn't know whether to be touched or enraged. I looked to Cassie. "Why didn't you tell me earlier?"

"Because I knew you'd be embarrassed." She laughed. "And you're totally blushing by the way."

"I know," I groaned. "I can feel it."

"And," Cassie said, "I figured you'd had enough embarrassment with that whole cowboy thing. And besides, it's not like you could take back her warning." She gave another snicker. "The ball was, after all, out of the sack."

I rolled my eyes. "Oh, shut up."

"If it makes you feel any better," Cassie said, "I think April meant to do you a favor."

"Some favor," I muttered.

I'd known April for years. Her heart was in the right place, but sometimes, her methods were a little ham-fisted for my taste. Reluctantly, I asked, "What did Joel say? Was *he* embarrassed?"

"He didn't *look* embarrassed. And he was still there when you came back, so…" Cassie shrugged. "I figured it would all work out."

I gave it some thought. Was I glad to know? Probably. But Cassie was right. Hearing this on Friday would've been my undoing. "I guess I should thank you for not telling me sooner."

She flashed me a smile. "You're welcome." Suddenly she burst out,

"Oh, man, I almost forgot to tell you."

"Oh no." I cringed. "There's something else?"

"Yeah, but you're gonna love this one. Guess who popped in for cookies this morning."

"Who?"

"Terry from the ice cream place."

My shoulders sagged. "And I missed her?"

"Yeah, but don't worry. I got the scoop."

Now, it was my turn to snicker. "The ice cream scoop?"

Cassie looked heavenward. "Forget the ice cream. I meant the scoop about Joel and Angelina. You wanna hear what happened?"

I leaned forward. "You *know* I do."

"Well, the way Terry talks, Angelina practically begged Joel to take her home."

I hesitated. After my stupid ballsack confusion, I wasn't taking any chances. "You mean like give her a ride?"

"Oh, she wanted a ride, alright." Cassie gave me a significant look. "And to be ridden, if you know what I mean."

I did know. And in this case, I could actually relate. With more than a little nervousness, I asked, "Did Joel take her up on it?"

"That's the best part," Cassie said. "He turned her down flat."

Relief coursed through me. "Really? How'd she take it?"

"Like a dog in heat."

I frowned. "Huh?"

"The way I hear it, she wouldn't take no for an answer. She starts rubbing on him and saying stuff like–" Cassie did a mock impression of Angelina. "'–Listen, Lover-boy, one night in *my* bed, and you won't *want* to go anywhere."

Lover-boy? I almost shuddered. "So what'd he do then?"

"At first, he's trying to be cool about it. But then, when she *still* won't take no for an answer, he tells her to piss off."

I felt my eyebrows furrow. "Piss off?"

"Yup," Cassie said. "Exact words, according to Terry."

"So then what happened?"

"So then, Angelina tells *him*, 'Hey, if that's your kink, count me in.'"

I felt my body go rigid. "You mean like–"

"Pissing on each other?" Cassie laughed. "Yeah. That's the way it sounded."

I almost didn't know what to say. *Talk about unsanitary.* "What did Joel do?"

Cassie gave a nonchalant shrug. "Well, what *could* he do? He whips it out and pees on her."

My jaw hit the floor. After a long, horrible moment, I managed to say, "Please tell me you're kidding."

Cassie burst out laughing. "Of course I'm kidding! Jeez. You should see your face."

I didn't *want* to see. I could still feel the heat burning across my cheeks. Somehow, I managed to ask, "So tell me. What did he *really* do?"

"He shrugs out of her buxom clutches and gets the hell out of dodge, leaves her standing there, panting after him."

I gave a little shudder. "Better panting than peeing."

"You're telling me," Cassie said. "So anyway, she finally flounces off, looking for Derek."

"Did she find him?"

"Nope. By then, he was long gone."

Probably, Angelina was lucky, at least when it came to Derek, because a few days later, it was *me* dealing with him. And, with Joel set to arrive any minute, it was a disaster waiting to happen.

□

CHAPTER 35

Standing on the front porch, Derek made a show of looking at the yard. "It's getting a little long, isn't it?"

Oh, crap. I gave the lawn a nervous look. "You mean the grass?"

"Well, I'm not talking about the driveway if that was your other guess."

God, what an ass.

Hoping to end this before it turned into a major issue, I said, "Sorry, I'll get it tomorrow, okay?"

He crossed his arms. "What's wrong with today?"

Joel was on his way to pick me up, that's what. But I'd be stupid to say so. And besides, it wasn't exactly the lawn-mowing part of the day. I said, "I can't. It's almost dark."

Derek consulted his watch. "Not for two more hours."

"Oh come on," I said, "be reasonable. It takes at least *five* hours to mow it."

This wasn't even an exaggeration. My lawn was three full acres, and all I had was a run-down push-mower. Even if I started now, and kept mowing after sunset, I still wouldn't be done until midnight.

Derek frowned. "It should've been done Monday."

I hated this. And yet, I'd asked for it, hadn't I? "Yeah, well, I was working Monday."

"Not all day, you weren't."

"How would *you* know?" I asked.

"Because the cookie shop closes at six. I do my homework, remember?"

Like I could forget.

Derek continued, "And what's your excuse for the other days?"

I didn't have an excuse, or at least, none I was willing to share. It was true that I'd been working my regular shifts at Cassie's, but mostly, I'd been spending every waking moment with Joel.

He'd made no mention of ending his camping trip, and I'd been living vicariously, enjoying the first thing that felt like a vacation in years.

When I made no response, Derek said, "You *do* know Monday was four days ago, right?"

As if I couldn't count. I gave him a look of mock confusion. "Really? I had no idea."

Derek crossed his arms. "Do you still want the job or not?"

I did. *Damn it.*

I gave my driveway a nervous glance. Joel would be here any minute. I could only imagine how delighted he'd be to find Derek standing here, giving me a hard time.

Eager to end this, I said, "I'll have it done tomorrow. I promise, okay?"

Derek shook his head. "Sorry, not good enough."

I made a sound of frustration. "Why not?"

"Because if my dad stops by and sees the sorry shape of this place, I won't hear the end of it. You know how he is."

Unfortunately, I did know. Until recently, it was Derek's dad who'd been handling all of the estate details. I knew exactly how he was. As bad as things were under Derek, they'd actually been worse under his dad.

It wasn't that the guy was unpleasant exactly. It's just that he micromanaged everything to the point of ridiculousness. And, unlike Derek, he wasn't someone I felt comfortable arguing with.

No doubt, if *he* were still handling things, I'd have already been docked for not mowing according to the set schedule. My stomach sank. The way it looked, Derek was going to take the same approach.

I couldn't afford to be docked. I needed the money.

I bit my lip. But Joel was literally on his way. We'd made plans, and I hated the thought of breaking them, especially last-minute. My own disappointment aside, it was so incredibly rude.

In front of me, Derek said, "So I'd get mowing if I were you."

"Oh come on," I said. "Just give me another day, okay?"

"Hey," Derek snapped, "this was *your* idea. Remember?"

What could I say? He was right. I'd practically begged him for the job. And, in my own defense, I was usually really prompt about it. But last week, things had been really crazy with all of those endowment meetings. And then, more recently, things had been crazy with Joel – crazy good, that is.

But if I wanted things to *stay* good – as in remotely peaceful – I needed to get rid of Derek, pronto.

"Fine," I said. "I'll mow tonight. There. Are you happy now?"

His lips pursed. "I'd be happier if I didn't have to micromanage everything."

Oh, for crying out loud. Like father, like son. I wanted to argue, but I didn't have the time. So what I said was, "I'll try to do better, okay?"

"Don't *try*. Do." And then, he turned away, stalked to his car, and sped off.

Gazing at the empty driveway, I tried to look on the bright side. At least, there wouldn't be a fistfight on the front lawn.

That was something, right?

Still, I'd have to cancel with Joel. I hated that.

I hated it even more a minute later, when he pulled up just as I was trudging toward the shed to get the mower.

□

CHAPTER 36

At the sight of Joel's car, I stopped and changed direction, heading toward him now instead of the shed. When he got out of his car to greet me, I said, "I'm really sorry, but I have to cancel."

He glanced toward my house. "Why? Is something wrong?"

"No. Not at all." I gave him an apologetic smile. "It's just a yard thing. You're not going to believe this, but I've got to mow tonight."

He said nothing as he studied my face, and I felt color rise to my cheeks. Cripes, next I'd be telling him that I had to wash my hair or something equally stupid.

I tried to explain. "It's like a job, actually. And it's got to be done on a certain schedule. Unfortunately, I'm already late." I rolled my eyes. "As I was just reminded."

"Yeah? By who?"

Damn it. I probably shouldn't have said that. I gave a dismissive wave of my hand. "You know, the estate people."

Joel's gaze hardened. "You mean Derek?"

I hesitated. "Him and his dad, actually."

"Your lawyers."

Funny, he hadn't phrased it as a question. Still, I nodded. "Right. But with this, it's more of an estate thing."

"Is that so?"

"Yeah." I tried to act like this was no big deal. "And Derek just reminded me that I'd better get it done, or–" I shrugged. "–you know."

Joel gave me another long look. "Or what?"

"What do you mean?"

"Let's say you don't follow the schedule. What then?"

I won't get paid. That's what.

And heaven help me, I needed the money. The nagging, I could deal with. But the lack of funds, now that was a serious problem, and it was getting more serious every week.

But Joel didn't need to hear about my problems, so in the most casual voice I could muster, I said, "Maybe it won't take *too* long."

I considered the best-case scenario. Maybe the mower would work just fine, and maybe if I walked really fast, I could get it done before midnight. After all, back when there'd been an actual lawn service, it didn't take *them* five hours to do it.

Of course, they didn't have a finicky mower that stalled all the time.

Joel's voice, quieter now, pulled me to the present. "There's something you're not saying. What is it?"

"Nothing." I glanced around the yard. Derek was right. It did look overgrown. If his dad happened to drive by, we'd both be in trouble. I gave a resigned sigh. "I just need to get it done. That's all."

Joel's eyebrows furrowed. "You're serious."

Obviously, he didn't get it, and no doubt, he was irritated, not that I could blame him. "I'm really sorry," I said. "If I'd realized sooner, I would've called."

"That's not the issue."

There was an issue? I knew it. Reluctantly, I said, "So what *is*?"

"You look worried, and I don't like it."

"Oh." His words warmed my heart. But I didn't want *my* worries to become *his* worries. So I said, "Yeah, well, I'm only worried because I hate to cancel last-minute. It's kind of rude, you know?"

Joel gave me a look. "Nice try."

"What do you mean?"

"I mean, it's more than that. I can tell."

Under his penetrating gaze, I started to squirm. If I didn't leave in like two seconds, I'd end up telling him everything. Hoping for a quick escape, I said, "I just need to get it done, alright? And the longer we talk about it, the longer I'll be mowing in the dark."

His jaw tightened. "You're gonna mow in the dark?"

"Not for sure. I mean, if I hurry, maybe I won't have to." I gave him a hopeful smile. "If you're not busy, maybe we can catch up tomorrow?"

"No. I've got a better idea."

"What?"

"*I'll* mow your lawn, and after, *you'll* tell me what kind of shit Derek's pulling on you."

I stared up at him. "I couldn't let you do that."

"Oh yeah?" He smiled. "Just try and stop me."

Suddenly, I almost wanted to smile, too. The offer was so sweet and unexpected. And yet, what I *should* tell him was that I didn't need any help, because everything was just hunky-dory.

But that wouldn't be true. And, I had to accept reality. I liked him. I *really* liked him. And I hated the thought of pretending to be something I wasn't.

I bit my lip. Against all logic, I wanted to say yes. But it wasn't the only thing I wanted. Over the past few days, I'd come to realize that I wasn't the only one who was hiding something.

Suddenly inspired, I said, "Okay. On one condition. There's something I want to know, too."

"Yeah? What's that?"

I met his gaze head-on. "I want to know about the fights."

CHAPTER 37

From inside the house, I heard the lawn mower running somewhere out back. To my relief, Joel had actually agreed to my terms, even if he didn't look too happy about it.

But I had a good reason for pushing the issue. We'd been spending a lot of time together, and in spite of my best intentions, I was falling for him in the scariest way.

How *he* felt, I couldn't be sure. But I *did* know that both of us had been dodging our share of questions – me when it came to Derek, the estate, and everything associated with it.

As for Joel, he'd been dodging questions about two primary things – the fights and how he made his money. This led me to an ominous realization. Those two things were probably related.

In spite of my earlier assumptions, he didn't seem to be hurting for money. And yet, he didn't seem to have a regular job waiting for him anywhere.

True, I could say the same for myself. Over the past few months, I'd been living in limbo-land, with a seasonal part-time job – two jobs if I counted the lawn thing – and a college career that I'd been forced to put on hold.

When Joel had asked me about college, I'd given him the same vague answer that I always gave. *"Oh that? I'm taking a year off."*

Like I had a choice.

But if anything, Joel's answers had been even more vague than mine. When I'd asked him point-blank what Mike had meant about seeing Joel "slaughter" someone at State, he'd replied with something along the lines of, *"Eh, the guy didn't know what he was talking about."*

What did that even mean? That Mike had mistaken Joel for someone else? That it wasn't a slaughter, so much as a maiming? Or that the altercation didn't qualify as a real fight?

I had no idea. But soon, I'd be finding out.

While he mowed the yard, I ran through the house, dusting the furniture and running a mop over the floors. It wasn't only that it gave me something to do. It was the fact that I didn't want added trouble if Derek's dad popped in for a spot inspection.

The way Derek had talked, that was a distinct possibility, and there was no way on Earth I wanted to get caught in any kind of violation.

The cleaning itself wasn't a hardship. I mean, I didn't mind cleaning my own place. But I hated the thought of doing it just because it was a condition of me living here – like some kind of temporary tenant, squatting in the guestroom until the real owner showed up.

I *was* the real owner – or at least, I would be, in four more years, assuming I could hold on that long.

I was just finishing the kitchen floors when I heard that dreaded sound, the doorbell echoing through the house. Fearing the worst – that it might be Derek's dad, coming to check up on me – I set the mop aside and rushed to the front door.

But when I flung it open, it wasn't Derek's dad. It was Derek himself. With barely a hello, he demanded, "What the hell is *he* doing here?"

Oh, crap. Maybe I'd been dreading the wrong person. But in my defense, I hadn't considered that Derek might stop by twice within such a short timeframe.

From the open doorway, I scanned the front yard. I didn't see Joel, but I could hear the lawnmower running smoothly out back.

Stalling for time, I said, "What do you mean?"

"As if you don't know." Derek made a sound of disgust. "What? You're farming out your work now?"

God, what an ass. I was *so* tired of being on defense all the time. "It's getting mowed. What do you care?"

"That wasn't the agreement."

I gave him an irritated look. "So *that's* why you came back? To make sure I was mowing the lawn myself?"

"No. I came with news about your car, not that you seem to appreciate it."

Obviously, he meant my mom's car, which was still being repaired.

"Fine," I said. "Is it done?"

"Hardly. You're looking at some major repairs."

I felt my eyebrows furrow. That couldn't be right. At the campground, Joel had said it was nothing big. I tried to recall what, specifically, the car needed. A new distributor cap or something?

My stomach churned with dread. "How major?"

"Worst-case scenario? A new engine."

I stared at him. That couldn't be right. Could it? My gaze narrowed. "Where's the car now?"

"What does it matter? It's not like you can drive it."

"I don't care. I want to know."

He stared at me for a long, tense moment before saying, "What's up with you, anyway?"

Well, that was rich. "What's up with *me?*" I gave a bark of laughter. "*You're* the one who's been a total jackass all summer."

Derek's mouth tightened. "What?"

This time, I wasn't going to back down. "You heard me."

"Alright. You really wanna know?" Derek took a slow, deliberate look around. "I show up here, to do you a favor, and I see that asshole out back, wearing no fucking shirt, like he owns the place."

I glanced toward the driveway. I couldn't help but notice that Derek's car was parked out front, right behind Joel's. And I *also* couldn't help but notice that Joel was out of sight, unless Derek had gone looking for him.

I crossed my arms. "Oh yeah? And *how*, exactly, did you see him?"

"What do you mean?"

"I mean he's not out front. So what'd you do? Skulk around the yard until you found him?"

"I don't need to skulk. This is part of my job."

"Sure it is."

"So, what is it?" Derek said. "Is he living here now?"

Right. Because I'd always been the kind of girl who invited random guys to shack up with me after knowing them for only a few days.

But I was in no mood to reassure him. "If he is, so what?"

"So, you'd be in violation of the terms."

"Of what? The estate?" I made a scoffing sound. "You're so full of it."

"You sure about that?"

Actually, I wasn't. But lately, I wasn't sure about a lot of things, *especially* when it came to the estate. Until a few months ago, I hadn't realized there were problems. Now, everything was a problem.

And Derek wasn't helping. I lifted my chin. "If you want to stop me, get a lawyer."

His jaw tightened. "As I keep reminding you, I *am* your lawyer."

"Yeah? Then why don't you act like it?"

"I am. Right now, in fact."

"Oh come on, Derek. You're not working *for* me. You're working *against* me."

"Is that so?" He shook his head. "Have you ever stopped to think that maybe, we're *trying* to look out for you?"

I gave a bitter laugh. "Or *maybe* you're looking out for yourself."

"What's *that* supposed to mean?"

I wasn't sure what I meant. But something was definitely off. I needed the chance to think. And besides, this wasn't the time to be discussing it.

Within the last minute or so, it had slowly dawned on me that I no longer heard the mower running, which meant that our argument could be interrupted at any moment.

Looking to end this now, I said, "Next time, save yourself a trip. Just give me the bad news over the phone." And with that, I took a long step backward, reached for the side of the door, and gave it a good strong swing.

It was supposed to slam shut. It didn't, thanks to Derek's foot, which stopped the door in mid-motion. He demanded, "What the hell is your problem?"

"At the moment? *You're* my problem. Now, get your foot out of my doorway."

"*Your* doorway, huh?"

"Yes. *My* doorway. *I* live here. Not you." I glanced at his foot. "So are you gonna move that or not?"

"Oh, I'll move it. But first, I've got a question."

I made a sound of annoyance. "What?"

"What are you gonna pay him with?"

"Who?"

"The asshole mowing your lawn." Derek gave me a smug smile. "Because I can tell you one thing. We're *not* paying you for that."

My stomach clenched. Stupidly, I said, "For what?"

"For this week's lawn care. Do I need to remind you? The maintenance contract is non-transferrable, which means that if you hire it out, you don't get paid."

I wanted to scream in frustration. But I didn't. Instead, hoping to call his bluff, I gave him a smug smile right back. "Nice try. But I didn't 'hire' him to do it. He's doing it as a favor."

"A favor, huh? So what *are* you paying him with?" His lips formed a smirk. "Pussy?"

My skin flashed hot, and then just as quickly, turned ice-cold. The comment was so wrong – and so completely unlike the guy I'd grown up with – that I didn't know how to respond, unless I wanted to slap him silly, which was seriously tempting.

But then, a new voice – Joel's voice – sounded from somewhere nearby. "Speaking of pussy…"

Derek gave a little jump and turned toward the sound. A moment later, I spotted Joel, walking from around the side of the house. He wore no shirt, and was covered in a thin sheen of perspiration.

If this whole scene weren't so awful, I might've spent more time dwelling on the fact that he looked like every girl's fantasy – or maybe just my fantasy, last night, in fact.

His thick, dark hair was slightly damp, and the muscles of his shoulders and stomach looked even more defined than they had in my dreams. I felt myself swallow as I tried to focus on what was really important – the fact that this was a powder-keg waiting to explode.

Derek turned to glare at Joel. "Are you talking to me?"

Joel stepped closer. "You see any *other* pussies around here?"

"No. But I see an asshole."

I spoke up. "Derek, seriously. You need to go, like *now*."

"Fine." He turned and gave me a stiff smile. "And you're welcome, by the way."

And you're not.

But I didn't say it, because I wanted him gone already.

Finally, I got my wish. Derek turned and stalked to his car. He yanked open the driver's side door, got behind the wheel, and slammed the door behind him.

A moment later, I watched in silent mortification as his car squealed in reverse, did a sloppy U-turn, and then roared down the long driveway, leaving an ominous silence in its wake.

I turned my nervous gaze to Joel.

He was still there, but he didn't look happy. □

CHAPTER 38

From the open doorway, I gave Joel a nervous smile. "I'm really sorry about that."

His brow wrinkled in confusion. "Why are *you* sorry?"

"Well, he called you a name for one thing."

"Forget that." He moved closer until we were standing within arm's reach. "Are you okay?"

"Yeah, sure." I gave a shaky laugh. "We fight all the time, so I'm kind of used to it."

Joel's gaze darkened. "That happens a lot?"

"No. Not really." I glanced toward the driveway, where Derek's car had been a moment earlier. "But he's been in a rotten mood all summer. Honestly, I don't know what's going on."

After a long, ominous silence, Joel asked, "You want me to have a talk with him?"

"No," I blurted. "Definitely not." In fact, that was the *last* thing I wanted. Trying not to be rude about it, I added, "But thanks. That's really nice." I ran a trembling hand through my hair. "But he's already gone, so..."

"So, I'll go after him, not a big deal."

That's where Joel was wrong. It *would* be a big deal. Already, it was a big deal. Looking to tone things down, I said, "It's fine, really."

"Sorry, but you're wrong."

I blinked. "What?"

"Talking to you like that? It's not fine. And you know it."

"Well, yeah. But you just saw the tail end." I tried to shrug it off. "He said some things. I said some things." I forced a laugh. "And you said some things..."

"Yeah. I did." His jaw tightened. "And he's lucky I only *said* something."

I didn't ask what Joel meant, because I could see it in his stance, along with the way his gaze kept shifting to his car, like he was thinking of making good on his offer – to have a "talk" with Derek.

I summoned up a smile. "I know. And I appreciate it, really. But can't we just forget it?"

Joel still wasn't smiling. "Forget it."

"Yeah. I mean, you're already mowing my lawn. You don't need to fight my battles, too." I deliberately brightened my tone. "When you're done, I was thinking I'd make dinner."

"I'm already done."

"Seriously?" I turned to study the lawn. With all of the Derek-drama, I hadn't even noticed, but the front yard looked surprisingly terrific. And I'd heard Joel mowing out back, so obviously, that part was finished, too.

Still, I couldn't quite believe it. "The whole thing?"

"Yeah. Unless there's more you haven't showed me."

I stared in amazement. "But you've only been at for a couple of hours."

Finally, to my infinite relief, Joel smiled back. "What? You wanna inspect?"

I felt myself swallow. That smile was almost my undoing. With a conscious effort, I pushed aside any thoughts of Derek. He wasn't here, thank goodness. But Joel was.

In the long shadows of the fading day, he looked utterly amazing. I didn't want to stare, but it was hard not to. Everything about him was pure perfection – from his beautiful face to his finely-cut shoulders and chest.

My gaze slipped lower, and I tried not to notice that his flat, defined abs glistened just enough to accentuate all those interesting ridges and valleys, the ones that, until now, I'd only been seeing in my dreams.

Catching myself, I forced my gaze to keep on going, as if I'd merely been looking down to inspect the chipped, white paint of the oversized porch.

Trying to get a grip, I studied the paint more closely and worked hard to focus on house repairs or something equally unsexy. But it was no use.

The only thing I wanted to think about was Joel.

"So?" he said. "Do you?"

Did I ever.

I gave a little shake of my head. "Do I what?"

"Want to inspect the lawn?"

"Should I?"

He gave a flick of his head. "Come on."

Soon, we were in the back yard, with its panoramic view of Lake Michigan. But now, I wasn't looking at the water, or even at Joel.

I was looking at the lawn. Like the front yard, it looked amazing. Confused, I turned to study the lawnmower, which he'd parked near the shed out back.

I turned my attention back to Joel. "How'd you do that?"

"Do what?"

I pointed to the mower. "Get *that…*" I pointed to the lawn. "…to do *that*?"

It was an honest question. Every time *I* mowed, the lawnmower sputtered in and out, making the yard look like a giant cat shaved by a monkey.

That was one reason it always took so long. Sometimes, I had to mow huge sections of it twice, just to make it look decent.

Joel shrugged. "It just needed some adjustments. That's all."

"Like what?"

"Nothing big," he said. "Fuel filter, air filter, sharpened the blade." He paused. "Also, the self-propelling mechanism was off, needed some tweaking."

"Tweaking, huh?" I smiled up at him. "What *are* you? Some kind of mechanical genius?"

"Nah, I'm just a guy."

Whatever he was, he wasn't just a guy. He was amazing in too many ways to count. His magic with the mower reminded me of how quickly he'd diagnosed the problem with my car, assuming he'd been right, that is.

Reluctantly, I said, "Hey, can I ask you a question?"

"About what?"

I bit my lip. "My car, actually."

"Yeah? What about it?"

"I just need some advice, that's all." I hesitated. "Derek said it might need a new engine. Do you think that's true?"

CHAPTER 39

My question hung in the air. In Joel's eyes, I saw slow anger, simmering just beneath the surface.

Instantly, I was filled with remorse. Of course, he was angry. Here, he'd just spent two hours mowing my lawn, and already, I was hitting him up for something else, even if it *was* only advice.

But did he realize that? I mean, he understood that I wasn't expecting him to fix my car, too?

Oh, God. What if he didn't? Regretting that I'd even mentioned it, I gave him an apologetic smile. "You know what? Sorry. Forget I asked."

"Why?"

"Because I shouldn't have."

"You shouldn't have what? Asked about the car?"

"Right. Definitely." I hesitated. "But just so you know, that wasn't a hint for more 'free labor' or anything. I was just curious what you thought, because you looked at it the other night."

I forced some cheer into my voice. "But you know what? It'll all work out. So, never mind."

He gave me an odd look. "What's wrong?"

"Nothing."

He waited, as if expecting a better answer than that.

When the silence grew too heavy, I finally admitted, "Alright, I can tell that you're mad, not that I blame you. I mean, no one likes a mooch, right?"

"A mooch?"

"You know. A freeloader. A user. Whatever." Feeling guiltier than ever, I turned away and gazed out over the lawn. "Already, you've done me a huge favor, and I don't want you to think I'm not grateful."

"It wasn't a favor," he said. "It was a deal. Remember?"

I was still looking at the lawn. "I know that's what you said. But it doesn't *feel* like a deal."

"Why not?"

"Because *I'm* getting the better end of it."

"That's your opinion, not mine."

Again, I turned to look at him. In spite of his words, the anger was still there. I could see it in his eyes, just as I could see the muscles of his neck, corded into tight knots.

When I made no response, Joel gave a slow shake of his head. "You think I'm pissed about the car?"

"Aren't you?"

"Yeah. But not at you." He studied my face. "You really don't get it?"

"Get what?"

Ignoring my question, Joel asked, "How have you been getting to work?"

"I've been riding my bike. Didn't you know?"

"No," he said. "I didn't."

"Really? Even though you've been stuck carting me around?"

"I wasn't stuck," he said. "I like carting you around. You think I'm out here picking you up because I thought your car wasn't working?"

"Well, yeah," I said. "Otherwise, like tonight, I would've just driven out to meet you."

"That's what *you* think."

I stared up at him. "What do you mean?"

"I mean, I *like* picking you up. And I like taking you home."

"Why?"

"Other than spending time with you?"

"Well, yeah."

Joel shrugged. "It gives me the chance to check things out, make sure everything's okay."

At first, I didn't get it. But then I recalled the very first time he'd brought me home. We'd arrived just in time to catch my uncle galloping off with that horse. "Is this about my relatives?"

"In part."

"I guess I should've mentioned, they won't be back for at least a month."

"Yeah? How do you know?"

"It's their pattern," I explained. "Whenever I catch them, they wait a few weeks before coming back. And one time, they didn't come back for two whole years."

"Because they lost interest?"

I winced. "No. Because they were living in Italy."

"Why Italy?"

"Who knows? But the timing was perfect. I was away at college, and with them out of the country, I didn't have to worry about them swiping my stuff while I was gone. So, in a way, I've been pretty lucky."

"You call that lucky?"

"Well, you know, glass half-full, right?"

Joel gave me a look that was decidedly glass-half-empty. "That's one way to look at it. About your car, where is it now?"

"I don't know. Derek didn't tell me."

His jaw tightened. "Right."

I hesitated. "So, what do you think? About the engine, I mean."

"I think the guy's full of it."

I felt a surge of hope. "You think so?"

"I *know* so."

I blew out a long breath. "Well, that's good. I'll call him Monday and get it worked out."

Joel didn't look thrilled. "Why not now?"

"It's a Friday night," I said. "No one will be working on it this weekend anyway." I tried to laugh. "And plus, I think I've had enough of Derek for one day."

"You want me to handle it?"

I studied his face. Was that a sincere offer? Even if it was, I knew better than to accept it. Still, I had to smile. "I'm pretty sure *you've* had enough of Derek, too. Besides, this will give him a couple days to cool down."

I glanced at Joel's bare chest. "Speaking of cooling down. Do you want a shower or something?"

"I don't *want* one, but I probably need one." He glanced toward the house. "Got a shower I can borrow?"

I had to laugh. "Actually, I've got like ten. You can take your pick." I paused. "But did you bring a change of clothes?"

"I always have a change of clothes."

"Really? Why?"

"Because things happen."

I couldn't help but wonder, what kind of things? But part of me knew. A guy like Joel? He was probably pounced on wherever he went. No doubt, he'd enjoyed the showers and bedrooms of countless girls across the state.

As we circled the side of the house to retrieve his things, I recalled Derek's snide suggestion, that I'd be paying Joel with, to put it crudely, pussy.

I gave Joel a sideways glance. True, I was ungodly attracted to him, and he'd done me a huge favor. But getting naked for lawn care wasn't exactly my style.

Joel did realize this, didn't he?

I gave myself a mental slap to the face. Of course he did. And I'd been stupid to even wonder.

In fact, thanks to April, he knew more than I wanted him to. So I pushed that thought out of my mind, and focused on the positive. Soon, Joel and I would both be getting the answers we wanted. And then, we could simply sit back and enjoy a nice relaxing evening.

Except, it didn't work out that way.

Not at all.

□

CHAPTER 40

I stared at the stranger on my doorstep. It was some guy in his late twenties, or possibly his early thirties. I'd never seen him before, and yet, something about him looked eerily familiar.

He was tall, with dark hair, dark eyes, and a lean muscular build that might've piqued my interest a couple of weeks ago, before I'd become so obsessed with another guy who looked remarkably similar.

I'd barely opened the door when the stranger said, "Where is he?"

Well, hello to you, too. Probably, if I'd been smart, I would've ignored the doorbell entirely. After all, it had brought me nothing lately but grief.

Joel was upstairs, taking a shower. And now, given my suspicions, I didn't quite know what to do. Should I welcome the guy inside? Or slam the door in his face?

Stalling for time, I said, "Where's who?"

The stranger flicked his head toward Joel's car. "The driver of *that.*"

I made a show of looking toward the driveway. Behind Joel's car was a pricey-looking sedan with dark tinted windows. The way it looked, the guy had serious money – or massive car payments.

Then again, I could say the same thing about Joel, or even myself, if my car wasn't older and broken down, that is.

I pushed aside the distraction and returned my attention to the stranger. "You *do* realize you can't just show up here, demanding to see whoever."

"Yeah? Why not?"

I gave the guy a closer look.

Ungodly attractive? Check.

Amazing body? Check.

A total jerk, just like Joel had implied? Oh yeah. That was a checkmark so big, I'd need a billboard to write it on.

I crossed my arms. "Because it's impolite. That's why."

Behind me, I heard Joel say, "Yeah *Bishop*. It's impolite." A moment later, he joined me at the door. "So shove off."

Bishop. Yup, that was Joel's last name alright. They were definitely brothers, although why the guy didn't go by his first name, I had no idea.

I was still pondering that when Bishop gave Joel a hard look. "Where the hell are they?"

In a voice filled with mock innocence, Joel said, "Where's what?"

Bishop's jaw tightened. "You *know* what."

Oh, crap.

I knew what, too. Or at least, I was pretty sure I did. Thanks to my internet research, I'd seen the brother who owned the Camaro. *That* brother had cryptic tattoos and even *less* civility. This brother was tattoo-free, but not much nicer.

And I could guess what he wanted – the guns in the trunk.

My gaze darted from Bishop to Joel as they stared each other down. Hoping to diffuse some of the tension, I said, "Isn't anyone going to introduce me?"

Bishop said, "No need. I'm not staying."

So much for a happy family reunion. But did he have to be so rude about it?

I said, "Good. Because no one invited you."

The guy's lips curved into the hint of a smile. "Who's impolite now?"

Next to me, Joel said, "You are, dickhead."

The guy shrugged. "So I hear."

Joel said, "How'd you find me?"

"Give me my stuff," Bishop said, "and maybe I'll tell you."

"Or," Joel said, "you can tell me. And *maybe*, I'll give you your stuff."

I spoke up. "Or maybe, you could do it at the same time. You know, like a hostage swap."

In unison, they both turned to look. Neither looked thrilled with my idea. I cleared my throat. "It works in the movies, right?"

"No." Bishop said. "In the movies, it all goes to hell."

Okay, so maybe he had a point. Still, I felt compelled to mutter, "Not in *every* movie."

Bishop looked unimpressed. "Then you and I are seeing different shows."

Joel said, "What are you doing here, anyway?"

"You *know* what I'm doing here." Bishop turned and glanced around the yard, as if assessing his surroundings.

I leaned closer to Joel and whispered, "You guys *are* brothers, right?"

"Supposedly."

"How many do you have, anyway?"

He glanced toward Bishop. "Too many."

In my view, there was no such thing. I would've loved to have a brother, a *real* brother – or better yet, more than one. I looked from one guy to the other. "You know, you guys really should be nicer to each other."

In unison, they both made the exact same scoffing sound. And for some reason, that made me laugh. "See? You're more alike than you realize."

But Joel was shaking his head. "No. I'm nothing like those pricks."

Well, that was interesting – and yeah, kind of rude, actually.

I looked to Bishop. He looked utterly unfazed.

In a surprisingly calm voice, Bishop said, "Well, *this* prick needs to talk to you. *Now*." His gaze shifted to me. "And preferably somewhere else."

I gave him an irritated look. "Don't you think that's kind of rude?"

"I'm not being rude. I'm doing you a favor."

Now, it was my turn to scoff. "Some favor."

Bishop looked to Joel. "Are you coming or not?"

"Forget it," Joel said. "I'm not going anywhere."

"Alright." Bishop shrugged. "You wanna discuss it here? Fine by me." He smiled. "I left Jake down the road. My guess? He'll be here in five, ten minutes. But hey, you do what you want."

My gaze snapped to Joel. From the look on his face, he was thinking the exact same thing I was. *"Well, this is just great."*

CHAPTER 41

Three hours later, Joel still hadn't returned. I felt my teeth grinding as I recalled what he'd said just before getting into his brother's car, leaving his own car parked in my driveway.

"I'll be back in a few."

For the hundredth time, I parted the front curtains and looked out over the darkened driveway. *A few what? Years?*

At this point, I didn't know whether to be worried or angry. Already, I'd called him twice. But he hadn't answered, and I hated the thought of calling him again.

After all, I wasn't his girlfriend or anything, and obviously, there was more to this situation than I knew. But why hadn't he called? Or at least sent me text? Was it *that* hard, to say, *"Sorry, I'm running late."*

For the tenth time, I pulled out my cell phone and stared down at the screen. *Ring, damn it.*

Suddenly, it did.

Startled, I dropped the stupid thing and winced as it hit the hardwood floor. I dove down and swooped it up, only to feel my shoulders sag. The phone was fine, but the caller wasn't Joel. It was Cassie.

Normally, I'd be happy to hear from her. But not tonight.

I answered with a distracted, "Hello?"

She hesitated. "Did I wake you? Oh, crap. I did, didn't I?"

"No. Not at all." But I *was* surprised to hear from her so late. I glanced at the nearby clock. It was past midnight. "Is something wrong?"

"Actually, yeah." She sighed. "Sorry to call so late, but there's a problem at the shop."

"What kind of problem?"

"You're not going to believe this, but a water pipe exploded in the back room."

"Exploded? Seriously?"

"No. Not literally." She gave a weak laugh. "Although you'd never know it from the looks of things."

"Oh no. That bad?"

"You don't know the half of it. I'll have to close for at least a couple of weeks, maybe longer."

The worry in her voice hurt to hear. "Oh, Cassie, I am *so* sorry. Do you need any help?"

"No. But thanks. Actually, I was calling for another reason. You're scheduled to work tomorrow, but I just don't see the point." With a note of false cheer, she added, "So congratulations, you've got the day off."

This wasn't good news, and not only because I was worried for Cassie. I didn't make a lot of money at the cookie shop, but it *did* help with expenses. So much for grocery money.

Damn it.

But even as the thought crossed my mind, I mentally kicked myself. The way it sounded, Cassie's business had taken a huge hit, and what was *I* doing? Worrying about a lost paycheck.

Mortified by my own selfishness, I said, "Are you sure I can't help? Not as an employee. But as a friend? I mean, you wouldn't have to pay me if that's the issue."

"It's not." She paused. "Well, actually it is. I mean, it's not like we're going to be selling any cookies. But the truth is, I've got to wait on the insurance adjustor before I do a single thing."

Hoping to cheer her up, I said, "At least you have insurance. So that's good, right?"

"I guess," she said, "but the deductible's a killer. A thousand bucks. I'll probably have to sell a kidney or something."

I almost didn't know what to say. *Poor Cassie.* "Are you sure I can't help?"

"I'm sure," she said. "But I *am* wondering something."

"What's that?"

"What happened with you and Joel? Are you guys on the outs or something?"

I tensed. "What makes you say that?"

"Because I just saw him at T.J.'s, and he wasn't with you."

T.J.'s? The bar? So *that's* where he was?

My fingers flexed around the phone. Trying not to sound as irritated as I felt, I said, "So, who was he with? A couple of guys who looked like they could be related?"

"Well, he *was* with two people. And now that you mention it, they *did* look like they could be related to each other, except..." She hesitated. "They weren't guys."

CHAPTER 42

It was already past two o'clock in the morning when I finally heard a car pull into the driveway. From my spot on the sofa, I opened my eyes just in time to see headlights bouncing off the far wall of the darkened front room.

After getting off the phone with Cassie, I'd opened the front curtains, but turned off all the lights. And then, I'd slouched onto the sofa and mentally rehearsed all of the rude things I was planning to say when that ass-hat showed his face.

Or who knows? Maybe he *wouldn't* show his face. Maybe he'd just slink over to his car and drive off without so much as a hello, or a goodbye for that matter.

My shoulders tightened. If so, that was fine by me.

It would save me the trouble of telling him where he could shove whatever excuse he was planning to give me, assuming that he'd even bother.

Outside, I heard a car door slam, followed by the muffled sounds of male voices, and then, even more slamming, like the idiots were getting in and out of the car – or *cars*, as in plural.

I didn't know. And I didn't care.

In what should've been good news, I didn't hear any female voices, which meant that the people in the driveway were probably Joel's brothers. Who knows, maybe they were his cover story. Maybe *that* was the reason for all the talking and slamming.

I rolled my eyes. Who was I kidding? Like he'd even go to that much trouble. Probably, they were just drunk off their asses.

It *was,* after all, past closing time on a Friday night. Probably, I should've gone out, too – drinking, dancing, or whatever. But where had I spent *my* evening? Home. Sitting here like a Cocker Spaniel, waiting for the lord of the manor to return.

Next, I'd be slobbering at his feet and fetching his slippers.

Pathetic.

Soon, I heard a car – or maybe more than one – drive off, leaving the night quiet once again.

Unable to resist, I stood and squinted toward the front window. From the shadows, I saw nothing. I heard nothing. I felt nothing, except a dull, depressing ache that made me feel like a giant loser.

For some reason, the night suddenly seemed ten times lonelier. How twisted was that? Reluctantly, I edged closer to the window and sighed as my most humiliating suspicion was confirmed.

Joel's car was gone.

I felt my jaw clench. *Fine.*

I didn't *want* to tell him off, anyway. He wasn't worth it.

Beyond disgusted, I trudged up the stairs, flicked on the lights in my bedroom, and made my way into my private bathroom. Looking to wash away my sorry mood, I started running a bath, only to pause in the middle of undressing when a new sound rang through the house, literally.

It was the doorbell.

What on Earth?

I was half naked – the *bottom* half.

When the doorbell rang again, I turned toward the sound. All things considered, I'd have to be a total idiot to answer anything now.

But as it turned out, I *was* a total idiot, because I couldn't seem to stop myself. I turned off the water, tugged on my shorts, and shoved my feet back into my sneakers. And then, I stalked toward the stairway with one goal in mind – to make him feel just as stupid as I did.

While stomping down the stairs, I recalled the details of what Cassie had told me earlier. She'd popped into T.J.'s for just a moment, in search of her landlord. While there, she'd seen Joel enter the bar with a blonde and a brunette who looked like they could be sisters. He'd had one on each arm, and they'd been smiling.

At the image, I found myself stomping just a little bit harder.

Great.

A sister act.

How nice.

From what Cassie had said, Joel's companions were, as she'd put it, quite attractive.

How lovely for them. If they wanted him, they could have him. It's not like *I* wanted him or anything.

Well, not anymore, at least.

When I reached the front door, I left it locked and called out, "Who is it?"

Sure enough, I heard Joel's voice, calling back, "It's me." He paused. "Joel."

A cold smile settled over my features. "Joel who?"

"You *know* who."

Yes, I did. It was Joel the Cocky Bastard who thought he could ditch me for a couple of hoochies and then show up here afterwards for sloppy seconds. I frowned. Or would it be thirds?

I shuddered at the thought.

What did he think? That just because he'd mowed my lawn that I'd forgive whatever slick trick he was pulling now. *Not likely.*

I leaned closer to the intercom. "Joel?" I paused as if thinking. "Huh. Sorry. Not ringing a bell."

In spite of my obvious sarcasm, his voice remained calm. "Will you open the door?" He paused. "Please?"

His calmness grated on me. What was I supposed to do? Open the door wide and give him a big, happy smile. *"Sure, come on in. You're so hot, I'd put up with anything."*

Suddenly tired of the drama, I gave up the pretense and said, "It's late."

"I know," he said. "But I wanna explain. Now c'mon. Open up. Alright?"

With a sigh, I disengaged the alarm, twisted the deadbolt, and opened the door. And there he was, looking just as good as the last time I'd seen him. That was how long ago? Five, maybe six, hours?

I stared up at him. To my surprise, he actually looked sober.

But so what? Maybe his drug of choice wasn't alcohol, but a couple of sisters in a back booth.

I crossed my arms and waited, wondering what on Earth he'd say now.

He glanced down at my clothes. "Were you sleeping?"

"No."

His mouth twitched at the corners. "Your shorts are on backwards."

I looked down and stifled a groan. *Oh, crap.* He was right. I should've noticed. Now that I was paying attention, they did feel kind of funny. So much for making *him* feel stupid.

Still, I lifted my chin and said, "Is that why you stopped by? To critique my clothing?"

"No." He glanced past me, toward the interior of the house. With a look that was *almost* apologetic, he said, "I forgot my phone."

CHAPTER 43

From the open doorway, I was still staring. "You forgot your phone? So *that's* why you rang the bell?"

I felt my eyes narrow. Oh, he could have his phone, alright. In fact, I could even tell him where to shove it – and it was nowhere near his ear.

In front of me, Joel gave a low curse. "I didn't mean it like that."

"Oh yeah? How did you mean it?"

"I wanted to call," he said. "*That's* what I meant." His expression softened. "Screw the phone. I don't need it."

He looked so sincere that I almost didn't know what to think. I had to remind myself that he hadn't been out saving orphans from burning buildings. He'd been out carousing with not just one, but *two* other girls.

Should I fling that fact in his face? Or wait to hear what he'd say?

I was still pondering that when Joel said, "I brought you something."

Confused, I glanced down. His hands were empty. Unless he meant the something in his pants, I couldn't imagine what he meant.

I gave him a stiff smile. "Oh yeah? What?"

He flicked his head toward the side of the house. "C'mon. I'll show you."

Reluctantly, I poked my head out of the doorway and looked to where he indicated. I didn't see anything, not even his car.

Until this very moment, I'd assumed that he'd driven off a few minutes earlier, and then returned for whatever reason. But now, I didn't know what to think. I asked, "Where's your car?"

"I moved it."

How nice for him. Apparently, he figured he'd be staying a while.

My jaw tightened. "Oh, really? Why?"

He studied my face. "Well, obviously, not for the reason you think."

"How would *you* know what I'm thinking?"

"Not hard to figure out." He glanced toward the side of the house. "Look, we had to move some stuff. That's all. And Bishop didn't want an audience."

An audience? Meaning me? At *my* house?

I *so* didn't need this. I gave Joel an annoyed look. "Listen, I don't want to be rude, but whatever you brought, I don't want it."

He gave me a smile that was almost cocky. "How do you know if you won't look?"

He could smile all he wanted. I wasn't buying it. What did he think? That he could just waltz up with a smile and some kind of present, and everything would be okay?

It wasn't okay.

And I was tired of the game-playing. I heard myself sigh. "You know what? I know exactly what you were doing, and I don't appreciate it."

He looked at me for a long moment, as if trying to decide how much I really knew. In a carefully neutral voice, he said, "What do you mean?"

Something in his eyes – a flicker of surprise with a twinge of wariness – told me that he knew exactly what I meant.

My heart sank as my worst suspicions were confirmed. "You *know* what I mean. But if you want to play dumb, that's fine by me." I felt myself swallow. "Just do it somewhere else, okay?"

He studied my face. "Who told you?"

Well, that was special. "None of your business. That's who."

"Who?" he repeated.

"It's a small town. Word travels fast, alright?"

He made a low scoffing sound. "Right."

I gave an exasperated sigh. "Look, it's the middle of the night. What did you think? That I'd fling open the door and invite you inside?"

"No." In a tight voice, he added, "but I didn't expect this."

No doubt, this was true. The guy was so good-looking that girls probably flung themselves at him regardless of how late it was or what he'd been doing.

I gave him my snottiest smile. "I just bet." In spite of my smile, I wanted to cry. "Now, will you please just leave?"

"If that's what you want." He turned away and began stalking toward the side of the house.

Stupidly, I waited in the open doorway, frozen by a mixture of despair and morbid curiosity. Soon, I heard the rev of an engine, followed by the sight of his car roaring down the long driveway and disappearing from view.

I took a deep, ragged breath. Well, that solved the curiosity thing.

And now, there was only despair.

I shut the door, trudged back upstairs, and finished filling the tub. I climbed in, only to discover that the water had cooled while I'd been downstairs talking to Joel. It wasn't cold, but it wasn't exactly hot either.

Given my finances, running a new bath was a luxury I couldn't justify. So I sat in the lukewarm water for less than a minute before climbing out, toweling off, and getting dressed for bed.

Somehow, I'd hoped that telling him off would give me some satisfaction. But it hadn't. The bed was cold, and my life felt empty.

I stared into the darkness, half-wishing that I'd ignored what Cassie had told me and let Joel in, anyway. Maybe the girls were friends. Maybe nothing had happened. Maybe I'd overreacted.

Or more likely, I was just being pathetic.

It was just past dawn when my cell phone rang. With a groan, I reached for it and checked the display. It was Derek.

I hadn't slept, or at least not enough to matter. I was tempted to let it go to voicemail, but then figured I might as well get this over with. After all, my mood couldn't get any worse – or so I thought until Derek started talking.

CHAPTER 44

"Listen," Derek said, "I don't know what in the hell you were thinking, but I don't appreciate it."

I rubbed at my eyes. "Huh?"

"Yeah. Nice trick you pulled. Who was the guy?"

The more he talked, the less I understood. "What guy?"

"The tough guy you hired to do your dirty work."

Tough guy?

Dirty work?

I sat up in bed. "Derek, seriously, what are you talking about?"

"As if you don't know."

"I *don't*," I insisted. "So either tell me, or let me get back to sleep."

"Hey, don't get pissy with me," he said. "*I'm* the one who's gotta smooth this over. And just so you know, Biff wasn't happy."

My mind was too muddled to think. "Biff who?"

He gave a derisive snort. "Very funny." And with that, he ended the call.

I flopped back onto the bed and stared up at the ceiling. Well, that wasn't weird or anything.

Derek was definitely losing it. Or who knows, maybe *I* was. Giving up on any hope of sleep, I climbed out of bed and got dressed. I'd been scheduled to work at the cookie shop, but now, thanks to that broken pipe, I wasn't.

But I still had plenty to keep me busy. In just a few short weeks, we'd be having the final meeting to select the recipients for this year's art-endowment.

I had paperwork to review, letters to write, and tours to arrange. I also had to finish the cleaning, and not only to avoid grief from Derek and his dad.

If I didn't get scrubbing, the place wouldn't be in any kind of shape for visitors, even if they were just traipsing through to eyeball my parent's stuff.

Normally, this was an exciting time. But today, I wasn't excited about anything.

It was because of Joel. I missed him. And I hated him.

But most of all, I hated myself. I should've known he was too good to be true.

Stupid me.

I decided to start with the cleaning, mostly because my mind was too foggy to tackle anything else. I was just lugging the vacuum cleaner out of the broom closet room when my cell phone rang with a call from Cassie.

As soon as I answered, she burst out, "Hey, I heard what happened with Biff. What was *that* about? And who was the guy?"

I almost staggered under the avalanche of questions. "What guy?" I set down the vacuum cleaner. "And who's Biff?"

"Oh come on," she said. "This is me you're talking to. Just tell me. I'm dying to know."

My mind was churning. "Yeah. Me, too."

She gave a small laugh. "Good one."

"I'm not joking."

She paused. "Are you serious?"

"Yes. I'm dead serious. And you're the second person to call today." I felt like I was in the twilight zone or something. "I don't even know a Biff."

"Sure you do," she said. "Big guy, red hair, owns the garage off Maple."

"Sorry, I have no idea who you mean."

"Oh, come on. He's the guy with the snowplow. Wears a lot of flannel."

Finally, it clicked. "Ohhhhh. *That* Biff." I'd seen him around town, but until now, I hadn't known his name. Still, I had no idea what Cassie was talking about.

I asked, "So, what'd you hear?"

After a dramatic pause, Cassie said, "I heard that last night, you and some tattooed guy practically jacked your own car."

I almost dropped the phone. *Jacked?* What did that even mean? As far as the rest, I knew only one person with a tattoo – April. And yet somehow, I doubted that the butterfly on her ankle had anything to do with *this* fiasco, whatever it was.

"Wait a minute," I said. "Do you mean my car was *stolen*? You're kidding, right?"

Cassie hesitated. "You don't have it?"

"My car?" I wanted to cry. "No. I don't."

Cassie paused for a long, silent moment before saying, "Huh. That's odd."

It wasn't odd. It was a nightmare. Desperate for more information, I said, "Look, I'm totally clueless here. Can you just tell me what you know? Like start from the beginning or something?"

Her voice grew quiet. "Are you okay?"

"I'm fine," I lied. "I'm just confused, that's all. So, will you just tell me? Please?"

"Alright," Cassie said. "This is what I heard. Late last night, Biff gets a knock on his door – not at the auto shop, but at his house. And it's some tattooed guy that Biff doesn't recognize. And this guy has a wad of cash, and he tells Biff he's there to pay the towing bill."

"What towing bill?"

"The one for your car. It was towed from some campground or something?"

I froze. *The campground. Joel. Joel's brother. His other brother. A guy with tattoos.* I heard myself say, "Oh, shit."

"What?"

My mind was racing. I recalled Joel standing on my doorstep. *"I brought you something."*

My gaze shifted toward the side of my house. There were several walls between me and what Joel had wanted to show me.

If I looked now, what would I see?

Cassie said, "Are you still there?"

"Uh, yeah. Sorry. I'm listening."

"So anyway," Cassie continued, "Biff tells the guy, 'If you want the car, come by the shop at eight.' And the guy tells *him*, 'I've already got the car. I'm just here to settle the bill.' So Biff looks to the street, and sure enough, there's your car, idling in front of his house."

"So the car was running?

"Right," Cassie said. "And Biff sees *you* behind the wheel."

"But I wasn't." Walking slowly, like someone in a trance, I started moving toward the front door.

"Yeah, well, it was dark and all." Cassie paused. "Maybe he just assumed it was you. I mean, who else would be driving your car?" She perked up. "He said you waved out the window, all cheery like."

Absently, I murmured, "Uh-huh."

"So it *was* you?" Cassie gave a shaky laugh. "Wow, you almost had me there."

At this point, I hardly knew what to say. "But Biff *was* paid, right?"

"Not just paid," she said. "Double. In cash."

My front door was now within sight. I kept walking, slowly, with a mixture of anticipation and dread. I mumbled, "Double?"

"Yeah. For all the trouble. Or at least, that's what the guy told Biff."

"But he was still mad?"

"Biff? Not hardly." Cassie laughed. "He thought it was hilarious. I mean, yeah, he was surprised and all, but trust me, he wasn't complaining. I just saw him at the donut place. In fact, he was the one who told me."

"Uh-huh." Silently, I opened the front door and walked through it. I was afraid to look. And afraid to *not* look. Slowly, I inched toward the side of my house.

When I rounded the corner, I heard myself gasp. Sure enough, there it was – my car, parked exactly where Joel had indicated last night.

He'd called it a surprise.

Well, it was definitely that.

□

CHAPTER 45

The sound of tapping jolted me awake. My eyes flew open, and I saw Joel standing just outside my car window. I shot up in the driver's seat and glanced around. It was dark outside. Already?

I rubbed at my eyes. How long had I been parked here, anyway? When I'd pulled up, it had been late afternoon. The way it looked, I'd been asleep for hours.

I looked to Joel's campsite. There was no fire. In fact, there was no tent. I felt my eyebrows furrow. When I'd arrived, the tent had been standing there just like before. Now, it was gone.

I looked back to Joel, who eyed me through the car window. From the look on his face, he wasn't thrilled to see me.

After last night, I could see why. I rolled down my car window and summoned up a tentative smile. "Hi."

He didn't smile back. "Hi."

I cleared my throat. "I, uh, came to thank you."

His expression didn't change. "You're welcome."

I pointed to my steering wheel. "So I guess this was the surprise, huh?"

Joel gave something like a shrug, but said nothing.

I forced another smile. "Hey, would you mind scooting out of the way?"

"Why?"

"Because I wanna get out."

"No need. I'm leaving."

I felt a twinge of panic. "What do you mean?"

"I mean, the trip's over. I'm heading out."

Now, it was more than a twinge. "To where?"

"Does it matter?"

Okay, I realized that I'd been pretty rude last night, but couldn't he see how everything had looked from my point-of-view? I studied his face. Apparently not.

I sighed. "Look, I'm sorry, okay?"

He shrugged. "Okay."

"Will you please just step aside? I really wanna talk."

"Yeah? I know the feeling."

I stared up at him. "What is this? Some kind of payback? Just because I wouldn't let you in last night?"

His jaw tightened. "I never asked to come in."

I cringed. He was right. He hadn't. All he'd asked was for me to come outside so I could see the surprise. And stubbornly, I'd refused.

I felt awful. Still, I had to point out the obvious. "It was the middle of the night. How was I supposed to know?"

"You weren't. That's why they call it a surprise."

"Well, maybe I *was* surprised, but not by that."

At Joel's blank expression, I plowed onward, "I was surprised you ditched me. You know, for those two other girls."

His expression didn't change. "What?"

Heat flooded my face. Was he really going to make me spell it out? Lamely, I mumbled, "I mean, is it any wonder I might've been a little miffed?"

"Miffed?"

I mumbled, "Well, yeah."

His eyebrows lifted. "*Two* girls? Like one isn't enough?"

He was totally missing the point. I looked away. "I dunno. Forget it."

"*Which* two girls?"

I was still looking away. *Oh, I don't know. Maybe the two chicks hanging off you at T.J.'s.* But I didn't say it. I couldn't. He'd only think I was spying on him, assuming that he didn't think that already. And besides, it was a little early in our relationship – if you could call it that – to get all crazy jealous on him.

For what felt like the millionth time, I reminded myself that he wasn't my boyfriend or anything. And even if he was, it's not like Cassie had seen them humping in the corner. Who knows, maybe they were all just friends. I bit my lip. Friends with benefits?

Maybe *I* was just a friend – or not even that, given the fact that he was leaving without saying goodbye. Through the glass of the passenger's side window, I studied his campsite. There was nothing there. And soon, he'd be gone, too.

At the sound of my name, spoken more gently than I might've expected, I turned to look. To my surprise, Joel's gaze had softened into something that looked almost affectionate. In a quieter tone, he repeated his question. "Which two girls?"

I'd never been one for playing games. For one thing, I wasn't very good at it. With a resigned sigh, I said, "Last night, someone spotted you with a couple of girls at T.J.'s." My own voice grew quiet. "And I guess I was kind of mad that you ditched me for them."

Joel studied my face for a long moment. And then, his lips twitched. "You weren't jealous, were you?"

"No."

He leaned down and rested his forearms on the window's opening. "Hey, lemme tell you something."

"What?"

"If it were me, and I saw *you* with two guys, I wouldn't've been happy."

My heart gave an embarrassing little leap. "Really?"

His gaze met mine. "You've gotta ask?"

My breath caught. I didn't know what to say. I was still dying to know who the girls were, but there was another question churning in my brain. "Are you really leaving?"

"That was the plan."

A spark of hope kindled in my heart. "*Was*?"

He looked toward his empty campsite. "The car's already loaded."

A wave of fresh disappointment coursed through me. "Oh." I looked around. "So, uh, where *is* your car?"

"At the storage place." He flicked his head toward the main road. "Across the street. You wanna give me a ride?"

I didn't, actually.

If I gave him a ride, he'd only be leaving that much faster. And yet, I couldn’t exactly refuse, not after everything he'd done for me. So I turned away and pushed open the passenger's side door.

When he circled the car and climbed inside, I reached forward to start the engine.

"Wait," Joel said.

I turned to look. "For what?"

"I wanna tell you something. Those girls – they weren't with me."

I searched his eyes. He looked so sincere. I wanted to believe him. But Cassie had seen them arm-in-arm.

At something in my expression, he added, "I mean, yeah, I was with them at T.J.'s, but we were just killing time."

Killing time?

While he'd been off at T.J.'s, I'd been at my house, waiting for him. I'd been worried. And angry. And just a little bit pathetic. The fact that he'd been merely killing time wasn't exactly a mark in his favor.

And then, there was the other thing. "But you had your arms around them."

"No," he said. "They had their arms around *me*." He gave something like a laugh. "They were dragging me in there."

I gave him a dubious look. "Against your will?"

"Pretty much. None of it was my idea."

"What do you mean?" I asked.

"Long story. But just so you know. Those girls? They're both engaged."

That made me pause. "Both of them? To who?"

"My brothers, actually."

"Oh." My heart suddenly felt ten times lighter. "Really?"

"Yeah. They came up with Jake and Bishop, who supposedly had to take care of something."

"Supposedly?"

"It sounded like bull to me. But the deal was, I had to keep the girls company."

"You mean because they're not from around here?"

"No." Joel paused. "I mean, yeah, that was the story Bishop gave. But you wanna know what I think?"

"What?"

"It was just a ploy to smooth things over." He gave a humorless laugh. "Like, we'd have a drink, they'd sing my brothers' praises, and we'd all be one happy family again." He made a scoffing sound. "Like we ever were."

"What do you mean?"

"Like I said, it's a long story. And trust me, you don't wanna hear it."

"You're wrong," I said. "I do." I hesitated. "Unless you'd rather not?"

"Forget them." His voice warmed. "Let's talk about us." □

CHAPTER 46

I met his gaze. "Us?" Technically, there was no us, but I really liked the sounds of that.

He leaned a fraction closer. "Before I showed up last night, do you know how ticked I was, knowing I had to stay away?"

His words sent a thrill up my spine. And yet, they didn't quite make sense. "Sorry, I'm not following. Why would you need to stay away?"

"Because I didn't want them anywhere near you, that's why." His jaw tightened. "They fucking ruin everything." He glanced away. "Sorry."

I almost wanted to smile. "That's alright."

"Nah," he said, "it's not. It's just one of those things, you know? They make me crazy, the whole lot of them." His voice softened. "And then, there's you."

My hand was resting on the center console. He reached out and closed his hand over mine. Soon, our fingers were intertwined, and I felt some of the tension slip away. I said, "There's me? What about me?"

"You're so sweet, it makes me forget."

"Forget what?"

He gave a rueful laugh. "Everything." And then, as if shaking off a lingering gloom, he said, "The good news is, they're gone. And they're not coming back."

"How do you know?"

Joel smiled. "Because I bribed them."

"With what?"

"What else? Their own stuff."

At this, I had to laugh. "You mean the Camaro? And those, um, collector's items?"

"Yeah. Those too."

"Wow, so you actually returned them? Why?"

"Because I didn't want anyone showing up on your doorstep."

My heart gave a wonderful little flutter. "So you did it because of me?"

"And, for me. Because I didn't wanna leave town."

"What do you mean?"

"You ever wonder why I was staying in a tent?"

"Well, yeah. At first. But then I figured you just liked camping."

"Nothing wrong with camping," he said. "But I was straight with you that first night. It wasn't just a vacation. I was lying low, looking to avoid their bull."

I couldn't resist teasing him at least a little. "So you were living off the grid, huh?"

"More like off their radar. I wanted some time alone. But then, something changed."

"What?"

His eyes warmed. "I met *you.*"

Through the passenger's side window, I glimpsed the glimmer of a campfire though the trees. But it couldn't compare to the glimmer in Joel's eyes when I whispered, "And I met you."

He leaned toward me, and I met him halfway. Our lips met in a kiss so sweet, it felt like coming home.

Now, more than anything, I wanted to pretend that our fight never happened. But I couldn't, because he was already packed and ready to go.

I pulled back and asked the question that I'd been dreading. "Are you still leaving?"

"That depends." His mouth twitched at the corners. "You still want me to?"

I gave an embarrassed laugh. "I didn't *really* want you to go."

He smiled. "Yeah? Could've fooled me."

I looked toward his empty campsite. "So, what now? If you're not hiding out anymore, what are your plans?"

"That depends."

"On what?" I asked.

"You."

I smiled, even as heat rushed to my face. "Can I confess something?"

"Sure, what?"

"I kept your duffle bag."

He gave a small laugh. "If you like it, it's yours."

I pretended to consider it. "Well, it *is* pretty nice. And I hear it *might* even include a cell phone." I met Joel's gaze. "But that's not why I kept it."

"Yeah? So why did you?"

"Well, I guess, if I'm being honest, maybe I was hoping for an excuse to invite you over, and see if we could smooth things out."

His gaze softened. "Baby, you don't need an excuse."

His words soothed my soul. And yet, I wasn't quite sure I deserved them. I gave his empty campsite a worried glance. "But I ruined your vacation. Want me to help you set everything up again?"

"Nah," he said. "I've got the campsite for another week, and the tent takes like five minutes to set up. If I had to, I could do it blindfolded."

I bit my lip. "Are you sure?"

"I'm sure." He flashed me a grin. "And besides, we had a deal. Remember?"

Like I could forget. Before his brother showed up, we'd been planning to swap secrets – me about the estate, and him about the fights.

I smiled. "I remember."

"Good," he said, "because I plan to collect."

"Speaking of collecting things…" I cleared my throat. "There's something I've got to say."

"Yeah? What?"

"Thanks, seriously. For everything, especially for getting my car back. Last night, I should've looked, and I feel awful that I ruined the surprise."

He gave me a boyish grin. "So you were surprised, huh?"

I laughed. "You have no idea. And just so you know, I'll pay you back."

"For what?"

"The towing, the repair, whatever." I paused. "Which brings me to a question. Who was the tattooed guy who picked up the car? Was that your brother, Jake?"

"Unfortunately."

My fingers tensed. Things were going so well, and I hated to the rock the boat. But this sibling animosity couldn't be healthy. I said, "I've seen some of his videos. Pretty crazy stuff."

Joel made a scoffing sound. "If you think he's crazy in those, you should see him in real life. The guy's a total tool."

The bitterness in his voice hurt to hear. No matter how messed up everything was, Joel was luckier than he realized.

I gave him a sympathetic look. "I know you keep saying that, but it was really nice of him to help."

"Nice?" Joel made a sound of derision. "He wasn't being nice. He was being a prick."

A tool. A prick. What next?

"Oh come on," I said. "That can't be true."

"Wanna bet? Last night, we're all at the storage place, and I turn my back for five minutes, and what does he do? He swipes the cap I ordered–"

"Wait. What cap?"

"The distributor cap. For your car."

"You had one? Like *on* you?"

"Yeah. Sitting on some boxes." At my perplexed look, he added, "It just came in. I ordered it last Saturday."

I was so touched, I almost didn't know what to say. "Really? You did?"

"Yeah, except Jake grabs the thing and drives off. I could've killed him."

I gave a confused shake of my head. "I don't get it. Why would you be mad?"

"Because I didn't know what he was doing. Just all of a sudden, he's gone. With Luna, the sap who agreed to marry him."

"What, you don't like her?"

"I like *her* just fine. It's *him* that's the problem. But last night, they both take off. And just when I'm about to go looking for them, they come back. With *your* car."

"But how?"

"The usual way," Joel said. "He breaks in, pops the hood, replaces the cap, and off he goes."

I stared at him. "And that's the *usual* way? You guys do this a lot?"

Joel hesitated. "I wouldn't say a lot."

I was almost afraid to ask. "About the garage, did Jake break anything? Like a window or door?"

"Nah. He told me he left it just like he found it."

If I weren't so concerned, I might've smiled. Apparently, there *was* some brotherly trust after all. "And you believed him?"

"Hell no," Joel said. "I drove out and checked, also made sure that Jake paid the guy."

Well, so much for the trust thing.

Pushing that thought aside, I said, "I need to pay him back."

"No. You don't. I already paid him."

"Oh. Okay. So I'll pay *you* back."

"That's what *you* think. It was a surprise, like a gift. You can't pay for that."

"But–"

"But nothing," he said. "I'm just pissed it was Jake, and not me, that found the place first."

"Oh, so *you* were gonna break into the garage?"

"That was the idea." He glanced away. "Which I should've kept to myself."

I had to laugh. "You're *all* crazy. You know that, right?"

"Hell yeah," Joel said. "Which is why I wanted them gone."

I saw his logic. But it still hurt to hear, for his sake, not mine. Tentatively, I said, "There's something I don't get."

"What's that?"

"Well, Jake retrieved my car, and saved you the trouble. Why would that make him–"

"A prick? Because he is."

"Yeah, but maybe this time, he was being nice."

"Nice? Jake?" Joel made a scoffing sound. "Dream on. He wasn't being nice. He was in a hurry to get his Camaro."

"But what did that have to do with anything?"

"I told him he'd get *his* car after I got yours."

"But why would you tell him that?"

"Because I figured as long as they were here, they could help me find the place, and maybe watch my back while I did it."

"But instead, he went out and got it himself?"

"Pretty much."

"Well, maybe it was some kind of peace-offering. Or maybe he wanted to keep you out of trouble."

Joel was frowning now. "What, you're sticking up for him?"

This reminded me of our last fight, back when I'd thought his brother was some poor slob, driving a beater. I no longer thought that, but this wasn't even about Jake. It was about Joel.

I squeezed his hand. "Hey, I'm on your side, totally. I just hate that you're fighting, that's all." In a quieter voice, I added, "I would've killed for a brother."

"Yeah? If you wanna trade, let me know."

"Except I can't," I said, "because I don't have one. That's my whole point. I'm just saying, maybe you're luckier than you realize." I summoned up a smile. "He's older right? So maybe he was looking out for his little brother."

Joel's eyebrows lifted, and I saw a hint of humor return. "Little, huh?"

I let my gaze drift over the length of him. He was tall and muscular, with large hands and long legs. Obviously, there was nothing little about him. At the sudden image that popped into my brain, heat flooded my cheeks and – to my total embarrassment – other places, too.

I cleared my throat. "You know what? Forget I said that." Suddenly desperate to change the subject, I said, "Hey, about the Camaro. Is that the car from that movie?"

"*Flashbang*? Yeah, that's the one."

"But why didn't you tell me?"

Joel gave me a wicked grin. "Because I didn't want you to know."

I rolled my eyes. "Oh, well that's nice."

"Hey, I wasn't looking to advertise it," he said. "And you've gotta remember, we'd just met."

He was right. At the time, we *had* just met, and we weren't exactly hitting it off. "But if the car was some kind of secret," I said, "why'd you take it out that night?"

"Because my own car was blocked in, and there was no way in hell I was gonna let you walk home in the dark." His mouth tightened. "Alone."

I had to smile. "So you pulled out a movie prop?"

"Hey, I'd have *stolen* a car if that's what it took."

I laughed. "Oh, stop it. You wouldn't."

"Wanna try me?"

"No," I said. "Definitely not."

Joel smiled. "Probably, I *should've* stolen a car. That Camaro? It was how my brothers found me."

"Because you drove me home that night?"

"Nah," Joel said, "because someone spotted the car outside the storage place, and then jumped on the internet to brag about it."

I cringed. "Oh."

"What?"

"I'm pretty sure that was April." I went on to explain how April had spotted the Camaro on her way out of town, and had called me afterward to tell me about it. I finished by saying, "So in a way, it's my fault you were found."

"Why *your* fault?"

"If only I'd put two and two together, I would've asked her not to say anything."

"Hey," Joel said, "you've got nothing to be sorry for." He gave my hand a tender squeeze. "And I like April. She looks out for you."

Yes, she definitely did, even if it meant warning guys that I wasn't a sack-jumper. But there was no way I'd be bringing *that* up.

Still, I had to smile. "Yeah, I like her, too."

"Speaking of cars," Joel said, "how about that ride?"

I gave a happy nod, and then drove him across the street to get his car. Five minutes later, I was driving back to my place, with Joel following in his own vehicle.

With him a few car lengths behind, I turned into my driveway, only to hit the brakes when I spotted them – my aunt and uncle, scurrying like rats, along the side of my house.

I sighed. *Not again.*

□

CHAPTER 47

I gave my uncle a hard look. "You're early."

He was standing next to Aunt Vivian, who was doing her best to look like this was just a casual visit, which made no sense whatsoever, because they were decidedly overdressed.

Joel and I had caught up with them in the back yard, where, as near as I could tell, they'd been making for the back door. Now, we were all standing on the back patio – with my aunt and uncle facing off against me and Joel.

I gave Joel a sideways glance. If it came down to a fight, I was liking my odds.

From my uncle's expression, *he* wasn't. He looked from me to Joel and back again. "Uh, early?"

I crossed my arms. "Yeah. By a few weeks."

His eyebrows furrowed. And then, with an obvious effort, he summoned up a hearty smile. "Yup. We sure are."

I made a scoffing sound. "You don't even know what I mean, do you?"

"Sure I do." But then, he leaned closer to Aunt Vivian and whispered, "Do *you* know?"

"Oh for heaven's sake," my aunt hissed. "You *do* realize, she can hear you."

My uncle's gaze shifted to Joel, and he swallowed with an audible gulp. From the corner of his mouth, he whispered again. "What about the big guy? You think *he* heard?"

This time, it was Joel who answered. "Yeah. He did."

My aunt gave a dramatic sigh. "There's no need for theatrics." She lifted her chin. "We decided to pop in for a little visit. What, is that some sort of crime now?"

I eyed their clothes. My uncle was wearing a black tuxedo. As for my aunt, she was wearing a long, emerald evening gown and lots of sparkling jewelry. She looked like she was dressed for the opera, with herself in the starring role.

I said, "Nice of you to dress up."

My uncle beamed. "Thanks. I wanted to wear my green tux to match, but your aunt said no."

Aunt Vivian gave him an annoyed look. "Ernie. Dear. I believe she was being sarcastic." She turned back to me and added, "Which we don't appreciate, by the way."

Talk about nerve.

"Wanna know what *I* don't appreciate?" I said. "These little visits. Just admit it. You're not here to see me. You're here to see what you can make off with."

My aunt gasped, "Well, I never!"

Joel spoke up. "Yes. You did." An edge crept into his voice. "But it's gonna stop."

Aunt Vivian turned to glare at him. "Who asked you, anyway?"

Now, it was *my* turn to speak up. "Me. That's who."

Suddenly, my uncle burst out, "Hey Melody! We brought you something." And then, with a flourish, he reached into the lapel pocket of his jacket and pulled out a small silver box, topped with a matching bow.

He held it out in my direction. "See, we weren't *taking* something. We were *giving* something." He gave my aunt a sly wink. "Right, Viv?"

She froze. "Um, well, you see…" And then, like a striking cobra, her arm shot out, reaching for the gift. Startled by the sudden motion, my uncle jerked back, and the box tumbled to the concrete. The lid popped off, and a small silver thing went rolling down the patio stairs. My aunt screeched, "Look what you did!"

Who? Me? Or my uncle?

I never found out, because already, my aunt and uncle were scrambling away, like kittens chasing a ball of yarn. Whatever the thing was, my uncle swooped it up and kept on running, with my aunt sprinting behind him.

I had to give her credit. For someone wearing heels and a long dress, she was no slouch in the running department.

When they disappeared around the corner of the house, I reached down and picked up the empty box, along with its lid. Attached to the lid was a small gift tag. I read it out loud. "To Bob and Marge. With love, from Ernie and Vivian."

I lifted my gaze to Joel. His body was rigid, and his mouth was tight. He was staring at the corner of the house, where my aunt and uncle had disappeared from view.

Hoping to lighten his mood, I said, "Well, Bob. What'd you think of that?"

His gaze didn't waver. "I think they need a talking to."

Maybe they did. But I'd had more than enough drama for one night. I reached for his hand and gave it a squeeze. "No. *I'm* the one who needs a talking to. Remember?"

Finally, he turned to look. "You said they wouldn't be back for a while."

"Yeah, well, they probably had some sort of special thing going on." I perked up as I realized something. "Hey, you know what that silver thing was?"

"What?" Joel asked.

"A little penguin. Aunt Vivian has this friend – Marjorie – who collects them. No wonder my aunt was so horrified. She probably had it made special or something."

As I talked, Joel's gaze kept shifting back to the corner of the house, as if he hadn't quite decided whether or not to give chase.

Hoping to keep him rooted next to me, I went on to tell him that Bob and Marjorie had a lake house twenty minutes away, and that they entertained *a lot*. I finished by saying, "So that explains the early visit." I gave a happy sigh. "There. Mystery solved."

At last, Joel turned and gave me his full attention. "You're happy about this?"

I smiled. "Nope."

He studied my face. "So why are you smiling?"

Still smiling, I tossed out a phrase I'd heard from him several times already. "You've gotta ask?"

Finally, he smiled and took my hand in his. Together, we circled the house, heading toward the driveway, so I could retrieve my keys from the car. But just as we reached the porch, Joel stopped to stare at the front door.

Following his gaze, I turned to look. Taped to the door was some sort of note. From my aunt and uncle? That would be my guess.

But that guess was wrong – unfortunately.

□

CHAPTER 48

With Joel standing a few feet away, I pulled the note off the door and gave it a quick read, only to feel myself pale with anger. I looked up and saw Joel watching me.

Concern darkened his features. "What is it?"

"Nothing."

Again, I looked down to study the note. I recognized the tight handwriting as Derek's. But even if I didn't, I'd still know that the note was from him, even though it was unsigned.

It was short, only four words. *Did you pay him?* Below those four words was a scribbled drawing of a cartoon cat.

In other words, a pussy.

I was still staring when the note disappeared, yanked out of my hands by Joel. I looked up to see him clutching it in his right hand, even as his gaze remained on me.

I gave the note a nervous glance. "You're not planning to read that?"

"The hell I'm not, after the look you just gave it."

"I gave it a look? What kind of look?"

"Like it hurt you." His voice softened. "And I don't like it."

"Yeah," I mumbled, "that makes two of us."

Joel rotated the note and gave it a long, silent look. When he looked up, his jaw was tight. "Who wrote this? Derek?"

"I guess."

"You *guess*? Or you *know*?"

"It's his handwriting. So yeah, I'm pretty sure it's him." I blew out a long, nervous breath. "Some joke huh?"

"Lemme ask you something. Do *you* think it's funny?"

I glanced away. "Not particularly. But I *do* like cats. So that's something, right?"

"Oh yeah. It's something." Joel gave the note another look. "Am I the 'him'? The one you're paying?"

"I guess," I said. "I mean, I can't think of anyone else, if that's what you're asking." I reached out and tugged the note from his hand. And then, I crumpled it up and shoved it deep into the pocket of my shorts.

Too bad we weren't camping. I'd toss it into the fire and laugh while it burned.

Okay, maybe I wouldn't laugh. After all, none of this was terribly funny. Still, I tried to smile. "You know what? I'm not even gonna think about it."

"Yeah? Well, *I* am."

I gave Joel a pleading look. "I appreciate that, honest, but this isn't what I wanted." I glanced toward my front door, which I still hadn't opened. "It's like every time you and I get a chance to talk, something stupid happens. I hate that."

"Wanna know what I hate?" Joel's gaze shifted to my pocket. "Shit like that. The guy needs a good ass-kicking."

"Maybe he does. But that would hardly be helpful." I sighed. "Can't we just forget it?"

"Here's another question," Joel said. "Before I showed up, was there anything between you?"

"I already told you. No. Never."

"You sure about that?"

"Definitely." And I was. Whatever Derek's problem was, it didn't stem from any romantic interest. I was absolutely sure of it.

When Joel said nothing, I said, "Oh come on. You have brothers. And *you* don't always get along, right? And just because someone leaves a rude note, it doesn't mean they have a crush on someone."

"A crush?" Joel said. "The guy's an asshole. And he's jealous. It's a dangerous mix. You know that, right?"

"But there's nothing romantic about it, so he can't be jealous."

Joel's mouth tightened. "There's more than one kind of jealousy."

"Yeah," I said. "I know. Like right now? I'm jealous that we're spending so much time talking about this."

At Joel's stony expression, I took a deep, calming breath. "Listen, I *so* appreciate that you care about this, but come on. Last night was totally crummy, and I don't want tonight to be, not for either of us. So can't we just put it behind us?"

Joel gave my pocket another long look. Finally, he said, "Alright. If that's what you want."

I breathed a sigh of relief.

And then, he added, "But only because you're gonna tell me what's going on."

Something in his eyes told me there was no point in arguing. After all, we'd agreed to swap secrets, and this was definitely part of it, for better or worse.

This is why, a few minutes later, we were standing side-by-side on the back patio. Together, we gazed out over the endless dark waters of Lake Michigan, illuminated only by the nearly full moon. The interrogation hadn't yet begun, and I wasn't looking forward to it.

But at least we were no longer arguing. After walking through my front door, I'd reminded myself that none of this was Joel's fault. If it weren't for Derek's stupid note, we'd probably be having a perfectly lovely time.

True, we'd both agreed to spill our secrets, but this wasn't the way I'd envisioned it.

The night was warm with a cool breeze coming off the lake. Even here, high above the water, I could hear the waves lapping at the rocky shoreline below the bluff.

Hoping to ease some of the tension, I'd gone into the kitchen and pulled out one of my birthday gifts – a bottle of cabernet from Dorothy the librarian. I'd filled two glasses – one for me and one for Joel.

Even if he didn't need it, I did.

With my glass in-hand, I watched him from the corner of my eye as he gazed out over the water. As for *his* wine, it remained mostly untouched, sitting on the wide railing in front of us. Next to his glass, I'd placed the half-empty bottle, which I'd lugged out here, just in case.

Watching him now, I couldn't help but notice the difference between *this* Joel and the pissed-off guy who'd yanked the note out of my hands.

He was a mystery, full of too many contradictions to count. He was sweet, but tough. Sensitive, but stubborn. Sexy, but slow to make any moves.

Was I complaining? I wasn't sure. April had been right. I wasn't quick to jump in the sack. But a sack with him? Now *that* would be something.

Already, I knew he was a great kisser. And from the little contact we'd had already, I knew that I loved the feel of his rock-hard body against mine.

Of course, this had been through layers of clothing. But it's not like we'd been wearing padded parkas or anything.

Even so, it was more than his body, or those soulful eyes of his, that made my heart flutter and thoughts run wild. It was a feeling that I couldn't quite describe, like I'd only scratched the surface of who he really was.

Joel's voice, quiet, but laced with steel, interrupted my thoughts. "So, are you gonna tell me?"

I gave a little jump. "Yeah. Of course." I turned to face him. "That's why we're out here, isn't it?"

Like me, he had turned inward, and was now facing me instead of the water. Feeling suddenly self-conscious, I tried not to squirm under his penetrating gaze.

I said, "I hope you don't take this the wrong way, but…" I hesitated. "Why is this so important to you?"

"You don't know?"

I *did* know, in the sense that I knew that he liked me. But that hardly seemed a plausible reason to take such an interest in my problems. Struggling to find the right words, I said, "I know that we've really hit it off." I gave him a shy smile. "And I know that I like you. A lot. And I *think* you like me…"

His eyes warmed. "You might say that."

Something about that look made me feel wonderful all over. Still, I felt compelled to finish. "But you hardly know me."

He shook his head. "I know you better than you think."

Feeling almost flirtatious now, I gazed up at him through my lashes. "So, what do you think you know?"

His lips curved into the hint of a smile, and he leaned a fraction closer. For a moment, I thought he might kiss me.

But he didn't.

Instead, he said something that drenched my warm, gooey glow with a cold, hard splash. "I think you're a nice person."

CHAPTER 49

I froze. *I was a nice person?* His words echoed in my brain. *Nice? Person?* Okay, it wasn't an insult or anything. But it was nothing like what I'd been hoping to hear.

Still, I tried to smile. "Thanks. I, uh, think you're a nice person, too."

He frowned. "What's wrong?"

"Nothing."

And it was true. Absolutely nothing was wrong. It was fine. I was just a little disappointed, that's all.

I mean, when *I* fantasized about someone, I never found myself thinking, *"Oh, take me to heaven, you nice person, you."*

I lifted my wine glass and took a long, steady drink before returning it to the flat surface of the railing. Already, the glass was half-empty. Or was it half-full?

In my current state-of-mind, I didn't want to speculate.

I cleared my throat. "So, I guess I'd better get talking, huh?"

Joel studied my face. "You *know* I meant that as a compliment, right?"

"Sure. I know." I ran a nervous hand through my hair. "And *I* meant it as a compliment, too." Pushing aside my disappointment, I said, "Seriously, you've been really great." I thought of my car, now sitting miraculously in my driveway. "And your brothers, too. They're, uh, also nice. For helping, I mean."

What the hell was I even saying? Only one brother had helped, and Joel hadn't been happy about it. But my mind was so jumbled, I could hardly think. *I was nice. Joel was nice. His brothers were nice. Cripes, who'd be nice next? Attila the Hun?*

Joel said, "Except they're *not* nice. You need to remember that."

Distracted by my own stupidity, I murmured, "Uh, right. What are they again?"

He frowned. "The opposite of nice."

Still preoccupied, I murmured, "Nasty?"

He stared at me for a long moment, looking almost disturbed.

Damn it. Now, too late, he had my full attention, and I was wishing that I could take back that last comment. That particular word, *nasty*, after all, did have certain sexual connotations. But at least it was more interesting than "nice."

The way *some* people looked at it, nasty was exciting. It was bold and daring. It broke taboos and shattered conventions. As for me, I'd never gone the nasty route, and probably wouldn't succeed at it, even if I tried.

And I knew why.

Joel was right. I *was* nice.

Boring.

Civilized.

Conventional.

Like a four-door sedan or a Saint Bernard.

My shoulders sagged. No wonder he was taking it slow. I was a nice person, heaven help me.

Joel reached for his own glass and took an even longer drink than I had. When he returned the glass to the railing, it was nearly empty.

Well, this was just great. I'd driven him to drink.

Looking to say *something*, I said, "Wow, you must really like cabernet, huh?"

"Something like that."

From the look on his face, the "something" was the need to wash away something unpleasant. I knew what it was – my stupid "nasty" comment. See? Even when I *used* the term, I was an utter failure.

Probably, he was picturing his brothers naked or something. From the look on his face, it was an image he didn't enjoy.

I could totally relate. Sure, they were great-looking at all, but *they* weren't the ones who kept me awake at night, with thoughts that made me blush in the light of day.

And now, I'd put the wrong X-rated images into Joel's head. No wonder he looked disturbed. If *I* had brothers, I wouldn't want to think of them as nasty, with all of the naked implications that went along with it.

Hoping to break the tension, I tried to make a joke of it. "Nasty brothers." I gave a nervous laugh. "Like with no clothes on or something. I mean, who wants to picture *that*, right?"

Now, it was *his* turn to freeze. "What?"

I cleared my throat. "I mean, because nasty and naked kind of go together, you know?"

He was still staring, looking even *less* happy now.

Desperate for a recovery, I blurted out, "Not that *I'm* thinking of them naked or anything."

He stared at me for a long moment. And then, in a tight voice, he said, "Good to know."

It was definitely time for me to shut up. If I were an airplane, I'd be going down in flames, big-time. I reached for the only parachute I had – my glass of wine. I lifted it to my lips and downed the rest of it. I returned the now-empty glass to the railing and looked longingly at the bottle. If I grabbed it and guzzled, would *that* be nasty? Or just pathetic?

Pathetic, definitely.

Reluctantly, I looked back to Joel. His expression was so cold, it gave me a shiver.

Talk about awkward. The more I talked, the less he liked it. At this point, I didn't even know what to say. What was that old phrase? When you find yourself in a hole, the first thing you should do is stop digging?

I mentally threw away my shovel, along with any hope of not looking like a complete imbecile.

After a long, tense moment, Joel asked, "Which one were you picturing?"

"What?" I felt my eyes widen in horror. "Oh, my God. You don't mean your brothers, do you?"

Joel gave a loose shrug. "You brought it up. Not me."

Suddenly, I was wishing I *had* dug a hole, the real kind, so I could throw myself into it and hide from my humiliation.

And now, heaven help me, I had to explain. It was either that, or let him think that I'd been dreaming of his brothers in the buff.

I tried to smile. "I brought it up, because you looked bothered by my stupid 'nasty' comment. It just made me wonder what you were picturing." I looked away. "So I was trying to lighten things up. You know?"

Right. Because nothing says "smile" like "Let's envision your brothers naked."

Joel's voice, softer now, reclaimed my attention. "That's not the thing that was bothering me."

I turned to look. "Then what was?"

"You looked hurt, and I didn't know why. I still don't." He studied my face. "What'd I say?"

He looked so sincere that I had to confess. "Don't get me wrong. I'm glad that you think I'm a nice person." I hesitated. "It's just that I know that's not very exciting." I tried to laugh. "But I guess we can't *all* be the life of the party, huh?"

"You think 'nice' is a bad thing?"

"No. Of course not. I mean, we all want nice friends, right?"

Joel leaned closer. "Let me tell you a secret."

"What?"

"I don't like you as a friend."

Even though I'd already suspected as much, his words were a balm to my jangled nerves. And yet, he was missing the point, so I tried again. "Right. I mean, I know, because we've kissed and stuff. So it's not like I think you're repulsed by me or anything."

"Repulsed? You're kidding, right?"

Damn it. The more I talked, the worse I sounded. "I'm just saying, nice isn't terribly sexy, you know?" My face was flaming now. If I was lucky, the darkness hid the worst of it. And if I was unlucky? I only prayed he had a tomato fetish.

Joel looked at me for a long moment. "You're wrong."

"I am?"

He nodded. "Wanna know what I think?"

"What?"

"Nice girls? They're sexy as hell."

CHAPTER 50

My breath caught. Suddenly, he wasn't looking at me like I was merely a nice person. He was looking at me like I was the only girl in the world.

That look only solidified something that deep in my heart, I already knew. I wanted him, and I didn't want to wait until some arbitrary timeframe when I knew him better.

After all, I knew everything that was important. He'd come through for me when practically everyone else had let me down. I hadn't asked him to, but he had. He was amazing – strong and thoughtful, with a wild streak that sent my pulse jumping.

In fact, it was jumping now, and not only because he was irresistible.

It was because I knew all too well that happiness could slip away at a moment's notice, and that if you didn't, at least once in a while, enjoy life's blessings when you had the chance, those singular moments could slip away, leaving you cold and empty, lost in a house that was way too big for only one person.

But tonight, I didn't feel lost, and he'd just called me sexy. So, with a whispered "thank you," I stood on my tiptoes and pressed my lips to his. His lips were soft and full, and so sweet that all of my doubts vanished in an instant. I leaned into him, loving the feel of his body, so hard and tight, as his mouth moved against my own.

I let my tongue dart out between our lips, and my pulse gave an extra little jump when our tongues met in the middle. He tasted like red wine and felt like forbidden fruit. I wanted more. So much more.

But already, he was pulling away, just like he always did. His hands slid from my back and settled on my hips, even as he took a half-step backward, as if to put some distance between us.

I wanted to whimper in frustration.

Why did he pull back? I studied his face, but found no clue. It was like the windows of his soul had been deliberately shuttered, blocking me from seeing anything inside. Breathlessly, I asked, "Is something wrong?"

When he didn't respond, I made a move to pull back further. But to my surprise, he didn't let go. In a quiet voice, he said, "You don't owe me anything."

I blinked. "What?"

"Forget what Derek said. It's bullshit."

I gave a confused shake of my head. "What are you talking about?" And then, my stomach sank as the realization hit home. "Oh, my God. You mean that thing about paying you with, uh…"

"Yeah."

Neither one of us said the word.

Pussy.

The word, still unspoken, echoed in my brain. I didn't know whether to be impressed by his chivalry or insulted by his assumption. Trying to sort things out, I pulled back again, now more forcefully. This time, he let go.

I stared up at him. "Let me get this straight. You think I was…" I paused, searching for the right way to say this. "…coming onto you as what? Some sort of payment?"

In front of me, Joel gave a loose shrug.

"Oh, my God. You did." I looked away, and a scoffing sound escaped my lips. "And just imagine how I pay the gas bill."

In a flash of insanity, it struck me that life would be a whole lot easier if I *were* that kind of person. I wasn't bad-looking. And I had family fame on my side. No doubt, I could pay a lot more than my gas bill if I were willing to get down and dirty to make ends meet.

Joel's voice, softer now, broke into my thoughts. "That's not what I meant."

Sure, it wasn't.

And yet, the snarky response died on my lips. He wasn't some bill collector from the gas company. He was Joel, the guy who'd been coming to my rescue non-stop. And what was I doing? Getting all pissy, just because he'd wounded my dignity.

I took a deep breath and plastered on a smile. "You know what? I'm not being fair." Again, I considered my car. And my lawn. And the thing with my relatives. "You've been really wonderful, and you deserve more than…" I made a vague gesture with my hands. "….this, whatever it is."

"No," he said. "I don't."

I gave him a perplexed look. "What?"

"That's not what I'm saying."

"Then what *are* you saying?"

"That I don't *deserve* anything. That's my point."

In my frustration, I didn't know who to blame for all the confusion. Me, for throwing myself out there? Him, for sending mixed messages? Or Derek, for injecting the slow-working poison that was paralyzing everything.

And I had to wonder, did Joel truly believe that I was trying to repay one service with another? If so, he was out of his mind. And besides, with as much as he'd done, a single so-called service would never be enough. I'd need more than one night, and maybe some props, like heated massage oils or crotchless panties.

The thought was so ridiculous that I almost laughed, but not in a good way. "So tell me," I said, "do girls *normally* sleep with you when you do something nice for them?"

"No."

"Well, that's a relief." Was it? I didn't know. At this point, I hardly knew even what I was saying.

He asked, "And you wanna know why?"

"Why?"

"Because I don't do nice things."

That was a lie. It had to be. I'd only known Joel a short while, and already, he'd done too many nice things to count.

I didn't bother hiding my disbelief. "Sure you don't."

"I don't," he insisted.

I studied his face. To my surprise, he looked utterly sincere. I felt my brow wrinkle in confusion. "But why not?"

"It's complicated."

"Oh, come on," I said. "That's just a cop-out."

"Maybe." He moved forward, closing the gap between us. "But forget that. Ask me the *right* question."

There was a right question? Whatever it was, I had no idea. "What question is that?"

"Why I did 'something nice' for you."

"I already know why," I said. "It was because you felt guilty. You know, for how rude you were in the beginning."

He gave a low laugh. "Trust me. I can be a lot ruder than that."

Now *this*, I believed. But I still didn't know what that had to do with anything now. "So?"

"So, I don't normally make up for it."

"Why not?" I asked.

"You want the truth?"

"Definitely."

"Because those other people?" Again, his voice grew quiet. "They weren't you."

My breath caught. "What?"

He nodded. "From the moment I first saw you, it was different."

I would've called him crazy, except I could totally relate. The first time I'd seen him was in the boardroom. Even then, I'd been unable to look away. But still, I had to ask, "Different how?"

"I don't know. I can't explain it. But you've gotta remember something."

"What?"

"In that meeting, I wanted to knock Derek on his ass. But I didn't." His gaze met mine. "Because of you."

He'd already told me something similar, but I wasn't quite sure what he was getting at now. "So you're saying, you stopped yourself for my sake?"

Joel gave a slow nod. "Then. And now."

At last, everything clicked. "So *that's* why you're turning me down?"

"That's what you think? That I'm turning you down?"

"Aren't you?"

"No." His eyes warmed. "I'm just saying, you don't owe me anything." His gaze dipped to my lips. "I can wait."

"Me, too." I gave a nervous smile. "It's just that, well, I don't want to. I mean, I know what April told you, and actually, she was right. But with you, that's not the way I feel. And just so you know, this has nothing to do with the lawn. Or my car. Or whatever else I'm forgetting."

He smiled. "Yeah?"

I nodded. "Yeah. Definitely."

He leaned forward until our lips almost touched. And then, in a low whisper, he said, "Well, too bad."

My mouth fell open. "Too bad?"

His eyes filled with mischief. And then, he kissed me, hard and hungry. I felt his tongue dancing against mine, and his pelvis pressing hard against my hip. His hands drifted lower, grazing the seat of my shorts. I gave a muffled moan, and pressed my hips so tight against his that I could feel his hardness surging against my stomach.

He wanted me, too. I was absolutely sure of it.

And yet, to my infinite frustration, he pulled away. *What the hell?*

He said, "But you *do* owe me something."

I was so breathless I could hardly think. "What?"

"You *know* what. So you'd better get talking."

I didn't know whether to laugh or scream. "God, you are such a tease." I wasn't even kidding. Already, I was slick with wanting him, and it was beyond obvious that he wanted me, too.

And yet, the way it looked, he wasn't going to back down. I let my gaze travel the length of him. I wanted him so bad I could taste it. Or maybe that was just the wine, lingering like that amazing kiss.

He flashed me a grin. "We can do this all night." He shrugged. "Or something else. It's up to you."

Talk about cocky.

And yet, the prospect was irresistible. So in a rush, I told him almost everything that was relevant – how Derek and I had been really close until recently, how Derek's dad controlled the estate, and finally, how the estate needed a lot of work and wouldn't be fully mine until I turned twenty-five.

The explanation didn't take nearly as long as I'd anticipated, maybe two minutes at the most, probably because I glossed over a ton of details, in particular the sorry state of my finances. But I had my reasons. If that wasn't a mood-killer, I didn't know what was.

I finished by saying, "So there you go. Are you happy now?"

"With what you just told me?" He gave me a smile. "Hell no."

"So why are you smiling?"

He leaned forward and brushed his lips against my ear. And then, in a voice filled with sin, he said, "Because in five seconds or so, I'm gonna carry your sweet ass upstairs, and give you something else to think about."

CHAPTER 51

Before I could say anything in response, he'd already swooped me up into his arms and started carrying me toward the back patio door.

And then, I was laughing. No. Giggling. "Wait. What are you doing?"

He didn't even pause. "You *know* what I'm doing. Now, tell me which way."

Already, we were at the patio door. "Oh, come on," I laughed. "You can't be serious."

"Why not?"

"Because it's too far."

With one hand, he opened the door and then pushed us through it. "That's what *you* think."

With me still cradled in his arms, he turned and pulled the door shut behind us. Soon, he was moving again, striding toward the main stairway.

I was still laughing, and it struck me how long it had been since the house had been filled with anything like this – the sounds of laughter, the anticipation of something wonderful, and the sensation of strong arms holding me like I weighed next-to-nothing.

At the stairway, he turned and began taking the stairs two at a time, shocking me with how easy he made everything seem. In utter amazement, I teased, "Do you do this often?"

"The steps? Hell yeah." He kept on going. "But like this? Nah." His voice softened. "Just with you."

The first half of his claim, I entirely believed. But the second half? That it was only with me? Well, that seemed way too far-fetched. Still, I loved the sentiment and pressed myself tighter against him.

Step after step, I felt his muscles moving against my side, smooth and effortless as we neared the top of the stairway. Obviously, he hadn't been lying. He was no stranger to steps. In my mind, I could practically see him, running up and down some stadium bleachers, shirtless and covered in a thin sheen of sweat.

Over the past week, my mind had been filled with thoughts of him, and now, some of those thoughts were becoming reality – a wonderful reality that felt more like a dream.

At the top of the stairs, he said, "Which way?"

I lifted my hand and pointed toward the open doorway down the hall. "There."

He moved forward, and soon, we were entering my bedroom, which was arguably one of the best bedrooms in the whole place. It was spacious and inviting, with large windows and a set of double balcony doors that overlooked Lake Michigan.

The lights were off, but the curtains were open, leaving the room bathed in a wash of pale, welcoming moonlight. Wordlessly, Joel moved toward my double bed and gently placed me on the quilt that I'd been using as a bedspread, ever since my first winter alone.

I realized that I was no longer laughing. I couldn't. Not anymore. I was too excited and breathless with anticipation. Desperately, I reached up with both arms and smiled when he lowered himself down next to me.

I turned toward him, and soon, we were kissing again. His lips were warm and wonderful, and I felt his hands caressing my back, and then move lower, skimming across the thin fabric of my shorts. His touch sent my pulse jumping all over again, and I wanted to be ten times closer.

I pressed my hips tighter against him, and felt the hardness of his arousal press against my stomach. If I weren't so lost in his kisses, I might've smiled. He wasn't the only one who was ready. I felt my own readiness inside me, slick and welcoming, wanting him with my body as much as with my heart.

Beyond eager, I reached between us with both hands and fumbled with the button of his jeans. But almost before I knew what was happening, his arms reached tighter around me, and he rolled us sideways until I was lying on my back with him on top of me.

My hands – so near to his pelvis just moments earlier, were now lying loose and empty on the soft fabric beside me. There was no way to reach that button now.

Damn it.

He lowered his head and nibbled at my earlobe. Into my ear, he gave a playful whisper, "Not so fast."

I was so excited, I could hardly speak. "I was fast?"

"Nah." His tongue grazed my earlobe. "But we're gonna take it slow anyway."

I didn't want to take it slow. I wanted him now, this instant. Breathlessly, I asked, "Why?"

"Because you're the sweetest thing I've ever seen. Which means…" His lips grazed my ear. "I'm gonna take my sweet time."

He moved downward, and I felt his lips tickle my neck and then my collarbone. He reached up with his hand and gently tugged at the collar of my loose T-shirt, exposing more skin to his lips and tongue.

His kisses were soft, and his tongue was teasing. There was nothing X-rated about any of this, and yet, with every kiss and every caress, my breathing became more shallow, and my hips became more insistent on rising against him in a desperate bid to lure him closer.

Just when I thought I'd go utterly insane, he shifted his body to the side until he wasn't lying so much *on* me, as next to me. With a slow, lingering touch, he reached for the lower hem of my T-shirt. With the fabric tucked between his fingers, he ran a warm hand up my torso, skimming across the side of my stomach and then higher, until my torso was nearly bare, and his hand curved around the side of my breast, which was covered only with a thin, silky bra.

He moved the cup aside, and I felt the exposed nipple harden in the cool night air. Or who knows, maybe it was already hard. All I knew for certain was that I ached for him, both inside and out.

I lifted my head, hoping to get a better look. I couldn't see his eyes, but I could see his mouth, curved into a slight, secret smile, like he was thinking of things he shouldn't say out loud.

I could *so* relate.

Still, I couldn't help but whisper, "What are you thinking?"

He lifted his gaze to mine, and in those soulful eyes of his, I saw raw lust, along with something more tender. It was the tenderness that almost did me in.

Yup, this definitely felt like a dream, a wild and wonderful dream, starring me and this incredible guy who, even now, was driving me crazy with anticipation.

He still hadn't answered my question, but he also hadn't looked away. So I waited, breathless and eager, until he finally said in a tone that was almost teasing, "I'm not gonna tell you."

"What? Why not?"

"Because," he said, inching his hand a fraction higher, "I want to keep you guessing."

Before I could even think to protest, I was rewarded with the feel of his fingers grazing my nipple. I gave a muffled moan and lifted my torso higher, desperate again for more of his touch.

His voice was quiet in the moonlit room. "See?"

"See what?"

"You." His fingers toyed with the nipple until it hardened so tight that it nearly ached. "So sweet."

In a breathless whisper, I admitted, "I don't feel sweet. Or even nice."

"Yeah?" He lowered his head and, through the thin fabric of my bra, traced the other nipple with the tip of his tongue. "How *do* you feel?" He moved the fabric aside and took the nipple into his warm mouth. And then, he sucked lightly. I gave a soft moan of pleasure and let my eyelids flutter shut.

I knew exactly how I felt – hungry and desperate for more. But I didn't know how to say it in a way that wouldn't sound ridiculous, so I settled on the next closest thing. "Happy."

His tongue was playing across my nipple now, teasing and tantalizing until I felt nearly crazy with desire. I could hardly breathe, and I could hardly think.

But I did know that it wasn't a lie. I *was* happy, happier than I'd been in a very long time.

I was even happier a moment later, when he moved lower on the bed, reached for my shorts, and gave them a soft tug downward. Soon, he was sliding them down my thighs, past my knees, and over my ankles. Silently, he tossed them onto the floor beside the bed, leaving me in just my panties and the jumbled fabric of my bra and T-shirt.

I couldn't even remember what panties I was wearing. But I *did* know they weren't anything fancy – just a basic cotton bikini in blue or maybe pastel pink. Hoping to see, I lifted my head for a quick glimpse. In the near-darkness, I couldn't distinguish the color. But I *could* see Joel's face.

He looked anything but disappointed. I felt myself smile as I wondered what *he* was wearing under those jeans of his. I said, "Now you."

He moved higher until we were almost within kissing distance. "Now me what?"

"Well, *my* pants are off…" Again, I lifted a hand toward his button. But already, he'd moved out of reach. I almost laughed. "You're such a tease."

He smiled. "I know."

And then, almost before I knew it, he was tugging down my panties and tossing them somewhere onto the floor. I felt his fingers, warm and smooth, stroke the inside of my thigh.

Breathless with anticipation, I savored the feel of his touch, gentle but persistent, as his fingers inched slowly higher, stroking and teasing near the intersection of my thighs. My hips rose in a silent plea for his touch to move higher, to zero in on that spot where I ached.

And when he did, I sucked in a breath of pure bliss. Dimly, I was aware that I was practically naked, and he wasn't. Not even close.

I *wanted* to see him naked. I wanted to *feel* him naked. I wanted to *be* with him naked.

But as his fingers moved, coaxing and teasing sensations out of me that I hadn't realized were possible, I didn't have the will to lodge any further complaint. So I let myself get lost in the sensations – the stroking, the teasing, and finally, the feel of one long finger sliding into me.

His voice drifted up to me. "You're so sweet."

No. I wasn't sweet. Not now. I was wet and ready, and desperate to have him inside me. But I couldn't say it, because my stomach was clenching, and my hips were convulsing as I rose up, meeting the magic of his touch.

Somewhere in the back of my mind, I considered lunging for that button of his, popping it loose and ripping down first his zipper, and then his jeans – making him as naked and wanton as I felt right now.

But soon, I didn't have to, because he was already doing it. In a haze of bliss and lust, I watched, breathlessly, as he stood and tugged down his jeans, along with his briefs, and then tossed them onto the floor.

He was massively hard, and I couldn't wait to have him inside me, even as the remnants of all those wonderful convulsions did funny things to my insides.

Gaining some semblance of control, I reached out and tugged at the hem of his T-shirt. I wanted to claw it from his body and leave it scattered in shreds on the bedroom floor. And then, I saw something in his hand, a little foil package that he must've retrieved from his pocket.

Knowing what it was, I sat up and snatched it out of his hand. "Let me."

He didn't argue, and I sat up straighter. Trying to be careful, I tore at the little package and pulled the condom from inside, leaving the foil container to fall wherever. Wanting to feel him first without anything between us, I reached out with my free hand and gave his hardness a long, smooth stroke.

I heard a muffled moan and looked up to see his eyelids drift shut and a soft smile curve his lips. I stroked him again, and gripped his shaft, and felt his hardness surge in my eager touch.

I didn't want to make him wait. I didn't want to make *me* wait either.

So I rolled the condom onto his length, and smiled with anticipation when he climbed onto the bed and positioned himself above me.

Beyond eager, I reached between us and guided his hardness to my opening. He lowered his hips just a fraction, giving me only a promise of what I wanted. I wanted *all* of him, every single inch. In a desperate bid to be closer, I lifted my hips, and sighed with pure bliss when I felt more of him slide into me.

He lowered his head until our lips met in a ragged kiss that he timed perfectly by giving me exactly what I wanted – his whole length, massive and hard, filling me completely, almost too completely at first.

But I loved it – the sweet ache of utter fullness. And then, he started moving – his lips, his hips, his hands. And I was moving, too. I reached up under his shirt and ran my hands along his back, feeling his muscles shift and move in time with our motions.

Desperate to feel his skin on mine, I yanked his shirt upward as far as it would go and pressed tighter against him. Next time, I silently vowed, I'd make sure that both of us were naked, completely naked, because even this, as wonderful as it was, felt like it wasn't quite enough.

I almost wanted to smile. *Next time.* There would definitely *be* a next time, as sure as the sun would rise and the tide would go in and out.

When I reached my next climax, he was right there with me, filling me, kissing me, claiming me, until I was utterly lost to everything but him.

We spent the next few hours in utter bliss, with more sex, a bubble bath for two, and finally, the sweet serenity of sleeping in Joel's arms, more content than I'd ever been in my whole adult life.

And I had him to thank – not just then, but early the next morning, when trouble, once again, arrived on my doorstep.

CHAPTER 52

I was standing in the front doorway, squinting in the morning sun. In front of me, Derek looked fresh and professional in a dark business suit with a classic red tie.

I didn't care how professional he looked. I still wasn't happy to see him, especially considering that Joel was still upstairs, after reluctantly – *very* reluctantly – agreeing to let me handle this on my own.

I gave Derek a cold look. "What are you doing here?"

Derek looked toward Joel's car, parked just a few paces away. He turned back to give me a smirk. "I see you have company."

In spite of my best intentions, I felt color rise to my face. Obviously, Derek knew exactly what I'd been doing last night, and who I'd been doing it with.

But so what? I was an adult. This was my house, at least for now. And I had nothing to be ashamed of. I lifted my chin. "That's none of your business."

Derek made a scoffing sound. "Right."

"It's not," I insisted. "And while we're on the topic, I didn't appreciate your note."

"Yeah? Well *I* didn't appreciate the thing with your car."

Now, it was *my* turn to scoff. "You're one to talk."

"Meaning?"

"Meaning, why'd you lie to me?"

"About what?"

"About the car needing a new engine."

"I didn't lie," he said. "It was a mistake. Beatrice confused the message."

Beatrice was the law firm's receptionist. She also acted as the receptionist for interviews related to the endowment. I liked her. And I highly doubted that she had anything to do with this.

"Oh, sure," I said, "blame *her.*" My tone grew sarcastic. "That's *ever-so* nice of you."

"You wanna hear what's nice?" Derek said. "Getting a call from Biff, telling me your car was stolen. Yeah. That was fun."

"Yes. It was." I smiled. "For Biff. Because he *didn't* consider it stolen."

"Yeah? Well, he should've."

"And besides," I continued, "the way, I hear it, he was actually pretty happy."

"Well, he wasn't when I got done with him."

My smile faded. "What do you mean?"

"It means that he surrendered the car without written authorization. You *do* realize he'll be billed for that."

"By who?"

"By the lawn firm. My time isn't free, you know."

"You can't charge him," I said. "It's not even your car."

"But I still had to deal with it. Long story short, we're billing him for an hour of my time."

"Fine," I snapped. "*I'll* pay it."

"Oh yeah?" His lips formed a sneer. "How?"

"What are you talking about?"

"I mean, you've got no money." His gaze dipped to my skimpy shorts and tank-top that I'd pulled on just before coming down. "So, unless you plan on paying the bill with something else…" His words trailed off as his gaze shifted to something just past my right shoulder.

Behind me, I heard Joel's voice. "You sure you wanna finish that sentence?"

In front of me, Derek's mouth tightened. "I was *only* going to suggest that she sell a painting or something."

What a crock. I couldn't sell a painting. The paintings, like everything else, were part of the estate. But I didn't argue the point, mostly because I didn't want to throw gasoline on the proverbial fire.

Even now, I couldn't bring myself to look behind me. When I'd left my bedroom, Joel had been half-naked, after practically jumping into his jeans to confront Derek.

I'd stopped him then, but would I be able to stop him now if things got ugly? I didn't even want to speculate. With my eyes still on Derek, I said, "You need to go."

"Yeah, whatever," he said. "I've got better things to do, anyway." And then, true to his word, he turned and stalked back to his car, got in, and slammed the driver's side door behind him.

When he fired up the engine, I finally turned toward Joel. He didn't look happy, but at least he was dressed.

In addition to the jeans, he was wearing the same shirt as last night and even shoes. He looked perfectly respectable. Still, I had to ask, "Why'd you come down?"

He frowned. "You've gotta ask?"

"But you told me you'd stay upstairs."

"Yeah, I did."

"So why didn't you?"

He moved closer. "You think I'm gonna sit up there and let him talk to you like that?" He joined me in the open doorway and eyed Derek's car as it sped down the long driveway. "Sorry. Not gonna happen."

Was he really sorry? I highly doubted it. And maybe I wasn't sorry, too.

In spite of all the drama, I actually felt kind of lucky, and not only because last night had been so wonderful. It was because if it weren't for Joel, Derek would probably still be here, berating me on my own doorstep.

I looked to Joel and said, "Probably, I should thank you for sticking up for me."

"Forget the thanks." He smiled. "But you *could* stop giving me grief about it."

He definitely had a point, which is probably why an hour later, we were swapping more secrets than I'd anticipated.

CHAPTER 53

We were just finishing breakfast out on my back patio when Joel said, "I've gotta ask you something."

Soon after Derek's departure, I'd whipped up a batch of scrambled eggs and toast, and brought everything out here so we could enjoy the fresh air and view.

I'd been reaching for my juice glass, but stopped in mid-motion. "Sure, what?"

"Are you in some kind of trouble?"

Suddenly, I wasn't thirsty. I set down my glass. "No. Why would you ask?"

Joel gazed at me for a long moment. "Why won't you answer?"

"I just did." I summoned up a smile. "Everything's fine."

"Yeah? Except you're lying."

I drew back. I might've been angry, except it didn't sound like an accusation. Mostly, it sounded like a statement-of-fact, which sadly, it was. "So what if I am?" I straightened in my chair. "And that reminds me of something."

"What?"

"You never told me *your* secret."

"My secret? What's that?"

"Well, you *do* remember the original deal, right? I was going to tell *you* about the estate, and you were going to tell *me* about the fights. But you never did. So now, I'm asking."

Joel stiffened in his chair. "Asking what?"

"See?" I said. "This is exactly what I'm talking about. You're acting all funny about it." I pushed back my chair and stood. "And you know what else? It's not fair, because I've told you a lot more than you've told me."

I froze. *Not fair?* Did I really just say that?

I knew all too well that life wasn't fair. Probably, I sounded like a kid objecting to her bedtime. I glanced around. And why on Earth was I standing? With a sigh, I sank back down.

Maybe he'd think I was just stretching my legs. I gave a mental eye-roll. More likely, he'd think I was crazy.

Lamely, I mumbled, "I'm just saying, it's your turn to tell *me* something."

"Fair enough. What do you want to know?"

I was so surprised that I almost fell out of my chair. Cripes, at this point, I'd need a safety strap or something. "Actually," I said, "I'm not sure where to start."

"Alright. I'll make it simple. You wanna know what I do?" His voice hardened. "I beat the hell out of people."

I tried not to flinch. After all, I'd suspected as much. "You mean like in regular fights? With an audience and stuff?"

"Not *regular* fights. Illegal fights. And yeah, there's an audience."

On some level, this was no surprise. I recalled Mike's star-struck reaction at seeing Joel along that lonely roadside. His words echoed in my brain.

I saw you fight at State.

You really slaughtered that guy.

Reluctantly, I asked, "Are you *still* doing that?"

"The fighting?" He reached up and rubbed the back of his neck. "I dunno. It's complicated."

I waited for him to explain. And when he didn't, I gave him a pleading look. "That can't be the whole story."

"It's not. But the rest of it's so messed up, you wouldn't want to hear it."

"You're wrong," I said. "I *do* want to hear it. Like, where do things stand now?"

"Nowhere," Joel said. "A few weeks ago, I was set to go legit, but the deal went south before it happened."

"What do you mean?"

"I was about to sign with this big sports agent, but the deal was squashed."

"By who?"

His jaw tightened. "My brothers."

I wasn't quite following. "You mean, like they talked you out of it?"

"Hell no. They screwed me over."

"How?"

"My brother Jake? He killed the deal."

My mouth fell open. I almost didn't know what to say. It was horrible. And yet, a tiny part of me *almost* wanted to send Jake a thank-you card.

Probably, this made me a terrible person, but there it was. I knew that Joel was tough. Really tough. And obviously, he could handle himself just fine. But there was something about him – a sweet, sensitive side that seemed at awful odds with the level of violence that Mike had described.

I hadn't known Joel for long. But I'd seen his face every time fighting came up. It wasn't the face of a guy who loved what he was doing.

Trying to get a better sense of the situation, I asked, "So, about that deal, is it killed for good?"

Joel gave a bitter laugh. "That's the funniest part. The guy tells me, come back in year, maybe it'll blow over."

"Maybe what will blow over?"

"Jake. That's what."

"Sorry, I'm not following. How, exactly, did Jake kill it?"

"Easy. He bribed the agent to drop me."

I felt my eyebrows furrow. "So Jake paid him off?"

"Yeah, but not with money. What that prick did was tell the agent that if he dumped me, Jake would stop messing with the agency's other clients."

Oddly enough, that made sense. I recalled Jake's fight videos. A bunch of them had involved sports stars, some pretty big names from what I remembered. From the little I'd seen, all of those stars had taken serious beatings.

It was easy to see why a savvy sports agent would do anything to make those beatings stop.

I looked to Joel. "So just like that, he dropped you?"

"Yeah. Just like that."

I almost didn't know what to say. "Wow."

"And then Bishop? *That* prick won't back me when I try to fight it.

Tells me it's probably for the best."

Finally, all the pieces were falling into place. "So *that's* why you're mad at them?"

"That and other things. My whole life, they've been screwing things up."

"Both of them?"

"Them and the other two."

"Wait," I said. "There's more?"

"Unfortunately."

He always said that. And just like always, I wanted to argue. No matter how awful his brothers might seem, I still believed that Joel was luckier than he realized.

At least, he *had* brothers. But this wasn't the time to quibble. So instead, I said, "The two I haven't met, what are *they* like?"

"They're dicks," Joel said, "just like the other two."

"Oh come on," I said. "That can't be true. I mean, there's gotta be *some* closeness there, right?"

Joel practically snorted. "Close? You wanna hear something funny?"

From the look on his face, I wasn't so sure. Still, I said, "Sure. What?"

"One of my brothers? Supposedly, he's got a place around here. "

I sat back in my chair. I hadn't seen *that* coming. "Really? Do I know him?"

"Hell, *I* don't even know him."

"What do you mean?"

Joel shook his head. "I haven't seen him in years."

And just like that, another piece of the puzzle snapped into place. "So *that's* why you're camping here? You were hoping to track him down?"

Joel glanced away. "I dunno. Maybe." Under his breath, he added, "It's probably a bullshit story, anyway."

"What story?"

"Nothing. Like I said, it's probably bull."

"Wait, is *that* why your stuff is in storage *here*, instead of in your hometown?"

"No," Joel said. "It's *here*, because my brothers are dicks, and I didn't trust my things anywhere near them."

"But what about your *other* brother–"

"That's all I know." He gave me a look. "Now, it's your turn."

CHAPTER 54

I glanced around the patio. "My turn? Already?"

"I told you about the fights," Joel said. "Now, you tell *me.* What are you afraid of?"

"I'm not afraid."

"The hell you aren't. So tell me. What's going on?"

I bit my lip. I wasn't looking forward to telling him. The whole thing was just so humiliating. But fair was fair, so I did what he asked. And this time, I didn't leave anything out.

By the time I finished talking, my mouth was dry, and my juice was long-gone. I'd explained everything – how taxes had consumed any funds set aside for maintenance, how I'd diverted the money meant for my own living expenses to pay for some of the bigger repairs, and how I was taking this year off from college to look after the place – and hopefully save some money in the process.

To give him examples of what I was dealing with, I rattled off a few of the minor things that were wrong with the house. I finished by saying, "And the worst part is, I can't do much about it until I turn twenty-five."

"Why twenty-five?" he asked.

"Because that's when I'll finally have control."

"Of what? The house?"

"Not just the house," I said. "The money, the artwork, the cars, everything."

No more Derek on my doorstep. No more pissy little messages from his dad. No more begging for permission to use my own things.

If I was lucky, the next four years would fly.

Concern darkened Joel's features. "In four years? Will you be able to hold on that long?"

"Sure." I tried to smile. "Almost definitely."

From the look on Joel's face, he didn't believe it any more than I did.

Looking to dispel the lingering gloom, I added, "There *is* one bright spot though."

"Yeah? What's that?"

"Well, there *was* some money pre-allocated for basic upkeep, like lawn care. I worked it out with Derek's dad so that *I'm* the one doing it."

Joel stared at me from across the table. "Let me get this straight. *That's* the reason you're stuck mowing the lawn?"

"I'm not stuck," I said. "It was my idea. And there was that old mower in the shed, so it mostly worked out."

Suddenly, Joel looked ready to explode. "That's bullshit."

His reaction surprised me. After all, it was only a lawn. I asked, "What do you mean?"

"I mean, what kind of asshole leaves you with a shitty, broken-down mower and hounds you when it's not done on time?" His eyes narrowed. "And what about Derek?"

"What about him?"

"You said he was like a brother."

"So?"

"So, what kind of shitty-ass brother is that? If *I* had a sister? There's no way I'd let that happen."

I gave him a long look. The sentiment was nice and all, but I'd seen firsthand how well he got along with his own siblings. Unsure how to respond, I picked at the crumbs on my empty plate.

Abruptly, Joel got to his feet. "You got a toolshed?"

I wasn't following. "What?"

"A toolshed," he repeated. "A place where you keep tools."

"Uh..."

"Forget it. I'll get my own."

I was almost afraid to ask. "Why would you need tools?"

"Because, a lot of what's wrong can be fixed in five minutes."

I highly doubted that. "What do you mean?"

"I mean, the leaky faucets, the loose doorknobs, the flickering lights. If Derek gave a rat's ass about you, he would've fixed those already."

"Wait." I stared up at him. *"You're* not planning to fix them, are you?"

"Hell yeah, I'm gonna fix them."

I felt my eyes grow nearly misty. And yet, there was no way I could accept such an offer. "I can't let you do that."

"Why not?"

"It just doesn't seem right."

"Yeah? Well, too bad."

I blinked. "What?"

"I said, *too bad.* I'm doing it, anyway."

In spite of everything, I had to laugh. "Too bad? *Again?* You say that a lot, you know."

"Nah." At last, he gave me the ghost of a smile. "Only with you."

We went back and forth a few more times before I finally gave in. For whatever reason, Joel seemed determined to do it, and I couldn't bring myself to argue beyond a certain point. Like the car thing, it felt like a gift I couldn't refuse.

The only *real* concession I wheedled out of him was that we'd put any repairs off until the next morning so we could enjoy the day together without anything hanging over our heads.

I didn't have to work, and it was shaping up to be a beautiful day – sunny and warm, with a light breeze coming off the water. It was the perfect kind of day to enjoy everything that the estate had to offer.

So that's what we did. We sunbathed on the narrow strip of beach just below my house. We pulled out the canoe and paddled along the shore line. We swam in the lake and made love afterwards in the boathouse below.

By sunset, I felt like a different person – blissful and carefree like I hadn't been in years. As for Joel, he seemed different too, like someone who was only just recalling what it was like to be happy.

Late that night, we fell into bed, warm from the shower and sated from sex.

The next morning, we hit the storage place to retrieve his tools. But inside Joel's storage unit, it wasn't the tools that claimed my attention. It was something infinitely more interesting.

CHAPTER 55

It was one of the most beautiful things I'd ever seen. The colors were perfection. The composition made me feel like I was part of it. The scene was so enchanting that I couldn't look away.

I called out to Joel, "Who did this? Do you know?"

He was outside the cluttered storage unit, rummaging around in the trunk of his car. "Who did what?"

"This painting. I checked for a signature, but I didn't see any."

I was still staring at it. If I had to classify its style, I'd say it was realism – except the reality was somehow more beautiful, like the painter was seeing things the way they *should* be, rather than the way they were.

Joel still hadn't answered my question. I turned to look and was surprised to see him standing directly behind me.

He gave the painting a cursory glance. "Why?"

"Why do I want to know?" Again, I turned to look. "Because it's beautiful."

It was an oil painting of a dark-haired woman with a couple of small children, all walking along the beach. She was in the center, wearing a yellow sundress and holding the nearest hand of each child. Both were boys. Each wore navy shorts and a short-sleeved, classic white button-down shirt.

Was it a mom and her kids? That was my guess.

The concept wasn't unusual. And yet, for some reason, I couldn't look away. Why was that? Maybe it was the facial expressions that drew me in. They conjured up feelings of love and absolute security – emotions I'd found sadly lacking ever since the death of my parents.

I was still looking at the painting. "Do you know if this was painted recently?"

While waiting for his answer, I gave the subjects' clothing a better look. The outfits weren't exactly modern, but they weren't terribly old-fashioned either.

It was the same with the hairstyles. The woman's hair was long and flowing. As for the boys, their hair looked delightfully disheveled, like they'd just been caught in a summer breeze.

Based purely on the clothing and hair styles, the painting had to be less than fifty years old, but its exact age remained a mystery. There was a timeless quality that made it impossible to place.

Even now, I couldn't stop staring. "You don't know who painted it, do you?"

When he still didn't answer, I turned to give him a questioning look.

He asked, "Why'd you uncover it?"

Instantly, heat flooded my face. Until just a few minutes ago, a large white sheet had been thrown over the painting, hiding it from view. I looked down at the sheet, now wadded up in my arms. "Sorry, I guess it's a bad habit." I gave an awkward laugh. "Family history and all."

Silently, Joel took the sheet from my hands and began to move around me, as if preparing to cover the painting up again.

"Wait," I said. "You never answered my question. Do you know who painted it?"

"Yeah." He tossed the sheet over the painting. "Me."

I did a double-take. "What?"

He looked toward his car. "You ready to go?"

"Not yet." My mind was reeling. "You said *you* painted that?"

"Yeah. Why?"

"Because you never mentioned it."

"Mentioned what?"

"That you were a painter." I looked toward the painting, now hidden from view. Even now, in my mind's eye, I could still see it.

I was an art history major and the daughter of a famous artist. I was familiar with practically all of the popular names and styles. Even if Joel had only copied the painting, it was an amazing reproduction.

I asked, "What did you paint it from?"

"What do you mean?"

"I mean, is it a copy of something? Like another painting?"

"No."

I hesitated. "A photograph?"

"No." Again, he glanced toward his car. "Ready to head out?"

I looked toward his car and then back to him. "Why are you so anxious to leave?"

"Because I've got the stuff we came for."

Right. The tools. I glanced around the storage unit. I saw oversized plastic bins, along with dozens of cardboard boxes, stacked nearly to the ceiling. I was dying to wade through the mess in search of more paintings. There had to be more, right?

Pushing that distraction aside, I turned back to Joel. "Just to make sure I understand…" I pointed to the covered painting. "You painted that on your own, I mean without copying anything?"

"That's what I said." His eyes were wary, and his muscles were tight. "What are you getting at?"

"It's *really* good."

He didn't even smile. "Thanks."

He didn't *sound* very thankful. In fact, he didn't sound pleased at all. I studied his face. "Why are you acting so funny about it?"

"Because it's private."

"Oh." The words felt like a slap, and I drew back, widening the distance between us.

Yes, I realized that I'd uncovered the painting without his permission. But in my defense, I'd assumed that it was covered for protection, not for privacy. It was a simple misunderstanding, and yeah, a mistake on my part.

Even so, his comment stung. *Private, huh?*

I recalled everything I'd told him yesterday about the estate and its problems. I hadn't done that with anyone else, not even Cassie or Aunt Gina. As far as *they* knew, I was doing just fine. But Joel knew the whole truth – the whole *ugly* truth, including the fact that I was broke.

That was private, too. But I'd shared it, anyway. And now, he was acting like I'd just been caught scrolling through his cell phone or cripes, rifling through his wallet.

How humiliating was this?

CHAPTER 56

Sitting in the passenger's seat, I gazed out the car window as the landscape zoomed by. There was something I needed to say, but I didn't know how to begin, or even scarier, how the conversation would end.

Already, my stomach was tied up in knots. Who was I kidding? I knew exactly how it would end.

Badly.

I didn't *want* it to end that way, but with Joel's current mood, I couldn't see any other possibility.

With lingering dread, I gave him my third or fourth sideways glance. He hadn't said more than a few words after closing the storage unit and getting into the driver's seat of his car, only *after* holding open the passenger's side door for me.

It was such a crazy mix of contradictions – the old-fashioned chivalry combined with his simmering silence. I still didn't get it. And the way it looked, he wasn't remotely interested in explaining.

Deciding to get this over with, I cleared my throat and said, "Hey, Joel?"

He didn't even look. "Yeah?"

"I've been thinking…" I hesitated. "I really don't think you should do this for me."

Still looking straight ahead, he said, "Do what?"

"The repairs and stuff. I just don't feel right about it."

It was true. I didn't. It was a funny thing, accepting favors. Sometimes it felt alright, like when there was *some* chance of doing a favor in return. But other times, it just felt wrong.

This was one of those times, and I couldn't quite figure out why. But

I *did* know that I was feeling strange and awkward about the whole thing.

Plus, I didn't want to owe him. Cripes, I already owed him – too much, in fact. There was no need to add to the list, right?

In the driver's seat, Joel said nothing in response. He didn't look. He didn't twitch. He didn't even change his expression.

I waited a few more seconds before saying, "You heard me, right?"

"Yeah, I heard you."

"And?"

"And…" He spared me half a glance, before returning his eyes to the road. "Too bad."

Too bad?

This time, it wasn't funny. I turned in my seat to stare at him. "I'm serious."

"Yeah? Me, too."

"What does that mean?"

"It means you agreed to let me do it. Too late to back out now."

"I don't care what I agreed to." I lifted my chin. "It's *not* too late, and I've changed my mind."

He hit the brakes – not hard, but enough to slow us down considerably. A moment later, he was pulling off to the side of the road. He cut the engine and turned to face me. "Why?"

"Why what?"

"Why the change?"

"Because you've done enough already."

"Bullshit."

I rolled my eyes. "Well that's just great. Your favorite one-word response."

"It's not my favorite."

"Oh yeah?" I said. "Then what is?"

"Fuck."

I stared at him. I couldn't even tell if it was a serious answer. I muttered, "Oh, that's nice."

He said nothing, and our gazes remained locked. The visual standoff lasted practically a whole minute before he said, "Just tell me. What's wrong?"

"With *me*?" I said. "Nothing. What's wrong with *you*?"

"Nothing."

I gave him my snottiest smile. "Bullshit."

If he was amused, he didn't show it. "Is this about the painting?"

"No."

His eyebrows rose just a fraction. "You want me to say it again?"

"Say *what* again? Bullshit?" I gave a bitter laugh. "No thanks."

He said nothing, and the silence stretched out. In spite of my best intentions, I started squirming in my seat. "Alright," I finally said. "Maybe I just don't want to owe you."

"You won't."

"Except I already do."

"No. You don't."

I gave him a pleading look. "Look, we can go round and round about this forever. But we both know that's not true."

When he said nothing, I started rattling off just a few of the things that he'd done for me. "You gave me a ride. You mowed my lawn. You even stopped me from getting robbed." I made a scoffing sound. "Twice."

His expression remained stony. "That was nothing."

"It wasn't nothing." With an effort, I softened my tone. "And besides, I just realized, I shouldn't be accepting so much."

"Yeah? Why not?"

Suddenly, I felt like crying. "Look, why does this have to be such a big deal?"

"Because this morning, you were good with it. Now, you're not. What changed?"

"I don't know." I blinked long and hard. "If anything's changed, it's you."

"Right." He closed his eyes for a long moment. When he opened them again, I saw the first sign of any real emotion. Regret? Uncertainty? I was still trying to decide when he said, "Just tell me. What'd I say?"

I blew out a long, shaky breath and reminded myself of all those wonderful things he'd done for me. And now, he was asking for something in return – the truth about what was bothering me.

All things considered, it wasn't too much to ask.

In a quieter voice, I said, "I just realized something. That's all."

His voice grew quieter, too. "Yeah? What?"

"I realized…" *Damn it.* How to put this? "Well, that we're probably not as close as I thought we were." I ran a nervous hand through my hair. "I mean, here, I've been boring you with all of my troubles, and I guess we're not really to that point yet."

"What point?"

Oh, God. He was seriously going to make me explain it? "You know, where we're sharing all these stupid, intimate details." I tried to smile. "So I guess I just figure it's time to dial it back a bit, you know?"

Watching me from the driver's seat, he grew utterly still, but said nothing.

Hoping to take the edge off, I gave a weak laugh. "I mean, I can't have you fixing my plumbing and stuff when we're just hanging out. It's not fair. To you, I mean. So now I feel all funny about it."

"Hanging out," he said. "*That's* what you think we're doing?"

I wanted to scream. Of all the things for him to zero in on, why that? In a moment of frustration, I blurted out, "Well, what *are* we doing?"

As an answer, he turned to face the road ahead. And then, to my infinite frustration, he fired up the engine and shifted the car into gear. A moment later, we were, once again, cruising down the lonely country road.

I sank down in the passenger's seat and tried to decide who I was more angry with – me, for not just letting it go, or him, for not understanding why I felt so funny about it.

The remainder of the short drive passed in stone-cold silence that grew more oppressive with every mile. I wanted to say something, but I didn't know what.

From the look on Joel's face, there was nothing he wanted to hear – not from me, anyway.

When we pulled up to my house, he got out of the car and walked around to the passenger's side door. He pulled it open and waited for me to get out.

If that wasn't a hint, I didn't know what was.

Silently, I got out of the car and then watched with growing despair as he climbed back into the driver's seat and shut the car door behind him.

My heart was begging him not to go, but my mouth refused to form the words, even as he fired up the engine and drove away.

Staring after him, I had to give him credit for one thing – he hadn't peeled out of the driveway like an angry teenager. But that was a cold comfort later that night, as I climbed into bed and tried to figure out exactly what I'd done wrong.

CHAPTER 57

Standing on my front doorstep, Derek gave me a knowing smirk. "Where's your boyfriend?" He turned and made a show of looking at the driveway, where Joel's car had been parked the last time Derek had stopped by.

That was how long ago? Three days? Or was it four?

Still half-asleep, I rubbed at my eyes. The morning sun felt too bright and too harsh. I squinted at my unwelcome visitor. "What?"

Derek turned to face me, and his gaze dipped to my thin rumpled shorts and matching tank-top. "You just getting up?"

I gave him an annoyed look. *His* clothes weren't rumpled. He was wearing a gray business suit and striped yellow tie. He looked fresh and wide awake, like he'd had plenty of sleep and the perfect double cappuccino.

Well, goodie for him.

I ignored his question and tossed back one of my own. "Is your phone working?"

"You mean my cell phone?"

"Yeah." I felt my jaw clench. "Your cell phone."

He reached into his pocket and pulled it out. Frowning now, he studied the display. "Yeah. Why?"

"Because next time, you can use that thing to call first, okay?"

He stiffened. "What are you saying?"

"I'm saying, I don't want you popping in here anymore."

At this, he had the nerve to look insulted. "Why not?"

"Because I want some privacy."

He was frowning again. "So he *is* your boyfriend?"

"And," I continued, "I'm tired of you giving me grief all the time."

"Boy, you're in a mood."

Yes. I was.

It had been two full days since my argument with Joel, and I still hadn't heard from him. Yesterday, I'd even gone to his campsite. It was utterly empty. No tent. No nothing.

Had he left town?

It sure looked that way. And I couldn't even call him, because right there, on my own kitchen counter was Joel's cell phone. He'd left it there when we'd driven out to the storage unit. Would he *ever* come back for it? I swallowed. Would he ever come back for me?

The odds weren't looking great.

The situation was so depressing that I wanted to crawl back into bed with an oversized stuffed animal and a pint of ice cream.

But I didn't have either of those things. I had Derek, who was literally the last person on Earth I wanted to see. And this included my pilfering relatives.

I mean, at my least my uncle might make me laugh.

As for Derek, he just made me want to hit something – like his face.

Oblivious to his danger, Derek gave a low chuckle. "What? Did he run out for donuts and forget to come back?"

At the mere thought, something squeezed at my heart. Oh sure, Joel had run out, alright. Unfortunately, no donuts had been involved. Was it over? It sure looked that way.

"Cheer up," Derek said. "Maybe the guy got lost." He lowered his voice as if sharing a secret. "Just between you and me, he didn't seem too bright."

I stared at him. *What a condescending prick.*

At something in my face, Derek took a small step backward. "Oh, c'mon, chill. I was just kidding."

"No, you weren't." I crossed my arms. "That's what everyone says when they're caught being an asshole."

Now, *he* was staring. "What'd you say?"

"You heard me."

"Yeah. I did." He frowned. "And that's a new word for you."

It was true. I hardly ever used language like that. And even when I did, I was usually alone. But what had all of that politeness gotten me? Nothing.

I gave a weary sigh. "Is there a reason you stopped by?"

"Yes. As a matter of fact, there is. I wanted to remind you of next month's meeting."

He didn't need to remind me. He meant, of course, the final meeting to select recipients of this year's art endowment.

This meant that in three weeks or so, I'd be spending the whole day meeting with the finalists in the boardroom while a parade of strangers traipsed through the house and ogled my parents' things.

In my current mood, I wanted no part of it.

Unfortunately, skipping wasn't really an option – since the meeting was taking place literally where I lived.

"I don't need a reminder," I told him. "And even if I did, why would you remind me now? That's weeks away."

"I'll get to that later," he said. "But you *are* planning to be there, right?"

"Of course."

He gave my clothes a quick glance. "And you're gonna be presentable?"

Oh, for God's sake. "No," I snapped. "I'm wearing this." I made a show of looking confused. "Don't tell me that's a problem?"

"Very funny."

Was it? I didn't think so, but then again, my funny bone had taken a serious beating since Joel's abrupt departure.

I told Derek, "Next time, just call, okay? Or text. I don't need a personal visit for these little reminders."

"It's not little," he said. "It's important that you be there, because I can't."

"What? You're skipping it?"

If only that were an option for me.

"Yeah," he said. "My dad's got me doing some research on the other side of the state, so you'll be pulling double duty."

I wasn't the least bit concerned. When it came to the actual decision-making process, I had nearly nothing to do with it. Mostly, my role consisted of being introduced as my dad's daughter and saying something nice to whoever came in.

Even in my current state-of-mind, I could pull that off with my eyes closed. In fact, I was kind of wishing my eyes were closed now.

I gave Derek an annoyed look. "Alright, fine. You told me. Is there anything else?"

His gaze narrowed. "Hey, if you want me to go, I'll go."

I waited.

He didn't go.

Instead, he said, "Next time I stop by, maybe you'll be in a better mood."

I thought of all the grief he'd given me over the last few weeks. "Or maybe," I said, "I'll slam the door in your face and remind you that you're supposed to call first."

And with that, I stepped back and did the unthinkable. I *did* slam the door in his face, and afterward, ignored the knocking and doorbell-ringing that followed.

Immature? Maybe. But somehow, I couldn't bring myself to care. When he finally went away, I stomped up the stairs and took a long, hot shower in hopes of washing away my irritation.

It did no good. I spent the whole shower thinking about Joel and our stupid argument. It wasn't only that I missed him like crazy. It was the grim realization that I'd revealed more than I should've.

It had been a risk, and not only to my heart. People would pay big money for the sad story that I'd so recklessly shared. I could practically see the headlines now.

Heiress Facing Financial Ruin.

Trouble with Blaire Estate

Stud Lover Tells All

I gave a small shake of my head. My imagination was running too wild for my own good. Even in my darkest thoughts, I didn't truly believe that Joel would be that cruel.

Or maybe I was just being naïve. After all, I'd trusted Derek, and look what a jackass *he'd* become.

I was just drying off when the doorbell rang again. Standing naked in my bathroom, I tensed.

Could it be Joel? The odds weren't *totally* terrible. After all, Derek had already stopped by, so that ruled him out. Plus, Joel had left his phone. If nothing else, he'd come back for that, right?

I dove for the clean clothes that I'd already laid out and scrambled to put them on. I flew down the stairs with no shoes and wet hair, only to find myself disappointed.

It was Derek again, delivering what? A freaking box of donuts. He told me it was a peace offering. I told *him* it was a stupid joke that I didn't appreciate.

I appreciated it even less when Derek made fun of me for my wet hair and disheveled clothing.

Some peace offering.

I refused the donuts and once again, slammed the door in his face.

It was getting to be a bad habit, but I couldn't bring myself to care. Just like earlier, I ignored his knocking, along with the doorbell, and tried to go about my business. After fifteen minutes or so, he went away at last.

Or so I thought. A few minutes later, just as I was finishing making my bed, the doorbell rang again.

Disgusted with the whole thing, I stomped down the stairs, determined to give Derek another piece of my mind.

But this time, when I yanked the door open, it *wasn't* Derek.

It was Joel.

CHAPTER 58

Standing on my porch, he looked too good to be real. I couldn't read his facial expression, but the rest of him looked incredible, even in basic jeans and a loose T-shirt.

I felt myself swallow. My hair was still wet, and I ran a nervous hand through the damp tendrils. "Uh, hi."

After what seemed like forever, he finally smiled. "Hi."

Something about that smile made me feel gooey all over, and I had to resist a sudden urge to throw myself into his arms.

After all, this might not be a social visit. Tentatively, I said, "Are you here for your phone?"

He shook his head. "Screw the phone. I'm here for you." His gaze met mine. "Unless you're gonna tell me to take a hike."

I smiled with relief. "I hate hiking." I paused. "No. Wait. That's not true. I *like* hiking. I just mean…" I gave a nervous laugh. "I wouldn't want you to hike alone."

What was I saying? I had no idea.

He reached for my hand. "I brought you something."

I looked down at our hands, now joined. I liked how they looked. Even better, I liked how they felt. I wanted to join more than our hands.

But then, his words sunk in. I looked up. "You brought me something? What?"

"A birthday present."

"But it's not my birthday."

"Yeah. But it was. And I never got you anything."

I shook my head. "You're wrong." My eyes were feeling almost misty again. "You gave me more than you realized."

"And you gave me something better."

"What?" I asked.

His voice grew quiet. "You."

I felt a big, stupid smile spread across my face. "And you gave me you."

His smile faded, and he shook his head. "No. I didn't. And I want to make it up to you."

"What do you mean?"

"Wait here," he said. "I'll be right back."

He released my hand and turned away. From the open doorway, I watched as he strode to his car, popped the trunk, and pulled something out.

It was big and flat, and wrapped in festive paper. He carried it from his car to the porch and held it out between us. He gave me a sheepish smile. "Happy birthday."

I stared at the thing. The size and shape looked eerily familiar. "What is it?" I asked.

"You *know* what it is."

I'd suspected. I'd even hoped. And a few minutes later, sitting beside Joel in my front room, I finally knew for sure.

I'd just removed the wrapping paper, and was now staring at the masterpiece underneath. I could hardly breathe. "I'm not sure I can accept this."

"Why not?

"Because it's too beautiful." I turned to study his face. "And I know that it must mean something to you."

"Forget that. *You* mean something to me."

Carefully, I laid down the painting, face-up on the ornate rug. And then, I threw myself into his arms and murmured against his chest, "I love it. Thank you."

His arms closed tight around me, and he whispered into my hair, "I'm sorry I was such an ass."

"You weren't," I said.

"Nice of you to say so."

I pulled back to study his face. "If you don't mind me asking, why were you so bothered?"

He glanced away. "It's complicated."

That wasn't the answer I wanted, but it seemed heartless to push it, especially after he'd given me so much already. But then, he surprised me with an odd question of his own. "You ever hurt people?"

I felt my brow wrinkle. "You mean, like hurt their feelings?"

"No. Like beat on them 'til they're half dead."

I stared at him. I didn't know what to say. Obviously, the answer was no. But surely, Joel knew that already. I hesitated. "That's not a serious question, is it?"

"No."

"Then why'd you ask?"

"So you could feel what *I* feel."

"You mean, when you fight someone?"

"Yeah. That." Joel looked away. "I fuckin' hate it."

"So why do you do it then?"

"Why else? For the money."

"Is it worth it?"

"I dunno." He shoved a hand through his hair. "I used to think so."

I was still trying to understand. "So, are you a pacifist or something?"

At this, he actually laughed. "Hell no."

"What's so funny? I mean, you told me you hated fighting."

"I hate fighting for money," he said. "But I'm no pacifist."

I had to ask, "What's the difference?"

"There's nothing wrong with fighting for what you believe in." He reached out and brushed a warm finger along the side of my face. His voice softened. "Or to protect someone you love."

My breath caught. "What are you saying?"

"I'm saying, if someone ever hurt you, I'd beat them to death and love every minute of it."

I swallowed. It was sexy and scary, and yeah, just a little bit confusing. He'd also used the L-word. Sort of. I wanted to say something in return, but I didn't know what.

Abruptly, Joel pulled back and said, "Anyway, fighting ran in the family, so here I am." He gave me a smile that didn't reach his eyes. "Creating things on one side, and destroying things on the other."

"By creating, you mean the paintings, right?"

Joel nodded. "You know what it was like, coming up after my brothers?"

"No. How was it?"

"It sucked."

"But why?"

"Like I told you, I'm the fifth one. By the time *I* get to school, everyone knows exactly what I'll be."

"What?" I asked.

"Nothing but trouble. Every teacher. Every principal. Every adult I ever met. I could practically read their minds. 'Oh shit, another one.'" He gave a wry laugh. "Man, they hated me on sight."

"All of them?" I asked.

Joel gave a small smile. "All except one. There was this art teacher – Miss Robins. Anyway, we're doing this painting project in junior high, and she tells me I have real talent."

"You do." I leaned forward. "*A lot* of talent."

Joel glanced away. "I dunno."

I reached for his hand. "Well, *I* do. Honest. I've never seen anything like it."

Joel gave me a dubious look. "Nice of you to say."

I shook my head. "I'm not 'saying' anything. I mean it. You know, there's this art foundation in my dad's name. Every year, we interview dozens of up-and-coming artists. I've never seen a single one with your talent."

I looked to the painting, lying there, face up on the floor. "Unless…" *Damn it.* I didn't want to say it.

"Unless what?"

I winced. "Unless you weren't being totally straight-forward about it."

At Joel's blank look, I said, "Don't get me wrong. It's absolutely beautiful, and I'll treasure it forever no matter what. But…" I felt my shoulders tense. *How to say this?*

"But what?" Joel asked.

I took a deep breath. "Don't take this the wrong way, but did you really paint that yourself? I mean, as an original?" In a rush to finish before he became angry, I added, "I know you were distracted when we talked about it, so I just wanted to double-check."

Joel squeezed my hand. "Baby, don't look so scared."

"I look scared?"

"Look," he said, "to answer your question, yes, I painted it. Not from another painting. And not from a picture. But I don't blame you for asking." He shrugged. "I mean, look at me. I'm no artist."

"But you are," I insisted.

"No. I'm not. Wanna know what I do? I don't create things. I destroy them."

"That's not true."

"Sorry, but you're wrong." He gave a slow shake of his head. "You wanna know something?"

"What?"

"You're the first nice girl I've ever been with."

The change of topic caught me off-guard. At the sweetness of the sentiment, I wanted to smile. But Joel wasn't smiling.

What was I missing? I asked, "Is that a bad thing?"

"For you?" He gave something like a laugh. "Probably."

"I'm serious," I said.

"You think I'm not?" He gave my hand another squeeze. "Remember what I said about the teachers?"

"You mean that they had preconceived notions about you?"

"That's one way to put it. But it was the same with girls. The nice ones? Their parents would get one look at me and run for the hills, dragging their daughters with them." He glanced away. "Not that I blame them. Shit, if I had a daughter? I'd be the same way."

"So, what kind of girls *did* you date?"

"The kind you don't *have* to date."

"Oh." Tentatively, I asked, "Did you like that?"

"Sometimes," he said. "Or, at least, that's what I told myself. And then something happened."

"What?" I asked.

He gave me a smile that melted my heart. "I met you."

And just like that, the gooey feeling was back. I don't know how it happened, or who moved first, but soon, we were in each other's arms – kissing and touching. Just like always, it felt like coming home, and I savored the feel of him.

The last two days had been miserable. But today, was heaven. And I was determined to enjoy it, especially because I had an idea.

Unfortunately, when I mentioned that idea to Joel a few hours later, the trouble started all over again.

CHAPTER 59

I gave Joel a perplexed look. "But why not?"

He was frowning now. "Because I told you, I'm no artist."

We were sitting out on my bedroom balcony, and I'd just told him more about the art endowment – how it paid a generous stipend, how only six artists were selected each year, and how several recipients from prior years had already experienced life-changing success.

I'd ended with the suggestion that Joel apply for one of the slots. Yes, it was late in the process, but not impossible to work out, given the fact that Claude hadn't yet made his final selections.

But to my disappointment, Joel had practically laughed in my face.

I was so confused, I didn't know what to think. "But you're really good."

He looked down to study his hands. I followed his gaze and saw what he saw, hardened knuckles with faint scars that could've only come from one thing – beating someone bloody.

I reached out and took his hands in mine. "Seriously, you *are*. And you should apply."

But he shook his head. "Sorry, not a good idea."

"Why not?"

He gave a bitter laugh. "Because it'll flame out. That's why."

"Oh stop it. It will not."

"Wanna bet?" His hands stiffened in mine. "If I told you I loved you, you'd leave me tomorrow."

I sucked in a breath. There it was again, the L-word.

Oblivious to the turmoil that he'd just caused, Joel continued, "Or maybe next week. Hard to say." His jaw clenched. "But it wouldn't be long."

I felt the beginnings of a real smile. "Joel–"

His eyes flashed in warning. "Stop."

I paused. "Stop what?"

"What I just said, forget it."

"But I don't want to forget it. I–"

"I mean it," he warned. "I didn't say it. And I'm not gonna say it."

I pulled back, letting our hands slide apart. "What's wrong? Are you angry with me or something?"

"I'm not angry. I'm realistic."

"No, you're not. You're talking like a crazy person."

"Yeah? Tell me something I don't know."

There *was* something that he didn't know, and I desperately wanted to tell him – three little words that had been growing in my heart almost from the beginning. In a softer voice, I said, "Joel, just listen–"

Abruptly, he stood. "I'm gonna get to work."

Confused, I stared up at him. "On what?"

His gaze drifted toward my bedroom, just beyond the open balcony doors. After a long silence, he said, "The kitchen faucet."

Screw the faucet.

That's what I *wanted* to say. But that was the last thing I wanted to argue about. So I said, "Alright. Then I'll keep you company."

"You know what? Forget the faucet. I'm gonna mow before it gets dark."

I gave him a perplexed look. "You mean the lawn?"

But already, he was striding through the balcony doors.

I stood and called after him. "But you just mowed a few days ago. It doesn't even need it."

He didn't pause. He didn't answer. He just kept on going. Desperately, I wanted to follow after him. But something in his stride told me it would be a huge mistake.

It hadn't escaped my attention that he'd zoomed in on the one job that wouldn't just take him outside, but would also prevent any further conversation.

If that wasn't a hint, I didn't know what was.

So I stood, watching like an idiot as he strode through my bedroom and into the hallway. A couple of minutes later, I was still standing there when I heard the sounds of the mower firing up outside.

I tried to look on the bright side. At least he'd gone for the mower, and not his car. That was an improvement, right?

CHAPTER 60

I felt like a stalker watching him from behind the front curtains, but I didn't know what else to do. I'd waited upstairs for at least an hour, hoping he'd come to his senses. But he hadn't.

So I'd come downstairs and nudged aside the curtains for a better look. His shirt was off, and his body was glistening as he pushed the mower from one side of the yard to the other. If he didn't look so angry, I might've enjoyed the view. But there was nothing enjoyable about this.

For someone who claimed that he wasn't an artist, he sure was temperamental. A wistful smile tugged at my lips. Funny, my dad had been the same way.

But he didn't mow the lawn. He played the drums. Badly.

I glanced down at my watch. In a couple of hours, it would be dark. Would Joel stop then?

And if he didn't, what would I do?

With an effort, I turned away in search of a mindless distraction. I found it in the laundry room, where I began folding a load of towels.

I'd just finished when I caught movement from the corner of my eye. I looked to see Joel, standing shirtless in the open doorway.

He gave me a wary smile. "Hi."

He looked so boyish that I had to smile back. "Hi. So, um, you're done?"

"With what? Making an ass of myself?"

I had to laugh. "At least you weren't drumming."

He shook his head. "Drumming?"

"It's what my dad used to do. But never mind that." I moved closer.

"Is everything okay?"

"I dunno." His eyes searched mine. "Is it?"

The way it looked, the storm had passed. I gave a happy nod. "It is now."

"I'm gonna take another shower. After that, you wanna start over?"

"Or if you want…" I smiled up at him. "We could start over *in* the shower."

So we did.

We had makeup sex in the shower and afterward, lay, clean and sated, on my bed. I was dressed in casual shorts and a sleeveless shirt. As for Joel, he'd thrown on a pair of casual shorts, but no shirt at all.

I snuggled against his bare chest, simply enjoying the moment.

The bed was made, and I'd left the balcony doors open to let in a summer breeze, along with the sounds of the waves, lapping at the bluff below.

As I lay, cradled in his arms, I might've felt absolutely content, except for the fact that I still didn't know what had set him off.

Reluctantly, I pulled back to look at him. "Hey Joel?"

He smiled. "I know."

"You know what?"

"That I owe you."

I still wasn't following. "You owe me what?"

"An explanation."

Carefully, I said, "I wouldn't say that you owe me one, but it would still be nice." I hesitated. "Earlier, what'd I say?"

"Nothing. It wasn't you. It was me." After a long pause, he said, "Wanna know what my dad used to call me?"

"What?"

"Cigar."

I felt my brow wrinkle. "Why?"

"Because I always got close, but never made it. Like I was cursed or something."

I ran a soothing hand along his shoulder. "Oh come on. That can't be true."

He smiled without humor. "That's what *I* used to say." He turned to look up at the ceiling. "Then I wised up."

"Why? What happened?"

"Life," Joel said. "It's like all these great things fall into my lap, but the moment I want them, *really* want them, they go up in flames."

"Is this about the deal with that sports agent?"

"Not *just* that. But it fits."

"How so?"

"Like get this. When the whole thing started, the guy's begging me to sign with him." Joel turned his head, once again, to face me. "He goes through the whole bit – fancy dinners, meetings with big stars, and promises like you wouldn't believe. But all along, I know it's a crock."

"Why?"

"Because this is *me* we're talking about. Cigar, remember?"

Already, I hated that word.

Joel continued. "Sure, I let him talk, but there's no way I'm taking it seriously, especially when the guy mentions underwear commercials."

I had to laugh. "Underwear commercials? Seriously?"

"Swear to God."

I let my gaze travel down the length of him. He had a body to die for and a face to match. No doubt, he *could* sell a lot of underwear. But this was no time to be distracted. "So what happened?"

"So I tell him to shove it."

"But wait," I said. "*You* backed out? I thought your brothers ruined it."

"Not *that* deal," Joel said. "The second one."

"There was a second one?"

"Yeah. After I tell the guy to shove it, he starts contacting me again, upping the deal, making it sweeter every time. Finally, he makes one of those offers you can't refuse."

"What kind of offer?" I asked.

"Total control. I don't do anything I don't want – no prancing around in my underwear, that's for damn sure."

Somehow, I couldn't see Joel prancing, but I got what he meant.

Joel went on. "And we're talking lots of money, probably millions."

"Wow," I said. "That much?"

"With endorsements? Sure. So I start thinking, 'Maybe my Cigar days are over, and holy shit, this is really happening.' And the more I think about it, the more I want it. So I call the guy and tell him we have a deal."

"What'd he say?" I asked.

"He was thrilled. Or at least, that's what he told me."

"So then what happened?"

"Oh, that's the best part," Joel said. "We get everything worked out, papers drawn up, the works. But the day I'm supposed to sign, I walk into his office, and where's the guy standing?"

"Where?"

"At his shredder."

My breath caught. "His paper shredder?"

"Oh yeah. And he gives me that look, like I just caught him screwing a goat."

I knew exactly what kind of look Joel meant. I saw it on my uncle all the time. But that was hardly relevant.

With growing trepidation, I asked, "Don't tell me he was shredding the contract?"

"That's exactly what he was doing."

I wanted to kill the guy. "Literally? Like right in front of you?"

"He wasn't being a dick about it," Joel said. "It's just that I got there early and, well, there he was."

"So, did he say anything?"

"Yeah. He tells me, 'Sorry no deal.'"

"Just like that?"

"Yeah. Except the guy takes an hour to say it."

I recalled the details from our previous conversation. "And he canceled it because of your brother?"

"Yeah. Some brother, huh?"

"Did you ever ask him about it?"

"Jake?" Joel's jaw tightened. "Yeah. I asked him."

"What'd he say?"

"He *claimed* he was doing me a favor."

I stared in disbelief. "A favor?"

"That's what he said, told me the agent was a snake, and that I'd thank him someday."

"And what did *you* say?"

"I told him where he could shove it. And then, I call Bishop, hoping he'll talk some sense into Jake. But what does *he* do? He says the same damn thing." Joel gave a humorless laugh. "Tells me it's for the best."

"So what'd you do then?" I asked.

"You *know* what I did."

He was right. I did. He'd taken something valuable from each of them and then, he'd skipped town. Trying to fill in the blanks, I asked, "So after the deal fell through, did you contact any other agents?"

"Hell no. Why bother? You think Jake wouldn't step in again?"

"But maybe it was something about *that* agent in particular."

"It wasn't the agent," Joel said. "And you want the truth? It wasn't even Jake. It was me. Cigar, remember? If Jake hadn't stopped it, something else would've."

"Oh come on. Stop saying that."

"Hey, I'm not complaining. I'm just telling you the way it is."

I couldn't quite agree. But there *was* something I wanted to say, even if Joel might hate me for saying it. I hesitated. "Have you ever wondered, if maybe it *is* for the best?"

Joel stiffened. "How so?"

"Well, because you hate fighting."

"So what?" Joel said. "Everyone hates their jobs, right?"

"Not always," I said. "My dad didn't." My voice warmed as I continued. "You know, he really loved what he did. He'd go out in his studio every morning and create the most beautiful things. And then, when his work was licensed, in reproductions and stuff, well, he did really great for himself."

This was a massive understatement, but hopefully, Joel got the point.

Joel said, "I'm not your dad."

I gave a little flinch. "Uh, yeah. I know."

Instantly, his voice softened. "I didn't mean it like that. I'm just saying, stuff like that? It's one-in-a-million, not even worth thinking about."

"But why won't you at least try?" I asked.

"Because, it's a waste. You know that story I just told you?"

"About the agent? Yeah, what about it?"

"Well, I've got a hundred just like it. Maybe not as big. But they add up."

I pulled back to get a better look at him. "So you won't even try?"

"Look, I'm not gonna die in a gutter or anything. I'm just saying, it's time to give it a rest."

"For how long?"

"I dunno. Maybe a month. Maybe forever. I'm still working on it."

As far as the endowment was concerned, he didn't *even* have a month. In only three weeks, Claude would be making the final selections.

Bracing myself, I said, "About the endowment–"

"Forget it."

"Just listen," I said. "Is it that you don't have any interest? Or that you don't want to get your hopes up?"

Joel looked at me for a long time, but said nothing.

I tried again. "Like, just out of curiosity, if you happened to be selected, you wouldn't turn it down or anything, would you?"

"Hell yeah, I'd turn it down."

"But why?"

"Because I don't want any special treatment."

"But I'm not the one who decides," I explained. "Claude, this art critic from Chicago, *he's* the one with the final say. And it's not like *he's* gonna give you special treatment."

When Joel said nothing, I tried a different approach. "Okay, about that whole cigar thing, let's say you won the lottery, you wouldn't rip up the ticket, would you?"

"With my luck? I wouldn't *buy* a ticket." He pulled me closer. "Don't get me wrong. I love that you care. But *I* don't. So just forget it, okay?"

But I *didn't* forget it. I had a plan, and Joel didn't need to know about it, unless it worked out the way I wanted.

I smiled against his chest. After everything he'd done for me, I owed him at least a chance, even if he wasn't willing to take it himself.

CHAPTER 61

On the phone, Derek sounded nearly unhinged. "Have you lost your fucking mind?"

Wincing, I held the cell phone away from my ear. I hadn't expected him to be thrilled with the decision, but even for Derek, this was a bit much.

He'd been out of town for almost a month now, and I'd come to appreciate how nice it was to *not* have him dropping by all the time.

As for Joel, he'd rented a cabin at the same campground where he'd been staying earlier, and we'd spent the last few weeks in utter bliss. We weren't living together, not exactly, but we'd had more sleepovers than I could count.

I loved him, and I was almost positive that he loved me, too – not that either one of us had said it.

On the phone, Derek was still ranting. "I miss one damn meeting, and you do *this*?" His voice rose. "What the hell were you thinking?"

I didn't bother responding. Instead, I waited, letting him rage to his heart's content. If it made him feel better, that was fine by me. I was happy, even if he wasn't.

I wasn't even worried. There was nothing that Derek could do to change the decision. Once I signed the award letters, the whole thing would be official.

Even now, Claude was finalizing the paperwork for Joel and the other five recipients. Among all of the winners, Joel was by far the best. He had the talent. He had the looks. He had a certain presence that even Claude had picked up on.

True, Joel hadn't presented his work personally, but Claude had remembered him from that whole painting fiasco, when I'd stupidly confused Joel with a stripper.

On the phone, Derek was still going strong.

As I only half-listened, I wondered what he'd say when he learned the rest of it – that I was planning to offer Joel the use of my dad's studio.

No doubt, I'd be facing another tantrum. But for once, I couldn't bring myself to care.

"Hey!" Derek barked. "Melody! You still there?"

Startled, I gave a little jump. "Oh. Are you done?"

"What's that supposed to mean?"

"It means you've been ranting for like ten minutes straight."

"I have not."

I glanced at my watch. "Uh, yeah. Actually, you have." I took a deep breath. "Look, I don't mean to be rude or anything, but can we can get this over with?"

"Why? You've got something better to do?"

"Gee, better than listening to someone yell at me? What do *you* think?"

In truth, I was waiting for Joel to finish oiling the hinges on the upstairs doors. I hadn't asked him to do it, but he'd insisted after some random comment I'd made about how squeaky they were.

I felt myself smile. He was always doing things like that – sweet, thoughtful things that made my life just a little bit better. And whenever I could, I tried to do the same in return.

Derek said, "You know, you're going to be a laughingstock, right?"

"Oh really? Why's that?"

"Oh come on. You gave your pretty boy an endowment."

Joel *was* pretty. And masculine. And the way it sounded, everything that Derek hated.

I sighed as a sad reality hit home. Sure, Derek was away now, but eventually, he'd be back. And then what? Would I be facing fistfights on the front lawn?

In a last-ditch effort to keep some peace, I said, "If you feel like listening, I'll tell you what happened."

"Go ahead." His tone grew sarcastic. "Unlike you, *I've* got plenty of time."

I seriously doubted that. Still, I sank down onto the nearest chair and calmly told Derek how I'd found that first painting in the storage unit, along with several others afterward.

I relayed how impressed the selection committee had been, Claude in particular, who predicted that Joel would take the art-world by storm.

When I finished, Derek gave a derisive laugh. "Wow, that was some sales job."

"It's not a sales job," I said. "I'm just telling you what happened."

"I wasn't talking about *you*," he said. "I was talking about *him*."

"What are you talking about?"

"Isn't it obvious? The guy's playing you."

"He is not."

Even now, Joel still didn't know what I'd done. And he especially didn't know that he'd been selected. He'd been out of town on the day of the big meeting, and hadn't returned until the next night.

Conscious of his crazy superstitions, I was waiting to tell him until I had the final paperwork in-hand. And then, I was going to whip it out with a flourish. *"Ta-da! You won!"*

In my mind, I envisioned the happy scene. Joel and I would celebrate, maybe even with champagne. And yeah, I might gloat at least a little, because it only proved that I'd been right all along.

Joel's cigar days were long-gone.

On the phone, Derek was saying, "Get real. The guy saw you coming a mile away."

"Don't be ridiculous. He won fair and square. And he would've won even without my involvement." My voice became earnest. "Seriously Derek, he's *that* good."

"Oh, he's 'good' alright."

"What's that supposed to mean?"

"It means, the guy just *happens* to ride in on a white horse at the exact time we're awarding the endowments? And he just *happens* to take up with you – the person who signs the award letters?"

I rolled my eyes. "Oh, please. Did you forget? *You're* the one who introduced us."

"I did not."

"Yes, you did. Remember? That whole scene in the boardroom? That was *your* doing. So if you want to blame someone, look in the mirror."

"No, *you* look in the mirror, because *you're* the one who did this."

"Sorry, but Claude selected him, not me. I'm telling you, Joel won on his own merits."

Derek gave a snide laugh. "What, the merit in his pants?"

"Oh, that's nice." I took a deep, calming breath. "You know what? I'm done talking."

"Yeah? Well I'm not."

"Fine," I said, "then talk to yourself, because I've gotta go." And with that, I disconnected the call and turned toward the kitchen, only to see Joel standing in the open doorway, wearing an expression that I couldn't quite make out.

CHAPTER 62

I stared at Joel from across the room. He still hadn't moved, and neither had I.

Had he overheard? And if so, how much? I cleared my throat. "So, you're done with the hinges, huh?"

He asked, "Is it true?"

I didn't know what to say. I stood, silently, as he strode forward and stopped within arm's reach. His gaze probed mine. "Is it?"

Stupidly, I said, "Is what true?"

"The art thing." His face was utterly unreadable. "You were just messing with Derek, right?"

This wasn't how I wanted to tell him. Stalling, I asked, "How'd you know I was talking to Derek?"

"Not hard to figure out." He studied my face. "What *was* that? A story to piss him off?"

I didn't know what to say. I hadn't been planning to tell Joel anything at all until the paperwork had been signed. But I didn't want to lie to him either.

Trying not to give too much away, I asked, "What if it *wasn't* a story? How would you feel?"

He shrugged. "I wouldn't care either way."

It was a lie.

I could see it in his eyes – a flicker of hope, along with a wariness that would've broken my heart if the news was bad.

But it *wasn't* bad. It was good. Really good. And suddenly, I was determined to make him enjoy it, whether he wanted to or not.

I gave him a secret smile. "Oh well, if you don't care either way…" I turned, as if to go.

He snagged my hand and tugged me toward him. "You're messing with me."

Laughing, I fell against his chest. "Am I?"

I felt his arms close tight around me. When he spoke again, I heard the hint of a smile in his voice. "Right?"

I pulled back to gaze up at him. In mock confusion, I said, "Wait, I thought I was messing with Derek."

"Derek isn't here," he said. "I am."

Yes. He was. And I was so crazy about him that I couldn't stop myself from smiling ear-to-ear when I finally announced, "You won!"

He shook his head. "No."

"Yes."

His mouth twitched at the corners. "You're shitting me."

I shook my head. "Nope."

"But how?" he asked.

"Oh come on," I said. "Do you *really* think I'd let just let it go?" Even now, I couldn't stop smiling. "You're amazing. So I took the painting you gave me and showed it to Claude at our final meeting."

Joel gave a confused shake of his head. "Who's Claude?"

"You don't remember? He's the art critic who picks the candidates."

Joel's voice grew quiet. "But I didn't apply."

"You didn't have to," I explained. "Thanks to Derek's little prank, your name was already on the list. And, they'd already met you, so anyway…" I gave him a big, happy smile. "Congratulations!"

Joel stared in obvious disbelief. "Just like that?"

Feeling embarrassingly smug, I nodded. "Just like that."

Technically, I might've been oversimplifying things just a little. There was still the matter of the paperwork, but really, that was just a formality. Although Claude was responsible for selecting the final candidates, I was the person who signed the actual award letters. And unlike that sports agent, there was no way on Earth that I'd be backing out.

Feeling insanely happy, I spent the next few minutes going over the basic details. In the process, I also reminded Joel that the award came with a generous stipend. I finished by saying, "So anyway, you'll be getting your first check within the month."

For some reason, this made him frown.

I asked, "What is it?"

He shook his head. "I don't get it."

"You don't get what?"

"It's a lot of money. How come you don't get any?"

I knew what he meant. The foundation paid generous stipends to six strangers a year, even as the house and everything else crumbled around me.

But things weren't that simple.

I tried to laugh. "Because I'm no artist."

But Joel wasn't laughing. "I'm serious."

Damn it. This was *his* moment, not mine. Hoping to ease his concerns, I said, "Okay, the truth is, the foundation was set up years ago while my dad was still alive. It was my mom's idea, actually. Anyway, that money is totally separate."

For Joel's sake, I summoned up a smile. "But that's a good thing."

He didn't smile back. "How so?"

"Well, for starters, it means the money won't get diverted into unrelated stuff." I gave a shaky laugh. "Like a new furnace."

If anything, his gaze grew *more* troubled. "That money, you should have some of it."

It was a sweet thought. And I loved him for it. But I hated that my own problems were interfering with what should be a happy moment.

I reached for his hand. "Just stop it. This is *good* news." I gave his hand a squeeze. "We should celebrate."

And so we did.

We made it a night to remember, with champagne on the patio, and mind-blowing sex afterward. That night, as I lay cradled in his arms, I considered how lucky we'd been to find each other.

He wasn't cursed. He was amazing. And it was long past time that good things flowed his way. I fell asleep with a smile on my face and love in my heart, even if I didn't quite have the guts to say it yet.

I knew why. I wanted him to say it back, or even better, say it first.

But would he?

CHAPTER 63

"You'll need a studio," I said. "You know, someplace to paint."

We were sitting in the breakfast nook, devouring pancakes and bacon. It was the day after I'd given him the good news, and I was still so excited, I could hardly contain myself.

"Yeah, about that," Joel said, "I've been thinking."

I leaned forward. "Me, too."

"You wanna go first?"

I nodded. "I was thinking that you might want to use the studio here. You know, that space above the guest house?"

To call it a space was a massive understatement. The studio was perfect, with an abundance of natural light and a breathtaking view of the water. I told Joel all about it and finished by saying, "But what were *you* thinking?"

He reached across the table and took my hand in his. "I was thinking you should keep the money."

I wasn't following. "What money?"

"The stipend or whatever you called it."

"But that's for you, to cover expenses."

"Hey, I've got plenty," he said. "Or at least, enough to get us through the year." He gave my hand a gentle squeeze. "Maybe two if we don't get too crazy."

I gazed into his eyes. *Us. We.* Of all his words, those two were the sweetest.

Still, I had to say, "That money's for you. Not for me."

"Alright," Joel said. "We'll call it rent."

"What do you mean?"

"I mean, I'll rent the studio and pay you for it."

"But you don't *have* to pay me," I said.

"I *want* to." He gave my hand another squeeze. "Now, say yes."

I considered all of the problems this would solve. I could replace the furnace, or at least have it repaired. And then, there were all those little things that I'd been putting off – like a new winter coat and more food in the pantry.

It would all be so nice.

And yet, it wouldn't be fair. I shook my head. "No way. That's for your own expenses, just like I said."

"Yeah. Expenses." Joel grinned. "Like a studio."

We went back and forth beyond the point of ridiculousness. In the end, we simply agreed that we'd work it out one way or another. But one thing we settled for certain. Tomorrow, we'd begin moving all of his painting supplies into the studio. And then, we'd move Joel into the guest house below.

The guest house was my idea. No one was living there, anyway. Even when Aunt Gina visited, she stayed in the main house with me, not out there by herself.

The way I saw it, the arrangement would be the perfect win-win. Joel would be living right there, below his studio, so he could paint whenever inspiration struck.

As for me, I'd have Joel within walking distance, or heck, hollering distance if the windows were open.

At last, everything was falling into place.

Later that same day, I finally heard back from Aunt Gina. We'd been playing telephone tag for the last few days, and I was eager to catch up.

Thirty seconds into the conversation, she blurted out, "Oh, my God, you had sex."

I almost dropped my phone. "What?"

"You did, didn't you?"

We'd barely said hello. How on Earth could she tell? I asked, "What makes you say that?"

"Aha!" she said. "I was right, wasn't I?"

I didn't know what to say. "Uh…"

Normally, I talked to Aunt Gina at least once a week. But the last few weeks had been so crazy that most of our correspondence had been by text. All this time, I hadn't mentioned Joel at all – partly because I didn't want to jinx anything, and partly because it didn't feel like a text-kind of conversation.

But now that things were going so well, I was dying to tell her all about him, except this wasn't quite the way I envisioned it.

"So, who is he?" She gave a little gasp. "Oh, my God. Was it the cowboy? Please say it was the cowboy."

"What cowboy? Oh wait, you mean the stripper?" I had to laugh. "No. Definitely not."

"So, who then?"

I was still laughing. "Hey, I haven't even said you were right."

"You don't have to say it. I can tell."

"But how?"

"You're laughing. And you've got a rosy glow."

"But you can't even see me."

"Yeah, but I can hear it."

Feeling suddenly naked, I wrapped my hoodie tighter around my torso.

As if hearing the motion, Aunt Gina said, "You can run, but you can't hide."

I had to smile. I missed her like crazy. And now, she lived five hours away. "Actually," I said, "there *is* someone I want you to meet."

"Oh yeah? So, it's serious, huh?"

It felt serious, but I still didn't want to jinx it. So I only said, "Well, actually it's a little soon to know."

"Is he cute?"

I considered her question. Joel wasn't cute. He was something else – something infinitely better, sexy and dangerous – and yeah, insanely beautiful. Still, I said, "Yeah. He's cute."

"How cute?"

"*Very* cute." I cleared my throat. "And the next time you visit, you'll get to meet him, since he'll be staying in the guest house."

"No kidding?" she said. "How'd that happen?"

I told her how Joel had earned one of the endowments, and how he'd be using my dad's old studio. I finished by telling her, "So, it just made sense for him to stay in the guest house, you know, because the studio's right above it."

My aunt paused. "But why wouldn't he stay with you?"

"What do you mean?"

"I'm just saying, why go halfway? Why not invite him to live in the main house?"

I *had* considered it. I loved having Joel near me. And from what I could tell, he felt the same way. But when it came to romance, I wasn't sure that living together was what I wanted.

I mean, we hadn't even said the L-word.

I said, "That's kind of rushing things, don't you think? And besides, I guess I'm kind of old-fashioned that way."

"Does *he* know that?" she asked.

"Does he know what?"

"Why you didn't ask him to stay in the main house."

"No." I paused. "I mean, we didn't really talk about it."

"Forget the guest house," she said. "Shack up. Live a little." She laughed. "If nothing else, it'll drive your lawyers crazy."

She was right. In truth, Derek was long past crazy already. Happily, he was still out of town, which was definitely a good thing.

"Don't worry," I said. "They'll go nuts enough with Joel in the guest house."

"Exactly!" she said. "So why go halfway? And besides, what if he's insulted?"

"Who? Derek?"

"Screw Derek," she said. "I'm talking about your hot artist."

I still wasn't following. "But why would *he* be insulted?"

"Because you're putting him up in the guest house, like a servant or something." Her tone grew teasing. "If you really like him, don't treat him like your sexy gardener. Treat him like a partner. Trust me. He'll like that."

Her words found their mark. Joel *did* take care of the lawn. And he'd been acting like a handyman of sorts.

Still, I said, "Oh come on, he wouldn't think that. He's not remotely insecure. If you met him, you'd know."

"Alright," she said. "Then I'm coming for a visit."

"Really? When?"

"This weekend."

I had to laugh. "When did you decide that?"

"Just now. I want to meet this sexy gardener of yours."

"He's not a gardener. He's an artist, remember?" I smiled. "And he's amazing."

"Great. Then I can't wait to meet him."

I was still smiling when I got off the phone. And yet, her advice haunted me the rest of the day. Was I treating Joel like a servant?

One way or another, I'd have to ask him.

CHAPTER 64

It was late afternoon, and we'd spent most of the day working to set up the guest house and studio above it. The building itself had three stories. This included the garage on the lowest level, living space on the second, and the studio on the third.

In the guest house, I'd washed the sheets, made the bed, cleaned the bathroom, and polished the furniture.

Now, I was wiping down everything else, hoping to make every inch of the space feel fresh and new.

As for Joel, he'd spent most of the morning moving his supplies from the storage unit into the guest-house garage. Already, the garage was bursting with covered artwork, along with boxes and bins, all in various stages of being unpacked.

As we worked, we called up and down to each other and found plenty of reasons to invade each other's territory.

I was wiping down the baseboards in the small kitchenette when I heard Joel say, "You know I'm a guy, right?"

I looked up. He was wearing tattered jeans and a white T-shirt with grimy splotches down the front. His biceps bulged as he lifted an oak kitchen chair and moved it out of my path.

I felt myself smile. "Really?" I gave his physique a long, lingering look. "I had no idea."

He set the chair aside and smiled down at me. "If I asked you to stop, would you?"

"Why would I stop?"

"Because it's not necessary."

"Sure it is," I insisted. "You want it to feel like home, right?"

At this, he laughed.

I gave him a perplexed look. "What's so funny?"

"Baby, if you saw *my* house growing up?" He paused. "Well, let's just say, clean baseboards weren't our thing."

Maybe that was true, but I refused to be discouraged. "Well, then you just don't know what you were missing."

His gaze warmed. "I do now."

I smiled up at him. "See?"

"But it's not the baseboards." He flicked his head toward the narrow stairway, just a few paces away. "Now c'mon. There's something I wanna show you."

"But I'm not done," I said.

"So take a break." He reached down and tugged me to my feet. He pulled me close and planted a soft kiss on my forehead. Into my hair, he said, "Or better yet, forget the baseboards."

"But–"

"Come on." He pulled away and guided us toward the stairway and then up the stairs to the third floor.

Inside the spacious studio, I glanced around. Already, he'd carried up a few plastic bins, along with at least a dozen boxes, stacked on top of each other.

But the place was still mostly empty. I knew why. It had taken a colossal effort just to move his things from storage into the garage below. Now, he'd need to lug the whole mess up the stairs before he could truly settle in.

Inside the studio, he led me to a far corner, where he popped the top off a large, grey bin. Inside, I spotted a few bricks, along with a sturdy-looking metal case, slightly smaller than a shoe box. He pulled it out and handed it to me.

Gripping the case with both hands, I asked, "Should I open it, or…?

When Joel nodded, I raised the lid and looked inside, only to feel my eyes widen. I looked to Joel and asked, "Is this yours?"

"Not mine," he said. "Ours."

Okay, now I was really confused. Again, I looked down. The box was filled with bundles of cash, secured with big rubber bands. I pulled out a random bundle and rifled through it. I saw mostly twenties, along with a few fives, some fifties, and a whole bunch of hundreds.

I looked to Joel. "Where'd you get this?"

"I already told you. From fighting."

"It pays *that* good? Seriously?"

He shrugged. "For some people."

Obviously, he was one of those people.

"And," he continued, "it helps when you bet on yourself." He gave me a crooked smile. "Assuming you win."

"So you bet on yourself?" I said. "Is that even legal?"

He moved closer. "Baby, nothing about it was legal."

I wasn't quite sure how I felt about that. Again, I looked to the money. "How much is this? Do you know?"

"The exact amount? Nah. Never counted."

"Why not?"

"*You* wanna count it?" he said. "Be my guest."

I *did* want to count it, but mostly out of curiosity. "But why did you say it's ours?"

"Because I want you to know, I wasn't lying. I can cover us." He flicked his head toward the cash. "And I can make more if we need it."

From fighting? No. I definitely didn't want that. And I knew in my heart that he didn't want that either.

"But you *won't* need it," I reminded him, "because you'll have the endowment money."

"No," he said. "*You'll* have the endowment money. Remember?"

"But that's not what we agreed on. I can't take your money."

"You're not taking it," he said. "We're sharing it. Like you're sharing this place."

Instantly, that reminded me of my aunt's admonishment. Pushing aside the money issue, I said, "Can I ask you something? You're not insulted, are you?"

"About what?"

I glanced around. "That you're living *here*. I mean, instead of the main house?"

Joel stiffened. "Why do you ask?"

Something about his stance made me wonder. Maybe he *was* insulted. "So you *would* rather live in the main house?"

Probably, it was a stupid question. Of course he would. Maybe the way he saw it, I was shuffling him off to the guest house because I didn't trust him or something. Or maybe he thought I was a snob. My stomach tightened. Or selfish, like I didn't want to share my own living space.

Just great. I was a paranoid, selfish snob. Maybe my aunt was right. Maybe I *had* insulted him.

But in front of me, Joel was shaking his head. "No. I wouldn't."

So he *wouldn't* want to live in the main house? That was a relief. Or, at least, it should've been. But for some reason, I felt compelled to ask, "Why not?"

"Does it matter?"

His evasiveness made me pause. "No. Not really." I tried to keep my tone casual. "I guess it makes sense, like if you want guests or something."

He gave me a look. "What kind of guests?"

Feeling suddenly unsure, I summoned up a smile. "You know what? Forget I asked." I forced a laugh. "Actually, that's a big relief. I mean, that you're not insulted or anything. My aunt – she was *really* worried about it."

Even as I talked, a funny thought occurred to me. Now, *I* was the one who was worried. How stupid was that?

Gently, Joel took the case from my hands and set it on a nearby stack of boxes. And then, he pulled me into his arms. He brushed his lips against my hair and said, "You want the reason?"

I couldn't resist. I nodded against him.

"I'm not gonna shack up with you."

I froze. His embrace was sweet, but his words were sour.

Shack up. My aunt had used the exact same term, but on Joel's lips, it sounded different, like something dangerous, and not in a good way.

I was still mulling that over when Joel said, "Your aunt's full of it. You know that, right?"

I pulled back to look at him. "You're not angry I asked, are you?"

"At you?" He shook his head. "No. But your aunt, she's gotta stop pulling that shit."

I frowned. "What shit?"

Joel's voice hardened. "She doesn't even know me."

"So?"

"So she's telling you to move me in?" His gaze darkened. "I could be anyone. A fucking ax-murderer, for all she knows."

"Except you're not."

"Yeah. But she doesn't know that." He gave a slow shake of his head. "This world? It's full of monsters, who'd like nothing better than to get their claws into something as sweet as you."

At the image, I almost laughed. "But *you're* not a monster."

"No." His voice grew quiet. "But I could be."

"But you're not," I repeated. "And besides, my aunt will totally love you."

His mouth lifted at the corners. "I'm not sure that's a mark in her favor."

"Well, I'm sure enough for both of us." I paused. "And about the whole living-together thing?" I gave a shaky laugh. "Forget I mentioned it, okay?"

"I will. And you wanna know why?"

"Why?"

Once again, he pulled me into his arms. "Because that's not your style." His voice softened into something sweet. "And I love you for it."

CHAPTER 65

Those three little words hung in the air. My stomach fluttered, and my breath caught. "What?"

"You heard me."

I pulled back to gaze up at him. Was he saying what I thought he was saying? The look in his eyes told me all I needed to know. I felt myself smile. Unable to resist, I teased, "But wait. You told me you'd never say such a thing."

"Me?" He gave me a sheepish smile. "Nah. *I* didn't say that."

I gave him a playful shove. "You did, too."

But Joel shook his head. "That was Cigar talking. Not me."

It took me a moment to realize that he was referring to that dreadful nickname, the one that had been inspired by a phrase I'd come to hate. *Close, but no cigar.*

The way it looked, those days were over. And finally, Joel was accepting the fact that good things could happen for him – *really* good things, judging from his current prospects.

I smiled up at him. "So, no more cigar, huh?"

"Forget the cigar," he said, pulling me close once again. "Now, tell me what I wanna hear."

Feeling suddenly shy, I said, "What?"

"You *know* what."

But before I could respond, he said, "Wait. Let me say it right." He lowered his head and brushed his lips against my forehead. "Melody?"

"Hmmm?"

"I love you."

I melted against him. "I love you, too."

His arms closed tighter around me. "You bet your ass you do."

I burst out laughing. "Well, aren't you the cocky one?"

"Nah. I just know a good thing when I see it." His voice grew quiet again. "You're my good luck charm, you know that?"

It was a nice sentiment, but he was giving me far too much credit. My own voice grew quieter, too. "No. It's all you."

I felt his hands in my hair and his lips on my forehead. "Sorry, but you're wrong. Before you? My life was shit."

"Oh come on," I said. "There had to be good things, too."

"Maybe. But they all ended the same way."

"How?"

He gave a humorless laugh. "In flames." He pulled back. "And as far as your question…"

"What question?"

"About guests," he said. "There's only one I want." He grinned down at me. "The rest can piss off."

I couldn't help it. A giggle escaped my lips. "Oh yeah?"

"Damn straight." His gaze warmed. "Because I don't want anyone here but you."

I felt my gaze shift to the floor below us. In the guest house there was a bed. And it was freshly made with clean sheets.

When I looked back to Joel, he was still smiling. "What?" he said. "You want me to prove it?"

I did, in fact.

A minute later, we fell, laughing, onto the double bed in the guest house. Something in Joel had changed. I could see it in his eyes, and I could feel it in his touch.

We were still fully clothed – me in shorts and a thin tank-top, and him in his tattered jeans and white T-shirt, with all those streaks of dust.

Maybe I should've cared. I had, after all, just washed the comforter.

But I didn't care. I couldn't, especially when he trailed his fingers along the side of my face and whispered so sweetly, "I love you."

I wanted to burst with joy. "I love you, too."

I didn't care how many times we said it, it would never be enough. We were laying side-by-side in the quiet room, simply gazing into each other's eyes.

It felt like one of those moments, a scene from a dream, where everything stands still, like a still image, to be remembered always. I heard myself say, "I can't imagine life without you."

He smiled. "Good, because I'm not going anywhere."

I smiled back, wanting to savor this moment, along with the certain knowledge that this was the guy I wanted forever, and the way it sounded, he felt the same way.

How wonderful was that?

Afternoon sun streaked through the gaps in the pale curtains, lending an unearthly quality to us and our surroundings. We undressed each other slowly, carefully, taking our sweet time in removing each other's shirts, and then the shorts in my case, and the jeans in his. Soon, we were wearing nothing at all.

Gently, almost reverently, he wrapped his arms around me and pulled me tight against him. Already, I was slick and ready. And as for his readiness? I felt it pressing hard against my pelvis as we lay there, still and silent, like two lovers about to take a vow.

He *was* my lover. And he was my friend. And, in the most unexpected way, he'd become the family that I'd been longing for.

Someday, I hoped we'd be adding to that family, filling the house with all the love and laughter that had been missing for far too long.

When he entered me at last, I felt a surge of such love and devotion, I almost wanted to cry. But I didn't. I was way too happy, even for that.

Side-by-side, and wrapped in that blissful embrace, we moved against each other, making his hardness surge and dance inside me, as we ran our hands along each other's backs, through each other's hair, and down each other's sides.

It was the most beautiful thing I'd ever experienced – from the sweet beginning to the wonderful end, when we reached that lofty peak and tumbled over, with words of love and the unspoken promise of forever.

The rest of the afternoon passed in a hazy blur of sweetness and love, and even some unpacking, when we could spare the time. When dawn broke, we were still awake.

It felt like the beginning of a wonderful future. And maybe it *would've* been, if only a mistake from the past hadn't come crashing in at the worst possible time.

CHAPTER 66

Cassie was laughing. "Oh, my God. And you *still* showed up for work?"

While helping her decorate a fresh batch of sugar cookies, I'd told her how Joel and I had stayed up literally until sunrise working on the guest house and studio.

It was still early morning, and I hadn't slept at all. I should've been exhausted, but I'd never felt more alive.

I said, "Oh, please. Like I'd leave you hanging, just because we lost track of the time?"

"Lost track, huh?" She gave me a sly look. "So *that's* what they're calling it?"

I felt that telltale heat rising to my face. Obviously, Cassie had figured out that work wasn't the only thing that had kept us from sleep.

I rolled my eyes. "Oh, shush."

I went on to tell her how, after my morning shift, I'd be driving to Chicago to sign the official papers for all of this year's art endowments, including Joel's.

She said, "Why Chicago?"

"Well, that's where Claude is, remember?"

"I know," she said. "But doesn't he normally come here?"

"Sure, normally. But with Joel at the house, I asked Claude if we could do it there instead."

"But why?" Cassie asked. "That's a three-hour drive."

"Yeah, but it'll be so worth it. Tomorrow, Aunt Gina's coming to town, and I have this big surprise thing planned for Joel." I smiled. "It wouldn't be much of a surprise if he was there when I signed the papers."

Cassie gave me a perplexed look. "But he already knows he's getting it."

"Sure," I said, "but this will make it official. And he'll be meeting Aunt Gina for the first time, so this will give us something fun to celebrate."

Cassie was frowning now.

I asked, "What's wrong?"

"Round trip, you're looking at a six-hour drive. And you haven't slept. Are you sure that's safe? And what about Joel? Isn't he going to wonder where you are?"

Her concern was touching, but totally unnecessary. "It's definitely safe," I said. "I'm not even tired. And as far as Joel, he'll just assume I worked all day." I grinned over at her. "Especially if I bring home cookies."

Cassie didn't look reassured. "Maybe you should leave now, so you don't crash on the way home."

"Oh stop it," I said. "I'm not gonna crash."

Cassie was in the middle of objecting again when a loud, pounding noise made both of us look toward the front of the shop. The store wasn't scheduled to open for another half-hour.

I asked, "Are you expecting someone?"

Cassie shook her head and then moved to the narrow doorway that led to the front room. She peered around the corner and sighed. "Oh, crap."

"What?"

She turned to me and said, "It's for you."

"How do you know?"

"Because it's Derek." She grimaced. "And he looks ticked off as usual."

Damn it. I didn't even realize he was back in town. I *so* wasn't in the mood for whatever was wrong *this* time. Still, I couldn't let him pound all day, so I strode to the door and called through the glass, "We're closed!"

"I'm not here for cookies," he called back. "I'm here to tell you something."

I called back, "So tell me later!"

He glared through the glass. "It can't wait."

"Oh, alright," I muttered. I opened the glass door barely a sliver and said, "But hurry up, because I'm on the clock."

He looked to the slim opening. "Aren't you gonna let me in?"

"No," I told him. "I'm working, just like I said. So just tell me, okay?"

"Alright, you wanna hear it this way? Fine by me. I just wanted to let you know that your boyfriend?" Derek gave me a nasty smile. "He's on his way to jail."

My jaw dropped. "What?"

"Sorry, I misspoke."

Relief coursed through me.

Derek was still smiling. "What I meant to say was *prison.*" He shrugged. "But oh well. See you later." And with that, he turned to go.

"Wait!" Desperately, I flung open the door. "You can't be serious."

He turned back. "Can't I?"

CHAPTER 67

Fifteen minutes later, I was pacing the back room of the cookie shop. And poor Cassie. Instead of getting any work done, she was listening to me rant about my own problems.

For the tenth time, I stopped pacing and studied the photos laid across the back counter.

Cassie asked, "So you *knew* what Joel did?"

"You mean the fighting?" I said. "Yeah, I knew."

She gave me an odd look. "Did you know it was illegal?"

"Well, uh, yeah. But I didn't think it was a big deal."

In hindsight, it all seemed terribly naïve. Seriously, what did I think? That Joel could go around breaking the law and there'd be no consequences, ever?

I'd just finished relaying what Derek had told me – that Joel was under some sort of suspended sentence. Apparently, he'd been busted for illegal fighting six months earlier. But, thanks to some high-dollar help from one of the promoters, he'd gotten off with barely a slap on the wrist.

Unfortunately, the slap had come with conditions. During a one-year term, Joel couldn't associate with a whole list of people who'd been involved in that particular fight.

Again, I looked down to the photos. They all showed basically the same thing – Joel hanging out in some bar with a bunch of guys who I didn't recognize. But thanks to Derek, I knew their names, and a little about their backgrounds.

A couple were fellow fighters, while a third guy was involved in the whole betting operation. All of them were on the list.

Looking at them now, I wanted to cry. How could Joel be so stupid? And why hadn't he told me?

Cassie asked, "When were these taken?"

"Like two months ago." I pointed to a beefy guy in a black dress-shirt. "See him? He got married the next day."

"How do you know?" she asked.

"Oh, that's the best part," I said. "I know, because these stupid photos were taken just before his bachelor party." I gave a bark of laughter. "And what does the guy do? He posts the photos online."

I mimicked his stupidity, "Oh, look at me. I'm getting married tomorrow." I gave a derisive snort. "Idiot."

Cassie's tone was gentle. "Oh come on. You can't really blame the guy."

I looked up. "Can't I? You *do* know what'll happen to Joel if the right person sees these?"

"No. What will happen?"

"Don't you get it? He'll be rearrested. Thrown in jail." My voice was shaking. "And then, the way Derek talked, off to prison."

"You don't know that for sure." Her tone grew hopeful. "Maybe he'd just get a warning or something."

I shook my head. "No. He won't. Derek's dad knows the prosecutor." My jaw tightened. "I swear, that guy knows everyone."

"But so what?" Cassie said. "That prosecutor – he probably won't even see the photos. I mean, not everyone scours the internet, right?"

"Don't you get it?" I wanted to scream. "He won't have to scour. Derek's gonna show him."

Cassie's mouth fell open. "What?"

I nodded. "Didn't I tell you?"

"Honestly," she said, "you were a little hard to understand. You were kind of…" She waved her words away. "Never mind."

"Hysterical?" I gave a bitter laugh. "Gee, I wonder why."

Again, I looked to the photos. The groom-to-be looked so happy. And I hated him for it. I looked up, meeting Cassie's gaze. "Wanna hear the worst part?"

She eyed me with concern. "There's something worse?"

"Oh yeah." I took a deep breath. "Apparently, there was this fight last year, where Joel really mopped the floor with some guy. And guess who he is."

Cassie shook her head. "I have no idea."

"Get this. He's a member of the Broadstreets."

Cassie looked utterly horrified. "The gang?"

It wasn't just a gang. It was a nightmare. A few months earlier, a huge sweep had landed most of them in prison – exactly where Joel might be, if things went terribly wrong.

I gave a sad nod. "And apparently, the guy didn't take it so great."

"What'd he do?" Cassie asked.

"Oh, nothing much," I said. "Just threatened to kill him."

"You mean Joel?" she said. "Is he worried?"

"I don't know." I rubbed at my suddenly tired eyes. "He never mentioned any of this."

"Then maybe Derek's lying." Cassie perked up. "He lied about the car, right?"

I let out a long, shaky breath. "I *wish* he were lying. But I saw the paperwork, along with a couple of news clippings. Unfortunately, this time he's telling the truth."

"What are you gonna do?" Cassie asked. "Like, is there some way to talk Derek out of it?"

"There is, in fact." I blinked long and hard. "I've got to get rid of Joel."

Cassie gave a little gasp. "You mean break up with him?"

My heart ached at the thought. But that's exactly what Derek had demanded. The jerk had even promised to send a moving truck to help things along.

But that wasn't all of it. "Not just that," I said. "I've got to pull his endowment."

"The art endowment? Is that even possible, legally, I mean?"

I gave another humorless laugh. "Oh yeah. I haven't signed the papers yet, remember? So technically, there's nothing to pull. I've just got to let Claude know that I'm vetoing Joel's name."

"You can do that?"

I sighed. "Oh yeah, it's one of the rare legal powers I actually have. Pretty ironic, huh?"

Cassie's voice grew quiet. "So you're gonna do it?"

"I don't know," I said. "But I can't let him go to prison."

"But you don't know for sure that he will. You know Derek. He's probably exaggerating."

I gave her a long look. "If you loved someone, would you take that chance?"

"You love him? Does he know that?"

A sad smile crossed my lips. "Yeah. We've, um, said it actually."

Cassie gave me a sympathetic look. "Oh, gosh, I'm so sorry."

"Yeah, me too." I couldn't help but recall Joel's dreaded nickname – Cigar. This would only confirm his worst superstitions.

There *had* to be another way. I just needed some time to think. Already, I had one idea, but I'd need to ask Claude about it. The only bright spot was that I'd been scheduled to meet with him today anyway.

I looked to Cassie and said, "I hate to do this, but do you care if I leave early after all?"

"Sure, no problem." Her eyes filled with sympathy. "So you're gonna tell Joel *now*?"

I shook my head. "No. And if I'm lucky, maybe I won't have to."

CHAPTER 68

When I finally turned into my own driveway, it was dark and drizzling. Pulling up to the house, I was surprised to see Aunt Gina's car parked out front. It should've been a welcome surprise, but in my current state-of-mind, I wasn't so sure.

As for Joel's car, I didn't see it, and maybe that was a good thing. Until I had something resembling good news, I'd be smart to keep my mouth shut. After all, there was no reason for both of us to suffer while I waited to hear back from Claude.

Distracted beyond belief, I got out of the car and made my way to the front door. When I opened it, I was greeted by the smell of something baking. I paused. It smelled surprisingly delicious.

From somewhere in the kitchen, Aunt Gina called out, "Melody, is that you?"

"Uh, yeah," I said, making my way toward the sound of her voice.

She called back, "Guess what I'm making!"

I stopped and gave the air another sniff. It smelled like pie. Really good pie. This made no sense. This was, after all, Aunt Gina, who wasn't exactly known for her culinary skills.

When I reached the kitchen, she looked up and gave me a big, happy smile. "Well? Aren't you gonna guess?"

I glanced around. I saw flour on the counter and apple peelings off to the side. "Is it apple pie?"

She clapped her hands together. "You got it!"

I didn't know what to say. I gave the oven a nervous glance. "So you made it from scratch?"

She laughed. "Don't look so worried." Her eyes brightened. "I'm taking a class."

"A baking class?"

"Not just baking. Cooking, too." She leaned forward. "I'm thinking of opening a restaurant." She brushed some flour off her dark shirt. "Or maybe a bakery. I mean, we're still on desserts, so I might be rushing it a bit."

In spite of everything, I almost smiled. This was vintage Aunt Gina. She went from zero to sixty in the blink of an eye. If this were any other time, I'd be thrilled to see her.

Now, I was just worried. Trying not to show it, I moved forward to give her a welcoming hug. "Boy, you really surprised me. I thought you weren't coming 'til tomorrow."

"Well yeah, that was the original plan." She pulled back to give me another smile. "But then I thought, 'I've gotta meet this guy of hers.'" She looked around. "So, where is he?"

I tried to smile back. "I don't know. I just got back."

"From work?"

"Sort of."

I'd been working alright, but not at the cookie shop. Mostly, I'd been trying to hammer things out with Claude.

Aunt Gina studied my face. "Is something wrong? You guys aren't fighting or anything, are you?"

"Nope." *Not yet, anyway.*

"Oh. Well that's good." She hesitated. "Maybe you should shower or something. You look kind of splotchy."

Funny, I felt kind of splotchy, too. And, I wanted some time to think. I agreed instantly, and turned away, with the promise to return after my shower.

Just before I reached the stairway, my aunt called out, "That guy of yours, he *does* like apple, right?"

I had no idea, so all I said was, "Well, it's everyone's favorite, so I'm sure he'll love it."

After showering, I returned downstairs and found Aunt Gina standing in the front doorway, waving goodbye to an unfamiliar white van.

Coming up behind her, I asked, "Who was that?"

She turned around to reveal an oversized white envelope. She gave it a little wave. "Special courier."

"Really?" It was long past business hours, and it couldn't be from Claude, because I'd just seen him. Maybe it was something to do with the estate? I was just reaching for the envelope when new movement in the driveway caught my eye.

It was Joel's car, pulling up to the house. At the sound of his car, my aunt whirled around to look. "Is that him?"

I bit my lip. "Well, it *is* his car."

She turned back to give me a puzzled look. "You don't sound too happy."

"Sorry." I summoned up a smile. "It's been a long day."

"How about this?" she said. "I'll pop out for a quick hello, let you introduce us, and then I'll take a nice long bath." She lowered her voice. "And give *you* two some time alone, if you know what I mean."

Heat flooded my face. "Really, that's okay."

My aunt laughed. "Oh come on. Don't be shy about it. If he's as hot as you say–"

"I never said he was hot."

"Sure you did." She paused. "Didn't you?"

I looked to the driveway, where Joel was getting out of his car. He was wearing jeans and a black T-shirt that clung to his muscles as he walked toward us in the drizzling rain.

My aunt turned to look. "Oh. My. God." She turned back to me and said, "Does he have an older brother?"

"Uh, yeah. But…" I winced. "He says they're awful."

"If they look anything like him, I'll take my chances." At something in my expression, she laughed. "Don't worry. I'm just teasing. I met someone. Didn't I mention that?"

I shook my head. "No. Who is he?"

She waved away the question. "Never mind that. Let's meet *your* guy."

Before I knew it, she was bounding out the front door to meet him. At the sight of my aunt dashing through the drizzle, Joel paused on the front walkway. His gaze drifted to me, and I gave him a tentative wave before reluctantly following after her.

Five soggy minutes later, the introductions were done, and we were all standing just inside the front entryway. My aunt glanced down at her clothes, which were still dusted with flour – except now the flour had congealed into a goopy mess, dripping down her shirt. "Oh, jeez," she said, looking back to Joel. "Normally, I make a much better impression."

He flashed her a smile. "Hey, I didn't notice a thing."

She almost giggled. "Liar." She turned back to me and said, "And I totally approve." She glanced toward the stairway. "Anyway, I'm gonna get cleaned up. Wanna meet back here in a couple of hours?" She smiled at Joel. "I made dessert. But it's a surprise."

She waggled a finger in my direction. "And don't *you* tell him either." In a stage whisper, she added, "Unless you can't resist."

In a flash, it struck me how wonderful all of this would be under different circumstances. Near me, I had the two people I loved best, and they seemed to be hitting it off.

The house was warm and scented with the aroma of fresh apple pie. Outside, it was still drizzling, which made everything seem extra cozy in here.

If it weren't for Derek's godawful threat, this would be the beginning of a lovely night. Now, all I felt was lingering dread.

I still hadn't heard from Claude, and the longer I waited, the more worried I became. He promised to call me as soon as he knew – or at least send me a text or something. *Where was it?*

My aunt turned and started heading toward the stairway before suddenly pausing. She whirled around and said, "Oh shoot, I almost forgot to give you this."

The envelope. She was still holding it.

As she moved forward, I held out my hand. "Sorry, I meant to grab that."

"Oh, it's not for you," she said. "It's for him." She gave Joel a warm smile. "Special delivery. Aren't *you* important."

She turned and handed him the envelope. As she did, I caught sight of not only his name on the front, but the return address in the upper left-hand corner. I felt my face pale. It was from my dad's foundation, and for once, I knew nothing about it.

A renewed sense of dread settled over me. Whatever that envelope contained, it couldn't be good.

CHAPTER 69

I snuck a quick glance at the soggy envelope. Joel was holding it loose at his side, still unopened.

I just prayed it stayed that way.

With growing despair, I watched my aunt walk toward the stairway. My heart was racing, and I wanted to holler out, "*Come back!*"

Aunt Gina was a bundle of energy. She'd be the perfect distraction for what I desperately wanted to do – sneak off with that envelope and see what it contained.

Yes, it would be intrusive, unethical, and a whole bunch of other things, but I was beyond caring. And besides, I was part of the foundation. Whatever the envelope contained, I should've been informed.

This had to be Derek's doing, which meant, of course, that the envelope was a proverbial bomb, waiting to explode.

Stalling for time, I turned to Joel and explained that Aunt Gina's early arrival had caught me by surprise. I finished by saying, "So anyway, sorry I didn't call to warn you. I guess I should've, huh?"

"It's alright." He eyed me with obvious concern. "Hey, don't look so worried. It's not a big deal."

I swallowed. "I look worried?"

I wasn't worried. I was terrified. But it had nothing to do with the change in my aunt's schedule.

All day, I'd envisioned telling Joel about Derek's threat. And all day, I'd imagined Joel's response. Joel was fearless. There was no way he'd back off just because Derek had waved some photos in my face and made mouth noises about knowing some prosecutor.

After all, if Joel had any sense of self-preservation, he wouldn't've been fighting at all, especially with it being illegal. I recalled our conversation from just a few days earlier. He'd actually mentioned fighting again if the money ran low.

Seriously, what on Earth was he thinking? That he could fly under the radar and not get caught? My shoulders sagged. Who knows, maybe he could've. But not anymore, because Derek wouldn't let that happen.

Joel asked, "Are you feeling okay?"

I gave a little jump. "What?

He reached for my hand. "You're shaking."

Distracted, I murmured, "Am I?"

Trying to keep it together, I gazed into Joel's eyes and wondered what would happen if the worst-case scenario played out. I envisioned him in jail – or worse, in prison, surrounded by enemies seeking revenge.

At the thought, I wanted to cry. Instead, I forced a smile. The smile felt funny, like my face was a lot smarter than I was. Somehow, I managed to say, "I'm just a little cold. You know, from the rain."

It wasn't even a lie. The house was warm, but for some reason, I felt chilled to the bone.

He pulled me close and whispered into my hair. "You want me to make a fire?"

The offer was a lifeline, and I decided to grab it while I had the chance. I nodded against his soggy shirt. "If you're sure you don't mind, that would be great."

He pulled back and said, "What do you have, like three fireplaces? Pick your favorite, and I'll get one going."

In what I hoped was a casual gesture, I tugged the envelope from his hand and said, "How about the family room?"

When he looked down at the envelope, I added, "I'll just set this aside to dry off." Before he could argue, I turned away and began walking toward the kitchen. I called over my shoulder, "I'll grab us some hot chocolate or something. Meet you by the fire?"

Without waiting for his answer, I hustled to the kitchen and filled the tea kettle with water. I placed it on the stove and turned the burner to its highest setting.

The hot chocolate was my excuse, but the thing I really wanted was the boiling water. The envelope had a normal seal, and I'd seen plenty of movies. A good dose of steam would loosen the glue easily, right?

Unfortunately, I never found out. The water hadn't even begun to boil when Joel's voice broke into my murky thoughts. "Want me to get that?"

Startled, I whirled around to see him standing within arm's reach. "The hot chocolate?" I tried to smile. "Thanks, but I've got it."

He smiled. "Sorry, but no."

I blinked. "What?"

He reached for my hand. "Come on. The fire's going. You let me worry about this, alright?"

Damn it.

Trying to sound happy about it, I asked, "But how could the fire be going already? It's only been like two minutes."

"I cheated," he said. "There was a starter log already there."

I stifled a curse. That's right. I recalled staging that stupid thing a few months ago. An instant fire with the flick of a match, it sounded oh-so wonderful at the time. Now, it was just an annoyance.

I glanced toward the kettle. "It's almost done," I said. "You go. I'll meet you there."

"That's what *you* think." He put an arm over my shoulder and guided me out of the kitchen. Short of throwing off his arm and bolting for the stove, I didn't know what to do except follow along.

The only bright spot was that I was still holding the envelope. I carried it with me, even as Joel led me to the family room and practically pushed me into the armchair closest the fire.

He smiled down at me. "I'll be back in a minute, alright?"

One minute? *Screw the steam.* As soon as he left, I ripped open the envelope and pulled out its contents – a letter and a check for fifty dollars, made out to Joel.

I read the amount again. *Fifty dollars?* That made no sense. Unless – oh, shit. That was the exact amount of that very first check, the one that Joel had ripped up at his campsite. This had to be Derek's doing.

This wasn't good.

Conscious of the time ticking away, I turned my attention to the letter, printed on the foundation's letterhead. Quickly, I scanned the few short paragraphs.

When I finished, I felt like throwing up.

There was no way on Earth I'd ever let Joel read this thing. It wasn't just inaccurate. It was a travesty. Worst of all, it was signed by Claude, who was supposed to be helping me – not ruining everything.

I lowered my head to study the signature. It couldn't tell if Claude had actually signed it, or if it was one of those auto-signature graphics that the foundation used for form letters.

Damn it. If only I had more time, I could sort this out. But I didn't, at least not now. I stuffed the letter and check back into the envelope and gave the room a nervous glance. I needed to hide this, but where?

My gaze landed on the fireplace, and I felt my jaw tighten. *Screw hiding it.* Before I could overthink it, I tossed the whole sorry thing onto the fire and stood to watch it burn.

But it didn't. To my infinite frustration, the stupid thing didn't burst into flames – at least, not soon enough, because a moment later, Joel's voice cut across the room. "What'd you do that for?"

Oh, shit.

I whirled to see him standing in the open doorway, giving me a perplexed look. And then, he was striding forward. Before I could process what was happening, he'd already moved past me and was reaching down into the fireplace.

I blurted out, "Don't!"

But he did.

CHAPTER 70

I watched in growing horror as he pulled the smoldering packet from the flames and turned to face me. When our eyes met, I didn't know what to say.

Silently, he looked down to the envelope. It was partially blackened and still smoking. He rubbed it against his damp shirt and then returned his gaze to mine.

For some stupid reason, I thought of my uncle and all of his ridiculous excuses. At that instant, I almost admired the guy, because no matter how guilty he looked, he always found *something* to say.

As for me, I had nothing. I mean, what *could* I say? *Oops?*

Joel's voice was quiet. "Tell me."

I tried to remember his question. "You mean, why'd I do that?"

"No." He lifted the envelope. "Tell me what's in here."

"It's nothing." I gave him a shaky smile. "Just a mistake. That's all."

His gaze hardened. "A mistake, huh?"

Desperately, I reached for the envelope. My fingertips had barely grazed it when Joel yanked it out of my reach. "Nice try."

"Seriously," I said, "it's nothing important."

Ignoring me, he opened the envelope and pulled out its contents, which of course, were utterly undamaged.

He looked at the check and then at the letter. His eyes quickly scanned the text. When he finished, he gave a bitter laugh. "I should've known."

"It's not true," I said.

"Uh-huh." He gave me a dubious look. "So that's why you tried to burn it?"

"Well, yeah," I stammered. "I mean, it's all just a mistake, so–"

"Right."

"It is," I insisted.

I recalled the letter's contents. To call it a rejection letter was a massive understatement. I couldn't recall every word, but a few of them definitely stood out.

Juvenile.

Simplistic.

Not of the caliber we're looking for.

It was all a lie.

I gave Joel a pleading look. "You've gotta believe me. Claude would *never* send out this kind of letter. Even with rejections – well, those are worded a lot nicer than this."

Joel gave a tight shrug. "Hey, nothing wrong with honesty."

"Except it's *not* honest. That's what I'm trying to tell you."

"What'd you think? That I couldn't handle it?" He released the letter, and it fluttered to the floor between us. "Forget it. It's nothing I didn't know."

"Oh come on," I said. "That is such a crock."

"You wanna know what's a crock?" he said. "That you'd try to hide it. What'd you think? That I'd cry in the corner because I got bad news?" He made a scoffing sound. "Trust me, I've had worse."

He was right. He had. Many times.

Again, that stupid nickname flashed in my brain. *Cigar.*

But this was different, because the letter was a lie. Joel had won on his own merit. Even without the endowment, he had an amazing future ahead of him. And somehow, I had to make him see that.

"Listen," I said, "I didn't want to say anything earlier, but I saw Claude today, and–"

"Yeah? Where?"

"Well, uh, Chicago actually."

He froze. "So you weren't at work."

"Well, I was," I stammered. "But then I wasn't. Anyway, just listen. I talked to Claude, and even if you don't get the endowment this year, your odds for next year are really, really good. Practically guaranteed."

His jaw tightened. "Fuck the endowment."

"What?"

"You heard me. I'm no painter."

"Oh come on," I said. "Now you're just being immature."

"Immature, huh?"

"Yes. And stubborn, too. You're not even listening to me."

"Yeah. And you wanna know why? Because I don't need your sympathy. You wanna coddle me like a baby? Fuck that. I don't need it."

His words sliced through me, but I tried again. "I'm not coddling you. I'm telling you the truth."

"No," he said. "You're telling me a bedtime story. What's next? You wanna tuck me and get me a bottle? Sorry, you've got the wrong guy."

No. I had the *right* guy. I knew that, even if he didn't. Desperately, I tried again. "Just hear me out, okay? Claude thinks you're *really* talented, and he's going to find you a new place."

Or at least, he was working on it right now. True, I hadn't heard back, but I knew Claude. For someone with Joel's talent, Claude would definitely find a way.

Joel's voice was tight. "What?"

"Well, the thing is…" I cleared my throat. "The whole guest-house setup, it's nice and all, but…" I bit my lip. *But what? Shit.* I had no idea.

But I can't have long-term guests?

But it's infested with termites?

But it's haunted with the ghosts of my dead parents?

I stared deep into his eyes, wishing I could just tell him the truth. *But if you stay here, Derek will make sure you end up gone, one way or another.*

And judging from Joel's reaction so far, I knew exactly how he'd take *that* bit of news. The last five minutes had only confirmed what I'd known all along – that he wasn't one to play it safe, that he'd resist any efforts of mine to protect him, that he'd resent me even more if he knew that *I* was the one who pulled the endowment.

Shit.

In front of me, Joel made a forwarding motion with his hand. "But…?"

I had nothing. Still, I yammered on. "Well, it's kind of remote out here. And, you'd probably be more inspired if you were closer to the action." I gave a shaky laugh. "The big city and all."

His voice was flat. "Chicago."

I swallowed. "Um, yeah."

He looked at me like I was a stranger. "You know, if you wanna get rid of me, just say so."

"I don't," I said. "You're reading this all wrong."

"Uh-huh. Wanna know what I think?"

From the look on his face, I wasn't so sure. Still, I felt myself nod.

"I think you're tired of slumming it, but you're too fucking nice to say so."

My stomach twisted. "That's not true."

"And you wanna know what else I think?"

"No," I murmured, "not really."

Ignoring me, he continued on. "I think that whole endowment thing was a crock. I think you pulled some strings to make me think I'm something I'm not."

"No. You've got it all wrong."

"Uh-huh. What'd you think? You could dress me up, put a paintbrush in my hand, and I'd be Mister Civilized?"

I stared up at him. "I don't even know what that means."

"Or maybe," he continued, "you were dumb enough to think my shit *was* any good. And so, you're thinking that I'm gonna be somebody, and you're all into me. But when you find out you're wrong, you're thinking, "Shit, how do I get rid of this guy?'"

"Except I'm *not* trying to get rid of you."

He gave me a hard look. "Aren't you?"

"No. Not at all." I glanced away. "But just think. If you took the place in Chicago for even six months, it would be a great opportunity."

Six months. By then, the suspended sentence would be officially over, and I could tell Derek to shove it. And then, Joel and I could start over, this time, without any interference.

Yeah, it totally sucked, but it was better than seeing Joel imprisoned or worse.

I gave him a pleading look. "I'd miss you like crazy, but you'd be so busy, the time would fly."

Maybe for him. But not for me.

Six long months – it felt like forever. Still, I summoned up a smile and continued. "You could paint, make connections, it's a really great opportunity."

As I rambled on, it suddenly struck me that Joel wasn't saying anything. Hoping that was a good sign, I kept going with my sorry sales pitch until I ran out of things to say.

When I finished, I gave him a hopeful look. "So, aren't you gonna say something?"

"Nope. I'm just waiting for *you* to say it."

"Say what?"

"That you want me gone."

"Weren't you listening?" I said. "I *don't* want you gone. This is totally for you, not for me."

He gave a bitter laugh. "Right."

"What's so funny?"

"You," he said. "Trying not to hurt my feelings. It's funny. Gotta laugh, right?"

In spite of his words, there was no laughter in his eyes.

As for me, I felt like crying. "This isn't a joke."

"Could've fooled me." And with that, he turned away and began walking out of the room.

I scurried after him. "Where are you going?"

"Well, it ain't to Chicago."

"Joel, just stop okay?"

But he didn't stop. He kept on walking and didn't pause until he reached the front door. And even then, he stopped only long enough to yank the door open and stride through it. Desperately, I followed him outside. It was still drizzling. But this time, I didn't care. "Come on," I pleaded. "Don't be like this."

Without pausing, he turned and started heading *not* to his car – thank God – but to the guest house. Relief coursed through me. Maybe he just wanted some privacy, or to discuss this where Aunt Gina wouldn't overhear us.

The grass was slick, and I was wearing no shoes, but I couldn't bring myself to care. His strides were long, and I was practically running to keep up. When he entered the side door to the garage, I followed after him, even as he silently strode to the stairway and started walking up it.

Maybe I should've stopped and given him some time to cool off, but something in my heart told me that time was running short. So I followed him up into the living area, and then watched with growing despair as he pulled out his duffel bag and began throwing things into it.

"What are you doing?" I asked.

"What does it look like? I'm getting my shit and going."

"You can't," I said. "Not like this."

"Why? It isn't 'nice' enough for you?" He paused and gave me his full attention. "Lemme tell you something." His gaze traveled rudely down the length of me. "Nice is overrated."

I flinched at the obvious insult. He didn't mean that. He couldn't. I said, "Joel, come on. Don't be like this."

He zipped up his bag and slung it over his shoulder. "Thanks for the good time," he said, heading toward the door.

The comment sliced through me. *Good time?*

Surely, I meant more to him than that?

I did. I knew it. And he meant more to me than he obviously realized.

I followed him down the stairs and once again out into the yard. He turned and started heading for his car.

With growing desperation, I lunged for his arm. It was slick with rain and colder than I expected. I gripped it like a lifeline and squeezed it tight until he had to either stop moving or drag me behind him.

To my infinite relief, he actually stopped. Turning to face me, he said, "What?"

Looking for any way to stall him, I blurted out, "What about the rest of your stuff?"

"Keep it."

"But your paintings–"

"That tattered shit?" He made a sound of derision. "Keep 'em, burn 'em, whatever. I don't care."

I gave him a pleading look. "But *I* do." I was still gripping his arm. Was I squeezing it too tight? Probably. But I couldn't bring myself to let go. I looked deep into his eyes and said the only thing I could. "I love you. You know I do."

"Yeah? Well sucks to be you."

The response was so cold, it gave me a shiver. "You don't mean that." I was crying now. "Come on. Don't go like this. Let's just talk it over, please?"

Finally, I saw a hint of uncertainty flicker in his eyes. Unfortunately, it was at this exact moment when I heard the rumble of a vehicle coming toward us.

I turned and saw the worst possible thing coming down the long driveway – a commercial truck emblazed with big blue letters along the side. And what did those letters spell out?

Full-Service Movers.

CHAPTER 71

I stood, frozen with dread, as the moving truck rumbled up to the edge of the driveway, where Joel and I were standing. I was still gripping his arm, and I had no intention of letting go.

The driver opened the door and stepped down from the truck. He looked to me. "You Melody?"

Unsure what else to do, I nodded.

He consulted his clipboard. "Good news. We had a cancellation."

I swallowed. "A cancellation?"

"Yeah. You weren't scheduled 'til Monday." He gave his clipboard another quick glance. "But we had a note here that you wanted the first opening." He gave me a big, friendly smile. "Guess it's your lucky day."

If this weren't so tragic, it would be hilarious. Today wasn't lucky. It was one of the worst days of my life.

In fact, it wasn't even daytime. I gave the guy a perplexed look. "I think there's been a mistake."

"No mistake here," he said. "We got the call this morning."

"But not from me," I said.

The guy looked to the house and gave a low, impressed whistle. "Yeah, I'm sure you got a business manager, huh?" He smiled. "Must be nice. Anyway, the crew's a few miles back, should be here in five, ten minutes. We'll get the stuff out in a jiffy." He pointed to the garage. "Is that the place?"

"No," I blurted. "Definitely not. I'm trying to tell you, nobody's moving."

"I know," he said. "We're taking a load to storage, right?" His brow wrinkled. "You didn't change your mind or something?"

"No," I said. "I mean yes." I took a deep breath. "What I mean to say is–"

Next to me, Joel muttered, "Fuck this shit." He pulled his arm from mine and began walking to his car. Over his shoulder, he told the guy, "Load it up. Take it wherever. To the dump, for all I care."

Before I knew it, Joel was halfway to his car. Desperately, I scrambled after him. As I moved, I called out, "Joel, will you please stop?"

To my surprise, he actually did. Slowly, he turned around and waited, with arms crossed, until I caught up to him. But when I reached him, I didn't know what to say.

Stupidly, I said the only thing that came to mind. "I love you."

He looked at me like I'd lost my mind. "You think you're the first girl to say that?"

Funny, it was a question I hadn't even considered. I heard myself say, "I'm not?"

He made a scoffing sound. "Hell no."

"But I mean it," I said.

"Yeah?" he said. "Good thing you don't hate me, huh?"

"What do you mean?"

He looked away. "I mean, fuck, what do you do to the guys you *don't* love?"

When he looked back, I swear, I looked straight into his soul and wanted to stagger back under the weight of his accusation.

In his eyes, I saw everything – the betrayal, the hurt, the fact that *I'd* done this to him.

But he had it all wrong. I had nothing to do with this current cluster. I bit my lip. Or, almost nothing. At least, not on purpose.

Damn it.

I gave him a pleading look. "Joel, please. It's not what you think it is."

He made a noise. It might've been a scoff, except it was too raw to convey normal human disbelief. With a slow shake of his head, he turned away, heading, once again, for his car.

I lunged after him, clutching his muscular forearm with my trembling fingers. I gave his arm a desperate squeeze. "Just wait, okay? I can explain."

Except, I couldn't.

If I told him everything, it might mean the death of him, literally.

Still, somehow, I'd make it right. I just needed some time, that's all.

To my infinite frustration, Joel wasn't inclined to wait. Gently, he pried my fingers from his rain-soaked skin. "Forget it," he said. "Not a big deal."

Lamely, I mumbled, "That wasn't supposed to happen. Not like that, anyway."

From somewhere near the front of the house, Aunt Gina called out, "Hey Melody! Ask him if he wants pie!"

Oh, for God's sake. Now, she was trying to help? Where was she an hour ago, when everything was going to crap?

But I wasn't being fair. At least Aunt Gina *was* trying to help. It was more than I could say for Derek, who seemed intent on ruining my life.

I turned and spotted her, standing in the open front doorway. With a pathetic smile, I waved her away, hoping she'd take the hint.

She didn't.

"Just ask him," she called. In an overly cheery voice, she added, "It's apple. Everyone's favorite, right?"

I made a sound of frustration. Didn't she get it? Pie wouldn't solve anything. A flame-thrower, now *that* might be helpful.

Still, I turned back to Joel, who, thank God, was still there. With a note of desperation, I asked, "Do you? Want pie, I mean?" I sucked in a nervous breath. "We could talk. And, uh, I think there's ice cream in the freezer."

Silently, Joel shook his head.

Of course, he didn't want pie. Probably, he wanted to strangle me. And all things considered, I couldn't exactly blame him.

I watched, helplessly, as Joel turned away yet again.

Short of throwing myself at him, I wasn't sure what I could do.

Sure, I could tackle him and beg him not to walk away. Or, I could beg him for just one more night alone – in his arms, in his bed, in his life.

Except I didn't want Joel for only one night. I wanted him forever. And more than that, I wanted him whole and happy, with no threats hanging over his head.

As I stared at his receding back, two little words echoed in my mind – six months.

If I could somehow bring myself to wait – for his sake, not mine – maybe I *could* have him forever. And maybe, just maybe, he'd eventually see that there was more to life than fighting or crappy nicknames or curses that weren't even true.

I blinked long and hard. Let's say I waited. How would he react when I finally told him the whole story? Probably, he'd hate me then, too.

I stiffened my spine. I'd wait. And then, I'd find some way to tell him. No matter how long it took, or what I had to do, I'd find some way.

He was worth it. *We* were worth it.

Already, he'd reached his car. Hoping to give him something to hang onto, I called his name one last time. When he turned to look, I said through my tears, "I know you don't believe me, but I *do* love you. And some day, I just hope you'll understand."

He gave a bitter laugh. "Don't worry. I understand plenty." And with that, he wrenched open the driver's side door, tossed his bag onto the passenger's seat, and slid in on the driver's side. A moment later, he fired up his engine and roared away, leaving me staring after him.

It was raining harder now, but I couldn't bring myself to care. Into the rain, I whispered it again – not three words, but two. "Six months."

If I lasted that long, it would be a miracle.

THE END

Other Books by Sabrina Stark

(Listed by Couple)

Lawton & Chloe

Unbelonging (Unbelonging, Book 1)

Rebelonging (Unbelonging, Book 2)

Lawton (Lawton Rastor, Book 1)

Rastor (Lawton Rastor, Book 2)

Bishop & Selena

Illegal Fortunes

Jake & Luna

Jaked (Jaked Book 1)

Jake Me (Jaked, Book 2)

Jake Forever (Jaked, Book 3)

ABOUT THE AUTHOR

Sabrina Stark writes edgy romances featuring plucky girls and the bad boys who capture their hearts.

She's worked as a fortune-teller, barista, game-show contestant, and media writer in the aerospace industry. She has a journalism degree from Central Michigan University and is married with one son and a pack of obnoxiously spoiled kittens. She currently makes her home in Northern Alabama.

ON THE WEB

Learn About New Releases & Exclusive Offers
www.SabrinaStark.com

Printed in Great Britain
by Amazon